Edna Buchanan has written seven novels, two of which have been nominated for Edgar awards, and three films have been made based on her novels. She won the Pulitzer Prize for General News Reporting in 1986. She lives in Miami Beach, Florida.

MARGIN OF ERROR

Just as Miami suffers the after-affects of a devastating hurricane, MIAMI NEWS reporter Britt Montero suffers post-traumatic stress after a shooting in which she was forced to kill a man. Then, into Britt's life comes major Hollywood star Lance Westfell, about to film an action movie. An obsessed mad woman stalks Lance, and mysterious accidents, mishaps and deaths push the production dangerously over budget. Britt and Lance become so close that both are now menaced by the obsessed fan — but is she the only one, or is someone else also determined to sabotage the film and murder its star?

EDNA BUCHANAN

MARGIN OF ERROR

Complete and Unabridged

ULVERSCROFT
Leicester

First published in Great Britain in 1998 by
Robert Hale Limited
London

First Large Print Edition
published 2000
by arrangement with
Robert Hale Limited
London

British Library CIP Data

Buchanan, Edna
    Margin of error.—Large print ed.—
    Ulverscroft large print series: mystery
    1. Montero, Britt (Fictitious character)—Fiction
    2. Miami (Fla.)—Fiction
    3. Detective and mystery stories
    4. Large type books
    I. Title
    813.5'4 [F]

    ISBN 0–7089–4189–3

Published by
F. A. Thorpe (Publishing) Ltd.
Anstey, Leicestershire

Set by Words & Graphics Ltd.
Anstey, Leicestershire
Printed and bound in Great Britain by
T. J. International Ltd., Padstow, Cornwall

This book is printed on acid-free paper

For Dr. Joseph H. Davis,
the world's most brilliant
forensic pathologist — and friend

Hollywood is a place where they'll pay you a thousand dollars for a kiss, and fifty cents for your soul.

— Marilyn Monroe

Acknowledgments

I am grateful to South Florida's best and brightest: Miami Homicide Lieutenant Gerald Green, Officer D. C. Diaz, the brilliant Dr. Eduardo Alfonso, and my wonderful and patient friends David M. Thornburgh, Renee Turolla, and Peggy Thornburgh. My Hollywood buddy, Peter Lance, and Marilyn Lane, Cynnie Cagney, Karen McFadyen, Bill Cooke, Bill Dobson, and Steven B. Waldman all generously shared their brilliance and expertise. So did Alex Justo and his sparring partner, Jorge Torres. Arnold Markowitz, *The Miami Herald*'s greatest natural resource, always manages to be there for me when it counts. I appreciate the help of Michael Clark and Gay Nemeti Robson of *The Herald* Library, and Arthur Stillman and John Hoover. My thanks to David Utley, Everglades District Manager of the Florida Division of Forestry, to firefighter Carl Aloi, and the man with the gun, Robert P. Hart, of the Metro-Dade Crime Lab's Firearms Division. Co-starring in this production, as always, are Leslie Wells, my editor, and Michael Congdon, my agent. What a sterling cast of characters!

1

I could smell the gunpowder. The dream was that real.

The dark woods disappeared as I awoke gasping, heart pounding: no gleaming gun or spilled blood in the moonlight, only the startled green eyes of my cat, staring from the foot of my bed. My heartbeat slowed down as I sat up, forehead and underarms sticky. The digital face of my bedside clock glowed in the dark. Three A.M. Hours till dawn.

I have never wished time away. No one knows more how little there is. What the hell is happening to me? I wondered. And why now?

The paper had offered me time off after the shooting, and the services of the company shrink. I had declined both. The best therapy for me was to continue covering my beat; I did not need corporate records linking me to a psychiatrist. Wouldn't that be a swell addition to my résumé?

I switched on the police scanner, thankful for instant company, a cacophony of voices: strangers at computer screens dispatching the

1

soldiers of the night to answer cries in the dark. I sat on the edge of my bed and listened, eavesdropping on men and women linked by radio, adrenaline, and a common purpose, the keepers of the peace on an unpeaceful planet.

Somebody had been stealing hookers' hearts — literally. Four so far, three in the Keys, then one in Miami. A Metro-Dade cop was checking out a man caught loitering near a drainage ditch where the last victim had been found a month ago. None of the missing organs had been recovered. What does he, or she, do with them? I wondered.

Detectives were on the way to the county jail, where two prisoners had been caught mining for gold — in the mouth of another inmate. They had removed two gold teeth and were prying a third loose when a guard interrupted.

There were several reports of shots fired in the Scott Project, no further reference.

High above it all, Air Rescue One throbbed toward the burn unit, its passenger a severely singed voodoo priest. His lit cigar had dropped into a bowl of gunpowder he was preparing for a ritual. And on the water, a Coast Guard rapid-response craft with portable pumps was racing to Government Cut to rescue two competing bait fishermen.

They had rammed each other during a fight for a prime fishing spot. Their cries for help as they took on water were broadcast over Channel 16. Sea Tow had been dispatched.

Trouble on land, air, and sea — a routine night in Miami. I sighed, measuring the heartbeat of this uneasy city and its restless inhabitants. Domestic warfare raged in a million-dollar penthouse overlooking the Atlantic. The battle, in progress for hours, had escalated, according to sleepless condo neighbors. Household items and clothing were now cascading over the highrise balcony.

Rotating my shoulders and rubbing the back of my stiff neck, I considered calling to complain that a dead man was disturbing my sleep.

I locked in on a northeast channel, curious heated exchanges between North Bay Village and Miami Beach police. They were fighting over a corpse. The object of their custody dispute was a late-night fisherman killed by a hit-and-run driver on the John F. Kennedy Bridge. Village cops had arrived first and determined that the accident had occurred on the Beach side of the span dividing the municipalities. Beach cops denied it. They pointed to shards of shattered headlight and a small chrome strip as proof that the point of impact had been on the Village side, and implied that somebody had dragged the body into their jurisdiction. Corpses generate voluminous paperwork. None of the cops wanted the task.

THE VICTIM NOBODY WANTS. My thoughts came printed in headline form, like poetry metered at so many beats per line. The next of kin was probably asleep somewhere out there, blissfully unaware that a stranger's knock at the door would soon change his or her life forever. Would hearts be broken? Dreams shattered?

Life is most often unfair. The man broken on the bridge, left like roadkill first by a motorist who was reckless or drunk, then by clock-watching cops eager to go home on time, probably did not deserve to die. Someone like him invariably turns out to be an honor student, a newlywed, or a good family man working two jobs to support aged parents. Unlike the man I killed. When it happened, I felt only relief and a sense of justice. No regrets. Why did he return to haunt me now?

What I did know was that there would be no more sleep for me this night. I stumbled barefoot to the kitchen to brew a pot of Cuban coffee. Billy Boots followed, and so did Bitsy, dragging her leash and scampering in circles around my feet, eager for adventure.

She is all I have ever inherited, a white toy poodle with the heart and history of a police dog. Most dogs want only to chew, run, and dig. Bitsy yearned for sirens and pursuits in the night. She used to ride Miami's midnight streets in the shotgun seat of a squad car, smuggled aboard by her original owner, a policewoman killed during the riots.

After inhaling half a cup, I felt my eyes focus, settled in my favorite chair, and punched the third button on my speed dialer.

'Homicide,' Sam Bliss answered. He is a middle-aged detective who has worked third shift for years.

'Hi, this is Britt. What's happening?'

'Jesus, girl. You ever sleep? Whatcha doing nosing around at this hour?'

'I'm always working. What's going on out there?'

'You know something I should?'

'Nope, just fishing.'

'SOS, same ol' shit. Otherwise it's quiet.' He dropped his voice. 'Betcher just getting in. Hot date?'

'You wouldn't believe my love life.' If I had one, I thought. 'What's new in the Oliver case?'

'You heard.' He sounded grim.

'No.' He had arrested Angel Oliver, a twenty-six-year-old welfare mother, for the

5

murder of her fifteen-month-old daughter, her eighth child. Cause of death: starvation. Baby Cynthia had never held a toy or seen a Christmas tree. She had lived her brief life in a cardboard carton. By the time a concerned neighbor alerted police, the baby was comatose. Rushed to a hospital, she died. She weighed six pounds.

'Let-'em-go Joe reduced it to manslaughter and set bond at twenty-five hundred.'

'Did she post it?' I scribbled notes on the pad by the phone. Circuit Judge Joe Turrell believed in the basic goodness of human beings and the inalienable rights of the accused. The more heat he took for being too liberal, the more leniently he ruled. Had Joe been a woman, he would always be pregnant. The man could not say no. He was a defense attorney's dream.

'Yep. Get this, the father of her six oldest sued for custody two months ago. Nice guy. Works construction up in Orlando. Says she was neglecting his kids and misusing his support payments. His new wife wants to raise them, but a judge saw 'no reason to take the children from their mother.' '

'Guess he'll get 'em now.'

'Don't count on it. Poor bastard came down over the weekend. His ex-mother-in-law kept the kids while Angel was in jail.

Wouldn't even let him see them. He's gonna have to hire another lawyer and start from scratch.'

'Somebody should start a spay-and-neuter program for unfit parents.' I reached for my coffee cup. 'That woman should be stopped before she has more babies.'

'Too late. That's why Joe reduced her bond.'

'Oh, no.' I nearly strangled on the steaming brew.

'Yep. She's nearly four months along.'

I began to feel better as we exchanged gripes and horror stories, bad-mouthing social services and the judiciary. Like liquid lightning, the caffeine had jump-started my brain cells.

I called the Surfside cops next, for the latest on their elusive cat burglar who prowled the dark to steal high-heeled shoes and fondle the toes of sleeping women.

'Definitely a foot fetish,' the sergeant muttered indignantly. 'Sickest thing I've ever seen.'

Then I called Miami Beach, where investigators were now handling the hit-and-run on the bridge. I showered, downed more coffee, ate a strawberry Pop-Tart, and was painting my toenails primrose pink when the scanner emitted an emergency tone. I cocked

7

my head to listen, tiny brush in hand, a glistening pearl-like drop of polish clinging to the tip. A shooting, possibly fatal, at the downtown Metrorail station. It was 5:15 A.M.

Just leaving homicide, Sam caught my call.

'You taking this one?' I asked.

'Looks like. My day starts when somebody else's ends.' He groaned. 'Supposed to take my youngest to school today. His mom's gonna be pissed off.'

'Somebody else's day apparently got off to an even worse start.' I wiggled my toes, hoping to dry the polish faster. 'What is it?'

'Apparently a security guard. DOA.'

'Anybody in custody?'

'Nope. I'm on the way. Gotta go.'

'Was it a shootout?'

'Won't know till I get there,' he said. Irritation crept into his voice. 'Gimme a break. Call me later.'

'I'll see you there.'

'Sure,' he said, without enthusiasm. 'Looking forward to it.'

I dressed hurriedly, trying not to smudge my wet toenails. Despite my rush I hesitated, closed the door, and returned to the bedroom. I slid the Smith & Wesson .38 from beneath the pillow next to mine. The weight was heavier and the blue steel colder than I remembered. This weapon, returned to me after the shooting investigation, saved my life. I should be grateful. Why, instead, did it make me sick to see it?

The front stoop was empty. Too early for the morning paper. My T-Bird chirped as I unlocked it with the remote. I slipped the gun into the glove compartment and snapped the door shut.

The faint promise of dawn smeared the eastern rim of a sapphire-blue horizon as I drove west, toward the dark across the causeway. The surface of Biscayne Bay mirrored Miami's sparkling skyline, reflecting a sight too beautiful to relate to what was ugly, brutal, and afoot on its streets.

★ ★ ★

Flashing lights splashed eerie shadows across pavement still adrift with the detritus of the night. Huddled groups of cops; medics packing up to leave. Sam Bliss stood out, tall, heavyset, and spreading around the middle. He wore his brown suit. Derisive colleagues called him the man with the blue suit and the brown suit. Ignoring them, he continued to alternate, brown suit one day, blue the next. Many homicide detectives spent their overtime on flashy cars and clothes, part of the image. Sam worked all the OT and every extra-duty job he could, but his wheels were compact and his wardrobe limited. His money supported a showplace home near Perrine, two acres amid orange and avocado groves, with a pool and a duck pond, a spread where his kids could ride horses and build tree houses. He was directing crime scene technicians at the moment.

The star around whom all the others revolved lay on his back in his own blood, staring sightless at puffy clouds drifting across a celestial-blue canvas. The new dawn had broken without him, pink and ethereal with shades of violet. A baby-faced young man, he looked startled that he had been suddenly cheated out of fifty years of life.

His blue uniform was neatly pressed, creases sharp. Shoes shiny. Holster empty. The killer was gone, along with the dead man's gun. An obscene round little mouth gaped open above his left eye, the bullet hole small and neat. The slug had exploded out the back of his head, taking a fist-sized chunk of skull with it. Bone and pinkish brain matter had splattered a stainless steel turnstile. A technician's small orange cone marked a single shell casing that lay on the pavement a few feet from the body. He had been shot only a block from police headquarters, just two minutes from

10

America's finest trauma center, but nothing could have saved him.

'He was still gasping when we arrived,' a paramedic said. His eyes were distant and he appeared oddly idle, lost without a patient to focus on. 'But he shut down fast. Used the paddles on him but he flat-lined.'

Soaring shadows and the flutter of wings drew my eyes skyward. The vultures had been back for months now, congregating down-town, cruising the hot-air currents, circling the spire of the old courthouse. Their small beady eyes missed nothing, nothing dead. Nature's cleanup crew. Had we not arrived first they would have swooped down to surround the fresh corpse.

A growing trickle of cars signaled morning traffic to come. The rising sun glinted off their glass and metal as sleepy motorists slowed to stare.

The corpse lay still, but his blood moved like something still alive, snaking relentlessly downhill, closer and closer to the knot of preoccupied cops focused on the official business of death. They cursed aloud as it inched precariously close, backing up and side-stepping to avoid soiling their shoes. Twenty feet long, the crimson ribbon glowed in the sun's first rays like a river seen from the air, continuing to widen and advance like some Blob in a horror film.

'Let's get this cleaned up!' bawled a short-tempered, unshaven Metrorail representative. 'We need to expedite!' He wanted the body gone, the mess removed before rush hour. Sam dug in his heels, refusing to request the on-call medical examiner until the techs had finished. This would be the doctor's third scene this shift. A tourist had drowned in a Miami Beach hotel pool; then the fatal hit-and-run on the bridge.

★ ★ ★

Bliss pulled on rubber gloves and straddled the victim, once the doctor arrived. They emptied the contents of each pocket into separately labeled brown paper bags. Not much: A $1 Lotto ticket and a cheap wallet.

'Eleven bucks,' he said, checking the billfold. The early morning glare exposed the weariness in his eyes. 'No witnesses so far.' He grimly scanned the block.

Other cops were canvassing among the street people. A young officer talked to one unkempt middle-aged man with ramrod-straight posture, several layers of clothes, and a tattered gym bag. We could hear his 'Yes, sir, no, sir,' responses to the cop's questions.

'Who called it in?' I asked Bliss.

'Anonymous, from a pay phone. We have to pull the tape.'

'Guess it wasn't robbery, since he still had his watch and wallet. Think it was a personal grudge?'

Bliss paused. 'Maybe it was robbery. Maybe his gun was all they wanted.'

The thought was chilling.

★　★　★

The dead guard was Randall W. Fairborn, age twenty-two.

'Don't put it in the newspaper until we notify next of kin,' Bliss warned. 'The security company says it's his mother, in Georgia.'

When I left, the Metrorail representative was arguing with the cops about the latest delay, the morgue wagon. The crew refused to rush breakfast for a passenger that would wait. They were at Denny's.

At Miami headquarters I sparred with Public Information Sergeant Danny Menendez, who refused me access to the taped 911 call that had reported the security guard's shooting.

'The homicide detective on the case has to hear it first and authorize its release,' he said. He sipped his morning coffee and shook his head. His uniform shirt was crisp and

13

starched, and he smelled of shaving lotion. He was right, of course, but I irritably insisted that the tape was public record, invoking the power of the paper's legal department.

He stiffly promised to pass my warning along to the chief and I flounced out. We usually get along pretty well. I was being a bitch, aware that my black mood would probably come back to bite me. It is not smart to antagonize the people I rely on for information.

I hit the Miami Beach and Metro-Dade police departments earlier than usual, yawning through stacks of overnight logs and computerized reports that strip away all heat and passion, reducing life-and-death events to cold, colorless codes on long grey printouts.

When I called from Metro-Dade headquarters to tell the day slot about the shooting, Gloria, the city desk clerk, said, 'I was just paging you. You'd better come on in. Fred wants you in his office, right away.'

Uh-oh. What did our city editor want this early?

'I don't know, but it must be important. He's asked for you twice already.'

Damn. What could be . . . ? Then I knew. Danny Menendez. That skanky weasel had complained about our skirmish. Ill-tempered cops jerk me around all the time, and I never snivel to *their* bosses. I hate crybabies.

Seething, I drove back to the office.

★ ★ ★

'How are you, Britt?' Fred Douglas's searching look made me squirm. Reporters were so much furniture to him. If we disappeared and the cops asked for our descriptions and what we were last seen wearing, he would have no clue. What was this? In my dark mood, I was certainly in no condition for close scrutiny. I must look like hell, I thought. That was how I felt. Shoving my hair back off my face, I wished I had used a comb and lipstick before our meeting. Something odd lurked in Fred's eyes. I vowed payback for Danny Menendez.

Fred leaned forward and pursed his lips, leather chair creaking. 'We've been aware, Britt, that it's been a tough few months for you.'

His concern made my eyes sting — because I am overtired, I told myself, not suffering from post-traumatic stress. That's what my friend Lottie Dane calls my 'flashbacks, black thoughts, and nightmares.'

'So I think we've come up with something you'll like.' His eyes crinkled and the corners

15

of his mouth curled up.

Oh, shit, I thought.

'I don't need any — ' I began.

'Hold it.' He raised his hand, eyes expectant. 'You're gonna thank me for this. You're gonna love it.' He could not keep a smile off his face.

It is cause for alarm when an editor predicts I will love something.

'You know they're filming *Margin of Error* here.'

I nodded warily. The first Hollywood epic to shoot on location in South Florida since the hurricane.

'Starring Lance Westfell.' Fred's eyes literally twinkled.

This had to be worse than I suspected. Mind racing, I nodded again.

'I suppose you've heard that he plays a reporter — actually, a government agent undercover as a reporter.'

Totally in the dark about the script, I nodded anyway, for consistency's sake.

'Well, the director, Phillip Hodges, feels that Lance' — I looked properly impressed at his casual use of the star's first name — 'needs to experience what it's really like for a reporter to cover the cops in Miami.'

Oh-no, I thought. Oh-no, oh-no, oh-no.

'And who better' — his hands formed a

flourish — 'than our own Green Eyeshade Award winner, Britt Montero, to introduce Lance Westfell to her beat and teach him the ropes?'

My head was swiveling right to left before he finished the sentence.

'Not a good idea,' I said emphatically.

Fred's eyes locked on mine, steel replacing the glitter. '*Excellent* idea.' His voice rose, becoming authoritarian. 'This project is important to the entire community.' On his feet now, he paced the length of his small office. 'Do you have any idea how much money Hollywood movie crews spend on location?'

He did not wait for an answer.

'This feature will be a shot in the arm to the local economy,' he went on. 'More importantly, it's an opportunity for us to show the rest of the world that Miami is back, that we are no longer a disaster area, that we've recovered from the storm.'

The painfully slow process of rebuilding was far from over. The city still struggled to recover from the hurricane and put life as it once was back together. Like me. We both knew that.

'Miami needs this shot at becoming the new film capital. We're even allowing the *Margin of Error* crew to shoot scenes here in

17

the newsroom. Only between midnight and eight A.M.,' he added hastily, in response to my startled look, 'so they don't interfere with the business of getting out a newspaper.'

'How nice. We'll still publish.'

'Now, Britt.' He tried to sound conciliatory. 'Half the people in this town would hock their grandmothers for this assignment, my wife and kids included. It'll be fun, a change of pace. Make it your top priority. Give him the tour, fill him in. Be nice.'

'Fred, this makes me really uncomfortable. I'm not the Chamber of Commerce. I don't have time to baby-sit some actor, and I won't turn my beat into a dog and pony show for some pampered Hollywood star,' I said stubbornly.

'Done deal, Britt.' His words rang with ominous finality. 'It's not baby-sitting; consider it a collaboration. The advance crew and Westfell arrived yesterday. I gave them your number here.

'This will be fun, making your rounds with a genuine film star instead of the same old cops and robbers. Enjoy!' he boomed as though he'd handed me a bonus.

'But whatever you do, Britt,' Fred warned, as I stalked out, 'don't let anything happen to the man. For God's sake, see that he's not mugged.'

18

'I thought this wasn't baby-sitting.'

He shrugged and picked up his phone, dismissing me.

★ ★ ★

My taste in movies, on the rare occasion that I get to see one in its entirety, tends toward lighthearted comedies, musical romps, and weepy romances, not slow-motion shootouts with flying body parts and exploding scenery. I encounter those on Miami streets every day. Lance Westfell. The only image I could conjure up was the larger-than-life actor striding across the big screen in tight-legged black Western garb, cracking a huge bull-whip. Would he bring it with him on the police beat? There are times I could use a bullwhip, a cattle prod, or, better yet, a hand grenade. I went back to the library and asked Onnie for Lance Westfell's file.

'I hear he's in town,' she chirped. 'I'd love to get his autograph for Darryl. He loved the movie where Westfell played a robot from another dimension, saw it four times. That boy walked like a robot for months. You gonna write about Westfell?'

'Only if he gets arrested. Or murdered.'

★ ★ ★

A message from Kendall McDonald was on my desk. I grinned in spite of myself. He missed me. Down off his high horse at last. My heart thudded in anticipation as I called homicide and asked for the lieutenant. Should I accept at once if he asked me to dinner, I wondered, or be cool?

'Glad you returned my call.'

Uh-oh. Something wrong here. His tone was businesslike, arm's length, without personal warmth.

'I wanted to pass along a few names and numbers, in case you hadn't made an appointment to see someone yet. I've checked them out, their reputations are all good.'

'You didn't have to go to all that trouble,' I said, deliberately distant.

'It's important,' he said.

'I'm pretty busy,' I said vaguely.

'Britt, you need this. You know I understand, firsthand, what happens to people in your situation. They tend to take risks, do things they ordinarily wouldn't. You can lose touch with your emotions, start feeling numb.'

'Puh-leeze,' I said flatly. 'That's not me. Why does everybody want to overdramatize this? I've got enough on my mind.' I told him about the Westfell assignment.

'Well,' he said, disappointed, 'don't go

20

Hollywood on us.'

'You know me. I'm not the type to go gaga over some superficial Hollywood heartthrob.' I should have said that I've met plenty of actors, most of them cops.

I did not bother to write down the numbers he carefully repeated, or thank him.

★ ★ ★

Lottie reappeared in the newsroom that afternoon, fresh from covering an erupting volcano in Nicaragua.

Frizzy red hair long and loose, wearing her cowboy boots, khaki cargo pants, and multi-pocketed vest, she was still high on adrenaline. She is the best news photographer I know. Too energized to light in one place, she circled my desk like a wild bird in a wind draft.

I studied her more carefully. 'Is your hair singed?'

'Dunno.' She pushed it back absently. 'Could be. Another rampage at Mother Nature,' she said in her Texas twang. 'You shoulda seen it, Britt. Bigger than the one we covered in 'ninety-two.' Her eyes narrowed and she dropped her voice. 'You look like shit. Trouble sleeping again? Shoulda been with me. Hot lava spewing, ash raining, rocks

21

exploding, thunderclaps from under the ground. You'da been more fun than Janowitz, that's for sure. That man sure can whine.'

Her face glowed.

'It was like being in an earthquake 'cept it don't stop; the ground keeps trembling underfoot. Ma Nature on another tear. Flares shooting, molten lava bombs bursting half a mile away. I love it.'

'Are the natives in a panic?' I asked, glad she was back.

'Hell, no, they're throwing tailgate parties to watch. It's like Fourth of July, 'cept, a-course, they don't have Fourth of July down there. They're all hiring on as guides to the press, and tourists are rolling in by the busload. They got themselves a whole new industry.' She stopped circling and crossed her arms. 'What's with you, Britt? Spit it out.'

I told her about my special assignment.

'Westfell! Are you complaining? I'd be happy as a five-year-old on Christmas morning. You are one sick puppy. Hey, I'll do it, I'll do it!'

I shushed her. 'Nobody else knows about it yet.' I was not ready for the teasing and smart remarks from the rest of the newsroom.

'That sexy, hot bod.' Lottie gave a mean little whistle that sounded like steam escaping from between her teeth. 'Did you see him bare-ass naked in *Dead by Sundown?*'

'No.'

'Hell, I freeze-framed it on my VCR, shot pictures, and blew 'em up. Big. Think we kin git him to sign one?' She raised her eyebrows. 'With a ree-al personal inscription?'

I sighed. Maybe Lance Westfell was lazy. Sally Field showed up to research a reporter's role years ago and accompanied one of the competition out on a story. That star quickly wearied of the mundane life of a reporter and departed in less than an hour, never to be seen again, except on the big screen for $6.50 a pop. I could deal with Lance Westfell for an hour or so . . .

That night I found that what I had feared was true. My toenail polish had failed to dry before my hasty departure that morning and was now one with my panty hose.

★ ★ ★

The next afternoon, on deadline, I hurriedly scooped up my ringing phone.

'Lance Westfell here.' The distinctive voice sounded oddly familiar, as though it should be in digital surround sound. 'Can I come over to the paper?'

'Now?' I said, caught by surprise. 'I'm sort of busy.'

'I won't get in your way, just want to watch.'

'Okay,' I said, impatient to return to my story.

'How do I get there?'

'Where are you?' Christ, I smirked, how will the superhero undercover agent manage to save the world when he can't even find his way to the newspaper?

'At the Sheraton.'

'Drive north, through downtown, then east toward the bay. When you see the water, look up. Fifth floor. Tell security you have an appointment. I'll be in the newsroom,' I said curtly. 'Unless a story breaks and I have to leave before you get here.'

There was a pause. 'Yes, ma'am. Later.' He hung up.

In a matter of minutes, as my fingers danced across the keyboard, an unnatural silence fell across the newsroom. Gretchen, the assistant city editor from hell, stared from the news desk. A copy boy froze in place. I looked up.

Lance Westfell stood at my desk.

'Are you Britt?' He wore blue jeans, a T-shirt, and charisma.

'Yeah.' I glanced around. 'Where's your entourage?'

He looked amused. 'Don't have one.' He

extended his hand. The grip was warm and firm. He was tall, but not as tall as I expected.

'Looks like I caught you in the middle of something.' He leaned over to scrutinize my computer screen.

'Just finishing.' I bashed the SEND button, and the copy vanished into the editing system before he could read the lead. He was the first to break the awkward silence that followed.

'I get the impression that you're not exactly starstruck.'

'I'm sorry,' I said stupidly. 'It's just that I'm very serious about what I do.'

'Don't apologize. That's good. That's good. So am I.' He nodded, his famous face solemn. His body formed a muscular triangle: broad shoulders, weight lifter's arms, and a chest like a Clydesdale over lean hips. Probably the result of years of steroids, I thought. The trademark tousled hair was black, curly and slightly unruly.

To my relief, the phone rang and I snatched it up but all I heard was heavy breathing, either an obscene caller or a gasping asthmatic who had mistaken my number for 911.

'It's him, isn't it? Is he out there?'

'Yes, Lottie.' Word travels at the speed of light in a newsroom full of snoops and gossips. 'Hold on a second.'

Gloria, the city desk clerk, was waving. Not her too, I thought. Instead of shouting across the room as usual, she minced self-consciously to my terminal. 'The police desk is on the other line.' She cut her eyes at Westfell. 'A multiple shooting.'

'Gotta hang up, Lottie. Shooting. See you later.' I punched in Jerry's extension. He monitors police radios in a small nook off the lobby.

'At least three down,' he said. 'A robbery. Somebody started shooting. I hear Westfell is with you.'

'Good guys or bad guys hit?'

'Can't tell yet. Pretty chaotic. What's he like?'

'I'll let you know.' I grabbed a notebook and looked up at Westfell. 'What timing. Let's go.'

2

We burst out the back door to the parking under the building. No steamy wet blanket waited to smother us on this glorious Miami winter day. The humidity had plummeted and

26

the clear air was astir with cool, comfortable breezes. Few surprises left after seven years on the police beat, I thought, but who could have foreseen this? Racing out to a crime scene with one of the nation's ten top box-office stars. Surreal.

The matinee idol climbed into the passenger side of my T-Bird. Light on his feet, he moved with the careless confidence of a professional athlete in shape. His presence, or merely his burnished physique, seemed to fill the car. The musky scent must be his shaving lotion, I thought, or was that testosterone? I floored it. We bounced over the speed bump with a tooth-rattling lurch and careened out on to the Boulevard, where I had to immediately slam on the brakes.

'This is the worst time of day to try to go anywhere in a hurry.' I fretted at the bumper-to-bumper rush-hour traffic. The star looked thoughtful. The dashboard scanner, locked in on the action, broadcast confusion at the scene, adding to the sense of urgency. I wheeled around a corner to use Second Avenue instead of the congested Boulevard, secretly pleased to see my passenger cling to the door handle, then fasten his seat belt.

Before he did, he took out a pack of Marlboros.

27

'Mind if I smoke?'

'No, but not in the car,' I said. 'No ashtray. It's full of change for meters and tolls.'

He put the pack away without protest. He wore a braided leather wristband with a hand-tooled silver clasp. No wristwatch. Time must be no problem when you're a star, I thought. The world waits for you.

He caught my sidelong glance. 'Nice car.'

'Not exactly a stretch limo.'

I didn't like the tone of my voice. I should be more friendly, I thought. He probably doesn't like this any more than I do.

'Bought it after the hurricane,' I offered. 'Already had one just like it, but it got totaled. Huge ficus tree flattened it during the storm.' I did not mention the ill-fated T-Bird before it, or the one before that. Just bad luck, but if he knew, he would probably execute an action-hero stunt leap from my moving car and call a cab.

He looked attentive but said nothing, so I babbled compulsively to fill the void. I hate it when I do that.

'It was at the home of a serial killer. I was trapped there, with him, in the storm.'

'Happened to me once.' He nodded.

'What?'

'Sure, in *Island of the Dead*. Except it was a typhoon. I had to kill the guy.'

28

'Me too,' I murmured. The man was talking about a movie, for God's sake. I suppressed a laugh. 'This was real life.'

'I heard. Phil, my director, and I had dinner with your publisher and Fred, your editor?' He shot me a half smile. 'Sounds like you could have used a stunt double.'

They had been discussing me?

'They come in handy,' he said. 'You see it?'

'What?'

'*Island of the Dead*.'

'Nope, don't think so.'

He shrugged. 'You'll have to catch it on late night. Or pick up the video, 'bout ten years old.'

How arrogant, I thought, for him to think I'd want to see his old movie, for him to assume a void in my life because I missed one of his early B films.

The scanner had reported the shooting location as 2734 NW 54th Street.

'Can you bring up that city directory, the cross-reference from the backseat?'

He reached over the seat and hefted the big, bulky blue book on to his lap with one hand.

'Check out Fifty-fourth Street, Northwest,' I said, veering around a slow-moving produce truck, 'for the name of the business at that address.'

He balanced the book on his knees and leafed through the pages.

I repeated the address. 'Look under the street name, then northwest.'

His large well-manicured index finger roved down one page; then he turned to another. 'Damn.'

'What?' I asked, hopelessly snarled in traffic.

'This gives the name of the resident at every address and their phone number.'

'Right,' I said defensively. 'A great tool for reporters. Even shows how long at that address. That a problem?'

His lip curled in that famous billboard poster sneer as he shook his head. All that was missing was the wicked-looking large-caliber automatic weapon cradled lovingly in his movie ads. 'The tabloid press and the paparazzi must use these things,' he said bitterly. 'I've had my moments with them. What about the right to privacy?'

'There *is* no privacy once the shooting starts.' I accelerated through an amber light a millisecond before it flashed red, then held my breath as three cars behind me followed.

'Nobody stops for red lights anymore,' I complained tersely, 'not since they were knocked out by the storm.' Some were dark for months. Legally, such intersections are to be treated as fourway stops. To Miamians, they present a *¿Quien es mas macho?* challenge. The lights have been repaired, but not their driving habits.

'Zippy Cash,' he said.

'What?'

'Zippy Cash. Looks like a pawnbroker at Twenty-seven thirty-four Northwest Fifty-fourth Street.'

'What chutzpah, an ex-cop owns that place!'

Clyde Zipper had a history of being too quick on the draw and had been forced to turn in his badge and gun after an off-duty barroom shooting. But he was best remembered for something else. An obnoxious prisoner, a career criminal who always filed complaints against arresting officers, deserved or not, charged that after a robbery arrest he had been viciously kicked and beaten in an interrogation room. He described his assailant as a huge white rabbit. Zipper had worn a rabbit costume that same day to an annual Easter egg hunt for underprivileged children at the PBA park. The evidence was purely circumstantial, and internal affairs never could prove a case.

★ ★ ★

I groaned as traffic slowed. Every motorist caught on the crowded Boulevard had switched to the secondary road.

'Funny,' my passenger said. 'I never thought about reporters having to deal with everyday annoyances like traffic. They just always seemed to be there, like cops.' He shrugged. 'But you've got no siren, no flashing lights.'

'What street are we at?' I had my eyes on the suicidal pedestrians darting between cars. I didn't mind the dirty rags and spray bottles. It's the bricks and concrete blocks that I object to. He called out the street signs, ticking off the numbers, navigating as we worked our way north.

Miami police had already cordoned off several blocks to divert traffic. Cops unloaded equipment from the trunks of patrol cars. K-9 officers had arrived, dogs barking and straining at their leashes. The street was blocked by flashing lights: accident investigators, traffic control, fire rescue, ambulances, and a hook and ladder. Parked behind an unmarked, I left a press card on the dash, shoved my handbag under the seat, and slipped the beaded chain with my press ID around my neck.

Lance Westfell adjusted his shades, donned a baseball cap with a Marlins logo, and yanked the brim down over his eyes.

The scene was a mess. Firefighters hosed down a wrecked car and a damaged bus. The barred front windows of Zippy Cash were shattered, the sidewalk awash in broken glass.

Danny Menendez from PIO was already there. 'Hey, Britt.' I knew nobody had died when he waved. He looked too cheerful.

'What the heck happened?'

'You know this is Zipper's shop?'

'I thought so. Is he involved?' I was vaguely aware of Westfell, standing quietly several feet away.

'He got hit, but it's not serious. Here's all I know so far, subject to change as we talk to more people.' Menendez turned his back to the sun and read from his own notes as I scribbled. 'Three armed kids pull a robbery, want guns. Well, they get 'em. Zipper sees what's going down, crouches behind the counter for cover, and starts to pull his thirty-eight. Unfortunately, he's put on a few pounds, and when he crouches, his gut twists his holster. His gun is only half out, and he shoots himself in the thigh. After he opens fire on himself' — Menendez raised an eyebrow at me — 'all hell breaks loose. The clerk draws his side arm, a Walther PPK three-eighty automatic, and a customer pulls his nine

33

millimeter. Everybody, including the robbers, starts shooting. Security cameras in the store catch it all on tape. Should be a hoot.

'The robbers apparently don't realize or don't care that the doors lock automatically. Customers are buzzed in and out and the button is behind the counter.

'Bullets are flying, looks like about twenty-five, thirty rounds fired. Display cases shattered, everybody is panicky, screaming, trying to get out. The perps and the customer can't find the buzzer. Zipper is in pain from his wound and trying to reload, and the clerk can't get to the button from where he is at.

'By this time, everybody wants out. Bad. They smash the front windows trying to escape but can't squeeze between the security bars. The customer loses an earlobe and is bleeding all over the place. Flying glass hits the clerk and one of the robbers. Woman driving by with her kids in the car loses her windshield to a stray bullet. She pulls over and they're all screaming. Zipper finally crawls through the blood and the broken glass, hits the buzzer, and the robbers split out the door. They pile into the get-away car, burn rubber, and slam into a Metro bus in the intersection.' He squinted at his notes.

'The number four route, bound for South Allapattah.'

'Wow. Anybody hurt on the bus?'

'Not seriously, but the driver is totally pissed. He leaves the bus to go call in the accident to his supervisor. Swears he only had six, seven passengers aboard, tops. Comes back and there's twenty-three people on his bus, all clutching their backs and their necks, claiming injuries.'

'You're kidding. Passersby jumped on the bus?'

'Musta seen their chance and took it. Swears he never saw most of 'em before. The robbers bail after the crash, take off running. Their car comes back registered to an elderly woman in Aventura. Must be stolen.'

'Think it could be FMJ?' FMJ, short for Full Metal Jacket, his street name, is a notorious teenage killer and carjacker, a fugitive since a crime rampage more than a year ago. He always shot his victims in the leg, his trademark, but everybody thought he had left town.

Menendez shrugged and thought about it. 'Nobody got shot in the leg except Zipper, and he popped himself.'

'How bad is Zipper hurt?'

'His holster was good solid leather, absorbed a lot of the impact. Slowed it down, flattened it out. The bullet ran out of a lotta gas before it could do too much damage. And he was using one-fifty-four-grain lead hollow points, not the copper jackets that do those jagged numbers. He was lucky.'

Menendez's name was being shouted out from half a dozen different directions, his pager chirping.

'Thanks, Danny.' I lowered my voice. 'Sorry I was such a bitch yesterday. Just a bad mood.'

'I figured.' He grinned. 'No sweat. I have to deal with that every month at home.'

'What?'

'PMS.'

'Damn, you son of a — ' Too late, he had disappeared into a crowd of cops, medics, and bus company officials.

'Bus passengers' lay supine on backboards or grimaced and held their necks. I needed witnesses, descriptions of the robbers and eyeball accounts from anybody who saw a crowd scrambling aboard a dented bus with no driver.

More people were clamoring for medical attention, claiming that they also had been passengers.

'Didn't I just see you come out of that delicatessen down the street?' I asked an 'injured' man.

He nodded solemnly. 'I went there to call my family, to tell them I had been in this terrible accident.'

A well-dressed young black woman told me she missed the gunfire but witnessed the aftermath. 'See that woman?' she whispered, pointing out a patient flat on a backboard. 'She's faking it; she was never on the bus. She was sitting on that bench across the street when it happened. I saw her.'

I crouched beside the 'victim', who clutched her purse to her bosom, eyes closed.

'Ma'am?'

Eyelids fluttered open.

'How do you feel?'

'Not good,' she murmured pitifully.

'Were you on that bus? Witnesses say you were across the street when this happened.'

'No speaka English,' she replied.

Gotcha, I thought. '*No te preocupes. Yo hablo español.*'

'*Sprechen sie Deutsch?*'

★ ★ ★

The irate bus driver argued loudly with the matriarch of an increasingly large Spanish-speaking family who claimed that they, too, had been on the bus. The blades of a police chopper, assisting in the manhunt for the robbers, beat the air overhead. The growing mob of spectators, school kids, and commuters pressed forward, eyes bright, eager to see the carnage at Zippy Cash. Cops tried to force them back.

Zipper's wife arrived, distraught and trembling despite police assurances that her husband's wounds were not life-threatening. Her strawberry-blonde hair was pulled back, exposing an inch of dark roots, and fastened with a white scrunchie.

'Is he really all right?' she pleaded.

'I didn't see him,' I told her, 'but they say he was talking, mad as hell, when they put him in the ambulance.'

'Sounds like him.' Marianne Zipper nodded, her smile tearful. She wore a T-shirt over black tights and athletic shoes, as though she had been working out. 'I always warned him that something like this was gonna happen sooner or later. You sure he's all right?'

I sensed a mood change in the crowd, the noise level, the focus, and felt uneasy. This was the victim's wife, for God's sake. Why was a gaggle of teenagers tittering and staring?

'Why can't he get a normal job like other people?' Marianne Zipper whined, wiping away the tears that coursed down her cheeks.

'First the police work, now ... ' Her voice trailed off. 'Is that ... ?'

I followed her gaze. In pursuit of the story, I had forgotten Lance. He stood three feet from my elbow, hands in his pockets, listening. 'Yeah,' I said. 'They're making a movie.'

'Hi,' she trilled, the long note almost musical. Her dazzling smile was not meant for me. 'I want you to know how much I loved *Lightning Force*.' She brushed by me to gaze up at Lance. 'The way you blew away those Russians and rescued that female spy and the little girl. You were great.'

Westfell smiled modest thanks.

'Would you autograph something for me?' Teeth flashed, eyes twinkled, lashes batted.

'Absolutely,' he said. 'Sorry about your husband.'

'Oh, he'll be okay.' She waved away his concern with an absent gesture. 'I've been through this before.'

She remembered me and turned. 'Can we borrow your pen?'

I handed it over.

'Good, a felt tip. Right here,' she said. Standing on tiptoe, she showed him where to sign her T-shirt, right over her left breast. 'Make it *To Marianne*, one word, two *ns* and an *e*.'

39

Once she broke the ice, everybody plunged in. Moments earlier, cops had been holding spectators back from the crime scene. Now they looked bewildered as the mob surged away, surrounding us.

TV news crews covering the crime suddenly caught on, swung into 180-degree turns, and stampeded toward the star. Wayman Andrews from WTOP reached him first and jabbed a microphone at his mouth, as a cameraman focused on his face.

'Can we do a brief interview, Mr Westfell? How did you happen to be out here today?'

Westfell began to look uncomfortable but stayed polite. 'I would be glad to, but this isn't the time or the place. It would be inappropriate. The publicist on the film will be happy to arrange it. I'm sorry.'

He turned and our eyes caught. People spilled across the street, pouring in our direction. The bloodied victims, the escaped robbers, the bus scam, and another rush hour from hell — all forgotten. Even the woman who claimed to speak no English sprang up from her backboard, scrambling toward us, shouting, 'Mr Westfell, Mr Westfell!'

'Let's get out of here,' I said.

'Right.'

We began to stroll to my T-Bird and wound up running for our lives, the mob hot on our heels. Like the robbers, we escaped.

I floored it. 'Weird,' I gasped, as we turned the corner. 'Reminds me of the riots, except they're not trying to kill us.'

'Maybe they are,' the star said in a guttural growl. 'Did you see my last film?'

Laughter dissolved the tension, my first clue that Westfell had a sense of humor.

'It didn't exactly do well,' he confessed. 'Bombed, in fact. That's why this one is so important.'

'Your fans . . . Does this happen to you all the time?'

The question seemed to surprise him. 'There is no safe place on the planet . . . My house has been broken into. A stranger showed up in my hotel room. Been stalked by crazies and paparazzi, and maybe some nice people, I guess, but how do you sort 'em out? Can't finish a meal, see a show, or take a stroll. People follow you into the bathroom. A woman followed me into the men's room at Spago last week. She was carrying a camera. There's one mental case, a real scary broad — ' He exhaled and shook his head quickly. 'Sometimes I wonder what it would be like to be anonymous, to be able to go anywhere. You won't believe this, but Lexie, my ex-wife — '

'The supermodel?'

41

'Right, and now film actress.' He looked pained and paused. 'Botswana. We were in Botswana once. A thousand light-years from civilization. Walking through a dusty market-place. Then all of a sudden it was just like what happened back there. I really wanted to do this today. I even entertained thoughts about wearing a disguise, a wig, or — '

'Groucho glasses,' I suggested. 'The ones with the nose and mustache.'

'Or a chicken suit,' he said.

'It must go with the turf. Entertainers want recognition.'

'Yeah,' he said, 'but people sifting through your garbage?'

'Where and when do you feel comfortable?'

He considered the question, gazing at passing traffic. 'Not often, maybe with other people in the business, but then you never know when one of them is writing a book. And my problem is, I'm not into the Hollywood scene.'

'Bummer.' I checked the rearview as I stopped for a light. 'Exactly what is this new movie about?'

He paused. 'We want it to be a killer thriller. A wild, blood-curdling, heart-pounding, steamy, suspenseful, roller-coaster ride of a story.'

I cut my eyes at him. 'Sounds like press

release puffery. What's the real story? I'm not writing about it,' I assured him. 'I won't give anything away.'

He shrugged. 'Shooting, chasing. You name it, we blow it up. Cars, powerboats, buildings, planes.'

'Exactly what the youth of America needs — a role model.' I was only half joking. 'I've written so many stories about people who got hurt by some impressionable jerk who got the idea from something he saw in a movie.'

'Such as?' he said. 'People like to use movies as a scapegoat for crimes that would have been committed anyway.'

'Really? What about the kids, all younger than twelve, who burned down the biggest lumberyard in town?'

'Kids play with matches all the time. Think about it. I did it myself, and you probably did too.'

'These kids popped a container filled with gasoline and nails in a microwave. The explosion ignited a fire that injured two firemen. Think they thought that up by themselves? Steven Seagal did it in *Under Siege*. Or the teenager who murdered two people 'just to feel the sensation of killing somebody' after seeing *Menace II Society*?'

'Hey,' he argued, 'the premise for *Margin of Error* is reality-based; the co-star is a winner. Meredith Page does not do dreck. She's had two Academy Award nominations. She'll be here next week, and I'm looking forward to working with her.'

'Sorry.' I meant it. Why was I picking a fight with him?

'That's okay,' Westfell said. 'My skin is thicker than that. Has to be in this business. You have to shoot me three times before I take offense.

'Besides, your newspaper is just as guilty. Publishing crime news gives people ideas. Like the one you wrote the other day about the rash of Lexus thefts. You wrote that the new models include an extra key in the owner's manual, usually kept in the glove box. Most owners don't even know it's there. But the thieves do, so they break into new cars, find the key, and take off.'

'But now the Lexus owners who read it are aware and can remove the key.' I was impressed that he had read my story.

'But you also told more thieves where to find it.'

'Car thieves probably don't read the News.'

'Probably don't go to movies either.'

I couldn't help smiling. He had me, but he didn't stop to crow about it.

'Now, Margin of Error revolves around a nuclear plant in Cuba and international sabotage designed to create a Chernobyl-like disaster that would make South Florida and the Caribbean uninhabitable for the next thousand years.'

'Our politicians and developers have already done that.'

His smile made me understand why fans thought him sexy.

'Is the movie company going to Cuba?'

'Nope, we're building the nuclear reactor set out in the Everglades. It'll pass for Cuba.'

'How did they get permits to do that on environmentally sensitive land?' I risked seeming confrontational again, but this sounded like a good investigative piece to me.

'It's nothing permanent; the producers promised that we won't disturb the balance of nature. We'll put everything back the way it was when we wrap. We're environmentally sensitive.' His tone had become defensive again.

An excellent outrage piece, I thought, but who would print it? Everybody — state, federal, and county officials, even the environmentalists and my editors — was playing footsie with the filmmakers.

'In the script, the Russians built the power plant, but since they pulled out of Cuba, maintenance and security are lax, which attracts the terrorists. Their plan could be the

45

most devastating act of terrorism to ever hit the United States, and the terrorists never even have to set foot on U.S. soil. What's scary is that there really is such a plant.'

'You stop 'em and kill 'em all at the end?'

'Every last SOB.'

'Too bad real life isn't that simple.' I swung the T-Bird into my space under the *News* building.

* * *

Westfell sat next to me at my computer terminal as I wrote the story. I made one last check before hitting the SEND key; the robbers remained at large. Local hospitals were on alert since one or more might have been hit, a good possibility with all that gunfire. If so, a car would roar up to an emergency room; the occupants would throw out the wounded and take off. The usual scenario. So far, it hadn't happened.

Westfell and I wandered down to the nearly deserted cafeteria and sipped coffee at a table with view. Miami Beach sparkled against the darkening sky across the bay.

'So, how does this pace, this job, affect your personal life?'

I usually ask the questions. This was unnatural. 'The beat is more a lifestyle than a

46

job,' I said reluctantly. 'Luckily, I don't have a husband or kids to worry about. Haven't been married.'

'Lucky you,' he said.

'Came close right out of college. But he hated Miami and this is my home. I love it here.' I thought of Kendall McDonald. 'There's been another relationship, on and off for a couple of years, mostly off. Our jobs usually conflict.' Time to turn this conversation around. 'You've been married twice.' I had done my homework too.

'Yep.' He leaned back in his chair, a Styrofoam coffee cup almost lost in his big fist. 'My first wife, Renee, and I met in college, at a Nature Conservancy meeting.'

'You always planned to be a actor?'

'Hell, no.' He shook his head, smiling ruefully. 'I was at Yale, planning on a law degree. Film crew showed up one day at the gym where I worked out. Shooting a commercial, asked me to audition for a part. Did it on a dare, landed the job, the money was good. Next thing I knew, I was in show biz.'

'What is Renee doing now?'

'Exactly what she always said she would. She stuck to her original goals. She's a protection ecologist working to preserve the rain forest and imperiled habitats in Brazil.'

'What happened? Why didn't you two work out?'

He sighed. 'She didn't want to live in Hollywood. I didn't want to live in the rain forest. I'm allergic to bee stings and mosquito bites. Tough on my kids. Spend as much time as I can with them. They're great, thanks to their mother. Brendan is fourteen, Shelley, twelve.'

'And what about the supermodel?'

'Wife number two. A mistake. A bad one.'

Nostalgic for the first wife, bitter at the second. Probably too recent, I thought.

'An ambitious woman,' he went on, 'a very ambitious woman. She wanted to be a movie star, and Lexie always gets exactly what she wants.' He took out a cigarette, looked for an ashtray, then glanced around furtively.

'This another no smoking zone?'

'Yeah,' I said. 'But who's gonna bust a superhero, the only man who can save the world?'

He lit up. Thick, curling lashes veiled his black eyes. There should be laws against men being that beautiful. He took a deep drag and exhaled, regarding me from behind the blue-grey smoke. 'This time it's just South Florida and the Caribbean.'

★ ★ ★

48

I drove him back to his hotel but declined his invitation to dinner. He did not have to feed me for showing him around.

''Bye,' I said, as he leaned in the passenger window to say good night.

'What time tomorrow?'

My jaw must have dropped. 'You want to do this again?'

He seemed startled. 'Sure. I should try to see as much as I can. We don't start shooting for a few days. I got a lot out of just seeing you work this afternoon.'

Doormen watched. Water spouted from landscaped fountains. A stretch limo rolled up behind my T-Bird.

'I bet,' I said. 'Will Marianne Zipper always remember this as the day her husband was shot or the day she got your autograph?'

He shrugged. 'Britt Montero.' The words rolled slowly off his tongue. 'One thing I learned today — the world is a more interesting place with you out there in it.'

He turned and walked into the lobby alone.

3

Half listening to the scanner, I hummed to the music from the car stereo as I drove home. Florida highway patrolmen on the police radio in rural South Dade were whooping it up, playing rodeo as they tried to corral a bull roaming loose on the Turnpike. Toto sang on the stereo about Africa, and all around me the night was star-studded and bejeweled. As I drove east across the MacArthur Causeway, a quarter moon floated near the Gemini Twins to the northeast, and to the south a sparkling cruise ship sailed majestically through Government Cut, the main shipping channel, carrying a thousand strangers toward open sea and a journey of infinite possibility.

★ ★ ★

The red light flashed furiously on my message machine. Six calls, three from Lottie.

I popped a frozen eggplant parmigiana in the oven, took Bitsy for a quick walk, then returned her calls.

'Where have you been?' she demanded. 'What happened? God almighty, tell me everything. Don't leave nothing out. Is he brokenhearted? Is he still in love with Lexie Duran?'

'I don't think so. From what I saw, I don't think he's comfortable sharing the same solar system with her.'

When Lottie heard I had declined the star's dinner invitation, she became absolutely apoplectic.

'He didn't mean it,' I assured her. 'He was trying to be polite. He doesn't like reporters. I wasn't dressed for it. I had to come home and take the dog out. I — '

'Sure, sure, sure. And you had to open your mail, wash your hair, and change your oil. Hell all Friday, Britt, you can spit out ten thousand and one reasons not to have fun. You are more stubborn than a dead mule. You've gotta get your act back together. Tonight coulda been the romantic highlight of your memoirs!'

'Get real, Lottie, the man dates movie stars and supermodels.'

'Surgically altered actresses and anorexic ice maidens. You are probably the first genuine red-blooded woman he's seen in years. He's hot.'

'He seems more intelligent than I expected. Did you know he went to law school at Yale?' The oven timer signaled that my meal was ready. I poured a glass of red wine, the phone still to my ear. 'He did say something really cool.' I repeated his final words to me.

She paused. 'Sounds like something I've heard before.'

'Sounded original to me.'

'So what is this dinner for one?'

'Mrs Paul's.'

She groaned. 'At worst, you woulda had the gourmet meal of a lifetime. At best you woulda had the night of a lifetime.'

'If he asks again,' I said slowly, 'maybe I will. He really sounded serious about researching his role. He's coming back.'

'Thank you, Jesus,' Lottie said.

'Next time you go to Blockbuster,' I said, 'could you rent *Island of the Dead* for me? It was way weird, out at the scene. The crowd, even the TV reporters, acted as though Westfell being there was big time, more dramatic and newsworthy than a real live shootout.'

★ ★ ★

I did not dream at all that night. A blessing.

Gloria paged me, a message from Lance

52

Westfell next morning.

I called the number. 'Margin Production.' The woman had an English accent and an attitude, decidedly cool and distant. 'Whom shall I say is calling?'

She warmed up and put me right through when I told her. 'Got tied up with some business here and went out to look at a house,' he said, speaking with the casual warmth of an old friend. 'I'm gonna lease it. It's great. Where are you?'

'Miami police headquarters,' I said.

'Any news?'

'Nothing huge.'

'Good, I didn't want to miss anything. I'll try to break outa here and catch you later.'

'Sure. The office can always reach me.'

'Guess what?' he added, sounding pleased. 'The County Commissioners want to give me the key to the county at their next meeting.'

'Last person they gave it to is still a fugitive. They're not too discerning.'

'True?'

'I didn't make it up.'

'You know how to hurt a guy.'

'That's life.'

'Save the story. Later.'

He hung up. I had the distinct impression that the only place I would see him again was on the silver screen.

I found Detective Bliss at his desk in the homicide office. He was wearing his brown suit. He had no new leads in the murder of Randall Fairborn, the young security guard. At homicide I was always on the alert for a possible Kendall McDonald sighting. My inquiring eyes wandered toward his office. It looked empty.

'One possible witness called in after your story in the paper,' Bliss was saying. 'She sounded credible, at first.'

'What changed your mind?' I sat in the chair next to his desk and balanced my notebook on my knee.

'She offered to come down and try to make an ID from mug shots, but couldn't make it this afternoon because she's lunching with the Virgin Mary. The two of them apparently have regular tête-à-têtes.'

'Whoops. Sorry about that. What about the nine-one-one caller?'

'Male voice. Could be a witness. Called it in at five-twelve A.M. Said' — Bliss paused to consult his notes — ' 'Better send somebody over to the Metrorail station at the government center.' The operator asks why, and he says, 'Somebody just took a bullet. They shot him, and I think he's gonna die. Better send somebody.' That's when he hung up.'

I leaned forward, as though something more could be discerned from staring at his notes. 'Sounds like he saw the victim, knew it was serious. You think 'they' is a figure of speech or he really saw more than one?'

'Your guess is as good as mine.'

'What did he sound like? Young? Old? Black? White?'

'No accent. No panic. Very matter-of-fact. Doesn't sound like he's disguising his voice. Possibly white male, between thirty-five and fifty.'

'Think it might be the killer playing games?'

'Anything's possible.'

'I'll mention in my follow-up that you'd like to talk to the caller.'

'Do what you can, appreciate it.'

'Did they print the phone?'

'Yeah, got lots of stuff, mostly smudges and smears. You realize how many people handle it every day? Even if we make a match, all he's gotta say is that he used that pay phone sometime recently. But the lab is working it.'

'What about the victim?'

'Didn't appear to have any alcohol or drugs aboard, according to prelim lab reports. Clean-cut. No record. On Apollo's payroll since September. Punctual, reliable, no apparent problems or incidents on or off the job. Talked to next of kin this morning. The mother. She's in town, plans to take her boy back home to Georgia.'

★　★　★

I drove to Randall W. Fairborn's apartment. The stucco two-storey building, a former motel, had long ago converted to efficiencies. The courtyard had a straggly palm tree and resounded with the sounds of noisy children at play. How, I wondered, did Randall Fairborn ever manage to sleep after working all night? His neighbors obviously spent a great deal of time sitting outside their crowded rooms. Milk crates and mismatched chairs, some ragged, stood outside each door.

I found Fairborn's name on the mailbox, climbed the stairs, and knocked on the peeling yellow door to apartment 7-G. Dread dried my mouth. Parents who lose a child to violence are never, ever the same again. Some react with rage and hostility, slamming doors, calling the cops, or attacking strangers who dare to intrude. Others are far too fragile to speak with an outsider. Only a messenger, I always pray that they seize this moment to tell their story, send a message, and perhaps even set into motion the events that will lead to justice. Resolution is so rare.

I steeled my heart, took a deep breath, and knocked again.

A stocky woman in her fifties cracked open the door. She wore glasses, a simple dark blue suit, and white blouse and was clutching a Bible. Her skin color was darker than her son's. She had been weeping.

'Mrs Fairborn? My name is Britt Montero.' I handed her my business card. 'I work for the *Miami News*. I wanted to talk to you about your son.'

She held the card gingerly as though it were something unusual and delicate, studied it through her bifocals, then lifted her eyes to mine for a long moment. Hers were swollen, red veins crisscrossing the whites. They already wore the look of irrevocable loss.

She nodded and opened the door wide. 'Come in,' she said softly. 'I wondered why nobody came.'

Stomach knotted, I stepped inside. Despite the decaying building and his single status, Randall W. Fairborn's tiny apartment was scrupulously neat. His mother had apparently been packing his possessions when I knocked. A cardboard box rested on the bed. The job was no major task. Her son did not live long enough to accumulate much. Some books and papers on the table. The door to the small closet stood open, exposing a second uniform on a hanger.

'I'm so sorry. I wrote the story in yesterday's newspaper.'

'I saw it. The man at the morgue gave me a copy when I asked him what happened to Randall. He said it would explain. I still don't understand.'

The only items on the closet floor were a worn but highly polished pair of shoes. She picked them up. 'He had another pair,' she said gravely, as though that was important for me to know. 'He was wearing them when . . . ' Her voice cracked but she swallowed hard and went on. 'He always took care of his things and kept them tidy. You can say that about him. Write that down,' she instructed, eyes moving to my notebook. 'Write it down. That boy took pride in his appearance. I taught him that.'

She clutched the shoes to her bosom.

'Lord Jesus,' she whispered, 'please tell me, why did God take my baby?' She stared at me. 'Why did God take my baby?'

I wanted to tell her that God did not take her baby, that it was a man with a gun, but I didn't. She sat heavily on the bed and I sat in the only chair. Randall was an only child, she said. He became the man of the family at age nine, when his father drowned in a fishing

58

accident. Randall took care of his mother, who did housework for a living. She saw that he went to church and to school. His first job was at age eleven.

He had come to Miami to study computer science at Miami-Dade Community College. That was why he took the night job in security, in order to attend classes by day. The books on the table were texts.

'He was so excited about coming to the big city,' Dorothy Fairborn said. 'He tol' me, 'Mama, get with the times. It's almost the twenty-first century, you got to know books and computers if you're going anywhere in this world. Know computers, you kin always get a job, anyplace.' His daddy didn't have the education. He worked in the sawmill. Randall wanted a good job. He wanted to wear a clean shirt to work. He wanted to make me proud.' Tears spilled over.

'That boy never caused nobody a minute's trouble,' she gasped. 'He was the sweetest soul who ever took a breath.'

She had no clue as to who killed her son, or why, she said. Rising suddenly, she resumed packing, as though moving, staying busy, kept her from shattering completely. She had come to Miami alone on a Greyhound bus and was exhausted.

'I kept telling him to stop sending money home, to eat right.' She shook her head. The cupboard contained only breakfast cereal, a jar of apple butter, and cardboard boxes of macaroni and cheese. The nearly empty refrigerator held apples, milk, and a grape-fruit.

I left her at the door, holding the Bible. The tinny music of an ice-cream truck wafted up from the street below, mingled with the shouts of the children. She asked again as I started down the stairs, 'Why did God take my baby?'

Parents who lose a child to violence are never the same. Neither are those who witness their pain.

★ ★ ★

Lance Westfell had appropriated my desk and was signing autographs when I walked into the newsroom. Clad in white trousers and a guayabera, he was adapting fast to life in the Miami lane. Onnie, my friend from the library, another single mother, stood at the head of the line, face aglow. I thought of Darryl, her precious little boy, and the woman I had just left.

★ ★ ★

'Britt!' Lance flashed his movie-star grin. 'Didn't miss anything, did I?'

I shook my head silently, pulled Ryan's chair up to my terminal, and went to work.

'Got a terrific house,' Lance was saying. 'Leased for three months. Waterfront, on Star Island. Mediterranean-style villa, gardens, a pool, a spa, a sauna, a tennis court, security, and a great sunset view of the city skyline across the bay. Even a well-stocked wine cellar.'

'Very nice.' I thought of Randall Fairborn's modest apartment, its tiny kitchen and nearly empty cupboards, and opened my notebook. Westfell would not stop talking, as I tried to focus on the story.

'Met your friend, Lottie. The photographer. A trip. She's dynamite.'

'Good.'

'What are we working on?' He rolled his chair closer to peer at my computer screen.

I wondered what he meant by 'we.'

'A follow,' I said brightly. 'Got some great quotes from the widowed mother of a murdered security guard.' I tapped in my password, glanced at Lance, and slugged the story MOTHER. He fell silent and watched me work. News broke before I finished: a telephone tip from a Miami Beach detective. A suspect had been

61

identified in the fatal hit-and-run on the bridge three nights ago. That was the good news. The bad news was that the man was now barricaded in his Miami Shores home, threatening suicide and surrounded by a SWAT team.

'Here we go again,' I said. Westfell appeared thrilled.

The suspect had cleaned up his car and taken it to a body shop, according to the detective. What gave him away was traces of human hair, flesh, and blood beneath the chrome strip that holds the windshield in place.

When a patrolman arrived, summoned by the shop owner, the suspect had leaped into his Ford Bronco and fled. With an increasing number of cops in hot pursuit, he raced home, roared into his driveway, and dashed inside. I have never understood fleeing suspects who seem to think, if they can just make it home, that they have won and the cops will go away. That is not how it works. Life is not a game of home free.

We parked down the block and approached on foot. The house, on a quiet residential street, actually belonged to the suspect's parents, the cops said. The son, age twenty-six, had done time for burglary, drug, and driving offences and swore he would never go back to jail. When he ran in the back door shouting that police were right behind him, his family ran out the front. They forgot to take along the family pistol, kept for home protection. Just as well. Who knows what bad things might have happened had family members come running out to greet the cops with it.

However, the first question police ask is whether there is a gun in the house. If the fugitive had not thought about the weapon, the cops brought it to mind by loudly demanding that he throw it out and surrender.

He refused.

Now he was armed, SWAT had mobilized, every house on the block had been blacked out, the neighborhood evacuated, and a hostage negotiator summoned. Sharpshooters were dressed in black and wore ballistic helmets. Protected from neck to groin by Kevlar vests, they crouched low, their .308-caliber Remington sniper rifles poised.

The arrival of Lance Westfell broke the tension. The SWAT cops were all eager to meet him. Since *Miami Vice*, most local lawmen no longer fantasize about heroically thwarting a major crime in progress. The favorite fantasy now is to make big bucks writing movie or television scripts. They mobbed the star and pumped his hand. What about the young man inside, holding himself hostage, gun to his head? I wondered.

Refusing to surrender, he had ignored orders from police, pleas from his overweight mother, and halfhearted cajoling from a kid sister who wore gold rings in her pierced nostril and appeared to be in her teens.

The father, police said, was out of town. Made sense to me. If they were my family, I would definitely be out of town myself.

Hostage negotiator Glenn Grimes strode our way. 'Glenn,' I said, notebook ready, 'can you fill me in about your — '

He swept by without a nod and joined the cluster around the film star. 'Mr Westfell,' he said. 'I hate to ask this, but we're having no luck with this kid. The mother says he's a big fan. Think you could help us out and give it a try?'

The mother and sister gazed imploringly from a distance, hands clasped prayerfully.

'Sure, I'll give it a shot.' Westfell did not seem surprised. I was. Were they serious? Was this *Candid Camera*? Were they already filming the movie? Was I the only one here who didn't know it?

Grimes, Lance, and the lieutenant in charge broke from the group and headed for the command post. The negotiator lifted the yellow crime-scene tape. Lance and the lieutenant ducked beneath. I followed. Or tried to.

The lieutenant blocked my way. 'Sorry, Britt, outside the tape.'

'But,' I sputtered, 'but Westfell's with me!'

'Sorry. No press inside the tape. That means you.' He added insult to injury when he tersely instructed a patrolman manning the police line to 'Keep an eye on her,' then turned to catch up to Grimes and Westfell.

Damn.

Lottie arrived, breathless. 'Did you hear? I met him! I met him!' She looked around. 'Where is he?' she demanded. 'I thought he was with you.'

We took turns watching, peering through the 500-millimeter telephoto lens mounted on her Nikon. The high magnification, and a device that doubles focal length, works as well as a pair of high-powered binoculars.

The barricaded suspect was refusing to answer the telephone, so SWAT was sending in Alex. Two hundred and fifty pounds, he stands three and a half feet tall. His heart is a battery pack, his face a camera that swivels and scans. A Star Wars-style robot, he works with SWAT and the bomb squad. His arms are metal; his hands are mechanical claws that can open doors and suspicious packages by remote control. He maneuvers on small tractor tires with a treadlike chain, is armed with water cannons that can reduce a bomb blast to a harmless fizzle — and is potentially deadly. A Remington semiautomatic shotgun is mounted on one of his steel claws. The cop watching through Alex's camera eyes can trigger the weapon by remote control.

Alex speaks, in the voice of the negotiator at his controls, and can broadcast both sides of the conversation. He can be a hero, never misbehaves in bedrooms or bars, and never has to be reminded to buckle his seat belt or wear a bulletproof vest. A heckuva cop, he would probably make a good husband.

He rolled up the front walk and stopped outside the front door. He spoke tonight in the familiar voice of a film star.

'Hello, Carl? This is Lance Westfell. I'm here in Miami to make a film, and these gentlemen out here think that you and I should talk.'

'Westfell?' A curtain moved in the front window. 'Are you really out there? I can't see you. Could you step into the light?'

Alex's camera swiveled toward the movement as his voice changed.

'This is Glenn again, Carl. We can't allow Mr Westfell to do that until you throw out the gun.'

66

'I want to talk to Westfell.'

'I'm here, Carl.' The actor's resonant voice was unmistakable.

'You should do more Westerns. They're your best work. I liked *The Last Gunfighter*.'

'Thanks, Carl,' Westfell said. 'So did I. But Wyatt Earp is dead now. No man makes it alone today with just a horse and his six-shooter. We all need help from others.'

'Great line,' I whispered to Lottie, impressed.

'I think it's out of the movie,' she said.

'That's why I'm concerned about you, Carl,' Westfell went on. 'I'm here to see you get that help.'

'I'd rather die than go back to jail.' Carl's voice grew ragged. The cops stirred ominously and a crouching SWAT member moved into position to lob in tear gas grenades. As though they would successfully startle the suspect into missing his own head if he shot at it.

'That's no answer, Carl.' Westfell's deep voice sounded warm and concerned. 'Suicide is a permanent solution to a temporary problem. Come out here so we can shake hands and talk man to man.'

'Can we have our picture taken together?'

The lieutenant nodded.

'Certainly,' Westfell said, into Alex's mike.

'My pleasure.' He glanced down the street in our direction. 'We already have a photographer here. She's a redhead. A knockout.'

I held my breath as the front door inched open. Alex rolled in reverse, about eighteen inches, shotgun claw raised. 'Carl, they would prefer that you just lob the gun out first.'

'Here it comes.'

'Hot damn and hallelujah!' Lottie said, as the gun plunked out onto the grass next to the stamped concrete walk. Formerly invisible, a figure in black SWAT gear pounced out of the hedge to snatch it up.

A muffled cheer arose from the assembled cops as Carl stepped out. He did not look sheepish, like most screwups who surrender. His eyes searched the crowd expectantly.

He was patted down but not cuffed until he and Westfell shook hands, then bear-hugged. They allowed Lottie to trot down the street to shoot the picture, but not me. The damn patrolman had his orders. I was furious.

'Is somebody taping this?' Carl bawled as he was led away. He was ensconced in the backseat of a patrol car when I was finally permitted down the damn street.

'My mom always said I'd be on *Cops* or *America's Most Wanted*,' he told me cheerfully.

'Hang in there, man,' Westfell told him; then Carl was driven off to face charges of vehicular homicide, leaving the scene of a fatal accident, and numerous misdemeanors. His mother and sister, gushing at the star along with half a dozen cops, didn't even wave goodbye.

'Westfell's the real deal,' Lottie whispered. 'Look how the cops love him.'

'Because they all want to write scripts,' I said, still bitter at being left out, 'or work as extras, paid consultants, or hired security for his new movie.'

'He was aces with that fruitcake.'

'Publicity stunt,' I muttered.

The chief even materialized to thank Lance for his help. Lottie shot them shaking hands, while I rolled my eyes and fantasized about switching captions so that under this one it would say DERANGED SUSPECT SURRENDERS TO MOVIE STAR.

'Britt? Lottie?' The star's big hands rested on our shoulders. How nice of him to finally acknowledge my existence. 'I can count on you two, can't I, to keep my part in this out of the newspaper?'

Lottie looked smug.

'I don't feel comfortable about press that comes from somebody else's misfortune. Deal?'

'I'll talk to my editors,' I said, knowing they would agree.

I wanted to canvass the neighborhood, now that the cops were pulling out, and tried the house directly across the street.

Lance frowned as he trailed me up the walk. 'Nobody lives here. It's all boarded up.'

'Don't be so sure.' I rang the bell.

'Just a minute,' someone called.

'Some people,' I whispered, 'are still shell-shocked from the storm, still hiding behind hurricane shutters.'

Nearly every block still has at least one shuttered house, where barricaded occupants live like moles, with no natural light.

A small pale woman opened the door, blinking in surprise. She wore a loose housedress and scuffs and had to be in her seventies. 'I thought you were my neighbor,' she said. 'She called to say they were at it again across the street.'

I introduced myself.

'And he's the actor,' she said, peering nearsightedly up at Lance. 'Saw one a his movies on TV the other night.'

'How did you like it?' he asked.

'Too many commercials.'

She motioned us to follow her into the living room. The only bright spot amid the

70

dark old-fashioned furniture was an arrangement of artificial flowers in a pink ceramic bowl on the coffee table.

'The trouble's over,' I said. 'The SWAT team came out, and the police arrested the son.' Lance and I sat side by side on the velvet sofa. She used the remote to mute the TV, which was tuned to the weather channel, and settled into a matching armchair.

'What's he got hisself into this time?' She faced us, hands in her lap, expression expectant.

'Looks like he was the driver involved in a fatal hit-and-run a few nights ago, and he fled from the police today,' I said. 'Is all this excitement unusual? Or have you had problems in the neighborhood before?'

'Oh, we've had problems. Started when they moved in 'bout ten years ago, just after my late husband had his first heart attack. Ernest passed away in December of 'ninety-two. That boy broke into every house on the block while he was still a teenager. His parents always asked us not to prosecute, and we tried to be good neighbors. But they never did offer to pay for anything he stole. And he didn't quit. I called nine-one-one so many times, it's on my speed dialer now.' She nodded at the telephone. 'Haven't used it lately, because I don't see out.'

'We noticed your shutters are still up.'

'I was going to take 'em down, but then Weaver the Weatherman said another disturbance was out there, stirring up trouble in the Caribbean, so I decided to wait till after hurricane season. Got arthritis now, and it's a hardship at my age to keep taking 'em down, then putting 'em up again. Thought I would take 'em down at Christmas, then put it off till after the New Year. But now hurricane season isn't all that far off, so might as well leave 'em up.' She smiled.

'Must be gloomy during the day,' Lance said.

She nodded. 'Have to leave the lamps on all the time, and the TV, to know what's happening out there. But you can't beat the security.' She looked wistful. 'Used to love to paint when I was a girl. Been thinking maybe I'd get me some brushes and maybe paint windows on the inside of them shutters, pictures of clouds, some trees and flowers.'

She offered iced tea, but I was on deadline. She invited us back any time and suggested that Lance do something about all the commercials.

'Living in the dark has got to be depressing,' I said, on the way back to the *News*.

'I know I'm depressed,' Lance said.

I do not know how I missed the expressway entrance — preoccupied, I guess. No big deal, not much traffic at this hour. I could drive back through the inner city. Northwest Second Avenue cuts through high-crime neighborhoods but my car was new, in good shape, and I was not alone; a superhero was riding shotgun.

'The chief seems like a down-to-earth guy,' Lance was saying, as he rolled down his window and lit a Marlboro. 'I'm liking this town more and more. It'll be great to move into the house. Hotels are so impersonal. A house makes you feel like part of the community, less like an outsider. I never expected such a warm welcome here. In LA, you get no respect. Did I tell you the University of Miami wants me to lecture on film history and help put together a film study program? And the Cultural Affairs Commission has invited me to be honorary adviser.'

I smiled cynically. 'Well, when they present you with the key to the city, check it out. It'll tell you where you stand. The

73

keys they usually hand out are plastic; they order them by the gross. Only really important people get engraved metal keys in velvet-lined boxes. They're expensive.'

'Thanks for the tip.'

His smoldering gaze made me jittery. Or was it my car? More specifically, the red light glaring from the dashboard. The battery light. I took my foot off the gas and the engine died. I suddenly became very aware that I had neglected to sign out a cell phone from the neat row of chargers plugged into the city desk and that I had taken my gun back into my apartment the night before.

'Car trouble?' Lance inquired. 'Looks like the battery.'

We were in the worst possible neighborhood. They call it the Hole, an area of gangs, street shootings, drive-bys, and robberies.

'This can't be.' I tried to restart the engine. 'This is a brand-new car.' I hadn't even replaced the emergency kit I always kept in the trunk. Flashlight, jumper cables, flares: I drove them around for years, and now that I needed them . . .

I turned to Lance. 'You don't happen to be carrying a gun, do you?'

'Hell, no.' He sounded startled. 'Why would I have a gun?'

'Well, you always do in the movies.'

'That's Hollywood. This is real life.'

'Humph, that's what I keep trying to get across.'

'What does that mean?'

'Oh, forget it. It's my fault for taking this route and forgetting a cell phone.' I remembered Fred's warnings and watched the rearview. Maybe Lottie would arrive to the rescue on her way back to the paper, but I knew better. She was too focused, too smart, to make the same mistake I did. I tried the car one last time: nothing. The headlights were out as well. As I opened the door, the interior chime didn't even sound.

'I'm going to find a phone,' I said evenly. 'Stay here, keep the doors locked.'

'You're not going anywhere.' He pushed his door open. 'Lemme have a look, it's probably something simple.'

'Too dark,' I said. 'You won't be able to see a thing, plus it will tip off the 'hood that we're in trouble. In case you haven't noticed, this is not Beverly Hills.' The anticrime sodium vapor streetlights were gone, used for target practice or stolen for scrap. 'I'll call the paper, have somebody pick you up, and try to get a tow truck.'

'Hell, no,' he said. 'We go down, we go down together.'

Nice line. It was too dark to see his expression.

'Okay,' I said. 'Hide anything you really want to keep somewhere in the car. They'll probably break in, but Lord knows they won't be able to steal it unless they steal a tow truck first.'

I scanned the street. 'Bring some money and a credit card.'

He made a questioning sound.

'Robbers on crack are enraged when victims don't have any money. That's when they shoot them.'

'Don't have any.' He shrugged. 'Never carry it. It's not me.'

'Wonderful,' I said. Made sense. The more money a man has, the less he needs it.

We bailed out, walking rapidly, with purpose, toward the Boulevard. We did not speak; our voices might draw unwelcome attention. There were garbage cans in the street, and the sidewalk was littered with broken furniture, discarded clothing, and trash. The few intact ghetto buildings were ringed by security fences wreathed in razor wire. I spotted a pay phone outside a boarded-up Laundromat a block and a half away but found it an empty shell, vandalized and dead.

Where is a patrol car when you need one?

'Beautiful night,' Westfell finally said softly. He was right. Even in this bombed, burned-out Beirut of a neighborhood, the air was soft, stirred by a playful breeze, and a canopy of stars outshone the city lights.

Movement from across the street caught my eye. 'Stay calm,' I murmured.

'I am,' he said. 'They're just kids.'

They were, just six to nine years old, four or five of them, nudging each other and staring. 'Spotters,' I said.

They scampered around the corner and disappeared, babbling and laughing among themselves, like some scruffy little herd of urban wildlife. I caught the word 'tourists'.

Oh, shit, I thought. They think we're tourists. Prime targets. Who else but tourists would wander into this neighborhood at this hour?

Ponce de León, our first tourist, discovered Florida as he searched for the fountain of youth. He named the place for its beautiful flowers. The natives responded by shooting him dead in 1521. They took him out with an arrow. Little has changed, except today the natives use lead.

'Let's get outa here,' I said, poised to run.

Too late. Two young men appeared, crossing the street toward us. Three more emerged from shadows at the corner we were

77

approaching. I did not turn, but heard the unmistakable sound of footsteps behind us. More than one set.

Fifty feet from the corner, too damn close to an open alley, we were surrounded. Lance, a big man, was no match for seven or eight youths, most likely armed. Probably doesn't even do his own fight scenes, I thought.

'Yo, what's up?' Lance swung forward to high-five the closest menacing figure. The kid jumped like a startled cat, taken by surprise. They were young, somewhere between the cradle and the electric chair. Their pants looked four sizes too big. They wore loose plaid flannel shirts over Raiders T-shirts and Raiders caps with price tags dangling. Price tags, the new status symbol. Some manufacturers, aware of the trend, now attach permanent plastic tags instead of flimsy cardboard, so they survive washing by fastidious gang-bangers.

'You him!' one screamed. 'Mako. Mako the shark!'

'The shark never lets go!' said another.

'You got it, dude,' Westfell said.

'Why you kill that punk-ass lawyer who stole the money?'

'It just wasn't his day.'

The sharper ones all talked at once in a melange of street-speak. Two others, slow or drugged, remained silent and uncertain. One skinny kid whose front teeth flashed gold was squinting, as though perplexed.

'You still got that car, wid the spikes on the hubcaps?'

'The trus and volves?'

'You really make it wid that big blonde?'

'Those tits real? Or did she have a boob job?'

'Whatcha doin' here?'

'This your woman?' The one wearing a red bandanna under his Raiders cap was in my face.

'Yeah, this is my woman.'

He stepped back as everybody turned to leer, and I managed a little wave.

'We not gonna take 'em?' mumbled Squinty Face, still looking puzzled.

'Fuckit, man, this is Mako, the man. Fu'get that shit.' Red Bandanna turned to Lance. 'You still got that big piece, the forty caliber?'

'A Desert Eagle, made in Israel.' Lance nodded. 'Yeah, but not with me at the moment. Glad we ran into you guys, we're doing a little research for the new movie, shooting here, in Miami.'

'Any gang action?'

'Yeah, you need a consultation?'

'Yeah, you hire us. We the Thirty-fourth Street Players,' Red Bandanna said, strutting back and forth in front of Lance. 'You put us on the payroll as advisers.'

'That's something to think about.' Fist under his chin, Lance seemed to think about it. 'You know how we like realism. Right now, we've got us a problem.'

'Who givin' you shit? They gonna deal with us,' said a skinny kid, inexplicably referred to by the others as Fat Boy. 'They hafta deal with us.'

'Just the fucking car,' Lance said. 'Piece of shit. Died back there, a couple blocks away. Think we need a jump.'

'*No problemo*,' Red Bandanna said. 'Felipe here, he be the mechanic.'

They escorted us back to the car, cock-walking, strutting in rhythm to some inner music, displaying their kick-boxing techniques, showing off, and rapping with 'Mako' about his weapons, his kills, and his blondes. I stubbornly scanned the streets, desperate for a squad car, convinced that this was about to turn bad.

It did not. Two of the gang met us at the T-Bird with flashy late-model cars. A screwdriver still protruded from the steering column of one of them. They left their headlights on and I popped the hood.

I mentioned to Fat Boy that I was a writer. 'For the *Miami News*,' I said.

'Like Lois Lane.' He nodded wisely.

'Sort of. You hear about that security guard? The guard down at the Metrorail station? I wrote that story.'

'Yeah.' Fat Boy looked deliberately vague. 'Yeah, guess he got capped by somebody collectin' guns.'

'Yeah,' I said mildly. 'That's right. They took his gun.'

Red Bandanna sniggered with ill-suppressed glee. 'Yeah, somebody, they need 'em.'

'Who would that be?'

'Maybe the PLO.' He shrugged. 'They collectin' guns. Must be expectin' trouble. Maybe wid the Brickell Boys.'

The Powerful Latin Organization. Unwilling to push my luck in our current situation, I merely raised an eyebrow and handed him a business card, in case he ever had any news to report.

Felipe was disgusted and disappointed to find nothing more challenging than the battery cable, which had come off. After a series of high fives, we were safely on our way.

'I don't believe that!' I whooped at Lance, as I turned right on the Boulevard, much to my relief. 'What just happened back there?'

Mako the shark was Lance's rogue cop character in a gang-banger movie called

81

Streets of Death. We had just met his audience. He shook his head. 'Reality succumbs again to the magic of twenty-four frames a second. Scary, ain't it?'

* * *

He hung around the newsroom until I finished the stories.

'I'm starved,' he said. 'Let's eat.'

I didn't argue. Fear always makes me ravenous. We drove back to his hotel. Water splashed and danced in ornate stone fountains surrounded by jewel-like flower beds. The uniformed doorman greeted Lance by name as I gave the T-Bird to the valet. The dining room was still open, with candlelit tables and sparkling crystal. We were seated in a private nook, the only ones there.

He smoked, casually perused the wine list, ordered a bottle, then asked about Dorothy Fairborn. 'She works cleaning houses,' I said, heartsick and weary at the thought of her. 'How will she afford to take her son home, much less bury him? Did you know it costs more to ship a dead body than to buy an airline ticket for a live traveler? Of course she doesn't know much about airline tickets yet. She rode a

Greyhound bus here to claim his body.'

'What you learn on this job,' he said quietly, 'most people never have to think about.' He flicked his Marlboro into an ashtray delivered by a waiter so obsequious he probably would have been thrilled to have Lance grind out the cigarette butt in his hand.

'You know,' he said, 'earlier, when you said you got 'great' quotes from the dead guy's mother, you struck me as so incredibly cold. I felt you were in no position to consider acting shallow.'

I didn't realize my feelings had been so obvious.

'But it's clear from reading your story and seeing you now that you genuinely care about these people. That is very interesting to me.' Leaning back in his chair, he studied me for a long moment. 'How do you sleep?'

'Like a baby,' I blurted, too quickly. 'At least I did, until — until the incident after the storm.'

'The shooting?'

'Yeah. Stories have never bothered me; in fact in some crazy way they made me feel . . . ' — I groped for the right word — 'valid, as though my job is important because I know I do right by the victims. I tell their side, which is all I can do. Sometimes there is nobody else to speak for them.'

Westfell was surprisingly easy to talk to. Maybe our shared experience had created some sort of bond.

'So,' I suggested casually, after we ordered stone crabs, 'tell me all about the super-model.'

He grinned ruefully. 'Between us?'

I nodded. 'Scout's honor.'

'She used me, simple as that. Modeling wasn't enough. Nothing ever is for Lexie. It made her crazy that Cindy Crawford got to star in a movie before she did. Her ambition is scary; you can actually feel it when you're with her, like something white hot that radiates from every pore. She's driven.'

He licked his lips thoughtfully and lit another Marlboro before he continued.

'First time I saw her was on the cover of that sports magazine, the swimsuit edition. You probably saw it. Everybody did.'

He rolled his eyes.

'When she put out the word that she wanted to meet me, I was intrigued. Who wouldn't be? She called when I was in New York. Said she was driving in from a shoot, the cover of *Vanity Fair*. Had a car, offered to pick me up so we could have a drink. I was game.' He shrugged. 'I got in the limo.' He made it sound so final. 'I got in the limo,' he repeated thoughtfully.

'She was gorgeous, that million-dollar face. She's one of the few that looks even better in person. Had her hair down and was wearing a full-length fur and high heels. The limo pulls away from the curb and she takes off the coat. In the middle of down-town Manhattan. It was all she was wearing, except for the high heels.' He paused to smoke and to reflect. 'That was one wi-i-ild ride. It was eighteen months before we ran off the road and crashed.' He sipped his wine and glanced up to see how I was taking all this.

I hoped my mouth was not hanging open. 'The coat should have been your first clue,' I said. 'Fur coats are only good on their original owners. So it really was love at first sight?' I adore hearing about other people's sex lives. Perhaps because mine is so dull.

'I was dazzled. She wanted to be a movie star. Lexie always gets what she wants.'

'What happened?'

'She got what she wanted.' He gestured casually with his cigarette. 'The wedding was eight weeks after that limo ride. My agent helped her get a small role in *Starlight Express*. The movie did well. Then I went to London to shoot *Ground Zero*, while she went to Vancouver for a slightly bigger role in *Deadly Sin*. We spent two weeks together before I went to Texas to shoot *The Last Gunfighter*, and she went to Hawaii to shoot *Dreams of Darkness*.'

His cigarette butt sizzled as he flipped it into a nearly empty saucer.

'When people keep leaving each other, even if they're really in love, eventually one doesn't come back.' His eyes shone with the look of a wounded spaniel.

I felt a twinge of pity, then wanted to pinch myself. Was he play-acting?

'There was also the little matter of the pool boy,' he added nonchalantly. 'And the football hero, an ex-boyfriend who, I later learned, was never entirely out of the picture.'

'How did you find that out?' I drowned a luscious hunk of stone crab in butter sauce.

'Skipped the wrap party on *The Last Gunfighter*, came home a day early. He was wearing my bathrobe, lounging next to my pool. The tabloids had a field day. Embarrassed the hell out of me and my kids. The whole world knows about it.'

As he signed the check, our waiter murmured something and tried to hand him a package. Lance declined, shaking his head and apologizing.

'What was that?' I asked, as we left.

'He's a would-be writer, wanted me to read his script.'

'Why wouldn't you?' I asked accusingly, rooting for the struggling artist. 'Somebody took a chance on *you* once.'

'And risk a lawsuit? Having somebody say I stole his idea? It's happened. Believe me, it's happened.'

'But it's so sad. The guy might be a great undiscovered talent.'

'I agree. But that's the business. It's hard, but you have to say no,' he said firmly. 'It's survival.'

★ ★ ★

He invited me to the bar for a nightcap after dinner. I declined. 'Great meal,' I said. 'Thanks. But I can't drive if I drink any more.'

His wistful eyes made the offer he didn't.

Was he a con man or just lonesome? I did not have to go home, but I did. When I strolled in at 2 A.M., the phone was ringing.

'Britt, where the hell have you been? I hope I know, and it was good. Have you heard the news? Put on your hard hat.'

4

Two a.m. phone calls are never good news. During a brief family vacation before flying to Miami to begin shooting *Margin of Error*, actress Meredith Page had been critically injured in an accident on a Telluride, Colorado, ski slope. Rescued by helicopter, she had been airlifted to a Denver hospital.

'You think Lance knows?' Lottie asked.

'I'm sure he doesn't. I just left him.'

I quickly told her about our encounter with the Thirty-fourth Street Players.

'Hell all Friday, Britt. Just like in his movies. That man's place of birth must be the planet Krypton.'

'Planet Hollywood is more like it.'

Did he need to hear the bad news now, or could it wait until morning?

'Better call him,' Lottie said.

Me, I would want to know. But then I always want to know . . . everything. Knowledge, good or bad, is power. Turned out to be a moot point. He was registered under the name Gardiner Bowles, his reporter/agent character in *Margin of Error*. No answer from his room. I had Gardiner Bowles paged in the bar. No response. Where was he? I left no message.

Page, an excellent skier, had been startled by a videocam-toting *paparazzo* on skis. She had swerved to avoid a collision and hit a hidden obstruction. The cameraman to blame for it had captured her spectacular cartwheeling spill on unpacked snow. By morning it aired during every newscast, along with touching footage of her grim husband and two bewildered small children arriving at the hospital where she was being treated. Her condition had been upgraded to fair. She would survive, but she would not be shooting a movie in Miami, or anywhere, anytime soon.

Lance called during my phone checks from home next morning. Hoarse and weary, he sounded as though he hadn't slept.

'Probably won't get to join you until late,' he said. 'You heard?'

'When I got home last night. Tried to call you.' Billy Boots, curled up in my lap, closed his eyes and purred as I scratched between his ears.

'Oh,' Lance said, his voice a raspy croak. 'Met some of our crew in the bar and went to South Beach. Ever been to one of those foam parties?'

'Once. Wouldn't do it again without a wetsuit and goggles.' Foam is the rage in South Beach. It is sprayed from the ceiling onto enclosed dance floors where strangers gyrate through wet wild bubble baths together. Shorter dancers risk total immersion, while bouncers armed with high-powered water guns stand by to blast revelers caught doing the wild thing beneath the suds.

'A real trip,' Lance said.

'What happens now? Do they postpone the movie?'

'Hell, no. We're here; the meter's running. We've got a schedule. Everybody has other commitments. The cameras have to roll. What have you heard? Maybe she's not hurt as bad as they say. You know how the press exaggerates. We could probably shoot around her until she recovers. If not, she has to be replaced. Damn shame. She was perfect for this.'

'All I know is what CNN is reporting,' I said coldly, miffed by his remark about the press. 'I'll check the wires when I get to the office, but multiple leg fractures don't sound like she'll work — or even walk — soon.'

'Son of a bitch!' His voice cracked with frustration and exhaustion. 'Who the hell goes skiing right before an important film? Damn! Everybody's job depends on the principals. I have a meeting at eleven with the producers, the director, the lawyers, and the insurance people. Should be a trip.'

'Try spraying them with foam.'

'Catch you later, woman.'

★ ★ ★

News was breaking in the southwest section, another *chupacabra* sighting. The mythical goat sucker, a cross between Big Foot, Dracula, and an alien — from outer space, not a third-world country — had struck again, animal carcasses scattered in its wake, all drained of blood.

The *chupacabra* is described by eyewitnesses, almost all Spanish-speaking and superstitious, as a four-foot-tall, hoofed, red-eyed, reptilian creature, with the oversized head and eyes of an extraterrestrial and the nasty fangs of something savage. If he is from outer space, it is definitely a third world planet, and like so many other aliens he brought bad habits with him.

Six goats, four pigs, and half a dozen chickens had been slaughtered and their blood drained on a Northwest Dade ranch during the night. The owners were at home and heard no commotion, as usual. A Spanish-speaking ranch hand discovered the

91

massacre, heard rustling sounds in the bushes, and swore he saw the *chupacabra* in the moonlight, blood dripping from his fangs.

County officials offered rational explanations as usual, including wild dog packs or 'something' escaped from a zoo. By the time I arrived, Everglades animal trackers, every TV reporter in town, and most of the local paranormal crowd, mystics, gypsies, psychics, and UFO chasers, were trampling through the underbrush.

Sergio, the witness, was retelling his story, rolling his eyes and sweating. '*Dios mío, los dientes*, the teeth.'

The cops had examined the carcasses, all with curious puncture wounds on the hindquarters.

By the time I drove back downtown, Dade County Animal Control and the police department had issued a statement identifying the culprit as an 'unidentified bad dog' still at large, attributing reports to the contrary as 'mass hysteria'.

A Kendall McDonald sighting briefly brightened my morning as I checked the overnight logs at the Miami police PIO. I glanced up from the press desk and there he was. *Buenísimo*. Lean, long-legged, and strongjawed, his grin deepening the cleft in his chin. So muy macho in his dark blue uniform that he could be national police poster boy of the year, if such a title existed. He had wandered in to see the commander. Happily, I was enjoying a good hair day, thanks to the low humidity, and was wearing my sandy silk slacks, a tailored white blouse, and my navy blazer, crisp from the cleaners. I had even added slick rosy lipstick, a touch of blusher, and my mother's antique gold earrings.

'See anything interesting?' His unimaginative opening line belied the expression in his silvery-blue eyes.

'Lining up a one-on-one with the *chupacabra*.' I smiled coyly.

'Where's your sidekick?'

I drew a blank.

'The tough guy, Westfell.' Was that a hint of derision in his voice? 'The matinee idol.' No mistaking it there.

McDonald's eyes swept the room, as though the star might appear to take a bow. Somebody did, but it was only Danny Menendez, bustling to the fax machine with his *chupacabra* press release.

'Westfell's not with her,' offered Menendez, who had seen me arrive alone. 'She already taught him everything she knows. Didn't take long.' He left, chuckling at his own stupid joke.

I was glad he was gone. So was McDonald. 'How are you, Britt? You getting enough sleep?'

I knew what he meant. 'Fine,' I lied. 'Couldn't be better.'

'You look terrific,' he conceded. 'Have you made your appointment yet?'

'No,' I said, too sharply. Why wouldn't he stop trying to push me into counseling I did not need? 'Things are working themselves out.'

I was grateful when he changed the subject, gesturing with the paper in his hand. 'The chief was so impressed by Westfell the other night that he plans to award him a special commendation. Strictly PR bullshit.' He paused. 'I hear you two are pretty tight.'

'Me and the chief?'

'No.' He grinned in spite of himself. 'You and Westfell.'

'We were at that SWAT scene.' Where was this going? I wondered.

'I meant his hotel.'

I stared, then swallowed. 'Having dinner,' I said shortly. How did he know? Off-duty cops working hotel security must have seen us and blabbed. Cops are the world's worst gossips. I hated explaining, sounding defensive.

He shifted as though leaving. I didn't want him to go. The leather gun belt he wore creaked. I felt wet and weak in the knees despite myself, remembering the sound it made when he stripped it off. Remembering his arms. I did miss him.

'I thought you weren't the type to be awed by some Hollywood heartthrob.'

'I haven't joined a fan club yet.'

'Be careful, Britt. Just take care of yourself.' The concern in his voice sounded real.

'Sure.' This strange, strained conversation was not what I had hoped for.

'See you.' He turned toward the door.

'When?' I hated myself for being so weak.

His silver-blue eyes caught on mine. Was the sadness in them for me or him?

'I'll give you a call,' he mumbled vaguely.

Biting back another 'When?' I swallowed hard, watched him make his getaway, and imagined a bullet hole, a big one, right between his shoulder blades. That made me hate myself even more, but it was either that or cry. Why was he so stubborn? Why were we both so stubborn?

★ ★ ★

Lance arrived at five. Jaded newshounds who had gaped the first time did not even look up. But I stared. He stalked through the newsroom with a macho stride, as though ready to crack his bullwhip on the big screen. His reddened eyes blazed with intensity. His strong jaw clenched, his lips curled down in anger. A husky bodyguard type, a slightly less vivid clone, hustled to keep up. He wore black, a T-shirt, slacks, and a blazer. Behind his shades, his eyes roamed the room, reminding me of the Secret Service, except for this guy's neat well-kept little ponytail. Lance, voice hollow, introduced him as Niko.

Lance was probably still hungover, I thought, wondering if he had caught any sleep. The clone nodded at me, smile impersonal, continuing to survey the room.

'Let's talk,' Lance said. Niko frowned when Lance asked him to wait there. The two of us walked out of the newsroom together.

'Cafeteria?' I said.

'No, private.'

'I know the place.' We sat on a concrete bench on a windswept outside patio off the third floor. The setting sun spilled blood-red stains across the rooftops of Overtown, scene of the last riots.

The man who wanted to talk said nothing.

'Meredith will be in physical therapy for some time, according to the news from Denver,' I finally said.

'Yeah.' His tone was bitter. 'They're holding a press conference tomorrow.'

'Who?'

'The producers, Richard Van Ness and Wendy Weintraub, people from the studio. To announce Meredith Page's replacement.' He lit a Marlboro, shielding the flame from the wind, and sucked in a deep drag.

'They already have somebody?'

'Yeah.' He stared at the sinking sun. 'Lexie Duran.'

'Your ex-wife?'

Taking a deep breath, he nodded and flipped his cigarette over the ledge.

I didn't understand. 'Why her?'

'My agent neglected to include co-star approval in my contract because our deal was always with Meredith Page, right from the start. The clause should have been inserted anyway. That son of a bitch. I have a gentleman's agreement with my agent not to steal from me. I forgot to make him agree not to be stupid.'

'Does Lexie Duran fit the role? Meredith Page has to be at least ten or twelve years older and she's beautiful but not . . . not as . . . '

'Flashy.'

'Right.'

'As written, our female lead is a brilliant nuclear physicist, a genius, familiar with the nuclear reactor in Cuba. She is the free

97

world's only hope to undo the sabotage in time. Can you picture Lexie Duran as a nuclear scientist?'

'It *is* a stretch.'

'They're flying in new writers to revamp her character and rework the script.' He chuckled without mirth. 'It's not gonna be the movie I thought it would be.'

'Maybe it'll be great,' I said.

He turned to look directly at me for the first time. Only a slight sliver of sun still showed above the horizon. 'Don't patronize me, Britt. You're the only person I can talk to in Miami, the only one with nothing to gain, no ax to grind.' He sighed. 'You know the situation with me and Lexie.'

'Just say no.' Where was the problem? 'Just don't do it. You're the star.'

'You don't understand the bottom line. That's all that counts in this business. It wasn't good for *The Last Gunfighter*. I did another big-budget movie, *Dark Journey*, my last project for WFI, World Film Industries, before coming over to Titan Films for *Margin of Error*. *Dark Journey* is in the can, about to be released. The suits at WFI are sweating it. A preview audience booed; we reshot the ending and added some scenes. It's being re-edited as we speak. Now the studio execs at Titan are skittish. If I don't agree to Lexie stepping in, they're making noises about taking the insurance payout and dumping the entire project.

'Bringing Lexie in to co-star after our bitter high-profile divorce is 'foolproof, hot-button casting', according to Alan Cappleman, head of the studio. They think the curiosity factor, the fans' prurient interest, guarantees big box office.'

'She must be uncomfortable too. Why would she agree?'

'Are you kidding? She couldn't sign fast enough. *Margin of Error* is a sixty-million-dollar production, her biggest film so far. Putting us together will send the tabloids into a feeding frenzy. That's right up her alley. She loves it, especially since she knows how much I hate it. It gives her another chance to work me over. I thought all that was finished.'

He lit another cigarette as the temperature dropped and darkness closed in over the city.

'Funny,' he said. 'We wanted to work together in the beginning. Spent a lot of time talking about the business, reading scripts, discussing projects. Never had the chance.' He gave a little snort. 'Now we can't stand being in the same room . . . And guess what, folks? We're gonna make a movie!' He sighed heavily and got to his feet.

'And I thought dealing with editors was tough.'

'Maybe one, two editors handle your story. How would you feel if it was a committee of egos, calling endless meetings to push their own cockamamie ideas?

'I'm worried about this film. Everything's taking a whole different spin. This was my chance to work opposite a serious, stage-trained, Academy Award-nominated actress. Sure, it's an action flick, but the script was really well written. I hoped it would be quality, that I'd finally break outa the mindless-action hunk image and be taken seriously. Now I'm playing opposite Lexie, who is not a trained actress, they're tearing up the script, and instead of a fine movie it's gonna be a public spectacle.'

'Life never goes according to plan.' I shivered, hugging my arms in the nighttime chill.

'Let's get some coffee.' He took a deep breath and stood for a moment, staring at the rising stars. 'Everything else may be going to hell in a handbasket, but, you know, I do like Miami. It's different here, Britt. Everything is softer, more seductive than LA.'

'Don't let it fool you,' I said.

5

Lance soon called it a night, striding off into the gloom with his own thoughts, his past, and Niko like a shadow on his heels. I decided to do the same and go home before Miami's good citizens began acting out their hostilities, frustrations, and bizarre fantasies, keeping me on the job all night.

Halfway to the elevator, my phone rang, I wanted out, but hesitated, went back, and picked it up.

'Are you the reporter?' The stranger's voice was tense. 'Detective Bliss gave me your number. He said you might be able to help me.

'Angel, my ex-wife, is charged with murder, but she still has custody of my children and won't let me see 'em.'

My chance gone, I put down my things, slid back into my desk chair, and flipped open a fresh notebook.

'I'm sure my kids ain't eating right,' Darnell Oliver whined. 'The woman never cooks, Lord knows what she's got going on there. That's why she won't let me see them, cuz they're big enough to talk and tell me what the hell she's doing.'

'You really suspect that your children are in danger?' Was he a concerned parent or a vindictive ex-spouse?

'No doubt about it,' he said forcefully. 'You know what she did to that little baby. She was probably out there dancing and drinking while that baby starved to death.'

'But HRS returned the other children after an investigation. The social workers must be satisfied that they are safe with her.'

'Yeah,' he said. 'And being a reporter, you *know* that HRS gives kids back to parents who kill them all the time.'

True. If Angel's track record was bad, so was that of the government agency charged with protecting children.

'All I want is a chance to take good care of 'em. My second wife is willin' to help me raise 'em to study hard and be good Christians. We got us a nice home, half an hour from Disney World. The judge must be crazy.'

'You pay child support?'

'Every week. Between that and hiring lawyers to fight this thing, it's breaking my back. All I wanna do is see my kids and give 'em a good home. Harry should be getting into Peewee League, and Misty

102

should be a Girl Scout, not taking care of the little ones and watching her mother bring home new boyfriends. Meanwhile, Angel is shuffling the banana and the kids ain't even eating right.'

'Shuffling the banana?'

'Yeah, you know, how they do on food stamps. Take a ten-dollar coupon to the supermarket, buy a couple of bananas, use the change to buy a six-pack.'

We talked at length. Sad, that this was how their high school romance ended. Teenagers themselves when they began raising a family, they quit school and married when she became pregnant. I wondered if she had been voted most likely to conceive.

'Are you the father of Cynthia, the baby who died?'

'Nah, we've been divorced for nearly four years. I was already remarried when she had that one. I didn't even know about the two youngest until last summer; that's when I first tried for custody of mine.'

'Who was Cynthia's father?' I didn't remember hearing a thing about him when the baby died and Angel was arrested.

'Who knows? She probably don't have a clue,' he said indignantly. 'Woman's a slut, pops those babies out once a year like clockwork. Ain't happy unless she's pregnant.'

103

'But why? When she can't even take care of — '

'Easier than working, I guess. A nut case. The woman is a nut case.'

I took his number and promised to check it out. No time like the present, I thought. Any task postponed on my beat may stay that way. The hot breath of breaking news constantly derails good intentions, swallowing all your time. When something matters, do it now, I always tell myself. Children matter.

Angel Oliver and her kids lived in a Title Eight government-subsidized apartment near the Orange Bowl. The aging neighborhood had grown even shabbier since the Dolphins and the Orange Bowl game moved twenty miles north to the new state-of-the-art Pro Player Stadium. The team took a major source of local income with it. The Orange Bowl lacked proper parking, and its neighbors had grown to depend on instant cash earned by renting parking spaces on their lawns and in their yards during games. Working families and retirees on fixed incomes squeezed in dozens of cars at six to ten dollars apiece. The old neighborhood sorely misses the Dolphins.

The front door of the first-floor apartment opened right on to the street. The doorbell apparently did not work. The clamor of children and TV inside did not abate when I rang persistently. When I rapped soundly on the wooden door, they grew quiet and it opened almost immediately. I saw no one, then looked down. A small boy, about age five, had one fist on the doorknob, and stared up at me with an expectant gaze. His silky hair was dark blond, with long, straight bangs that brushed his eyebrows.

'Are you Mommy's friend?' he asked.

Before I could answer, he demanded, 'Did you bring me anything?'

The evening was chilly, but he wore no shirt and was bare-foot, in baggy shorts.

'Is your mom home?'

His siblings clustered behind him, including two big-eyed girls of about seven or eight. One had darker hair and they were not dressed alike, but seemed to be twins. Two smaller children were barefoot and in diapers, one of whom appeared in dire need of a change. The smallest, a runny-nosed rug rat, sat on the floor clutching a bottle. Another little one was gnawing on a half-eaten banana, reminding me of Darnell Oliver's accusations.

They all gazed up at me, expressions grave, except for the tyke who opened the door. He simply looked curious.

'Is she here?' I took a step inside.

'No.' The boy persisted. 'Did you bring anything?'

There were mattresses on the bare floor and little furniture, except for a top-of-the-line twenty-seven-inch color television apparently hooked up to cable.

'Well, I didn't know for sure you would be here, but I might have something.' The others, shy and cautious, quietly closed in around us to watch, expressions still grave. I groped in my purse for the individually wrapped hard orange candies I use when I miss meals and my energy flags.

I came up one short but scrabbled at the bottom of the bag until I unearthed another. Each politely took one. Nobody grabbed. One of the twins, who picked up the baby's bottle when it fell, even unwrapped one for him.

'Can he have that? He won't choke on it, will he?' I was asking a seven-year-old, clearly more experienced in child care than I was.

'Don't swallow it, Beppo,' she told him. 'Just suck on it.'

If they didn't choke, was this good for their teeth? Did they brush? Were these babies all home alone?

'Who's taking care of you?'

'Misty.' The boy licked his lips.

'Harry!'

A girl of eleven or twelve stepped out of what had to be the kitchen. Wearing a spattered apron, she had a long wooden soup-spoon in one hand. She shared the same silky bangs and big eyes of the others but wore the harried look of an adult.

'You know you're not supposed to open the door! You're not supposed to let anybody in!'

Harry shoved back his bangs in an exasperated manly gesture. 'Stop it, Misty. It's okay. She brought us something.'

'Just you wait,' she warned ominously. To me, she said, 'You have to come back when my mother is home.'

The others gathered around her, staunch little troupers, trying to look contrite, distancing themselves from me, except for Harry, who stood his ground, pouting, and the baby, who had crawled out of his diaper. One twin even spit out her orange drop and held it in a sticky palm as though it were something about to be confiscated by the police.

I needed to reassure Misty, I thought, and get into that kitchen to see if there was any food for the children. She pursued the baby, snatching him up with maternal expertise as she deftly readjusted his diaper. That gave me the chance to sneak a look in the narrow alley-style kitchen with greasy spots and holes in the wall. The countertop seemed reasonably clean and was spread with slices of white bread and a package of lunch meat. She must have been slapping bologna sandwiches together. The soup simmering on the stove smelled like Campbell's.

'Why is this door open?' Angel Oliver demanded as she walked through it. Thin and blonde, she wore a short black leather jacket and looked far too young and pretty to be the mother of so many children or a pregnant defendant facing manslaughter charges. Her pregnancy, in fact, did not show at all. She and the children shared the same rosebud mouth and big eyes, though her brows had been tweezed into a thin line and the lashes thickened by mascara. A tiny gold angel dangled from a chain around her neck, but she affected the wary, suspicious demeanor of a mother bear who has just surprised a stranger stalking her cubs.

'Did you bring me anything?' Harry asked, tugging at her skirt.

'What's going on here?' his mother demanded.

'Harry let her in,' shrilled one of the twins, pointing a small finger at the culprit. He quit tugging at his mother and tried to look innocent.

He wasn't the only one. 'Hi there.' I greeted her with the phony warmth and sheepish grin of a burglar caught in the act.

'Are you from MRS?' she asked crisply.

'No,' I reassured her. 'My name is Britt Montero, from the — '

She knew. Didn't even wait until I could spit it out. 'Get out of my house!'

'I was hoping we could talk — '

'Get *out* of my house! Who gave you the right to come sneaking in here talking to my children when I'm not home?'

She flung open the door and gestured for my exit.

'I didn't realize that you weren't here at first.'

She glowered at Harry, who gazed back adoringly, her little man of the house.

'I was hoping we could talk.'

'I have nothing to say, to you or your newspaper. Get out! Before I call the police!'

'Call them,' I demanded, sick of being shouted at. 'I'm sure they would find it very interesting to hear that the children were home alone.'

She glared venomously.

'Listen, I thought you might want to talk, to tell your side.'

'You didn't ask for my side before you wrote that story! You just printed whatever

109

the police said, all that garbage, the lies they told you, then you put that picture in the newspaper for everybody to see.'

As mug shots go, it actually wasn't all that bad. I've seen a lot worse.

'I tried. I left a message with your mother, who wouldn't talk to me, and it wasn't possible to reach you at the time; you were in — '

All the little eyes and ears watching and listening kept me from using the word in front of them.

'You couldn't be reached,' I repeated.

For a moment I thought she would relent. I was wrong. 'Get out,' she said, her children gathered protectively around her. 'Before we throw you out.'

What was she going to do, for Pete's sake, have the little ones bite me on the ankle? Starve me the way she did that baby? I left, but not without a final shot.

'The children's father is concerned about them. Why won't you let him — '

'Daddy?'

'Daddy?'

The word echoed from one little mouth to another. 'Daddy?'

'That son of a bitch! Did he send you?'

'Why won't you let him see the children?'

'Out! Get out!' she screamed, as she sprang

110

forward and swung the door shut, nearly slamming it on me.

From the other side I heard her turn on Misty. 'You were in charge! You are the oldest. You're responsible! Why did you let him open that door?'

Most children in tough circumstances act older than their age. I know a little about that myself. I had just made life tougher for one of them, the little surrogate mother trying to hold it all together. I vowed to try to make it up to them somehow.

As I drove away, I opened the windows and the moon roof, letting the cool night, the stars, and the neon wash over me as I thought of how Lottie yearns to be a mother and how some people who would be great parents never have the chance, while those who should not be allowed near a child are usually the most prolific. The higher power who weaves the fabric of our lives together has a definite mean streak.

Later I dreamed of dark woods again, about the gun and the blood glistening in the moonlight. But this time the man I killed wore the face of the young security guard. I screamed, or was that his mother? When I awoke I could still smell the gunsmoke, the dream was that real.

6

I dozed off after dawn, oversleeping well into the safe light of morning. Luckily, it was my day off. My plan had been to jog the boardwalk at sunrise, to enjoy the weather, the most exhilarating of the year. Instead, I awoke groggy, jogged Bitsy around the block, took a quick shower, and slipped into my good military-style navy blue dress with epaulets and gold buttons. Lance had moved into his leased house and wanted me to see it. He also had more questions about reporting. So we planned to talk, then go to the *Margin of Error* press conference at eleven. Later, he would be presented with the key to the county during an afternoon commission session at Metro-Dade Center.

Despite my initial reservations, I actually looked forward to the day. Experiencing, even vicariously, the adulation showered upon him would be a welcome change to my usual reception. Nobody loves a police reporter. I wondered as I showered how Angel Oliver would have reacted the night before had

Lance been with me. She certainly wouldn't have threatened to call the police. Movie stars can be handy tools. Every reporter should have one.

Breakfast was to be yogurt from my refrigerator, but — too late. What was in the carton had grown a long grey beard. I drank coffee and nibbled a slice of raisin toast instead.

★ ★ ★

The security guard at the Star Island entrance dutifully noted my destination and tag number. Obelisk-shaped white deco lamps lined the narrow bridge from the causeway on to the island. Posh home to stars and multimillionaires, the island appeared more lush and more pristine than usual, probably because I was still thinking of the dismal garbage-strewn street where Angel Oliver and her children lived.

Gloria and Emilio Estefan, Vanilla Ice, and Leona Helmsley are among the rich, famous, and infamous residents of the multimillion dollar walled estates where gated drives are bordered by towering royal palms and luxuriant tropical landscaping. One spoiled German tycoon air-conditioned his open backyard and pool area, to better

113

enjoy it year round. Money is no object on Star Island. Don Johnson intended to build there, at the pinnacle of his *Miami Vice* fame, but dropped his plans in a fit of pique because the deal was reported in the newspapers. He sued, saying he would be mobbed if fans knew where to find him.

I cruised down Island Drive and found the house.

Lance was living large.

Stately palms lined the winding driveway. Sculpted hedges and fruiting and flowering trees were everywhere. Between them I caught flashes of turquoise bay, the bright blue of a pool, and a shaded tennis court.

The house was a Mediterranean-style villa with arches, columns, and breezeways. Three shades of brilliant bougainvillea and a fiery Mexican flame vine intertwined incestuously as they spilled over the walls. One of the heavy double front doors stood ajar. I pushed it open and stepped into the dimly lit entryway.

'Hello?'

There was a stir, the rustle of someone moving nearby, more a disturbance in the air than footsteps.

'Lance?'

Again, a flurry of energy and a flowery fragrance.

'Hello, there,' I called.

A woman appeared from a shadowy passageway.

'Hi.' I gasped. 'You startled me.'

Her smile was confident, controlled. 'You were looking for . . . ?'

'Mr Westfell.' She must be his assistant or a public relations person, I thought.

'I'm Stephanie, Lance's fiancée.' Her curly lashes dipped shyly at the revelation. Was she blushing? 'May I help you?'

I stared, startled again. 'I didn't know he was engaged. How nice to meet you.'

The hand she offered was soft, but the grip firm, as her intelligent, clear grey eyes locked on mine. In her thirties, pretty, in a wholesome collegiate way, sturdy build, brown hair in a pageboy, pearls, nice manicure with pink polish.

With the Lexie disaster such recent history, Lance's engagement surprised me. Something he had neglected to mention. This pleasant woman looked mature, more June Cleaver than supermodel. No one would ever picture this one naked, wild, and crazy in a limo. She would fit right in at the PTA or in a church choir. Good for Lance. Maybe he was growing up.

'And you are?'

'Britt, Britt Montero. I'm the police

reporter for the *Miami News*. I've been helping him research his role.'

'Of course.' She cocked her head and smiled. 'He's spoken about you. You've been such a help. We're so grateful. He thinks he's got it down pat now and asked me to thank you. He won't be needing any more help.'

She steered me toward the door.

'He doesn't want me to come to the press conference? Or to Metro-Dade Center this afternoon?' What is this? I thought, irritated. I could have used the extra sleep, or jogged the boardwalk, or joined the ten o'clock aerobics class at the Spa.

'No.' She looked apologetic and a bit embarrassed. 'I just got into town,' she whispered confidentially. 'You know how it is, we need a little quiet time together. We've missed each other so much.'

'Sure. But he should have called to tell me,' I griped. All dressed up with no place to go. It was my day off and I had driven all the way over here. This would teach me. I knew better than to get involved with these self-centered Hollywood types.

'I know,' she commiserated, shaking her head. 'Men! You know how they can be. Poor Lance is so busy he forgets his manners. Thank you so much for coming.'

She stepped to an ornate hand-carved

mahogany sideboard set with a breakfast buffet of fruit and croissants and picked up a small sharp knife. Slowly she sliced a Key lime, the lady of the house intent on her little wifely duties. Dismissed, I headed for the door.

Should I go to the press conference anyway? Nah. The beach beckoned; I would take a book and nap in the sun. To hell with Lance.

I crossed the flower-bordered brick driveway and climbed into the T-Bird. I had started down the drive when Lance suddenly appeared around the side of the house. I glimpsed him in the rearview mirror but did not stop.

'Hey!' he yelled. 'Where ya going?'

Sends his lady friend out to blow me off, then has the chutzpah to wave. I floored it. The car lurched forward and I caught a flash of movement out the corner of my eye. Lance was sprinting across the lawn, to cut me off at the gate. Instinctively I stopped accelerating, but didn't hit the brake.

The man was fast. He beat me there and lunged in front of the car. Would Fred fire me if my bumper broke both of Lance's legs? I thought of Meredith Page and slammed on the brake.

The T-Bird stopped just in time. Lance had

both hands flat on the hood, out of breath.

'Britt! Whatcha doing!'

'What does it look like?' I snapped, rolling down the window as he came alongside. He wore a white cotton crew-neck sweater and linen slacks.

'Where ya going?' He looked perplexed. 'You coming back?'

'No.' Now I was perplexed. 'Your fiancée gave me the message: you've got it down pat, and you don't need any more help.'

'Fiancée?' He took a step back and stared down at me.

'Stephanie.'

'Jesus Christ! No! Where was she?'

'In the house.' I shrugged. 'She answered the door.'

He pointed a finger directly at me. 'You! Stay right there. Niko!' He was still bellowing his bodyguard's name as he ran back to the house and skidded through the front door.

What the hell was going on here? Grumpy and irritable I turned off the key, got out, and followed him.

Nearing the front door I heard shouts, Lance and Niko, scuffling, thuds and screams from inside. A lover's quarrel? The woman had just arrived in town. This did not bode well for their relationship. What was wrong with these Hollywood people?

In the foyer, I nearly stumbled over a small painting that had been knocked off the wall. A shrill running scream echoed from upstairs. I followed the sounds through an archway into a formal dining room, looked up, and saw Niko and Stephanie struggling on the landing. He was trying to force her down the stairs. Lance was on the phone, agitated and gesturing, at the top. Niko caught Stephanie in a bear hug and swung her around, her feet high off the floor, as she shrieked and struggled. One of her sandals flew off and landed halfway down the flight.

'Lance! Lance! Don't let him do this!' she howled. 'Please! Don't! Don't!'

I could not stand there and watch them manhandle a woman.

'Put her down!' I shouted. Starting up the stairs, I snatched up her shoe and considered whacking Niko on the kneecap with it.

'No! Be careful. Stay back!' Niko warned, his arm out like a traffic cop. 'She's dangerous!'

Dangerous?

My eyes darted back to the sideboard. The lime slices were still there, oozing juice. The knife was not.

'Niko! Be careful! She's got a knife!'

He heard me and tore at her skirt pocket. The knife clattered to the floor.

I saw the glance he and Lance exchanged.

Sirens were already approaching.

Two Miami Beach cops burst in the front door, guns drawn.

'In here!' I said.

'Is that her?' one yelled.

They should have been able to figure that out, since Niko had her in a headlock at the moment.

Who was the villain here? Was this how Lance broke off romances? No wonder his love life was rocky.

Stephanie was pitiful, clothes and hair disheveled, sobbing hysterically as they handcuffed her. 'This isn't necessary. Officer, you don't understand!' she wailed. They marched her down the stairs. 'We're going to be married! We love each other. This is just a misunderstanding! Lance!' She arched her neck, looking back over her shoulder at him. 'Lance, please don't let them do this!'

Eyes cold, arms folded, Lance ignored her tearful pleas.

She was advised of her rights and locked in a cage car as more cops and Lieutenant Simmons, their supervisor, arrived.

Lance and Niko both talked at once, about arrests, hospitals, and restraining orders against Stephanie in both LA and New York.

'Florida has aggressive stalking laws,' the

lieutenant told them. 'We can get an injunction, a court order, charge her with aggravated stalking, hang a weapons charge on her for the knife, breaking and entering, trespassing — '

'No, wait, wait.' Lance cut him off. 'Just a minute, guys.'

Niko reeled as though slapped. He knew what was coming.

'Look,' Lance said. 'We don't need this kind of negative press. We haven't even started shooting yet. If she's arrested there's no way to keep it out of the tabloids.'

Niko sighed, exasperated.

Simmons looked dubious. 'This . . . uh . . . an on-and-off-again relationship?'

'Hell, no,' Lance said. 'Never on. The only relationship we have is in her mind. Her name is Stephanie Carrollton, better known as the fan from hell. Started out innocently, organizing a fan club, then weirded out. She showed up in LA, broke into my house, even stole my Ferrari once and, when the police stopped her, said we were engaged. She landed in a psych ward that time. Her family took her back to Boston, had her in treatment, but then she showed up when I was in New York. Got into my hotel room somehow and tried to commit suicide.'

Hard to tell if the cops were buying his

story 100 percent. I wasn't sure I was. Stephanie was absolutely convincing. She had fooled me.

'I was married at the time,' Lance was saying. 'We come back to the hotel and find Stephanie unconscious in our bed — wearing Lexie's nightgown. That was a trip.'

'Sick chick,' said one of the cops, who turned to gaze out at the squad car. I handed him Stephanie's shoe.

'Not bad-looking, but sounds like a candidate for the puzzle factory,' said another.

'She into drugs?' the lieutenant asked.

'Beats me.' Lance shrugged and ran his hand through his hair. 'If she's not on medication, she should be. I had no idea she was in Miami.'

'She's into Lance,' Niko said. 'Classic obsessive. She could definitely be dangerous.'

Lance looked sheepish. 'I just don't like her showing up here, and I hated it in LA when she took off with my car.'

'It doesn't take much for somebody like her to switch from suicidal to homicidal,' Niko argued.

'What do you want us to do?' The lieutenant looked perplexed.

'I called my lawyer right after I called you,' Lance said. 'He's trying to contact her family, have them get her under control and back into treatment up there.'

Niko clearly didn't agree but, resigned, he brought out a Polaroid to photograph her. Copies would be posted at the Star Island guardhouse and circulated among the local cops and security staff working on the movie.

The lieutenant said he would try to persuade Stephanie to let them take her to county hospital for a psychiatric evaluation. 'But,' he warned, 'you understand that without criminal charges it's strictly voluntary. She can walk any time.'

'Do what you can,' Lance said. 'Let's just try to keep it low-profile.'

The lieutenant said he would, then looked at me. 'What about her?'

All heads swiveled in my direction. 'No arrest.' I shrugged. 'It's probably not a story.' At least not in a newspaper run by starstruck management. 'It would make a helluva gossip column item, but chances are Eduardo won't hear about this, at least he won't from me.' Why did I feel uncomfortably like a conspirator?

No time left for a full-blown tour of the house, but Lance quickly pointed out the media/screening room with five overhead television screens, the sunken bar, and the glass walls with a 180-degree view of the city, then he pulled on an off-white sports-coat. We were now running late for the press conference at the Inter-Continental Hotel.

I insisted on taking my car, so Lance rode with me. Niko, clearly uneasy about the arrangement, followed in their rented Lincoln Town Car.

'All right,' I said, as we cruised across the causeway in my T-Bird, 'tell me straight now. Be honest, just Lance to Britt. You had a little romance, an affair, with Stephanie, right?'

'No fucking way. Think I'm crazy?'

'A one-night stand?'

'Absolutely not, I swear. Not so much as a wink, a drink, or a cup of coffee. Never said or did a thing to encourage her. Quite the contrary. I've had her arrested, committed, and threatened by my lawyers. Remember? I must have mentioned something to you about a scary broad. The mental case? Well, you just met her. And thank you very much. If I hadn't stopped you, you were outa there. I wouldn't know why, and who knows how and when I would have met up with her in the house.'

'Has to be creepy,' I conceded. 'But she said you two wanted to be alone.'

'Britt, don't you think I would have told you if I was engaged or involved with anybody?' His look was reproachful.

124

'You know me better.'

'No, I don't. How was I to know? You saw the cops. She is very believable. How can this woman afford to follow you all over the country? Does she work? How does she live? What does she do?'

He rolled the window down, looking sullen, and lit a cigarette, again without even asking if it was okay. Jet skiers tried to pace us in the blue bay, and a V formation of pelicans glided lazily overhead.

'This is it,' he finally said. 'This is what she does. I think I'm full-time for her. She was one reason I was happy to go on location. Don't know why I didn't think she'd show here. Distance hasn't stopped her in the past.'

A generous trust fund from her grandfather supported Stephanie comfortably, he said. The well-educated daughter of a mainline Boston family, she was able to do as she pleased.

'That explains it,' I said.

'What?'

'Her shoe. It was a Salvatore Ferragamo.'

'Didn't know you were into fashion.'

'I think it's obvious that I'm not, but my mother is. She coordinates fashion shows. *Her* obsession is trying to properly accessorize me, coordinate my wardrobe, and make me over. So far, she's failed.'

'Shouldn't try to fix something that ain't broke. She did a good job the first time. Why mess with success?'

His smile was sexy. He'd apparently gotten over his little fit of pique. I fixed my eyes on the road, but my inquiring mind wanted to know. I knew that Lottie's would, too.

'How did Lexie react when Stephanie showed up in your bed, unconscious?'

'She thought it was a hoot — and scary,' he said, as I turned south on the Boulevard, past the Bayside marketplace. 'She's had bad experiences herself. She took self-defence lessons, learned to handle a gun. She's a crack shot, with her own weapon. Customized, so it doesn't mess up her manicure.' He sighed. 'I didn't need this now. Today is stressful enough. All the shit with this movie, and seeing Lexie again. It's not gonna be pretty.'

★ ★ ★

A gauntlet of cameras waited. We were late, but Lexie Duran was even later. A publicist whisked us into a staging area, where we joined director Phillip Hodges and producers Wendy Weintraub and Richard Van Ness. Hodges was tall and boyish, curly haired and in his early forties. Wendy Weintraub, small,

126

middle-aged, and mousy, wore olive drab and no trace of makeup. Odd that a woman so colorless produced big, bold, bright technicolor movies full of action and excitement.

'We were worried,' she told Lance plaintively. 'You're late.' She looked pointedly at me, as though I must be the reason.

'Everything all right, Lance?' Van Ness sounded more suspicious than concerned. Tall, with white hair, glasses, and a bit of a paunch, he was in his fifties and wore expensive casual clothes.

'Sure, sure.' Lance helped himself to a cup of black coffee from a silver pot. When he introduced me, the only flicker of interest or recognition came when he mentioned where I worked. Publicity, now that meant something to them.

'It's already too late for the news at noon unless they do a live feed. Is ET here? Where's Lexie?' Wendy asked in a nasal whine, checking her watch for the second time in less than a minute.

Lance ignored the question.

'She just got in a couple of hours ago,' Van Ness said. 'Give her a break. She'll be here.'

The stage was arranged as if for a panel discussion, with microphones and water glasses at each place.

Everyone but Lance took their seats, and

the director and producers began fielding questions, withholding the identity of the new co-star, heightening the suspense, promising to introduce her shortly. Watching from the sideline, with Niko and Lance, I saw Lottie down front with the other photographers. She gave me and Lance a thumbs-up. A few cursory shots were snapped, but everybody was waiting for the stars.

Van Ness orchestrated the proceedings, so puffed up by his own importance that had somebody stuck a pin in him he probably would have flown backward a hundred yards. Finally, he pompously introduced 'the star of our film, Mr Lance Westfell.' Lance acknowledged the applause, camera shutters whirring, and took his seat. Before he could finish saying how happy he was to be in Miami, excitement erupted at the back of the room.

Lexie Duran. Like a flame, in a sleek red dress short enough to be illegal in many rural north-Florida counties, she waded directly through the press corps instead of waiting offstage to be introduced.

'Here she is now!' Van Ness boomed into his mike, wearing a phony look of surprise, as though this hadn't been set up. 'Our new co-star, Miss Lexie Duran!'

Every camera swung into a 180-degree

turn, cutting Lance off mid-sentence. No one could take their eyes off her as she sauntered slowly to her seat, waving like Miss America, flashing her million-dollar toothpaste-ad smile, radiating charm, confidence, and sex appeal.

When she sat, adjusted her skirt, and crossed those impossibly long legs, I thought Wayman Andrews from WTOP would have a heart attack.

She had certainly upstaged Lance Westfell. Exactly what she had in mind. She was good.

Lance looked wistful for a moment. I was probably the only one who noticed. Did he yearn for their lost love or his stolen spotlight?

Questions flew fast and furious. Lexie smiled and laughed. Each time Lance spoke she crossed or uncrossed her legs, tossed that lush mane of tawny hair, or licked her full crimson lips, attracting the cameras like heat-seeking missiles.

Yes, she loved Miami. Yes, she was 'so excited' about the new movie.

'Do you foresee any difficulties in working with your ex-husband?' asked the Channel 7 entertainment reporter.

'It's the bravest thing I've ever done.' She laughed and glanced coyly at Lance. 'Seriously, as a professional actor,' she said, flashing perfect teeth for the cameras, 'you don't let your personal life interfere with your work. I'm looking forward to this movie.'

'What about you, Lance?' another reporter asked.

'We're all grown-ups,' he said evenly. 'And we all share the same goal, to turn out a terrific product.'

'But the love scenes?' The first reporter persisted, turning back to Lexie. 'Don't you think that will be awkward, given your history?'

Lexie smiled, drooping her eyelashes, a trick she did so well on the national hair-color commercial that first ran during the Super Bowl. 'Of course not,' she purred into the bank of microphones. 'We've already rehearsed.'

'So that's what that was,' Lance quipped, his rueful expression drawing laughter. From my peripheral vantage point, I caught the split-second glint of malevolence in Lexie's eyes as he sat grinning, momentarily back in the spotlight.

The press corps loved it.

★   ★   ★

'Sheesh, I need a drink,' Lance muttered as he, Niko, and I left the hotel. Lexie and the others still held court inside.

'Not yet, amigo,' Niko said. 'It's onward and upward, to Metro-Dade county hall.' I left my car at the hotel and we took the Town Car driven by Niko, who seemed happier with that arrangement.

'Didya see what Lexie was doing?' Lance grumbled. 'Didya see the stunts she was pulling? Her and that son of a bitch Van Ness. What love scenes?' His voice rose. 'What freaking love scenes? There are none in the script as I know it.

'This day has got to get better.' He leaned back on the plush seat, closed his eyes, and sighed, repeating it like a mantra. 'It's gotta get better.'

★ ★ ★

The commission chambers atop Metro-Dade Center were jammed. Meetings are televised live on cable so our citizenry can see their elected leaders in action. The shows often have more comedy, drama, and intrigue than prime-time network programming. Lobbyists, lawyers, and taxpayers wheel and deal at tables on an open-air patio outside, watching the show on monitors as they await their turn. Today, fans of all ages had joined the usual crowd.

They mobbed Lance as we crossed the patio. Cheers and applause rang inside the paneled chambers. The mayor hammered his gavel to interrupt discussion of the controversial high-rise sprinkler issue.

'Let's take a break now to recognize an esteemed visitor to our city' — he beamed and straightened his tie — 'someone we hope will enjoy his stay as much as we enjoy having him. We want him to feel at home in the Magic City, so he returns often; therefore we are taking this opportunity to proclaim Lance Westfell an honorary citizen of Dade County and hereby present this token, a key to the county. The world-famous world-class star of *The Last Gunfighter*, *Ground Zero*, *Dead by Sundown*, and many, many others, Lance Westfell!'

Lance took the key and stepped up to the mike. He appeared happy and relaxed, without a trace of the harried, headachy expression worn moments ago. Must be show biz, I thought, or perhaps positive energy drawn from the enthusiastic crowd. Waiting for the applause to subside, he scrutinized the key, pretending to bite it, in a test for authenticity.

'The real thing,' he announced directly to me. 'Not plastic. Lock your doors,' he warned, waving it high. 'What will this open?' he demanded, turning to the mayor and the commissioners.

'The hearts of every Dade County resident,' the mayor said quickly. That man is never at a loss for words.

'I know you're dealing with important issues here, so I won't take up your time,' Lance said. 'I simply want to thank everybody for our wonderful reception in your beautiful city, which will shine in our movie. I hope we do you justice. This is just the beginning. Hollywood has discovered Miami. Thank you for this honor.'

He exited down the center aisle to an ovation, grinning and pumping hands. It was a love fest. He should run for office, I thought. Look at Sonny Bono and Clint Eastwood. He could not do worse than the politicians we have. Our commission meetings are a three-ring circus anyway. We could use a ringmaster proficient with a bullwhip.

As Lance approached where we stood, Niko, who never took his eyes off him, said, 'Thanks for warning me about the knife this morning.'

'I'm glad it turned out all right.'

He forged ahead, parting the sea of fans as we fought through the crush and clamor toward the elevator. Nearly there, I reached out, caught his shoulder, and spoke in his ear.

'Stephanie didn't stay at the hospital,' I said urgently. 'She's here!'

7

Lance did not see her. He was grinning at several giggly teenage girls and pumping the hand of a fresh-faced young woman in pink. Stephanie was pushing through the crowd about four feet from his right elbow, smiling, her eyes fixed on him.

The elevator doors had opened. Niko shouted his name, moving fast. As Lance turned, Niko wheeled him around and hustled him inside, one big hand on the small of his back. The young woman in pink, still clinging to Lance's hand, was swept inside as well. Niko shoved me aboard and seemed about to eject the woman in pink but Stephanie bounded forward, face alight. Hard to believe she was the same hysterical woman marched off in handcuffs that morning. Did she ever quit?

Niko lunged forward, blocking her as the doors slid shut between them.

'Lance! Lance!' Stephanie called. The elevator was glass enclosed, in the center of an atrium. We stared at Stephanie and she stared back, mouthing words unheard as the car slowly descended. The last we saw of her were the toes of her Salvatore Ferragamos.

'I knew it, I knew it,' Niko muttered in exasperation.

The cute blonde girl had an upturned nose, big blue eyes, and a gaze fixed adoringly on Lance.

'It's okay,' he assured her, assuming that our abrupt departure had startled her.

'I've seen all your movies,' she chirped, as though nothing had happened. 'Saw *Island of the Dead* seven times.'

'Now there's a fan,' he said. 'Glad you liked it.'

I paid scant attention, wondering, as Lance and Niko had to be, about Stephanie. When and where would she next appear? Were those expensive shoes of hers pounding down the stairwell at this very moment? Would she greet us in the lobby as we disembarked? The blonde girl fumbled in her purse, in search of a pen for an autograph, I assumed. Instead she came up with a spray-top bottle. I hoped she would not use hair spray or perfume in these tight quarters. She did not. She sprayed a healthy blast directly into Lance's face.

'What the . . . ?' His hands flew to his eyes.

Her arm extended rigidly from her body, teeth on edge, her eyes narrow slits, she kept spraying with the enthusiasm most Miamians reserve for fire ants or palmetto bugs.

'What is tha — ?' I didn't complete the word because Lance shoved me into the corner, his broad back planted in front of my face, shielding me from the spray.

The control panel was handy, so I mashed the red emergency button. A shrill alarm bell sounded as the elevator jolted to a stop between floors.

'Drop that! Drop it!' Niko demanded. I heard someone grunt as they scuffled, his ponytail flying. More spray hissed wildly, mist arcing into the air, as they fought for the bottle.

What was that stuff? The droplets smelled sweetish and sickening. Not mace, not tear gas. The sounds of their struggle evoked flashbacks of that night in the woods when I fought to survive. The walls spun. I wanted the hell off this elevator. Now!

The bottle escaped their clawing hands, catapulted free, and fell. Lance lurched backward, protecting me. Niko kicked it into a corner. It was unlabeled, the contents milky.

He and the girl bounced off the walls, she whimpering as he wrestled her to the floor.

'What is that stuff?' he demanded. 'What the hell is that shit?'

'Let me go, you son of a bitch!' she panted, sprawled ungracefully, legs splayed, his knee on her chest.

'What's in the fucking bottle? What is that stuff?'

'You bastard! Let me up!'

He glanced from the floor where he held her. 'You okay, Lance? Let's get this thing moving and get out of here.'

'Yeah,' Lance said. Hands trembling, I jabbed frantically at buttons, but the elevator seemed frozen in place. The girl's darting eyes fixed on the bottle, just out of her reach. Niko couldn't let her go. Lance stood in the same position, hands to his face. Fighting claustrophobia, trying not to inhale, I hit the lobby button. The elevator lurched and began its descent.

Niko took his knee off the girl, snatched up the bottle, sniffed the contents, and tasted some on a finger, as she sat up. Her twisted pink skirt exposed pale, slightly flabby thighs.

'I'm going to sue you,' she spit venomously at Lance. 'Your goon attacked me. I'm calling the *National Enquirer*. I'll make a hundred thousand dollars from this! I'm suing.'

Lance said nothing.

'What is this shit?' Niko demanded,

shoving the bottle in her face.

The elevator door opened at last. The cop assigned to maintain security at commission meetings stood waiting, baton ready. I hoped he would swat her in the teeth with it. I was tired of all this.

She scrambled to her feet and rushed out. 'Help, officer. I've been attacked! Officer!'

His response was skeptical and knowing. A middle-aged man in suspenders, a video camera balanced on his shoulder, stood behind him. The man had been taping Lance's appearance for his hospitalized teenage daughter, a fan. After the key was presented, he had rushed to the lobby to tape Lance's departure. He had been filming our descent from a vantage point on the outside portico and had alerted the police officer.

Amateur video, phenomenon of the nineties, the new national pastime. Americans are everywhere with their trusty InstaCams, capturing plummeting planes, violent cops, crooked politicians, and each other in action. Amateur video, beloved by tabloid TV — and me, at the moment.

His playback clearly showed the woman wielding the spray. More good news: Stephanie was being detained outside the commission chambers until Lance could leave the building.

The cop ushered us into a private office to escape the growing crowd. He closed the door behind us and asked if everybody was okay.

'No,' Lance answered. 'I think I have to go to the hospital.' He blinked. 'My eyes burn like hell, and I can't see.'

'That shit could be acid,' Niko said, voice tight.

Something roiled in my stomach.

At first, Lance refused to lie on a stretcher but the rescue squad prevailed. 'We've gotta irrigate your eyes, Lance,' the medic said, 'and we can't do it with you sitting up. Time is important here, buddy. We don't want any permanent damage.'

'Do what they say. Do what they say,' Niko urged, helping Lance, whose eyes were squeezed shut, down on to a gurney. 'We're going with you, amigo.'

'You got my key to the city?'

'Yeah, yeah. Don't worry. I've got it,' Niko said.

Before we rolled, the paramedics administered anesthetic drops to Lance's eyes. I sat up front with the driver. Niko rode in back, gripping Lance's ankle as a medic inserted a plastic tube into an IV bottle of saline solution and washed out Lance's eyes. He did one, then the other, then began again. Each time he had to force the lids open.

A Channel 7 news crew pounded up as we were about to pull away, a reporter from the other paper and Channel 23 hot on their heels.

'Where are they taking him?' a reporter cried.

'Cedars!' I shouted, as the rescue truck roared away from the curb, siren wailing.

The driver turned to me. 'You know we're going to Bascom Palmer?'

'They'll figure it out soon enough.'

I watched, wincing with Lance, as the medic held open his right eye and drowned it in saline solution.

'Hear you're in town to make a movie,' the medic said cheerfully as he forcibly pried open Lance's left eye. Lance's fists clenched.

The famous eye institute, only two miles away, seemed so far. In emergencies it always does.

★　★　★

I held his hand as they rolled him into the ER. 'You didn't have to shield me,' I told him. 'Niko and I are supposed to watch out for *you*. We're the ones paid to throw our bodies in front of yours and take the bullets.'

140

'Who told you that?' He managed a smile.

'My editors. They warned me not to let anything happen to you.'

Three doctors were waiting, alerted by radio. I recognized Dr Alonso, a famous corneal surgeon. It was a comfort to see him, immaculate in a white lab coat, brilliant, the best, but his look of concern made the gravity of Lance's situation clear.

How would this look in the national press? Lance's movie was to be the lynchpin in Miami's comeback from the storm, the tourist murders, the violent crime statistics, the mass felony arrests of University of Miami football players, and the Panthers losing their shot at the Stanley Cup. We were going to look so good. Damn, I thought. Lance does not deserve this. Neither do we.

'Anybody check the pH?' Dr Alonso asked.

'Didn't have any litmus paper aboard,' a medic said.

They whisked the patient into an examining room. No waiting with this type of injury, no litany of insurance questions first. Corrosive chemicals could be burning their way into the inner eye, and every second counts. Being Lance Westfell did not hurt either. More nurses than you would have expected to see on duty in the

141

entire hospital suddenly became extremely busy in the immediate area, sneaking peeks at the superstar, who did not look so heroic at the moment.

'Check the pH of that bottle's contents,' the doctor snapped.

'What does pH mean?' Niko asked.

'Tells us whether it's acid or alkaline,' the nurse answered. She dipped a small, clear strip of paper into the milky substance.

'Don't let it be acid,' Niko beseeched.

'Actually,' she said brightly, 'the chances of permanent injury are far less if it is acid. Both can cause the same initial damage, but acid won't penetrate. An alkaline isn't neutralized as quickly by the body, so it continues to seep into inner layers.'

'What would be alkaline?' I took notes.

'Bleach, chlorine, lye.' She shrugged. 'With them, the aftermath is worse.'

Chills rippled up and down my arms. I blinked at the thought of a million optic nerve fibers shutting down, short-circuiting the electrical impulses to the brain. The test paper turned yellow-orange and she disappeared into the examining room. Before the door closed behind her I heard a doctor leaning over Lance say, 'It's a little off, six point four.' I had no idea what he meant but hated the sound of it.

'I can't believe I let this happen.' Niko's fists were clenched together as he rocked back and forth. 'Son of a bitch! He wouldn't listen. He wouldn't listen. He's been too exposed ever since we got here. I warned him. He can't just walk around in crowds without at least three security people on him.' The pain on his face was real.

'You can't beat yourself up,' I said. 'Stephanie had us all distracted. Who would have thought?'

'I can't believe this,' he said. 'Women. I hate tussling with them. You can't deck 'em, and they're hard as hell to hold on to. I'd rather fight ten men. I hate this, twice in one day. I shoulda seen — '

'Nobody can see everything.' I tried to keep us both from panicking, tried not to look at the clock, knowing I should call the paper. 'How long have you worked for Lance?'

'From the beginning.' He hunched in his chair, hands to his head. 'We played ball in high school. Lance was quarterback, I was left end. Got out of the Marines just about the time he first got into acting. I studied acting too, got into martial arts. We wound up working out at the same gym. I had some problems, he got me squared away. Saved my life. First starring role he had, I was his stand-in. Been stand-in, trainer, security, ever since. He's good people, the best. I shouldn't have hesitated, man. I should've broken her fucking neck.'

A Miami cop interrupted. They had information on the contents of the bottle. The chief had assigned his best man to the case and he was en route.

★   ★   ★

Lieutenant Kendall McDonald exuded no sense of urgency, concern, or even surprise at seeing me. I flew halfway down the hall to meet him as he sauntered toward us. Niko was right behind me.

'Any word on what the stuff was?' I asked anxiously. 'Was it acid?'

'Still baby-sitting the matinee idol, huh?' he drawled.

'Yes,' I said impatiently.

He frowned and looked thoughtful. 'Isn't this your day off?'

'Yes.'

He raised an eyebrow.

'McDonald!' I wanted to pound his chest. 'Did you find out what it was? The doctors need to know. Now!'

'I'm sure the cowboy will survive.'

'This is frightening for him, for all of us. If you know anything, spit it out.'

144

He shrugged. 'Her name is Karen Sawyer. Fan and wannabe actress/model.'

'And?'

'Upon hearing that aggravated battery is a first-degree felony, she suddenly became cooperative.'

'And?' I wanted to clutch his throat to force out the words. Niko seemed about to do so.

'When she heard the matinee idol was in Miami, Ms Sawyer paid a visit to a friendly Santeria priestess and invested in a super-powerful love potion.'

'Love potion?' Niko and I chorused.

'Guaran-goddam-teed to work. Spray the object of your affections, and he is yours for life.'

'What was in it?' Niko demanded, as I sighed with relief.

'We talked to the priestess. Interesting concoction. Mother's milk, rose water, a few herbs and roots. Nothing toxic.'

'Thank God.'

'Mother's milk?' Niko grimaced.

McDonald fought a grin. This is serious, I thought indignantly. What is wrong with this man?

'It definitely did not work,' Lance mumbled, when told of the love potion. The alcohol-based rose water had stung his mucous membranes, but his sense of humor remained intact. No permanent injury but, Dr Alonso explained, the doctors had to 'flip his eyelids over to be sure no residue remained in the little cul de sacs of his upper lids.' Each tiny crevice in his lids had to be cleaned out with Q-Tips. I winced. Lance was a trouper. McDonald did not mind at all. In fact, he smiled a lot.

'He should be fine in twenty-four to forty-eight hours,' Dr Alonso said. 'The conjunctival fornices have been explored and found to be uninvolved. We'll treat him topically. Three sets of eyedrops, including cortisone and an antibiotic. The third will enlarge the pupil and inhibit ciliary spasms, so the movement of the pupil is not painful,' he explained. 'We will need to see him again in a day or so. We could keep him here.'

'He won't want to stay in the hospital,' Niko said.

'He's already indicated that,' the doctor said. 'We can discharge him, then see him again to remove the patches.'

'Patches?' Niko asked.

'The surface skin of his eyes is so irritated that he'll have to wear them for twenty-four hours or so. The poor guy. I saw *The Last Gunfighter*,' the surgeon said. 'He was really good.'

Niko nodded. 'Is there a way to get him out of here without the press all over him? We don't want pictures.'

'I'm sure we can arrange something,' the doctor said.

McDonald's bedside manner stunk. 'The chief asked me to express his regrets,' he was telling Lance, who was seated in a wheelchair, patches covering both eyes. 'He's at a chiefs' meeting in Tallahassee or he'd be here himself. But he wanted me to assure you that the department is at your disposal and will continue to be, should you need protection in the future — from fans intent on spraying you with mother's milk or anything else.'

He struggled to keep a straight face.

'That guy's got an attitude,' Niko growled as McDonald departed.

'You know how cops are,' I said.

'Uh-oh.' Niko leaned out into the corridor. 'Look who's here.'

'Who?' Lance gripped the armrests of his wheelchair.

'Sorry,' Niko said. 'Wendy and Richard Van Ness.'

Lance relaxed. 'Could be worse. I thought you'd spotted Stephanie, Lexie, or the bad blonde with the bottle.'

The producers burst into the room, Wendy

dressed like a wren, Van Ness in tennis whites.

'Lance! What the hell happened?' Van Ness blurted, shocked at the sight of his star.

'I got the key to the county.' Lance shrugged. 'I was warned. Apparently it's the kiss of death. At least I'm not a fugitive yet.'

'How could you let this happen?' Wendy whined at Niko.

'It looks worse than it is,' Lance said. 'No damage, the docs say I just have to wear these for a day.' He gingerly touched the patches over his eyes.

'We were staggered when we heard,' Van Ness said dramatically. 'Lexie is alarmed. We were playing tennis . . . What the hell is wrong with this town?

'Sure you're okay, champ?' He clamped a bony fist on Lance's shoulder. Lance reacted, startled by the sudden touch. 'Where's the doctor in charge?' Van Ness boomed. 'We need to talk to the doctor. No problem starting work this week, is there, champ?'

'No problem.' Lance was stoic. 'Tell everybody it's no big deal. Stung like hell. Just thought it should be checked out.'

'Definitely. We're here for you, champ. Anything you need. Anything.' He and Wendy set out to track down the doctor, seeking assurances that Lance would indeed be ready to work in a matter of days. How heartwarming, I thought.

'What are the chances of keeping this out of the press?' Van Ness asked me when he returned reassured. 'That's your department, isn't it?'

'About as much chance as winning a murder conviction in LA. Reporters are already downstairs. Somebody shot video of the whole thing. I plan to write a story myself,' I added.

Van Ness looked annoyed. Wendy glared.

'Love potion? Mother's milk?' Van Ness grimaced and fingered his mustache. 'Ludicrous. Makes our star look silly.'

'Security is a problem,' Wendy said, turning on Niko.

'Right. I'm handling it,' he replied.

'Hope you do a better job than we've seen so far,' she said.

★ ★ ★

We returned to Star Island in a hired limo. Lance leaned back in the seat, hands on his knees. 'You were right all along, Niko. I should have listened. Light me a cigarette, will you?'

'Don't worry about a thing, amigo.' Niko lit a Marlboro and passed it to Lance. 'From now on I'm armed. The permit can be expedited through the governor's office, but I'm gonna be packing, starting now. We'll have three people on you at all times, front, back, and flank. I'm point man. If it's okay, I want to call Pauli, Dave, Frank, and Al in LA. They catch the next flight out, they can be here by morning. We'll have at least one off-duty cop stationed at the house at all times. Maybe somebody on the gate.'

It seemed to me like an overreaction, but this could have been worse. What if she had had a gun? Or if it had been acid?

Lance exhaled and looked pained. I wondered which hurt more, his mucous membranes or the total loss of his privacy and spontaneity. 'Whatever you say.' He sounded bleak.

'I got the number of a registry to bring in a nurse until the patches come off.'

'No, Niko. No.' Lance leaned forward, deep voice intense. 'I'm with you on everything else, but . . . no. I'm spooked. I can't see a damn thing. No fucking strangers in the house while I'm like this. Britt?' He groped in my direction, and I took his hand. 'You're the only person I can trust here, aside from Niko. Stay at the house to help out? Just till I can see?'

No way, I thought. I had to write my story,

then pick up my mail, my messages, and my dry cleaning. I had to go feed Bitsy and Billy Boots and walk the dog. I had to wash the car, write out my bills, and balance my checkbook.

'Sure,' I heard myself say. 'You can count on me.'

'What the hell's going on up ahead?' The limo driver slowed down.

No chase cars had pursued us from the hospital because the doctors and the producers had called a press conference as we beat it out the back door and the pack had fallen for it.

But now, traffic jammed the Star Island entrance: TV trucks, marked news cars, and camera crews. Choppers throbbed overhead. I recognized one as a local TV station's 'Sky Spy'.

'We've got us a welcoming committee,' Niko said, guiding Lance's hand to the ashtray. He instructed the driver to go on by, as though headed for South Beach and used the car phone to warn the security man at the guardhouse to clear traffic; we were about to barrel through without stopping.

The driver turned back west. A motorcycle cop cleared a path. Our driver floored it and the gate lifted just in time. Though our windows were tinted, shouts went up as we roared through. I recognized many of my colleagues and some freelance paparazzi among them.

'Vultures!' Niko muttered.

Since the streets are public thoroughfares, no one can be barred from the island. Security is limited and the guard chiefly a deterrent. His task: inquire as to destination, record the time and tag number, then raise the gate. He did his job now, but in super-slow motion. Laboriously, he wrote the destination of the news car behind us on his clipboard, consulted his watch, and strolled to the rear to copy the license tag, number by number. Then he trudged back into the guardhouse, in no hurry to press the button. He did slow them down.

They must be screaming, I thought, as I watched out the rear window.

Other reporters were already on the island, camped out on the swale. Lance slid down in his seat as Niko jumped out, door locks snapping behind him. Had the garage door opener not been in the Town Car, still parked at Metro-Dade Center, we could have driven directly through and into the garage. Instead, Niko dashed to open the gate, besieged by cameras and reporters with microphones. In the dusky twilight it was easy for the press to initially mistake him for Lance. They looked so much alike, particularly with his ponytail tucked inside his collar. An overweight paparazzo, whose specialty is stalking stars for the tabloids, leaned dangerously out of a rented chopper overhead.

We pulled into the driveway. Niko closed the gate, then opened the garage. As the door closed behind us, paparazzi were coming over the walls.

Lance and I sat waiting in the dark as Niko hit the lights and went inside to check the house and close the drapes. This had to be what it was like when his marriage to Lexie was breaking up, I thought. What chance did they have? I often pursue people reluctant to talk to a reporter, but on my beat it is usually only once that scandal, crime, or twist of fate makes someone newsworthy for a brief moment in time. What must it be like, I wondered, to live day in and day out with the wolf pack on your scent, most ravenous at times of personal crisis but always circling?

'You're home,' I told Lance cheerfully.

Niko and I exchanged a glance as we helped Lance into the house. To my relief, he did not say it, but I knew what he was thinking. I could have easily been part of that pack. To be on the other side was oddly disorienting, especially for someone who has always believed her path to be righteous.

That feeling would not make writing my story any easier.

With Lance comfortable in a chair, his feet up, I called my landlady, Mrs Goldstein, who agreed to take care of Bitsy and Billy Boots. Then Niko made calls while I fixed tea for them and Cuban coffee for me and heated soup in the gloriously appointed and well-stocked kitchen. Surrounded by shiny chrome and marble-topped ambience, I stirred the soup with a long spoon and thought of little Misty Oliver, stirring soup and fixing sandwiches in a grease-spattered, ill-furnished, government-subsidized apartment, struggling to mother her ever-increasing number of small siblings. Suddenly I wanted to sob. But I didn't. What was wrong with me?

Niko was watching, an odd expression on his face. 'I have to file a story,' I said briskly, glancing at the clock.

The city desk put me right through to the last person I wanted to talk to.

'Where have you been, Britt? Where is Westfell?' demanded Gretchen, the assistant city editor from hell. 'They said you were with him. How far are you from writing?'

'I'm at Star Island,' I said. 'He's here and he's okay. I can do it right now.' I could send the story by modem from a computer room off the kitchen.

'What about art?'

I knew what she meant but pretended I did not. 'The cops must have a mug shot of the woman available by now.'

'I meant Westfell. Villanueva can shoot it. He's there right now, outside the Star Island house.'

'Westfell doesn't want pictures,' I said tersely. 'He's wearing patches over his eyes.'

'Great!'

'He is not comfortable.'

'Talk him into it, Britt. You can do it.'

'No chance.' I wouldn't even try.

Niko listened from the kitchen door, one eye on me and the other on Lance.

'No,' I repeated. 'But there is good art out there somewhere. I've got the name and number of a man who shot the whole thing on videotape.'

'They're already promoting it, as an exclusive on *Hard Copy* tonight,' she snapped.

'A lot of people were snapping pictures when Lance left the commission chambers. I'm sure Karen Sawyer, the woman who did it, is in some of them, in the same frame. The ones shot near the elevator. He was talking to two teenage girls. Both had dark hair; one

155

had a flowered blouse. Sawyer's the blonde, to their left, in a pink dress, carrying a shoulder bag. That was less than a minute before it happened.' Stephanie might even be in the same shot, I thought, but did not mention her.

Gretchen's final words were conspiratorial. 'Go let Villanueva in, Britt. You know you can talk Westfell into it.'

Niko showed me how to use the sophisticated computer setup. I tapped out the story, questioning Niko and Lance about what they remembered, and checked with the cops on Karen Sawyer. She had been charged with assault and battery.

'Hey, guy,' I called in to Lance, 'your true love's got a record, minor stuff, here and in California: petty larceny, DUI, and one for soliciting.'

'She should get a refund. The potion still ain't working,' Lance muttered.

'I don't think I want to meet any more of the women in your life,' I said, as Niko and I helped Lance up to bed. 'You know, you're taking this pretty well, actually.'

'Ah, it ain't so bad,' he said. 'I had to wear contact lenses, red ones, for *Night of the Red Death*, back when I was starting out. Scratched up a cornea and had to wear a patch for a couple of days. The best thing about these is they come off tomorrow.'

Niko got him stripped down to shorts while I fixed a light supper and sent it upstairs in the handy electric-powered dumb-waiter. We ate in Lance's room, listening to TV news reports. His king-sized circular bed could be rotated to face either Biscayne Bay or a huge TV screen. Too bad he could not see either one.

Stoked on coffee, I took first watch. Niko promised to spell me at 3 A.M. I dragged a comfortable chair up to his bedside. 'Can I have a cigarette?' he asked.

'I'm surprised you smoke.' I shook a Marlboro out of the pack and put it in my mouth. 'You work out, you're in great shape, you're a health-conscious guy.'

'You one a those militant ex-smokers?'

I struck the match and lit up. He licked his lips.

'Nope.' I exhaled. 'I kicked it in high school. Never really liked it. Only tried it because everybody else did. Then it became uncool, but I guess smoking is making a comeback in movies.'

'Never went away,' he said. I brought the cigarette to his lips. They moved like those of a blind baby searching for the comfort of its mother's nipple. He took it in his mouth and

157

sucked down a deep drag.

'Nice,' I said. 'Smoking in bed. Hope this place has smoke alarms. We can try for two trips to the ER in one day.'

'I'm counting on you to beat out the flames.' His lips curled in a half smile.

'Hate to see them use a fire hose on you, after all you've been through today.' I positioned the ashtray near his fingers.

'Unlike most people,' he said, one arm under his head, 'I didn't smoke as a teenager. Had to learn for my first movie. Looks good on camera. Dramatic, sexy. Remember how Bogart used to dangle a cigarette out of his mouth? They still call it Bogarting, he was that good. Can you picture Bette Davis without a cigarette?'

'My favorite is that scene in *Now, Voyager*,' I said softly, 'where her lover lights two cigarettes, one for each of them.'

'Paul Henreid. Right. Suggestive and intimate. You light a woman's cigarette, she looks up into your eyes, steadies your hand with hers.'

Almost made me want to start smoking.

'Remember James Dean with the pack in the sleeve of his T-shirt?' he said, sinking back on his pillow. His biceps were like those of a sculpted Roman gladiator. Had I seen him as one in a movie? 'In Paris and South Beach,' he was saying, 'in the outdoor cafés, everybody lights up. Hazy blue smoke can set a scene. Look at *Die Hard*. You can tell the good guys from the bad guys just by the way they smoke.'

'You're right. I hadn't thought about that.' I liked the way his abs moved when he exhaled and the fact that he could not see me watching.

'If it hadn't been Sir Walter Raleigh, some actor would have invented it. The action pauses, you light up. Gives you all kinds of business. Tamp down the cigarette, scratch the match, toy with a lighter. George Raft could do more with a cigarette . . . You've got the angry exhale — '

'My mother is good at that one.'

' — and the seductive inhale. Smoking is a terrific device. You can be flirtatious, or hyper, or menacing like Cagney and Edward G. Robinson. Decadent, sophisticated — remember David Niven?' He reached for the ashtray, dropped his cigarette, and lost it in the bedclothes. 'Uh-oh.' He groped with both hands.

'Now that's sophisticated.' I snatched it from between sheet and comforter and brushed away the ashes. He had swung his feet off the far side of his bed and sat there looking sheepish. 'It's okay, it's okay,' I said.

'I've got it. This one was more Larry, Moe, and Curly than David Niven.'

Smiling, he settled back on to his pillow.

'Want me to read to you?' I browsed though the stack of books and scripts on his bedside table.

'I think I'll just go to sleep.' He yawned.

'Okay. Just speak up if you need anything. I'll be right here. If I'm not, Niko will be.' I leaned over and pecked him on the cheek. 'Pleasant dreams.' Don't know why I said that. My mother always did when she tucked me in at night. Maybe because my recent dreams had not been pleasant.

I curled up in the big comfortable chair and began to read the *Margin of Error* script, careful to turn the pages quietly. I had never read a movie script before. I instantly envisioned Lance as the hero. He and the female lead shared no love scenes in this script; the character Meredith Page was to have played was a nuclear physicist with a husband in the military and a young son menaced by terrorists. I wondered how the new writers would change the relationship. When I finished, I switched off all but a soft night-light. The room was comfortably cool and smelled of rose petals, a potpourri in a crystal bowl on the dresser. I did not fight the drowsiness; sleep had been so elusive lately. Should Lance stir or need anything, I would hear.

La mala hora, the bad hour of my life, invaded my dreams. Again, that dark rutted road, a sea of night closing in around me. Then the captive moon, ripe and full, sailed free from cloud cover, spilling silver across the treetops and the face of the man who wanted me dead. Fighting his iron grip, the weight of my gun in my hand, an explosion lighting up the night. Blood in the moonlight. Smoke trailing from the barrel.

I awoke disoriented and gasping in the dark. In that moment between dream and reality, the brutal struggles between a man and a woman in the elevator and on the staircase down the hall replayed at warp speed across the wilderness of my mind. Or was it my own struggle to survive in a place surrounded by darkness and death?

Lance was sleeping peacefully, naked from the waist up. I stared at his broad chest and muscular arms in the faint glow from the nightlight. His sheet was rumpled. Eyes covered. Trapped in darkness. Helpless.

Like someone in a dream, I arose and locked the door.

8

I peeled the sheet back and touched him. His head jerked, instantly awake. 'Who's that?'

'Shut up,' I said. 'You don't need to know.'

'Britt?'

'I said, shut up,' and roughly cut off his words with my mouth.

'You've got me at a disadvantage here,' he mumbled, voice ragged from sleep.

He reached out for me and touched my bare breast. 'Whoops.' Startled, he was already aroused.

So I deliberately joined the ranks of women who had been attacking him in one way or another all day; Stephanie, Lexie, Karen Sawyer. He did not resist, as I tickled, bit, tortured, clawed, tormented, and assaulted him. Shuddering, he reached for me as I pulled away, just out of reach. 'I can't chase you,' he muttered. 'I can't find you.'

'I know,' I whispered. Then startled him again.

'Want to tie me up too?'

'No.' I smiled and rudely freed the captive

bulge in his under-shorts.

'Just asking.'

How incredibly exciting to make love to a helpless man. Totally free, a role in a fantasy, not something actually happening. I could ravish him, as beautiful and powerful a man as I had ever seen, but he was lost in the dark and I was invisible. His mind's eye saw me only through other senses. Never had I felt so uninhibited, so sexually aggressive — and busy, as though I were an incubus plundering the sex and sapping the strength of my helpless victim before vanishing at dawn.

'I have to see you.' His body glistened with perspiration, though the night was cool. 'I have to see you.' His hands went to the tape holding his eye patches in place. I jerked his fingers away roughly.

'No.' Straddling his body, I pinned his hands. 'You can't. Take those off and I disappear.'

'But . . . okay . . .' He could have flung me across the room one-handed, but this was an agreeable victim. 'You can put a choke collar and a leash on me and lead me around, whatever you want.' His voice was husky. 'Just don't stop.'

My hips slowly rotated above his erect penis. My hair fell across his face. I felt his heart pound. 'What is it that you want?' I whispered in his ear, catching the lobe unmercifully between my teeth.

'Please,' he begged. 'Please.'

The man was far from helpless. He filled the dark places in my psyche with his presence and the wet places in my body with his own. We had sex until we were raw. Then we did it again.

'When I first saw you I knew we would be together,' he whispered, 'but I never thought it would be like this.'

'What movie is that from?' I disengaged myself and padded barefoot and naked into his bathroom. His bedside clock said nearly three.

'Can I have a cigarette?' he called.

I thought a moment. 'No.'

'Hold me?'

Ignoring his pleas to come lie down beside him, I cleaned him up with the efficient, impersonal touch of a nurse, straightened his bed, got dressed, unlocked the door, and resumed my seat, somewhat gingerly.

A rap at the door came at exactly three. Niko opened it and I smiled. 'He's been good,' I said softly. 'He's been dreaming.'

I walked down the paneled hall to a charming guest room decorated in Laura Ashley prints, opened the French doors to a balustraded balcony, and gazed across black water at the city burning bright and wicked in the night. After a few minutes I stepped back inside, closed the doors, stretched out on the bed, and was asleep at once.

* * *

I awoke at seven, refreshed, energized, and hungry. The room was cheerful, the bed soft and comfortable, and the morning face of the city reflected innocently from the bay. Oh, shit, I thought, glimpsing my not-so-innocent face in the mirror. Did it really happen? My sore bottom told me it did. What was I thinking? No excuses. I was cold stone sober. Lance, I thought. Oh my God. I took some deep breaths out on the balcony, resisting the urge to make a run for it before Lance awoke. I didn't even have a car on the premises. The movie crew would be in town for a while. How would I explain my disappearance?

The oval tub in the guest bath was equipped with a Jacuzzi and stocked with delights like French milled complexion soap, honey-almond shampoo, bath foam, and ginseng body lotion. I used them all, then donned a soft fleecy robe that hung on the back of the door. This leased estate had all the perks of a world-class hotel.

The house was quiet, so I crept downstairs, brewed a pot of coffee, found some bacon, and began scrambling eggs. While I was at it, I squeezed some orange juice. The kitchen lacked nothing. My most domestic adventure in years would have been almost pleasant, surrounded by opulence, had I not been haunted again by the hungry eyes of Angel Oliver's children and by my own aberrant behavior the night before.

Shame did not curb my appetite. I wolfed down breakfast, then fixed trays, slid them into the dumbwaiter, and hit the button. I dashed upstairs to meet it, ducking into my room first to slip into my dress.

★ ★ ★

'Good morning,' I said cheerfully, smiling sweetly as I opened the door. Miss Goody Two-Shoes. Wholesome was my middle name.

Niko was watching the morning news. Lance was sitting up in bed, smoking a cigarette, wearing a robe.

'Is it a good morning?' Lance said. What did he mean by that?

'The sun is shining,' I said, glad he couldn't see me. No way to know what he was thinking. He said little.

166

Niko arranged Lance's plate: eggs at three o'clock, bacon at twelve, toast at nine. He neglected to mention the salt shaker at five. When Lance knocked it to the floor, we both moved to help but he scooped it up himself.

'Amazing what you can find if you grope around long enough,' he said, and smiled.

I ignored his remark. Apparently he had said nothing, but Niko was not stupid. He looked curious as I poured coffee, keeping my distance. Luckily I was saved by the bell. The front gate. He checked a small monitor on the massive wooden desk.

'It's the guys. They're here.' Niko picked up the attached telephone.

I trotted downstairs to let them in, eager to get lost in a crowd.

Pauli, Dave, Frank, and Al. Huge, muscular, and fresh off the red-eye. Dave and Al were fair-skinned and blond. Pauli wore dark sunglasses and was shiny bald, as though his head had been shaved and polished, with a nose broken so often that it now rested on his upper lip. Frank was black and short-haired with wide shoulders. Wearing windbreakers and lugging black duffel bags, they resembled a mean lean pro football team taking to the road.

They took the stairs two at a time while I

went to brew more coffee and take care of the flowers. Most funerals have fewer. The off-duty Miami Beach cop at the gate had been checking out and accepting deliveries.

One stood out. Red roses, with a silver Mylar I LOVE YOU balloon. Niko zeroed right in on it as the beef trust came stampeding down the stairs. He opened the card. 'Sweetheart, I should be there taking care of you. We'll be together again soon. Forever. I love you. Always, Stephanie.'

⋆ ⋆ ⋆

Niko arranged to retrieve the Town Car from Metro-Dade Center and have my T-Bird brought from the hotel. The press conference there seemed so long ago, yet it was less than twenty-four hours.

Lance interrupted my goodbyes. 'Hang in awhile longer, would you, Britt? Just till the patches come off?'

No hint in his voice of what had happened between us. I casually agreed, then drove home to change clothes. Only one way to deal with this situation, I told myself: Pretend it never happened. If I did not mention it, perhaps Lance would not either. He had had a stressful day, been traumatized and medicated — too bad it

168

was with nothing more mind-altering than eyedrops.

Mrs Goldstein was watching for me, excited and full of questions. She'd read the paper and seen the TV reports. Her inquiring mind wanted to know much more. Her husband, at age eighty-one, even climbed down from the roof he was patching over one of the units.

'How is he?' she wanted to know.

'Oh, he's good, very good,' I said, wondering what they would think of me if they knew the truth.

She wanted me to persuade Lance to autograph a picture for Seth, her teenage grandson, a star reporter for the Eastside Junior High *Gazette*, in Hopewell, New Jersey. I promised to try.

I changed into a pale silky blouse with tiny mother-of-pearl buttons right up to my chin, matching slacks, and a flowery vest. Prim and proper, I noted, studying myself in the mirror.

★ ★ ★

This time we arrived at Bascom Palmer in the Town Car with Niko, Al, and Pauli, no sirens.

Dr Alonso removed the patches as though unveiling a work of art.

169

Lance studied me for a long moment. Forgetting my embarrassment, I smiled. His vision was fine but he would need sunglasses for a few days. His eyelids were still red and swollen; I wondered about his private parts.

The doctor seriously suggested that Lance wear safety glasses when greeting fans in the future. Made sense in this city, where to many motorists a stop sign means time to reload.

Lance had agreed to let Lottie shoot his first pictures since the incident. She was waiting and returned to Star Island with us in the Lincoln, happily chatting up Lance and his bodyguards. She and Pauli had crossed paths years ago when he worked for Stallone and she had photographed the star for a magazine assignment.

She shot more photos at the house, where two maids and a housekeeper were now on the job.

'Life is simpler on the police beat,' I told Lance, as he signed a picture for Seth Goldstein. 'It's easier to tell the good guys from the bad guys.'

He thanked me, almost formally, for my help and I left.

'So what was it like, sleeping under the same roof with Lance Westfell?' Lottie demanded, as I drove her back to her car.

'Tell me everything.'

'I'm not good at playing nurse,' I confessed.

'But wasn't I right about him?' she said. 'The bigger the star, the more down to earth.'

'Sure, with paparazzi scaling the walls and bodyguards everywhere.'

'Celebrities that big have to build walls around themselves,' she said. 'It ain't an easy life. But when push came to shove, he turned out to be real. He protected you when he had no idea what that woman had in the bottle. Lord knows what woulda happened if that love potion had landed on you.'

She grinned. I said nothing and she cut her eyes at me. 'You okay, Britt? You ain't telling me something?'

I was lucky. Late for another assignment, she had no time to give me the third degree.

I was off until next morning but stopped by the office. I got some coffee, emptied my mailbox, printed out my messages, and sat at my desk, relieved to be back to normal.

The first letter I opened was handwritten and began with a grabber.

I want to expose one of the most violent and dangerous criminals Miami has ever

171

seen, a sadistic monster who will stop at nothing.

That person is my mother.

The next one began:

I AM MISSING!
I need to be found! I miss my home and my family. Please help me. If you can't, or won't, please, please let me know at once. You are my only hope and I am desperate. I am praying and anxiously awaiting your answer.

Signed, Jane. Postmarked Miami, no return address.

I sighed. Jane? Jane Doe? Would she wonder why she did not hear from me? Would she write again?

I returned a phone message from Sam Bliss, who sounded weary, as always. 'What are you doing in so early?' I asked.

'Meeting with people from our gang unit. I think that tip you passed along was good. The PLO is stockpiling guns.'

'Why?'

'You know why as well as I do.'

'Sure. Guns are power. Guns are money. They can be sold. They can be traded. But there has to be something more.'

'Yeah, keep this between us right now. But our intelligence is that they *do* have a problem with the Brickell Boys.'

'They always have. Why is it heating up now?'

'Why? Why? Why? You sound like my kids. Word on the street is that some of the Brickell Boys got lucky pulling a routine burglary, apparently stumbled on an extensive gun collection that included four assault rifles.'

'Oh, hell.'

'My sentiments exactly.'

'Think it was the PLO who hit Zipper's store looking for matching firepower?'

'Maybe, maybe not. They had a skirmish outside a dope house in Liberty City the other night, and looks like the assault weapons changed hands.' He chuckled. 'Appears the Brickell Boys got hijacked; somebody stole their toys. We've got two with minor wounds but they're not talking.'

'So they hit Zipper's, trying to recoup?'

'Looks like it. Apparently, they're not comfortable being outgunned by the enemy.'

'Who is?'

'Those assault rifles are in big demand, on the street for inner city warfare or to sell to some of the back-to-Cuba movements.'

'How did they stumble on that kind of firepower? Where was this burglary?'

'Didn't hear it from me?'

That was the question he had been waiting for me to ask. 'We never talked.'

'Private home, in the Roads section.' He paused. 'Monica and Wallace Atwater.'

'You're kidding!' Wealthy civic and business leaders, he is a former stockbroker, a financial planner, and top dog in the Chamber of Commerce. She is executive director of the Tourist Development Association. 'What were they doing with those kinds of weapons?'

'Home and personal protection. That's what they say,' he said smugly.

'I love it, great story.' The Atwaters sang baritone and lead soprano in the noisy chorus of politicians and prominent citizens who blamed news reports, not young men with guns, for Miami's tarnished image. They accuse the media of 'exaggerating' the crime problem, and I am a prime target. My recent story on a Boston tourist carjacked in the Design District drew a TDA protest from Monica Atwater, claiming I 'unfairly smeared' the district because the man from Boston was not actually murdered there. As she accurately pointed out, his killers did not shoot him four times and push him out of his moving Cadillac until they had driven a good four blocks outside the district's unofficial limits.

'You can probably pick up a copy of the burglary report tomorrow.' Bliss's voice dropped to a whisper. 'Here's the case number.'

I jotted it down. 'Did you find the murder witness, the nine-one-one caller yet?'

'*Nada*. Thought maybe you'd get a call after your story.'

'Nope, but I've been off. If anything comes in, I'll let you know.'

Two messages from Darnell Oliver. I pushed them aside to return to in the morning when I was officially back on the job.

I shuffled through the rest of my mail and snatched up my ringing telephone as I scanned an FBI bulletin.

'What size shoe do you take?' the caller asked.

'Six,' I replied, without thinking. 'Why?'

'What kind of shoes are you wearing now?'

'What? Who is this?'

'High heels? Or is it sandals?' the caller whispered, breathing hard.

'Is this a joke?' I spun around, scanning the newsroom. None of the smart alecks were there. Only Ryan, at the desk behind me, focused on his terminal, at work on a story.

'No, you wrote about me.'

It couldn't be. Maybe it was. 'What is

wrong with you? If you want a sick relationship with women's shoes, go buy a pair. You can even buy them used at the Salvation Army or Goodwill.'

'It's not the same. It's better when you know who wore them.'

'You belong in jail, you pervert!' I slammed the phone down. 'Britt?' Ryan's voice was soft, behind me. 'Who was that you were just talking to?'

'Nobody,' I said. 'Just some weirdo.' It takes one to know one, I thought.

9

His grandparents nagged the twenty-five-year-old man to find a job and support himself. They told him to move out and said he was 'no good'. They were right. He reacted by stabbing his granddad seventeen times and bludgeoning Grandma to death with a plaster statue of the Virgin Mary.

The manhunt ended at the nearest pawnshop. The story kept me busy for most of the morning, but not too busy to stop by headquarters to pick up a copy of the Atwater burglary report.

Police don't issue press releases about this sort of crime. People like the Atwaters will shove aside old ladies who shuffle between them and a camera lens, but they definitely prefer low profiles on their private peccadilloes. Police brass, ever conscious of politics and promotions, try to accommodate the rich and powerful by fixing tickets or keeping a lid on a DUI arrest or some other embarrassing *faux pas*, but foot soldiers from the ranks always rat them out.

Journalists live for the opportunity to tweak the pompous. As somebody once said, Good reporters comfort the afflicted and afflict the comfortable.

Editors were clustered around the city desk when I spilled the story. Gretchen's classic nose wrinkled, as I expected. 'But it's only a burglary, Britt.' Pursing her lips, she smoothed her sleek blonde coif. 'Hundreds happen every day, thousands. Since when do we report them?'

'Depends on what's stolen and from whom. These are the same people who appeared on CNN last week to tell the world that we have no crime problem. If Miami is as safe as they claim, why does Monica Atwater, in her posh, well-patrolled, upper-income bedroom community, find it necessary to keep an AK

Forty-seven under her bed and an Uzi on her nightstand?'

Everybody else on the desk agreed that the story belonged on the budget, leaving Gretchen conspicuously silent.

The story would not rate a front page headline. At best, it would appear somewhere below the fold, inside the local section, but it was front page in satisfaction.

★ ★ ★

Monica Atwater returned my call immediately, since I had not left word what it was about.

'Sorry to hear about your burglary.'

'I have no idea what you're talking about.' The voice was as brittle and cold as ice.

She quit stonewalling when she realized I knew chapter and verse, then argued that it would be irresponsible to report the crime and that, if forced to do so, she would call her 'good friend' the publisher to prevent it.

'Did the gold charm bracelet they stole have sentimental value?' I asked sympathetically.

'As a matter of fact, it did,' she snapped.

'What about the AK Forty-seven?'

A long pause. 'My husband is a collector.'

'But I thought one was taken from under

your bed. Is that where he keeps his collection?'

'He's out of town a great deal. It was there for my personal protection.'

Perfect quote. 'But I thought you, Mr Atwater, and your organizations speak out against private gun ownership on the grounds that it isn't necessary for personal protection.'

She hung up.

I punched the redial button. 'We were cut off,' I said cheerfully.

'No, we weren't,' she said, 'and I'm calling your publisher.' This time she slammed the phone down so hard it hurt my ear. I tried Atwater's office, but his wife's dialing finger must have been faster. First his secretary said he was on another line; then she came back to report him gone for the day.

The story would be stronger if police could actually link the Atwater guns to a homicide. I wondered if there was a way to actually tie the stolen weapons to the young security guard's murder. But the connection was tenuous at best, a street-level arms race. The theory might or might not be true, much less provable.

Before finishing the story I called Bliss to see if anything was new. 'Gotta go,' he said. 'A nurse from county ER called. One of Angel Oliver's kids just came in. Nurse knew the history, saw the name, gave us a call.'

'Which one is it? Is it serious? What kind of injury?' I pictured Harry, his big eyes and solemn little face.

'Dunno. Don't think it's life-threatening, but if she hurt one of 'em, it could be enough to revoke her bond, and give the rest of 'em to the father.'

'I'll meet you there,' I said.

I turned in the Atwater story, aware it would not make the early edition. Every editor up and down the line, maybe even the publisher himself, would scrutinize my copy, and it would be vetted by the paper's in-house lawyer. Some would not be happy, but hell, news was news.

★ ★ ★

Angel seemed to be pouting. She wore black jeans, a scoop-neck tee, and an attitude. She was flanked by Bliss, in his blue suit, and an HRS caseworker, a plump middle-aged woman with a file folder in her hand. A baby wailed behind the curtain.

The detective and the social worker were taller and outweighed her, but from the body language it looked like Angel was holding her own. She wasn't backing down. I was on borrowed time — hospital personnel would soon make me as a reporter and bounce me out of there — but I hung back, hoping Angel wouldn't spot me until I got a handle on what was going on. A doctor behind the curtain with the patient said something, and they all turned. Angel spoke with him briefly, then scooped up a toddler in diapers, one of the little ones, smaller than Harry. The runny-nosed little girl, red in the face from crying, quieted in her mother's arms. I saw neither blood nor bandages.

Angel tossed back her loose blonde hair and wheeled away from them, straight toward me. No one attempted to stop her or take the child. Then she saw me and hit the brakes.

'What's she doing here?' She spun, glared at Bliss, and stamped her foot. 'You called her! What is this? You're just trying to make me look like a lousy mother!'

She did a pretty good job of that herself, I thought.

'You won't get away with this! I'm calling my lawyer!' Still clutching the tot, she veered away abruptly, giving me a wide berth. 'Stay away from me and my kids,' she muttered, 'or I'll kick your ass from here to Homestead.'

She stomped off, mad as hell, shaking her bootie in those tight jeans, the big-eyed baby gazing placidly back at me over her shoulder.

'There is no reason. I would say she did exactly the right thing,' the social worker was telling Bliss as I approached. He scowled in disgust.

'Is the baby all right? Where is she going?' I asked.

'You're that one from the *News*, aren't you?' The woman shifted the file to the far side of her body as if to protect it from my prying eyes. 'This is a confidential matter.' She studied me disapprovingly over the rims of her eyeglasses.

'Murder isn't confidential,' I said sweetly.

She shot an angry glance at Bliss, who looked more rumpled and weary than ever, and marched off.

'Where did Angel go?' I asked him, as we walked out together.

'To the pharmacy to fill a prescription and then home, I guess,' he said morosely. 'I shouldn't've jumped the gun, I shoulda had a patrolman check this out before I wasted my time.' He squinted at his watch for a long moment.

The child was suffering from an earache and fever. Angel got scared when the fever reached 102 and brought her to the ER. Doctors found no signs of neglect or abuse and HRS saw no reason to take action,

182

despite the family history.

'This shift is killing me.' Bliss walked like his feet hurt.

'I thought working days for a change would agree with you.'

'My body clock is all screwed up, dunno if it's two A.M. or two P.M.' He sighed. 'Can't get used to it, and it's messing up my off-duty jobs.'

★ ★ ★

On the way back to the newsroom I thought about all the child-related cases that end badly and resented more than ever the cloak of confidentiality that inept social workers often use to cover their mistakes. They, I thought, are the biggest dangers to kids in jeopardy. I decided to see whether anybody at the top was even aware of the Oliver children or if they had slipped between the cracks.

But, first, a message to see Fred. I marched back to his office. Had to be heat about the Atwater story. Sure enough, I knew it. A printout of my story lay on his desk. I was tired of all this shit, special treatment for people with friends in high places.

'What's the problem?' I began, coming on

strong. 'What about the 'aggressive, take-no-prisoners, kick-ass journalism' you always preach?'

He looked up, puzzled, and slowly removed his glasses. 'What about it?'

'You see a problem with the Atwater story?' I sat in front of his desk, looked him right in the eye.

'No.' He grinned. 'Nice work. I just can't believe what jackasses those people are.'

I leaned forward. 'Is that why you called me in here?'

'No. The director, Phillip Hodges, called. He would like you to be available, on hand while they're shooting, for technical advice, local stuff, and so on.'

I relaxed in my seat and crossed my legs. 'Do I get on-screen credit?'

'I doubt it.' He smirked. 'Why don't you have your agent call him?'

I smiled. 'My beat's pretty busy. I don't think I'll have the time.'

'Evidently they appreciated the time you spent with Lance and want you around.'

What the hell did that mean?

I shook my head.

'Well, Britt.' He pushed his chair forward as though getting back to work. 'I don't have to tell you about all the people who would cheerfully murder for the opportunity, or remind you how important the success of this project is to the community, to all of us. This may be Miami's chance to join the Hollywood big leagues.' He studied the schedule on his desk. 'I could have Barbara DeWitt or Howie Janowitz help them out. They both know the city well.' He looked up. 'Which do you think would do a better job?'

'But they've never worked the police beat.' I heard the indignation in my voice, alarm bells sounding in my brain. Did I really hate the idea of another reporter hanging out with Lance and the film crew instead of me? Yes, I did. That surprised me.

Fred looked smug. 'Well, Britt, why don't you play it by ear? They'll start shooting in the newsroom soon. I'll tell the desk you're free to work with the film crew whenever you like. You'll be under no pressure from them. So I can tell Hodges you're available?'

'I guess so,' I said casually. 'When I'm not busy.'

I returned to my desk, knowing I'd been had and wondering what, if anything, Lance had to do with it. Then I called Linda Shapiro, the HRS regional director. We had butted heads in the past, especially when she was Youth Hall administrator. Recently promoted, she was committed to avoiding the scandals that ousted her predecessor. Her

185

bosses in the state capitol wanted no more bad press or dead children, most likely in that order. She reviewed the file and called me back.

'I've talked to the father of most of them, and he's genuinely worried about the kids,' I told her.

'We've heard from Darnell Oliver ourselves,' she said, shuffling papers. She did not sound impressed, either by his concerns or mine. 'All I can tell you is that we've thoroughly investigated this case and checked out the mother's home three ways from Sunday. Our caseworkers have determined that the children are clean, well nourished, and apparently well cared for. We found no evidence of abuse or neglect and we have no plans, unless something unexpected occurs, to move them out of the home. Future custody, of course, depends on the outcome of the mother's case. We're keeping tabs on it until it's adjudicated. I suggest you do the same,' she said. 'I can't discuss the case any further.'

Same old runaround. 'So you'll wait until something terrible happens,' I said coldly.

'Don't you try to scare me, Britt, I'm already scared. Working with kids is very scary. That's what I do all day every day, and between you and me, sometimes I just look at the whole damn system and I'm overwhelmed by fear that we've failed. There's a multitude of children out there who are totally lost. What's worse is, nobody even knows or cares that they're lost.'

The unexpected revelation, a rare personal glimpse, caught me by surprise and I quit sniping. As we said goodbye, Gloria, the city desk clerk, waved frantically. 'You have a call!'

She looked excited, unusual for her. I answered with a feeling of dread, hoping it wasn't a cop shot or a plane down. I was feeling weary and depressed myself, as though it were contagious.

'What's happening?' Lance asked cheerfully.

My stomach did a back flip. 'You're starting to sound like a reporter.'

'I miss the police beat. What's going on?'

His tone was casual. Relieved, I filled him in on the homicidal grandson, Angel Oliver, and the Atwater saga. He chortled at the last one. 'What a coincidence.'

'What do you mean?'

'Monica and Wally. I met them recently, at the advisory committee meeting.'

'Right. Friends of yours, huh?'

'I hope so. I promised to lend them my house for a fundraiser, an AIDS benefit.'

'Eeeuuuwh. You should have asked me first.'

'Not a good cause?'

'A good cause,' I conceded. 'But these people are not truly altruistic, they're just out to promote themselves and see their pictures in the newspaper.'

'Isn't everybody?'

'You sound so cynical. I hate seeing you involved with them.'

'Funny, they say the same thing about you.'

'I don't doubt it.' I laughed and worked my stiff shoulder muscles. 'How's the moviemaking coming along?'

He sighed. 'Problems.'

'Any word from Stephanie?'

'She's not in the house at the moment, I hope. But she sent some tapes and a video.'

'You're kidding. What's on them?'

'Music, poetry. Haven't heard 'em myself. Niko and the guys are going through them, just in case there's something in there we need to know about.'

'What are you going to do?'

'Send them to my lawyers, see what they say.'

'What about her family?'

'They say they don't know where she is.'

'No return address on the tapes?'

'No, or we woulda sent them back

unopened. Hey, any chance you'd meet us, some of the crew and me, for a drink later?'

What did he really have in mind?

'I don't usually hang out with actors,' I said lamely.

'I never hang out with reporters.' When I didn't answer, he said, 'Think about it. We'll be at Smash, in the VIP room. I'll leave word at the door.'

★ ★ ★

I cleaned off my desk, went home, walked Bitsy, then daubed on black mascara and hot pink lipstick and careened east. Skate punk reigned over the pastel neon of South Beach, boom boxes blasting as 'bladers and 'boarders hurdled makeshift ramps and garbage cans.

I reluctantly relinquished my keys to the valet, taking a fond last look at my T-Bird, aware it could be aboard a freighter bound for Port au Prince within the hour. With all its power, the US government is totally unable to block illegal traffic: stolen cars streaming out, illegal aliens pouring in.

The brick-red sidewalks outside Smash vibrated with the sounds from within. To my surprise, the doorman discovered my name on his clipboard.

I had never been to the VIP room before. In fact I had never been to Smash, or Grab, the adjacent restaurant. They are among the ever-evolving South Beach enterprises, catering to the 'beautiful people', those into body piercing, tattoos, and leather. An Adonis-like man smiled and I smiled back before realizing that he was wearing what appeared to be skin-tight leather trousers without a crotch. Frenzied dancers were being driven to a fevered pitch by pounding metallic music. Partners were moshing, thrash-dancing that resembled violent shoving matches. Solo dancers bounced endlessly as the band blasted their brains into Swiss cheese. Earplugs were probably considered uncool, I thought wistfully.

The secluded VIP room offered some refuge from the sonic assault. The stylish Victorian nook was adorned with stunning models, both male and female, red plush couches, mood lighting, and a voyeur's view of the floor below.

Niko was watching the crowd, listening to the music, his back to the wall. He saw me first, caught my attention, and steered me to Lance, who was sequestered at a table with several people and surrounded by a phalanx of muscle. His small group appeared unaware of the rampant dementia below.

Phillip Hodges looked out of place, pale, serious, and artistic, hair in his eyes. He and Lance were in deep conversation with three other men. One was dressed like Niko, entirely in black. A scar zigzagged like a lightning bolt down the right side of his face, ending in a split at his lower lip, and his skin looked tanned and hard. Next to him sat a pleasantly pudgy fellow with hair receding in front, long in back. A gold earring dangled from one lobe, and he wore black nail polish — either that or he had recently slammed all his fingers in a car door. He was introduced as Ziff Bodine, special effects and makeup; the face with the scar belonged to stuntman Trent Talon.

Third in the group was assistant director Rad Johnson. Bearded, intense, and in his thirties, he wore a little red scarf knotted jauntily around his neck, like the one sometimes worn by Pulitzer, Lottie's rescued greyhound. I didn't like the way Johnson studied everything but my face. Lottie's dog displays more character and honesty in his eyes.

All were helping themselves from bottles of Chivas Regal and Jack Daniel's on the table and a magnum of Dom Pérignon chilling in an ice bucket. 'Great bone structure, look at those fabu cheekbones!' Bodine splashed champagne into my glass. 'You're Scandinavian?'

'Only by first name. My father was Cuban, my mother's people were Miami pioneers, English ancestry.'

'Cuban! Get outa town!'

Talon exuded the edgy tension and had the crazy eyes seen in both the best undercover cops and the most dangerous criminals. The risk takers. No surprise when Lance called him the best stuntman in the business. 'You should see this guy work,' he told me. 'He jumps outa tall buildings, crashes cars, runs through fire, gets blown up and blown away.'

'Not often enough,' Talon muttered over the rim of his glass. The split in his lower lip transformed into a giant dimple when he smiled. 'Lance hates seeing me make a living. He likes to do his own stunts.'

'I wanna share the fun.' Lance looked casual, no sign of a meaningful glance or lascivious stare. I felt relieved.

Hodges appeared to be brooding.

I asked him how work was progressing.

'Trouble,' he intoned morosely, sipping his Scotch. 'The worst is the bloody nuclear reactor. My God, the thing keeps sinking in the muck. Our crew's the best. They've done everything to shore it up. It's already cost more than three times the budget for the damn thing, and it isn't right yet. Van Ness was apoplectic this afternoon. You should have heard Wendy.'

'No way to locate it someplace else?' I sampled my champagne.

'It's our most elaborate set,' Johnson said sarcastically, as though addressing a simple-minded child. 'The whole story line revolves around it.'

'At least the story line as we knew it.' Hodges glanced meaningfully at the others. Script revisions were apparently still under way, at the producers' orders.

'Yeah, for all we know,' Lance said, exhaling smoke, 'we won't even need the reactor. This movie may wind up being *Supermodel Saves Miami*.'

'We lost a backhoe this afternoon,' Hodges lamented into his drink. 'Damn expensive piece of equipment, just disappeared into that miserable, muddy swamp, and one of our crew wound up with a nasty compound fracture, had to move him to higher ground on an airboat, then fly him out by chopper.'

I resisted the urge to whip out my notebook. They had already made it clear that shop talk was off the record.

'The damn location scout said the area

193

would be perfect. We went crazy getting all those permits,' Hodges said bitterly.

'Not a good idea to mess with the Everglades,' I said. Lance watched me, smoking, eyes hooded. 'It's a strange, ancient, mystical place. The 'Glades are like nowhere else. Full of old Indian burial grounds. Primeval. Weird. Inexplicable things happen out there. That's the swamp that swallowed a DC Nine, and all hundred and ten people aboard. Remember? They searched for weeks and never found a single body.'

'Get outa town.' Ziff's eyes were bright. They all stared at one another.

'Sorry.' I shrugged. The champagne was great. The only one taking hits from that bottle, I was beginning to enjoy myself.

'We should have the 'Glades whipped by tomorrow,' Hodges said hopefully. 'We're constructing platforms.'

'Damn straight. We built the whole goddam Sahara in Arizona for *Sandstorm*.' Johnson shoved his red face at mine.

'That must have been like building a swamp in the Everglades,' I said.

'Or a mountain in the Himalayas,' Lance said. We exchanged smiles as Johnson poured himself another drink, sloshing some on the table.

'I love it.' Ziff shivered with delight and

refilled my glass. 'Tell us more scary stories about the Everglades.'

'She could help with that other thing,' Lance offered.

'Right,' Ziff said. 'We have this scene. What exactly would the chunks look like when somebody's brain' — he shuddered delicately and gestured with both hands, dark nails agleam — 'sort of explodes?'

What was the cocktail conversation like at the other VIP room tables? I wondered, trying to recall the last time I had seen spattered brains.

'Depends how big the pieces are. I got one on my shoe once . . . A bit like dissected shrimp, only a bit greyer.' I waved away the untimely offer of an hors d'oeuvre.

'Good, good.' Ziff scribbled in a small notebook.

Talon had wandered to another table for a few words with a platinum blonde in a black leather bustier.

'What a town, what a town.' Lance looked relaxed, moving to the music. Behind us, a couple necked feverishly on a couch. They were both guys. I saw somebody snorting coke down on the dance floor. The man in the crotchless leather pants had scaled the stage. He did a swan dive and was crowd surfing, passed like a volleyball above a sea of hands.

Lance leaned in my direction to watch.

'Did you know,' I said in his ear, 'that Hodges called my editor to ask that I hang with the crew while you're shooting?'

'No.' His eyes remained focused on the scene below. 'Your name came up at a meeting and I suggested that you could probably give us some valuable advice, but it wasn't my idea.'

The din below increased in volume, the revelers apparently intent on partying until they puked. Niko shot an uneasy glance our way as Lance stood and stretched.

'Let's split.' Lance nodded toward Niko, who picked up the signal.

I was relieved; the champagne had made me giddy. Hodges and Lance were ready to call it a night. So was I. But Ziff, Johnson, and Trent were all for forging on, to a popular new spot featuring cybersex, where customers in comfortable armchairs in front of personal computers indulge in sex with electronic partners. Earphones amplify every sound and headsets make the graphics and action seem real.

Since I was the native they asked my advice, assuming I knew all these places intimately, that my life was an endless round of South Beach party scenes.

'It is safe sex,' I said helpfully. 'Or you could go to TNT, WOW, or Crescendo.'

We swept out of Smash, surrounded by a flying wedge of muscle. A few dancers shouted out Lance's name and he waved. For a millisecond, a face in the crowd caught my eye, but when I turned to look, she was gone. Could it have been? No one else in our group reacted. Had she been there, they surely would have seen her. I had been drinking and my eyes were playing tricks on me, I decided. Smash was full of long-haired women. It couldn't have been Stephanie.

Lance and I stood close, our first moment alone, in a secluded doorway shielded by the others as Niko called up the cars.

'You took advantage of me,' he said quietly, his voice deep and intimate.

'Excuse me?'

'Maybe you forgot.' He shrugged. 'I guess I wasn't that memorable.' His questioning eyes caught mine.

I felt dizzy, the soft night, the champagne on an empty stomach. I swallowed. He squinted. 'Are you all right to drive?'

I took a deep breath.

'We're gonna walk a little,' he announced aloud.

Niko looked pained but was game.

We walked. Niko forged ahead, discreetly

out of earshot. Al and Dave trailed discreetly behind us, several feet apart. The Town Car, Frank at the wheel, rolled alongside at minus five miles an hour. Like characters out of a big-screen gangster epic we, and our bodyguards, strolled past stout-hearted drag queens, tourists, and outlaw kids roving like jackals through a neon apocalypse. Surreal.

For sure, I told myself, we would not be mugged. Window shopping might be fun, I thought, but then glanced into the shop we were passing. Condomania. A window display featuring glow-in-the-dark condoms, a body-sized prophylactic, and a bouquet of inflated condoms molded to look like flowers. Thank God, I thought, that the Design Review Board had refused them permission to erect their four-foot neon logo.

I tried to focus on Lance. He was talking about work, my work. 'I'm really into it,' he was saying. 'If I could just be anonymous and take a year off to try something else, I would like to be a reporter, or even a news photographer.'

'You would not be impressed by the editors, the pay scale, or the benefits,' I said. 'So, you've worked with Ziff, Trent, and Rad before?' I giggled. 'Ziff, Trent, and Rad. Sounds like the Seven Dwarfs.'

'No,' he said patiently. 'No resemblance to Grumpy, Doc, and Sleepy. Ziff is great, started in makeup, moved into special effects. Aged me thirty years in two hours for *Ground Zero*. Of course,' he added, 'Lexie could do that in twenty minutes. And Trent? The man moves so fast he could play Ping-Pong against himself. Best in the business.'

We loitered at the rim of a sandy beach, watching the nearly full moon climb a charcoal-clouded sky over the Atlantic. The few lights in the darkness winked from freighters far out at sea. Ocean, moon, and endless sky. The moment might have been romantic, had it not been for Niko, Frank, Al, and Dave.

I began to laugh and could not stop.

'That's it.' Lance looked stern. 'You're not driving home.'

Niko drove, Frank following in my T-Bird.

The two rows of small garden apartments were bathed in darkness except for the security light Mr Goldstein had installed.

Lance strolled with me to the door. 'So this is your place.' He looked around as I inserted the key.

'It's been fun,' I said.

'C'mere, babe,' he coaxed, tucking his big fist under my chin. 'I won't bite you, unless you want to be bit.'

'No biting,' I said flatly. I knew where that could lead, still embarrassed about that episode. And what would become of Niko, Frank, Dave, and Al, waiting out by the curb? 'You either,' I warned Bitsy, who had scampered out and was scrambling crazily around our feet. I kissed Lance on the cheek, went inside, and peeped back out.

If Mrs Goldstein was watching me come home, she got her money's worth this time, I thought, as the security light illuminated the famous Lance Westfell's departing profile.

From shadow behind the curtain I saw the Town Car pull away. I was still watching as another car rolled by slowly. Looked like a Taurus. Red, I thought, impossible to be sure in the dark. Some odd instinct rooted me in place. Shortly, in the time it took to circle the block, the same car rolled by again. Someone looking for an address? Probably a late-night pizza delivery for some insomniac with the munchies. I left the window, took Bitsy's leash off the hook behind the door, snapped it to her collar, and stepped outside.

The night was clear and cool, even a bit chilly. As I locked the door behind me, footsteps rapidly retreated. Bitsy heard them, too, and alerted. A car door opened, then closed, just out of sight.

Curious, I followed the sounds out to the

street. The Taurus idled, double-parked at an odd angle. Looked like a woman behind the wheel. My natural instinct was to approach the car and see who it was, but something made me hesitate. Suddenly the driver hit the gas, peeled out, and raced down the dark street, burning rubber.

I turned, took Bitsy inside, and double-locked the door behind us.

10

This time I was not alone in those dark woods at the mercy of the man who wanted me dead; weeping children crept through the shadows. Twice, I awoke, and in a fugue state of halfsleep reached for the gun beneath my pillow. But the touch of cold steel offered no comfort, only served to make my dream more real. This is dangerous, an inner voice whispered as I struggled to determine whether I was awake or sleeping. The gun frightened me, but I was so much more frightened without it.

Awake and lucid, I revisited my three hard-and-fast rules about owning a gun: Know how to use the weapon, know when it is legal to use it, and, most important, be psychologically ready to do so. I lay awake in the dark, listening to the night and remembering people I knew, including two police officers, whose hesitation cost them their weapons and their lives. For the first time, I understood.

The Oliver children haunted my day. My champagne hangover didn't help. It felt as though a Cuban terrorist had exploded a car bomb inside my skull. I was lucky that my beat was relatively quiet. By afternoon I was ready for another shot at Angel Oliver. Her beef was that the press had never reported her side, only the charges against her. If I promised to tell her side, whatever that was, she might be tempted.

What self-serving statements could she offer, what excuse could she have? Who else could be to blame? She had starved her baby, for God's sake. And whatever her feud with Darnell, how could she justify shutting him out of their children's lives? I felt the absence of my father, executed by a Castro firing squad when I was three, every day of my life. Every child is entitled to a dad, especially one who cares and wants to be part of the picture.

I took two aspirins, told the desk where I was going, and drove to Angel Oliver's apartment. It was already after four and the children should be home from school. Chances were she'd be there.

I drove across the river and past the gates of the Orange Bowl. The neighborhood, aging buildings with few shade trees, looked grubbier than ever, in contrast with the pristine and well-kept stadium, padlocked and waiting for the big game that will never be played inside its walls.

I knocked; again the sounds of child's play abated. This time the door inched open just a crack. 'Mommy?'

Heck, I thought, she isn't here. Harry peered up at me.

'Mommy's not home,' he said, quickly adding that she would be. Soon.

True, or what he had been coached to say if a nosy social worker showed up?

He closed the door firmly. Good boy, I thought. Never let a stranger in the house, ever. I sat in the T-Bird parked across the street, on an angle, debating whether to wait or leave a note. Hopefully, she would be home soon. She was probably out shuffling the banana. The afternoon sun beat down unmercifully, and the car became unbearably hot with the windows up. Sweaty and sleepy, head throbbing, I yearned for crank windows that I could roll down without starting the car. Impossible to find a late-model car without push-button windows these days. My objection is that they do not perform well underwater; they short-circuit, trapping people inside submerged cars. Happens all the time in this seaside community, criss-crossed by waterways, bridges, and the world's worst drivers.

Two urchins, street kids about nine or ten, were thunking a basketball against an adjacent building. Just a matter of time before they thunked it off my T-Bird, I thought, annoyed. I saw a shadier parking space open up half a block away and was about to move the car when a Metro bus lurched to a stop at the corner and Angel got off, lugging two Burger King sacks. She headed down the street toward her front door, as the bus wheezed away from the curb, spewing an exhaust trail so heavy it looked like a mosquito spray truck. Angel wore cutoffs and a multicolored striped pullover. My timing had to be good, I thought. I needed to persuade her before she could disappear inside and slam the door. I opened my door, as a car parked down the block sprang to life.

I eased out of the T-Bird. Angel was two doors from home. Her step was not as bold or her body language as feisty as when her cubs were threatened. She looked almost vulnerable. I stepped into the street. That was when I saw it, a new cream-color Pontiac Bonneville, cruising ever so slowly down the block. The occupants, four or five teenagers, were all focused on Angel.

Oh, shit, I thought. Purse snatchers. They want the little handbag swinging from her left shoulder.

What did they expect to score from a welfare mother in this neighborhood? I thought indignantly. The little bastards were about to knock her down and rip off her purse. Probably even take the BK bags and steal her kids' dinner. Dammit.

Riveted on her, they neither saw nor cared about me. I was glad I had stowed my own purse in the trunk.

'Angel!' I shouted across traffic to warn her.

She did not hear me. Shouting again, I began to run toward her. She stopped and turned. I expected one of the punks to bail out at any moment to take her down on foot. I glanced at the oncoming car. Nobody emerged, only gun barrels suddenly bristling from the passenger-side windows. The most menacing was long and fitted with a cone-shaped device. The guns glinted in the sun. These were no purse snatchers. This was a drive-by. Angel saw them at the same instant.

Everything happened in slow motion.

I was screaming, still running toward her. She scrambled for the door, groping in the little purse for her keys. A plume of smoke erupted from the car, followed by the loud crack of gunfire. A row of grackles on a telephone line overhead leaped into open sky with raspy cries, beating the air with their wings. One of the little boys shouted; then both dropped and rolled like pros, as their basketball thudded slowly into the street. Halfway down the block an elderly man hit the sidewalk on all fours, his groceries scattering as he tried to crawl beneath a parked car. Angel still fumbled for her keys as I reached the door. I twisted the knob, pounded it with my fists.

'Open it! Open it!' I screamed at her. Earsplitting cracks kept coming, as fast as the two gunmen could pull the triggers. Concrete exploded overhead. Clouds of dust and grit showered us. Angel whimpered, keys in her hand at last. Sparks cascaded off the side of the building as a round smashed into a power meter. Glass flew out of two parked cars out front. The gunmen had been shooting high but were correcting their aim. A slug buzzed like an angry wasp, then shattered concrete inches above the door. Something glanced off the frame of my sunglasses, and for an instant

I thought I was hit. They drew up almost abreast, still shooting, so close I heard cries from the occupants, saw them bouncing oddly around inside the car. We're dead, I thought, forcing my body against the door, which suddenly flew open. Screaming and cursing, we both fell inside on top of Harry.

The other children lay frozen on the apartment floor, the older ones, accustomed to drive-by shooting drills at school, shielding the preschoolers.

Angel clutched Harry as I swung the door shut, gunshots still slamming the building like sledgehammers.

'Stay down! Stay down!' I gagged, choking on the dust.

A hole the size of a quarter opened in the door, and another the size of a tennis ball appeared in the wall across the room. The same slug kept going, breaking glass in its path. Misty was on the floor, her body across the baby, eyes closed tight, both hands clamped over her ears. I thought the firing would never stop. Would they ever run out of ammo?

Suddenly it was quiet. Ears ringing, I breathed again, despite the thick haze of dust. The shooters were gone as quickly as they had appeared. I crept to the broken front window to be sure. White smoke drifted slowly down an eerie empty street that smelled of cordite and sulfur.

Angel sobbed and let go of Harry, who got to his feet. I wanted to hug him myself for opening the door. He never cried. Solemn and dry-eyed, he studied the concrete chips and dust on our clothes and in our hair, then blinked.

'Did you bring me anything?' he demanded.

Angel hugged him. 'I did, baby, I did.' Whimpering, she groped on all fours for the scattered burger bags. The other children began to stir and run to their mother. Astonishingly, no one was hit.

'Stay away from the windows.' My knees shook. 'They could come back. Maybe they just went around the block.' They could be reloading.

I shoved a chair against the door while Angel dialed 911. Then Misty and I turned the table on its side and gathered the rest of the kids behind it until the police came.

★ ★ ★

'Britt, how'd you get here so fast?' the first cop asked. His second question was for Angel. 'You got some kind of beef with gangbangers?'

'No,' she said, still sniffling. 'It was my ex-husband.'

My head swiveled on that one, and I winced. The chunk of flying concrete that bent my sunglass frame had bruised the side of my face.

'That son of a bitch!' Angel raged, as anger took the place of fear. 'That son of a bitch! He tried to kill me!'

'Who?' I said.

'Darrell, that bastard!'

'That wasn't him,' I said impatiently. 'They were teenagers.'

'He's responsible.'

'Did you see him?' the cop asked.

'No, but he put them up to it,' she said stubbornly. Face pale, lips a determined line, she acted like she believed it. 'He's trying to kill me.'

It irritated me to think she might send the cops off on a wild goose chase, allowing the real culprits to escape. She reminded me of the Cubans who blame every cataclysm in life on Fidel Castro.

'He's some redneck shit-kicker, a construction worker in Orlando,' I told them privately. 'Most of these kids are his; he wouldn't risk hurting them. The shooters, they're gang-bangers.' I suggested they advise Bliss, who knew Angel's background.

The detective whistled when he arrived and saw the mess. So did Lottie, who had heard the shooting report go out on her scanner and was already en route when the office dispatched her. I was glad to see her, feel her hug, and listen to her concerned murmurs about the bruise above my temple.

Gang unit detectives also showed up. So did TV news crews, demanding to know why I was inside the roped-off area and they were kept out.

The apartment house looked like it had been hit by mortar fire in Beirut. Heavy-duty rounds from the bigger gun had gouged out chunks of the building.

Angel's popularity took a major nose-dive among her neighbors, particularly the Spanish-speaking people next door, left without power because of the smashed electric meter. A parked Chevy Lumina was another casualty. Slugs had penetrated both doors, then struck the building.

Cops fanned out to be sure that no innocent neighbor had been blown away by a stray bullet while showering or watching TV.

The two small boys who had been playing near my car had seen the whole thing.

Adrenaline-charged and hyper, they now danced about, bright-eyed and excited.

I did not know whether I would recognize any of the suspects. Their guns had commanded all my attention.

'I think one was an AK Forty-seven,' I told the cop writing the report.

'She right, she right! It an AK Forty-seven. Bam, bam-bam, bam!' One of the urchins crouched, spraying the crowd behind the yellow crime-scene tape with rapid fire from an imaginary weapon. The other nodded, clutching his basketball.

'They will flat-out kill you dead.' The cop shook his head. 'Saw 'em in 'Nam. Excellent gun for the jungle.'

Our eyes caught for a moment, as we shared an unspoken thought about this place we lived in.

'This one had something attached,' I told him, mouth dry, as I tried to describe the conelike device.

'One of them things, you know . . . ' the boy said. 'You know, Tyrone, whatcha call it?'

'Flash suppressor,' the boy with the basketball said, proudly enunciating each syllable, jutting his chin with an air of superiority.

The cop nodded, taking notes.

'Why were they using it?' I fumbled with

my own notebook.

The cop shrugged. 'In daylight? Probably just cosmetic. Every time you fire, a foot of flame shoots out. A suppressor reduces the flash by about twenty-five percent, so it doesn't mess up your night vision as much. Mighta been on there when they got the weapon, and they don't know enough to take it off.'

'The one in the backseat had a smaller gun.' I still felt numb.

'Nine millimeter.' Tyrone casually bounced his basketball.

'You sure?' the cop said. 'How do you know it was a nine millimeter?'

'I seen 'em.' The boy clamped a skinny hand on his hip and struck a pose.

'Right,' the cop said, lifting an eyebrow.

Nearly forty rounds had been fired. It had seemed like more to me. Only a few expended cartridges were scattered in the street, which explained the bellowing and all the bouncing around inside the car. Because the guns were only partway out the windows, the shooters were spraying themselves and each other with red-hot shell casings.

'Like getting burnt wid a hot spoon,' Tyrone announced, nodding wisely. He caught the cop's sharp glance and quickly added, 'That what my cousin Billy say.'

Ordinarily, this shooting, though nearly a massacre, would not be considered newsworthy since no one died. But this was a slow news day, and even without casualties the cops made it top priority because so many children, a pregnant woman, and a newspaper reporter had been in the line of fire. And, of course, the guns were still out there, in the hands of people unafraid to use them.

Even McDonald showed up. Why was it my destiny to have him always see me at my worst? He looked grim, tilted my chin, eyeballed my bruise, and asked if the medics had checked it out.

'I'm okay,' I said. If he had his way I'd be in therapy three times a week and en route to X-ray right now. I was lucky. My dime-store sunglasses had deflected the flying concrete chip. They could not be resuscitated.

* * *

'Amazing nobody got hit,' Bliss said later.

He could not have been more amazed than I was. I shivered in the sun, acutely aware of its comforting warmth through my clothes. Inexplicable. A single stray shot often kills or maims a totally innocent victim blocks or buildings away. It happens every day. I

213

remembered so many stories, so many deaths. Yet we were in their sights, the targets of that deadly barrage, and we escaped unhurt. Instinctively, I wanted to thank God for sparing us, but would that betray all those struck down? Had God abandoned them? Was anyone listening out there in the universe? Was anybody paying attention?

The car I heard start just prior to the shooting must have been the Bonneville. I had watched and waited for Angel. So had they.

'They were definitely after her,' I told Bliss. His own initial theories included random target practice, a gang initiation, or something Angel had brought on herself.

'One other possibility,' he said, lowering his voice.

'The ex-husband?'

'Nope. Planned Parenthood. They'd have a motive.' He suppressed a grin.

I ignored his sick humor. 'She can't stay here. They could come back.'

The sharp-eyed little boys had abandoned basketball for the moment and were eagerly helping the cops find expended cartridges, which were being marked and numbered. I reentered the apartment to say goodbye, Lottie trailing after me.

My knees were shaky, my appetite gone,

but Angel's kids were wolfing their burgers as though nothing out of the ordinary had occurred. She was feeding the baby.

'That was stupid,' she said flatly, back to her old obnoxious self. 'Why did you run right in front of them?'

'I don't know,' I said testily. 'I thought somehow I could stop them from shooting you.'

'Working for the News doesn't mean you're bulletproof — or accurate. But thanks.' She wiped the baby's chin.

'You're welcome. Any idea why they were shooting at you?'

'I told you. It was Darnell.'

'Anybody else have a reason?'

'Nobody.' She shrugged and shook her head.

People who claim to have no idea why somebody tried to kill them are usually liars. They know. They are hiding something. When you piss somebody off that much, you know it.

'Why would Darnell do this?'

'Cuz he's a mean son of a bitch. Cuz he doesn't wanna pay child support. Cuz he's violent. That's why I got me a restraining order against him. Too bad that piece of paper don't stop bullets.'

'You have a restraining order?'

She nodded.

'I didn't know that.'

'There's a lot of things you don't know.' She cut her eyes at me sarcastically.

'I came here because I want to tell your side,' I said. 'Will you call me? Then we can talk.' I handed her my card and she took it.

Her eyes narrowed slightly when Lottie shot pictures, but she never objected and even provided the children's names and ages.

* * *

'Gawd, what beautiful kids,' Lottie said, as we left the apartment. 'To think, they almost lost their mama. I like her.'

'How could you?' I asked irritably.

'Hell all Friday, Britt. Look at those kids. The woman's doing the best she can. It ain't easy.' She paused and lowered her voice. 'Lordy, looky there, at that handsome stud giving you the eye. I think he wants your body.'

She waved to McDonald, who flashed a dazzling smile and beckoned me to his car, where he was using his two-way. My heart went *thumpita thumpita* as I joined him. He looked happier than I had seen him in a long time. I smiled back.

'Guess what?' He gazed fondly into my eyes. 'Our guys just arrested one of your Hollywood friends.'

11

I wanted to go home to change my clothes, wash my hair, and try to do something about the plaster and concrete dust permanently packed into my sinuses.

Instead I went back to the office, wondering how to charge a new pair of sunglasses to my *News* expense account. A message from Lance awaited me.

'You won't believe the day I had.'

'Tell me about it,' I said, fingering the swollen side of my face, the skin around my neck itchy from the dust.

'Worst damn — '

'I know, I heard.'

'What?'

'Rad's arrest.'

'Whoa. Where'd you hear that? Van Ness and Wendy said it was gonna be hushed up.'

'Surprise.'

'How'd you find out?'

'My job.'

'Writing a story?'

'Of course.' I waited for him to explode, intimidate, or attempt bribery. 'It *is* a story,' I said. 'Assistant director of major Hollywood epic busted during a brawl with two transvestite hookers at a Biscayne Boulevard crack house.'

'You have to do what you have to do.' He sounded philosophical.

'Damn straight.'

'Putting it in the newspaper won't make us the most popular people on the set.'

'Us?'

He laughed. 'Sure. They'll assume I whispered in your ear.'

His voice suddenly made me all weak and mushy, wanting him to hold me and whisper in my ear. Was it because I had the hots for him? Because Kendall McDonald was acting like such a jerk? Or because I had just survived a near-death experience and needed validation that I was still among the living? 'That's not fair to blame you for being my source.'

'I'm a big boy, I can take it.'

'You're not trying to talk me out of writing it?'

'Could anybody?'

'No.'

'Just what I thought,' he said. 'Britt?'
'Yeah?'
'Was he really wearing women's panties?'
'That's what the cops say.'

★ ★ ★

Van Ness and Wendy testily refused comment, referring me to the project's publicist, who sternly lectured that by persisting in the pursuit of this minor story I was about to forfeit my rare and privileged relationship with the filmmakers. The story of my life.

Johnson had posted bond, but I couldn't find him. A search of his rental car had yielded enough drugs to warrant felony charges. A mixed bag of pills in his glove compartment included roofies, the date-rape drug Rohypnol, according to the cops. Never again, I vowed, would I chugalug drinks from strangers with such gay abandon. Was Rad the supplier for the entire movie crew? I wondered. Maybe that's what assistant directors do. I recalled Ziff's manic energy, Trent's raw edginess, and even wondered if various pharmaceuticals might be helping Lance through all his stress and pressures. As I sipped coffee and pondered my lead, he called again.

'Hey, you're on TV!'

I glanced up at the three silent monitors mounted over the city desk. There I was on the news. I have seen myself looking better.

'What's that in your hair?'

'It's not confetti.'

'Niko came in and said you were on the tube. Hold on.' He came back on the line. 'He says that guy you're talking to is the one who was at the hospital, at Bascom Palmer.'

'He's right. Lieutenant McDonald. That's him.'

'You okay?'

'Yeah.'

'What the hell happened? Wasn't that much action when I went on the beat with you. Wish I'd been out there.'

'Oh, sure, you could have been shot at too. The studio would have loved that.' Did he have any concept that this was real life where dead was dead?

'Who's the little blonde?'

'That,' I said with emphasis, 'is Angel.'

'The baby killer? She doesn't look that bad.'

'They never do. Why did you call before, if Van Ness or Wendy didn't ask you to find out if we knew about Johnson?'

He hesitated before answering. 'I can't just call and say hello?' He sounded hurt.

'Sure.'

'Good. But I did have reasons. I called for a favor, and to gripe about my day. Nobody shot at me, but they might as well have.'

'What?' I tried to sound sympathetic while wondering what the favor was and whether he understood that I was fighting a dead-line.

'Lexie doesn't want to be a mother.'

'What?' I pushed away from the VDT screen.

'The script is changing as we speak. Two more new writers; now we've got a chief and three assistants hacking away at it. Van Ness is wrapped around Lexie's pinky. She's playing him like a violin, and he's pulling the writers' strings. She doesn't want to play the mother of a ten-year-old. Not her image, she says. He agrees. So now the kid is out of the picture.'

'Roland Starrett? He's so cute.'

'His parents aren't. They manage him. He's their meal ticket. They're mad as hell, threatening to sue.'

'He'll get paid anyway, won't he?'

'Yeah, they have to buy him out, but his parents say this damages his career, that child actors have a short work life and he turned down another movie role and a TV series to do this. They want what he would have been paid for all three, plus damages.'

221

I made sympathetic sounds as I watched the clock.

'Then some nut sneaked into the wardrobe trailer out at the port where we were shooting today and slashed a lot of the clothes. Hopefully they can be replaced. If they can't, we may have to reshoot what little we've done.'

'Who do you think did it?'

'I know what you're thinking, but she hasn't been seen.' He sounded thoughtful. 'Stephanie never pulled that kind of stunt before. But it'd be a relief if it was her; then we'd know we don't have some lunatic in the crew.

'But worst of all, remember Walder? Broke his leg out at the nuclear reactor site?'

'The guy from the Coast?'

'Yeah. He's got gangrene.'

'Whoa, I betcha it's from the bacteria, acrochilia or something, in the muck out there. Harmless except to frogs unless it mixes with hydraulic fluid. Survivors from another big jet crash out there years ago lost limbs to gangrene after minor injuries. This guy was in an accident, a backhoe or swamp buggy, right? I bet that's it. Transmission fluid probably has the same effect. Stirred up with the bacteria in the swamp, it turns into something really nasty. How's he doing?'

'They've got him in a hyperbaric chamber. Flew his family in from LA. The union refuses to let anybody work at the site until the reactor is stable.' He sighed. 'It's listing again. They're talking about blasting now. If they can blast down to solid coral rock, they can anchor the thing.'

'I really don't think they should. Is that the favor? I'm not making a buy for you. No blasting caps, no dynamite, no way — '

'The AIDS benefit. I wanna make sure you'll be there.'

'Isn't it, like, fifteen hundred dollars a ticket?' He had to know I don't travel in those circles.

'I don't mean buy a ticket. You'd be, sort of, hostess.'

'But the Atwaters will be there. The high rollers, the movers and shakers. Probably your producers. I don't think they'd be comfortable — '

'Screw them. I'm letting 'em use my house, my name.'

'Do I have to work in the kitchen?'

'You don't even have to know where it is.'

'I already know.' This was tempting. I lunged for the brass ring. 'I know Lottie would love to go. So would my mother.'

'Great. Bring 'em as my guests. We'll have a table.'

The day did not turn out an absolute bummer, after all. Lottie was delighted, and my mother — who called, frantic, after hearing I had been shot at and missed — hung up thrilled and totally gaga about what to wear to the season's big event.

And the cops had news. The shooters had abandoned the Bonneville in a West Dade canal. Finding it was no major feat of modern police work. The canal was a popular dumping spot for hot cars, so popular that two other rusting hunks were piggy-backed beneath the Pontiac, spotted because its backside was sticking up out of the water. No surprise that it had been stolen from South Beach a few nights before.

Mrs Goldstein, who had also seen TV, welcomed me home with her special chicken soup, a hug, and some news of her own.

'A lovely girl, a friend of yours, was here today looking for an apartment. She said you sent her, but I told her we don't have a vacancy. She wanted to know all about you.'

Somehow I knew before she told me.

Stephanie.

I was already beat-up and bruised, and now Lance's stalker was sniffing at my trail. No point calling the cops. If snooping was a crime, I'd be doing hard time. No reason to pester Lance. He had his own problems. What could he do anyway? The woman had shadowed him for years, and he had not been able to stop her. Maybe Stephanie had now satisfied her curiosity about me. If not, I would handle her myself, try to talk some sense into her.

My chance came next morning. Gloria said a woman had called several times but left no message. Next time I picked up the telephone it was her.

'Ms Montero.' She sounded perky. 'I've been trying to reach you.'

'You've got me.'

'This is Stephanie Carrollton, Lance's fiancée? We met at his home?'

'Of course I remember.' Who could forget her banshee screams and departure in police custody?

'I thought we should talk, woman to woman.' She sounded earnest.

'I think so too, Stephanie.' I rubbed my forehead and leaned forward in my chair.

'I'll get right to the point. I've seen you with Lance and thought that before you begin to harbor any illusions or false hopes, you should be aware that he is not available. We have been, and still are, very much committed to each other.'

'Stephanie, I don't believe that is the case, or that it ever was. I think deep down you know that.'

'You're wrong. Every relationship has its ups and downs. We're working things out.'

The only background sound was some faint easy-listening-type music. 'Where are you?'

'Why should I tell you?'

'Your family is concerned. I think you should contact them.'

'They want to keep Lance and me apart,' she said impatiently. 'They've never wanted us to be together. But they're going to have to accept the fact that Lance is my family now. We belong together, especially at this time. I'm sure you've seen the stories. This film is very important to his career.'

'Stephanie, you have to accept the fact that he doesn't feel the same way you do.'

'That's not true!' She sounded sincerely indignant. Talk about illusions and false hopes. Had I not known better, I would have believed her myself. 'Lance wanted me to come down here. When he sent for me — '

'He sent for you? How? When?'

'We communicate in our own special ways,' she said softly.

'Stephanie, you will only get in trouble if you persist in this. You're gonna wind up in jail, or a hospital, or hurt. This is a dangerous city. You shouldn't be running around out there alone.'

'Don't you threaten me,' she said angrily.

'I'm not. I'm telling you straight, woman to woman. You have got to get a life. Think about all the wonderful things you could do. You're healthy, attractive, and have the means to live anywhere, do anything. You could have it all.'

'Lance is all I need.'

Over his dead body, I thought. 'He doesn't feel the same.'

'You're wrong,' she said stubbornly. 'The first moment I saw Lance, my whole future flashed before me. He knew it too. Mystics have told me that we were married more than once in past lives. We're soul mates. We share a destiny. Some things are meant to be. We will be together.'

Oh, Lordy, I thought. 'Stephanie, you need help. You have to see someone.' The words echoed inside my head: the same ones I'd heard from people who care about me. Clearly, Stephanie was not about to listen any more than I had. Was I as deep in denial as she was?

'You're just like all the rest of them. My family, and that Niko.' She spat out the words. 'And Lexie Duran, that tramp, and all the others. None of you can keep us apart.'

'Look, Stephanie,' I said, getting tough myself. 'I am not your problem. But I will be, unless you leave my landlady alone and stay away from my place. Is that clear?'

'You were nearly killed,' she said bitterly. 'Too bad they missed. Just stay away from Lance. Or you may not be as lucky next time.'

Oh, swell, I thought, as she hung up.

12

Stephanie's threats had a definite impact. I instantly accepted when Niko called to say Lance was inviting me to lunch.

It was neat to simply inform the desk that I was doing lunch with the film people. Me, the reporter who normally eschews lunch hours out of fear that I'll miss something. No problem. Fred had kept his word, though Gretchen looked grim.

Niko called from the lobby, and I went down to meet them.

The Town Car was nowhere in sight. Today it was a white Rolls-Royce Corniche convertible, with red leather upholstery and the rag top down. Lance looked very South Beach, strikingly handsome in a ribbed cotton sweater and white linen slacks. He sat in the driver's seat.

'Hey, I'm taking you to my favorite restaurant.' Niko held my door as I slid in next to Lance; then he climbed in back, with Dave.

The convertible emerged into sparkling sunshine, and a brisk breeze riffled our hair. It had been years since I had ridden in an open convertible, since about the time unruly Miamians had begun pitching bricks and Molotov cocktails into passing cars.

But this was the exhilarating sort of day that lifted spirits and evoked feelings that all was right with the world. The spirit was contagious.

'God invented convertibles for this kind of weather,' Lance said, wheeling out toward the Boulevard.

'Henry Ford might dispute that.'

The red Taurus I saw pull out from behind the *News* building reminded me of something.

'I forgot to mention,' I said. 'Stephanie called today, and she has been to my apartment, talking to my landlady.'

'Niko,' Lance said, braking slightly. 'You hear that?'

He and Dave leaned forward so I could fill them in.

'And if I'm not mistaken,' I added, fastening my seat belt and checking the side mirror for the Taurus, now gaining on us, 'there she is.'

Their heads all swiveled.

'Watch it!' I warned. My foot automatically mashed a non-existent brake pedal. Even a Rolls-Royce has no controls on the passenger side. Lance swerved to avoid a lumbering Metro bus, as its driver and passengers peered down, goggle-eyed at the super-star who recklessly zoomed on by.

'Now I know why you usually have other people drive,' I said.

'I can't believe it,' Lance muttered. He grinned and hit the gas. 'Let's lose her.'

Oh, no, I thought. This was why I always prefer driving my own car, even though it puts a damper on dating.

We flashed onto the MacArthur Causeway, traveling east toward the Beach, the Taurus in hot pursuit.

'Where are we going?' I imagined Stephanie creating a huge scene in some crowded swank restaurant like the Delano or Joe's on trendy South Beach and our departure in a glut of police cars, paddy wagons, and paparazzi. The idea made me queasy. I related somehow to Stephanie and, despite her animus, would take no pleasure in seeing her manhandled and hauled away again by the cops.

'It's a surprise,' Lance answered, as he swerved across two lanes and hit the gas. At the peak of the high west span, surrounded by turquoise water, the pastel towers of Portofino and South Point rose against the eastern skyline.

Stephanie might be crazy, but she was not stupid and she was certainly resourceful. South Beach is a short strip of real estate. This convertible would not be hard to spot. She would track us down.

I touched Lance's shoulder. 'Maybe we should go back. No point in creating a situation.'

'No way! No problem.' He grinned like a man with a secret. Maybe we were en route to his Star Island house. But then why did he bother to pick me up? I could have driven there myself, or Niko could have come for me.

I glanced back, the rushing wind lifting my hair. The Taurus, a good half mile behind, had just crested the high rise of the west bridge. Lance veered to the right. An irate cabby leaned on his horn. Lance smiled and waved. The driver recognized him, tooted back, and flashed a thumbs-up. Teenage girls packed in a Buick screamed 'Lance!' in unison. They and other drivers slowed to let him across and into the right lane.

What was he doing? He slowed, then left the causeway, bumping across weeds and green grass onto Watson Island. All that was out here was an airstrip for Chalk's seaplanes and a heliport for sightseeing tours. 'This doesn't go anywhere,' I protested.

'Oh, yes, it does.'

The Taurus had tied up the fast lane and was signaling, trying to cross three lanes of traffic.

Lance hit the brakes, and we skidded to a stop on the tarmac. 'Let's go, Niko! Come on.' He grabbed my hand and tossed the keys to Dave. 'We'll call when we need a pickup!'

Dave nodded and slid behind the wheel, blond hair shining in the bright light.

The three of us ran toward a waiting Suncoast chopper, propeller already churning. Lance scrambled aboard, helped me in; then Niko followed. 'Let's go! Let's go!' Lance said.

The pilot nodded and we spiraled into a crystal-blue winter sky, with breathtaking Biscayne Bay, Miami, and the islands below. As we rose we could see Dave pulling out onto the causeway headed east for Star

Island. He waved as we hovered for a moment. The Taurus was careening across the grass after a feat of death-defying lane hopping. It stopped, the door opened, and Stephanie scrambled out. She stared skyward, right arm out-stretched. We were too high to tell, but it seemed to me that she was calling Lance's name.

I could not help laughing with elation at the beauty of it all, the cool crisp air, the vivid blues and greens, the clouds, the sea, and the glittering city. There was the *Miami News* building, staid and solid on the bay. I visualized the stuffy newsroom I had just left and laughed again.

'Wave! Wave!' Niko said, pumping his arm at Stephanie. We were all grinning. He had the pilot radio back to base that anyone inquiring should be informed that we were bound for Bimini.

'Bimini?' I asked.

'Nope.' Niko looked smug.

'You know we'll pay for this,' I said, gasping for breath. 'She's mad as hell already.'

'Forget her. She can't touch us,' Lance said. 'Nobody can. Let me see that now,' he added, inspecting the bruise, now a lovely shade of lavender, on the side of my face.

'You were right,' Niko said. 'She does need a stunt double.'

The view intrigued me: the Coast Guard base; ships and small boats trailing rooster tails on the bay. We skimmed a thousand feet above the traffic streaming north and south on US 1. The vivid hues of Architectonica stabbed at the sky; Haitian freighters meandered along the Miami River; flags fluttered over the US Customs building. The look, the colors, and the geography of Miami never fail to move and excite me.

'Isn't it beautiful?' I settled back. 'I thought we were going to your favorite restaurant.'

'I forgot to mention, it's in Key Largo.'

★ ★ ★

We followed the narrow ribbon of US 1 south as I tried to ignore the throb of the rotors, which awakened something primitive deep inside me, making me think about sex.

Below, the deep blue of the Atlantic on one side and the brilliant turquoise of the Gulf of Mexico on the other were divided by a single silvery strip of concrete, the overseas highway.

We landed in a waterside parking lot and dined at the road-house where they claim the movie classic *Key Largo* was filmed.

'That's why I had the urge to come here,' Lance said, as we relaxed over drinks at a wooden table overlooking the water. Niko sat at the bar ten feet away, drinking coffee.

'What?' I had been imagining Stephanie, at the helm of a powerboat halfway to Bimini. Or pulling into the parking lot behind us. I did not doubt her powers of persuasion.

'You remind me of a young Lauren Bacall.' He reached across the table, brushed my hair back off my forehead, and gazed through me with dark, smoldery eyes.

'No resemblance,' I blurted. 'I'm shorter and — '

He cut me off, that famous, slightly sneering mouth shaping and relishing each word. 'I mean the essence of the woman, the way you carry yourself. I saw it in that TV news clip yesterday, even after the shooting. You know who you are, where you are. Your eyes have a look, as though they've seen everything and nothing is a surprise. It makes me want to try to surprise you.'

Who is writing his lines? I wondered.

'A heady comparison,' I said, 'but I don't see it.'

'Even the voice,' he said. 'You have to admit your voice is husky.'

'It is,' I acknowledged. 'But people don't call me 'sir' on the phone.'

He watched me closely. 'Always in control, as though you can handle anything. You don't take any guff. I bet you give as good as you get. A sense of humor. A woman of the world. Or is it all a façade? Sometimes, off guard, your eyes look haunted.'

'I don't do much self-analysis,' I said. 'No time.'

'You're an exciting, fascinating woman.'

I felt as though I were being dissected, like a bug.

'A bit insolent,' he continued. 'And you behave like a man.'

'What?'

His mouth twisted in a sly smile; he knew what I was thinking.

'No games. You look people straight in the eye when you talk to them. And you always look like you're expecting something to happen at any moment.'

'It usually does.' Time to change the subject. 'I thought actors only talked about themselves.'

'You have no idea how boring that is. Does the haunted look relate to that incident after the hurricane?'

I sighed and nodded. 'Is it that obvious?'

'Something's bothering you, something more than the usual everyday cops-and-robbers routine.'

'It shouldn't haunt me,' I began, toying with my drink. 'But it does. I'm not sure why. I've reported hundreds of deaths, mostly murders, seen the dead lying in the street, on slabs in the morgue, in their coffins. Bodies still bleeding, decomposed corpses no mother would recognize, people frozen in rigor mortis. It was my job. I always slept like a baby because I knew I did right by them. Told their stories because they couldn't. You know, crime survivors can form support groups, lobby lawmakers, and fight for justice. But death seals lips. Nobody speaks for them. So it was my job to find out all I could, then tell their stories in black and white, printed on our consciousness.'

'How was this one different?' Interested and attentive, he was surprisingly easy to talk to. And I surprised myself, spilling things I had discussed at length with no one.

'Obviously, I had never been the one to pull the trigger, to look into a man's eyes after I fired a bullet into his head.'

Suddenly my mouth was dry and my eyes were wet. What was wrong with me?

'He was trying to kill me. He was the man who had betrayed my father and caused his death, he was a serial killer who had kidnaped, raped, and murdered teenagers. Nobody deserved to die more than he did. He is not mourned. The only people who may regret his death are the shrinks who would have loved to pick his brain and publish papers about him. *He* would have loved the attention, matching wits, playing cat and mouse with them. He would have enjoyed the process, while the taxpayers footed the bills. I'm glad he's dead and will never have the chance. My father . . . ' — my voice kept cracking but I had to get it out — 'I never knew my father because of him. It ruined my mother's life.' I began to sniffle. 'But I don't think I went there to kill him. I had my gun. But it came down to kill or be killed.'

I stared at the tablecloth, fighting tears. What was wrong with me? I looked up, directly into Lance's eyes. They looked soft.

'People even congratulated me, said I saved the state and the victims' parents the cost and the ordeal of a trial. One set of parents even sent me flowers when the shooting was declared justifiable.' I gulped. 'Their twelve-year-old son was dead — and they sent me flowers.'

My eyelids burned. A tear skidded and dropped ungracefully off my nose. I fumbled in my bag for a handkerchief. Lance pulled one from his pocket and handed it over. It was monogrammed and smelled good. I gave up delicate dabbing at the tears and loudly blew my nose.

'I wasn't upset,' I insisted. 'Everybody said I did the right thing.'

'Would you say you're upset now?'

'Not really.' My voice quavered.

'Jesus Christ,' he said. 'I wish you could see Silverman.'

I sniffed and blew my nose again. 'Who?'

'My therapist. He's in LA.'

'Not you too.'

'Somebody else has suggested . . . ?'

'Everybody: my bosses, Lottie, McDonald; that's what — '

'McDonald, that cop?'

I nodded and unfolded his handkerchief, searching for a spot that wasn't already damp.

'So he's the one,' Lance said, pointing a finger, 'that you were involved with.'

Since I didn't trust my voice, I kept nodding.

'Shit.' He smiled and shook his head. 'That explains a lot.'

'His attitude?'

'Yeah. You coulda mentioned it. I thought I was losing my manly charms. Cops usually like me. I played enough of them.'

I tried to smile back at him. 'Sorry. And I'm sorry about all this, I didn't mean to spoil lunch. I never fall apart. I don't know what's wrong with me. I must be manic depressive. I was so happy a little while ago, on the way down here.'

'I know manic depressives. Manic depressives are friends of mine, and you, sweetheart, are no manic depressive. What you are is human. You just need to talk it out with somebody. Seeing a therapist is no disgrace, no sign of weakness. Where I come from these days, anybody who isn't seeing a therapist needs to.'

I sipped some water. 'You see one?'

'The guy's great, helped me through some rough spots. The rags-to-riches syndrome, too much, too soon; Hollywood; Lexie. How did you think I got to be such a together guy? How did you think I handled all this?'

'Drugs,' I said in a small voice. 'I assumed Rad Johnson was your supplier.'

★   ★   ★

We talked and walked the beach all afternoon, then flew back through a fiery sunset reflected in water like a mirror. Lance held my hand and I toyed with the leather bracelet on his wrist.

'From my gunslinger days,' he said. 'Wore it in my first Western.'

240

'The one where you kept cracking the bullwhip?'

'No.' He looked surprised. 'You didn't see *The Bandits?*'

'I don't think so.'

'The least you can do, woman, is watch my movies.' He pretended to pout but the blow to his ego was real. I really had to go to Blockbuster.

'Look,' I said, changing the subject. A necklace of lights, the Julia Tuttle Causeway, glittered to the north as we hovered over Watson Island. 'See there, on the south side. That's where the Pieces of Eight case started.'

'Pieces of Eight? Sounds romantic.'

'Eight dismembered body parts washed up. Never identified them or solved the case. And right down there is where a drunken cabdriver named Captain Jerry crossed the median and killed himself and five tourists.'

'Thank you for the guided tour.'

★   ★   ★

Stephanie was not waiting for us, but Dave was, standing next to the convertible, wearing a nylon windbreaker. We zipped across the darkening causeway back to the *News*.

'See you later?' Lance asked, as we pulled up in front of the building.

'Later?'

'We're shooting in the newsroom tonight. Hope you'll be there, to give another guided tour.'

'But you don't start until after midnight,' I said.

'If you can make it.' He shrugged.

He and Niko urged me to call the police at the first sight of Stephanie. Hopefully this time they would hold her long enough for a judge to issue the commitment order sought by her family's lawyer.

'They can't be trying very hard,' I said. 'She's not all that difficult to find. I mean, we keep seeing her. Maybe they're simply relieved that she's down here, out of their hair.'

'If she shows up, don't even try to deal with her,' Niko warned. 'She's dangerous. Let the police handle it.'

Lance planted a kiss on my forehead, and they zoomed off into the growing darkness. I took the elevator to the newsroom, mind racing, wondering how to explain my six-hour lunch. I didn't need to. Nobody had even missed me.

13

I did feel better after unburdening myself to Lance. That was all I needed, I told myself: to talk it out with a friend. Now I was fine.

Messages waited. 'Britt,' Gloria said, her expression odd, 'some woman called, said she wants you fired because you went to Bimini with her husband.'

'I haven't been to Bimini, with or without somebody's husband,' I said innocently.

'And a guy called, wanted to know what kind of shoes you were wearing. When I said I didn't know, he asked what kind I had on. Is he a . . . ?' Her eyes rolled.

'Yes,' I said. 'Just hang up if he calls again.'

'But you know the publisher's policy, to make the paper reader-friendly and be helpful and courteous to every caller no matter who they are or what they say.'

'Then transfer this guy to the publisher's secretary.' The woman, a prim spinster, had held the same job since leaving a convent thirty years ago.

Gloria looked doubtful.

'Or you could simply say that you are

243

wearing four-inch metal spike heels with open toes, crimson polish, and that you want him to — '

'Okay, okay!' she said. 'Never mind.'

Since nobody had missed me for six hours, I left again. Went home, walked the dog, took a catnap, changed clothes, returned to the paper, and made some phone checks.

The guys in the sports department were crowded around a TV watching the Panthers roughhouse at the Miami Arena. Cries of 'Rats on the ice!' meant our team had scored.

Phillip Hodges showed up first, stalking the newsroom, pacing, frowning, and looking creative. He was accompanied by his chief cinematographer, who kept whipping out a light meter. I waved but stayed at my desk, working.

Fast-moving crew members appeared precisely at midnight, rolling in with lights, poles, and scaffolding. They brought racks of clothes, equipment on dollies, and huge metal camera cases on wheels. They changed the time on all the clocks in the newsroom, efficiently positioned lights, covered the big picture windows, and, in effect, turned night into day.

Impressive, especially in this city, run by highly paid professionals unable to even synchronize the traffic lights.

The newsroom, which had slowly emptied except for the few diehards who work until 2 A.M., began to fill up again, as though the internal rhythm of the building had been accelerated to warp speed. Ziff Bodine arrived, lugging a satchel and wearing another belted safari outfit. All he lacked was a pith helmet. He greeted me like an old friend and pulled up a chair. His fingernails were still glossy black. 'I have some scrumptious gossip,' he confided.

'Great,' I said. 'Exactly what I need.'

'Especially since it involves you, girlfriend.'

'Uh-oh.'

His voice became intimate and he rolled his chair closer, as extras drifted around the room and settled in at desks. Most appeared too well dressed and well mannered for roles as reporters and editors. 'Well, Van Ness and Wendy were absolutely livid when you wrote about poor Rad's unfortunate encounter with those nasty crack house hookers and the police. He wants to stay on as AD, so they had a meeting and he agitated them even more. He's so angry about your story — which was picked up, by the way, and reported out on the Coast — that you emerged as the villain, as if you are to blame, not him, for landing his tail in jail.'

'Kill the messenger, of course,' I said. 'Obviously, I sent him to the crack house. Par for the course.'

'Well, don'cha know, Van Ness declared you *persona non grata*, barred from the set.' He grinned slyly. 'Until someone pointed out that we were shooting at the *News*. And that even he did not have the authority to ban you from your own newspaper. Get outa town! Don'cha love it?'

'Yes,' I said. 'Thanks for sharing. I really didn't plan to be here tonight.' I hit the SEND button, dispatching my story into the editing system. 'But now a SWAT team couldn't budge me.'

'Get outa town.'

We high-fived.

Lexie made an entrance, trailing an entourage, dramatic as always, like a rare exotic bird. She wore a blue dress and dripped aquamarines, like glistening drops of water, from her throat and wrists. Van Ness rushed to greet her and stuck to her like something impossible to scrape off the sole of your shoe.

'I didn't know she had any scenes here at the paper,' I murmured to Ziff.

'Her part is growing by leaps and bounds,' he said knowingly. 'You *are* planning to join us when we blow up the warehouse, aren't you? We're doing it Sunday morning, less traffic.'

'You're blowing up a real building?'

'You betcha, sugar. Moviegoers want happy endings or lots of very large explosions.'

'I thought you would build a set, like the nuclear reactor.'

'No way. They did a deal for this warehouse near down-town. It's been condemned to build a new hotel. We're doing the demolition.'

'Lance will be in it when it blows up?'

'Gardiner Bowles, his character, will. It's a toss-up on who actually does the run through the building as the charges are detonated. Lance loves to do his own stunts; you know, that macho image. It's not really dangerous, been done a hundred times, but the studio chiefs get antsy at the thought of singeing even a hair on that bad boy's gorgeous head.'

My phone rang. Who would call this late?

'Gloria?' asked the voice.

'No, this is Britt.'

'Good. Would you like someone to worship at your feet?'

'Hold on.' I covered the mouthpiece with my palm. 'Ziff? Would you talk to this guy?'

★ ★ ★

247

I opened my ladies' room locker, added a little blusher, and brushed my hair. The six-stall six-sink bathroom is adjacent to a shower and a mirrored locker room with a sofa, coffee table, and chairs. The place was empty and half lit, a bit spooky at midnight. While in a stall, I heard the *shwoosh* of the door. Heels clicking on the tiled floor. Someone from the film crew, I thought, but by the time I flushed and stepped out, she was gone. I took a final look in the mirror, slammed my locker door, and snapped the little padlock.

On the way back to my desk, I encountered Lance outside the wire room. He was trying to stretch his too-tight black jeans by doing deep knee bends as Niko hovered nearby.

'Didn't think you were here when I saw Ziff at your desk,' Lance said.

'I was working on a story.' I glanced into the newsroom. Ziff was chatting happily on my phone. Was he still talking to the same caller? He was. As we watched, he leaned way back in my chair, raised his right foot, and thoughtfully studied it from several angles while speaking into the phone.

'He's talking to one of my crank callers, a fugitive with a foot fetish.'

Ziff grinned, then laughed.

'Looks like they don't wanna be disturbed.'

Lance grimaced and did another deep knee bend. He looked red in the face. 'They must've bought 'em a size too small.'

'Or too much *arroz con pollo*,' Niko said.

Lance shot him a dirty look. 'The other two pair that somebody sliced up were fine.' He took a deep breath. 'Tell the sound-man my voice is gonna register a few octaves higher.' He turned to me. 'I still haven't seen where they print this newspaper.'

'The pressroom,' I said. We walked toward the employee elevator, Niko trailing behind.

'What were you working on?'

'The rat patrol is rounding up suspects, busting them on the street and in parking lots around the arena, confiscating their rats.'

'Say again?'

I pushed the elevator button. 'Whenever the Panthers score, fans throw rats on the ice.'

'I noticed.'

'The tradition started after a rat wandered into the home-team locker room. Scott Mellanby, the forward, beat it to death with his hockey stick. When he scored two goals that night, everybody decided rats brought the team luck. Fans started throwing toy rats. Long tails the best, to wind up for a good fling on to the ice. Some are pretty cute.'

We stepped on to the padded freight

elevator, and I hit 3.

'Nice-size rubber rats with good hang time sell for about three-fifty. Then there are matched sets, the Rat brothers, Wilbur and Orville. They're not recycled after they're picked up; that would be tacit approval. The league frowns on throwing anything on to the ice. Arena concessions don't sell rubber rats for the same reason. But for street salesmen, they're big business. Factories in Taiwan are working overtime. They have to make it now because next year they're gonna ban the practice. This is the last hurrah, and at the moment they're in such demand that a truckload of rubber rats got hijacked at gunpoint a while back. Fans will do anything to get them.'

We stepped off on 3, but instead of a right turn into the cafeteria, we hung a left and descended a short, dimly lit stairway. 'So why are they arresting people?' Lance's voice and our footsteps echoed off the concrete block walls.

'Money. Panther officials pressured the police to stop rat sales outside the arena. Fans have only so much disposable income, and they want it all spent on T-shirts, mugs, and hats at their souvenir stands inside.'

'So little old ladies are getting mugged,' Niko said, 'while the cops arrest guys for possession of rubber rats?'

'You've got it. Our system at work.'

The double doors into the bowels of the newspaper loomed ahead. Air space actually separates the vast three-story pressroom from the rest of the building in order to contain the noise and the vibration. The shudder can still be felt underfoot in the newsroom when the presses roll.

We pushed through the doors into what sounded like the path of a runaway freight train. The sound was deafening. The final edition was rolling.

Catwalks skirted the towering two-storey presses, one midway, the other at the top, accessible from the main deck by ladder. Dressed in dark blue uniforms, the pressmen wore steel-toed safety shoes, face masks, and ear protectors, like those used at the pistol range. Paper hats protected their hair from the inky mist, floating particles and splashes spewed by the presses. Blinking red lights flashed digital readouts monitoring the viscosity of the ink and the number of papers printed on each press.

'Looks dangerous!' Lance said in my ear.

'It is!' I shouted back. 'People have lost fingers, hands. There's zero tolerance when the presses are running. See? There's the

ON/OFF/SAFE switches in the control room. Over there is another emergency power switch to shut it down fast if anything gets caught up in the machinery.

'The paper moves between the roller and the inked plates,' I shouted, 'one roller to another; then by conveyor belt up to the mail room on the fifth floor, where they're bundled; then slid down spiral chutes to the loading docks.'

'We're gonna shoot a scene down here later on!' Lance bellowed in my ear.

'I didn't see it in the script.'

'Something new.' He wore a rueful expression. 'There's a lot that's new!'

'I hope they don't have you running in, yelling, 'Stop the press!' It doesn't happen.'

The rhythmic pounding and gut-wrenching vibrations were overwhelming. I caught Lance's glance. He was thinking the same thing.

'Let's get out of here!' I shouted. We burst back out into the hallway.

'It's like an earthquake in there,' Lance said, as we climbed the stairs. Slightly breathless, in the shadowy corridor above, as Niko wandered on ahead, Lance leaned in front of me, barring my way, and kissed me. Warm, sweet, and gentle accelerated to hot, wet, and urgent as his body pushed mine against the cool, unyielding wall.

'Careful,' I warned, catching my breath. 'Your pants are too tight already.'

'I won't bite, unless you wanna be bit,' he said, backing off.

Lost for a moment, I regained my senses.

'Good,' I said briskly. 'Want to see the plate-making room next?'

'Let's save that for another night.'

This time I gave him my handkerchief, in case my lipstick had rubbed off on him. I could see he didn't have one in his pants pocket.

★ ★ ★

'Lance, there you are!' Wendy ignored Niko and me. 'They need to do sound checks and get you into makeup.'

Whisked off to a chair at the back of the newsroom, Lance was fitted with a giant bib by a makeup woman with a huge carrying case packed with tubes, vials, and jars.

Ziff, still on the phone, laughed conspiratorially. 'Uh-oh.' He caught my eye as I approached. 'Britt wants her phone back.' Listening for a moment, he leaned over to scrutinize my feet.

Shaking my head vigorously, I viciously mouthed the word *no* at him.

'Can't do it,' Ziff told the caller. 'Gotta go now . . . Anytime. Bye-bye.'

'I'm glad you two have bonded,' I said, 'but just remember, he's wanted by the law, so don't get too chummy.'

'What did he do? What did he do? Tell me all about it,' Ziff cried eagerly. 'Was it something really gross?'

★ ★ ★

As the night wore on, I learned that shooting a movie involves more waiting than action. Ziff filled his idle time by selling ghoul pool tickets for five bucks apiece. The names of show business celebrities, age seventy or older, were written on folded slips of paper and drawn from a box. If the celebrity you drew died within thirty days, you won. When there was more than one winner, they split the pot. When there were no winners, the pot grew. 'Like the lottery,' Ziff explained.

'That's sick,' I said.

'How many do you want?' he asked, pencil poised.

'I don't gamble,' I grumbled. 'How can you enjoy winning because some beloved show business figure died?'

'Everybody's gotta go sometime.' Ziff pouted.

'I won eleven hundred dollars on Gene Kelly,' Maureen, the wardrobe mistress, said fondly.

★　★　★

The scene they were shooting tonight was the first between Lance and Lexie. Did the old chemistry still linger? The inquiring minds of the entire crew, down to the caterer, the wardrobe mistress, and the Best Boy, a nice old fellow named Norman, all wanted to know, watching so eagerly it made me wonder how many were stringers for the *Enquirer*.

Van Ness, Wendy, and a gaunt middle-aged scriptwriter hovering at the edge of the action all seemed to think that casting former lovers in the roles of former lovers was pure genius.

'The love scenes will tell the story,' Maureen predicted, handing over five dollars for the ghoul pool and selecting a name from the box. 'Hell,' she said, unfolding it. 'I got Ann Miller again. That woman will outlive all of us.'

Gossip flew, while camera tracks were laid out across the newsroom. I heard that Rad Johnson was still officially aboard as AD, though not listed on today's call sheet; that Lance's old studio was trying to woo him back; and that Lexie was rumored to be dating Stallone.

The gaunt writer, Kirby Walters, a script doctor from LA, complained bitterly about his accommodations. He had been promised at least two rooms, he griped, at the small Collins Avenue hotel where three floors had been reserved for *Margin of Error* crew. Instead, he had been lodged in a cubicle with an alley view and no place to plug in his laptop. Standing by like an expectant father, he explained the newly written scene that was about to be shot.

Cassie Malone, Lexie's character, appears unannounced in the newsroom in search of Gardiner Bowles. (No clue as to how somebody who looked like Lexie could slip unnoticed past newspaper security.) Cassie, a slick con woman, is an old flame. The back story, Walters said, was that they had once worked on assignment together, to recover a fortune in stolen drug money from the cartel. They had become lovers, but when Bowles was wounded, cornered by Colombian hit men, Cassie left him for dead, took the money, and ran.

Not bad casting, I thought. The latter in many ways matched Lance's description of their divorce.

Cassie now needs Gardiner's help, but he

has other priorities, an important mission. She really believed he was dead, she insists, which was why she bolted with the money. She learned he was alive, she says, when she glimpsed him at a recent press conference. She has invested her stolen fortune in a major resort hotel venture in Cuba. Ironically, her partners, Spanish businessmen, are now trying to cut her out of the deal. When she confronted them, somebody tried to kill her. She cannot turn to the courts or the authorities because her investment is illegal under US law. When Gardiner refuses to help her, she threatens to expose him and blow his cover as a reporter.

Technicians played with spotlights as Hodges, the director, crouched in front of them. Desktops were rearranged and Polaroids snapped, for continuity and so their former states of disarray could be accurately restored, part of the deal with the paper. Hodges joined the cameramen in a long slow dolly sweep down a track, stopping frequently to mark the floor where the cameras would pause to shoot certain angles.

Lance and Lexie waited on far sides of the room, avoiding eye contact as the production manager rehearsed the extras until they achieved the right voice levels. I joined Lance's camp, along with Niko, his assistant, a makeup person, a script girl, Ziff, and others. Lottie also showed up to watch, after an evening of line dancing at Desperadoes. Our separate sections were like the bride's and the groom's sides at a wedding. Or ringside at a prize fight.

They really do say 'Action!' and snap the striped board. Take One. Lexie walked into the newsroom on cue, wearing as scared, uncertain, and vulnerable an expression as could be mustered up by an immensely rich and famous supermodel. She scanned the newsroom for Lance. Her face was to flood with relief when she saw him. Instead it looked more like the expression I wear when I change the sandbox. Taking a deep breath, she walked toward him. Takes two and three and four and five, the cameras shooting from every conceivable angle. No dialogue, just her.

Then they shot Lance at his desk, with the reporters and copyboys, all extras, busy in the background. When he glanced up and saw her, his expression was to change from startled recognition, to longing, then firm resolve.

Except the first time it was more like Oh, shit.

They shot it over and over until the director finally got what he wanted.

'Lordy,' Lottie murmured, 'he still loves her.'

'In the movie,' I said. 'That's acting.'

'Didn't know he was that good.'

By the time the stars finally exchanged dialogue, I was mesmerized.

CASSIE:

'I didn't know you were alive.'

GARDINER:

'You didn't wait around to find out.'

She then related her problem with the bad guys, over and over, with many retakes due to forgotten or bobbled lines. Finally, she got it right.

GARDINER:

'How did you get involved with these people, Lexie?'

Shouts of 'Cut! Cut!'

'It's Cassie, Lance, not Lexie!'

He got it right next time, but a phone interrupted, ringing in mid-scene. 'Cut! Cut!

Somebody get that!' Hodges shouted. 'And get those phones turned off!'

The offending phone was mine. I tried to shrink into the woodwork. Who the hell would call the newsroom at 4 A.M.?

Security, they said, looking for me.

'Delivery for you,' the guard at the employees' entrance said. 'Flowers.'

Now I understood why Lance had wanted to be sure I would be there. Who else could persuade a florist to deliver at that hour? I asked the guard to send them up.

'You better come down,' he said.

I went, smiling until I saw it.

The arrangement waited on the security desk. A wreath. Wilted flowers, spray-painted black. REST IN PEACE, the ribbon said. My stomach churned. Suddenly I felt bone weary and wanted to go home. Fantasy is so much more fun than real life.

YOU WERE WARNED said the unsigned black-bordered card.

The security guard had thought it a joke, the delivery man said that was what his boss understood as well. Niko thought we should make a police report. I did not. I considered Stephanie more annoying than a threat. We agreed not to trouble Lance with it while he was working.

The last scene of the night, squeezed in before dawn, was Lance, gun in hand, dashing up the cement stairs from the pressroom. Lexie and her entourage had gone, the last press run was history, and there was no noise, only Lance's increasingly heavy breathing. Hodges and Van Ness seemed perverse, ordering take after take after take. Each time Lance charged at top speed, hurtling the steep steps two at time.

He was so winded and red in the face after ten or twelve takes, I worried that he might have a heart attack.

Breathing hard, he slumped against the wall for a few moments as they paused to reposition the lights before the next take. He gasped for air, glancing at Niko and me as the makeup woman blotted his brow.

'Quick,' I suggested. 'Have another cigarette.'

★   ★   ★

When they finished for the night, the crew swept through the newsroom putting everything back the way it was. Lance seemed weary and preoccupied. It was my turn to buy lunch, so I invited him for a late one, at my favorite place. He said he would call, and we parted at dawn. I drove

261

home alone, too tired to worry about Stephanie.

★ ★ ★

My phone rang at one.

'Ready?' Lance wanted to know.

'Give me an hour.'

I drove through the guarded gate to his house at two thirty. The temperature hovered at 70 and the weather was breezy with whitecaps on an emerald-green bay. Puffy cumulus clouds and wisps of cirrus drifted in a rich blue ceramic sky.

Lance was waiting, dressed casually as I had suggested. A cotton pullover, jeans, baseball cap, and shades.

He swung into the passenger's side without hesitation. I like a man who has no problem with me driving. 'Where's Niko?'

'I escaped my captors.'

'Swell. Are they bound and gagged in the wine cellar?'

'I felt the need for unsupervised play.' He shot me a meaningful glance, then looked startled as I turned west on the causeway, toward the city.

'When you said casual,' he said slowly, 'somehow I thought we might be going to your place.'

'Wrong.' We breezed up on to the Dolphin Expressway, then south on I-95, got off at Brickell, and shot across the Rickenbacker Causeway to Key Biscayne.

'So, you're recovered from the stair scene?'

'I better be. They'll probably wanna shoot it another thirty, forty times tonight. And *if* it makes it past the final cut, you may actually glimpse it for two, maybe three seconds.' He shook his head. 'Last time my heart rate was that high, I was naked.'

I ignored his look. At the far end of the island I turned into Cape Florida State Park, down an unpaved road into a nearly empty parking lot. Deserted wooden picnic tables and barbecue pits were scattered through a strip of woods bordering a sandy ocean beach.

'There's a place out here?' he asked, as we got out.

'Yes.' I unlocked the trunk and lifted out my big wicker picnic basket. 'Right here.'

The site was perfect. Absolutely deserted. We spread my pink linen cloth over the rough wooden table. Matching napkins. Real silver. A thermos of hot soup, a bottle of cold wine, roasted chicken, French bread and fruit, beneath moody Australian pines, with the sounds of the surf pounding the beach and the wind playing in the treetops.

'My new favorite restaurant,' Lance called it.

Mellow from the wine, we strolled the sand after lunch, following the surf to the Cape Florida lighthouse. 'This was the scene of the crime. The first murder that we know of in Key Biscayne took place right here.'

'Somebody kick sand in a beachboy's face?'

I shook my head. 'Seminole Indians had been forced down the coast and they attacked. Wounded the lighthouse keeper, killed his assistant, burned, and looted. 'Bout a hundred and sixty years ago.'

'They still in jail awaiting trial?'

'So you're familiar with our justice system.'

I opened a bag of what was left of the bread, tore it to shreds, and we fed it to the seagulls, laughing and ducking as they swooped down, squawking, catching crusts in midair, quarreling and screaming until only crumbs remained.

Lance found a perfect trumpet shell, all swirls and spires, presented it with a flourish, and I slipped it in my pocket. Then we sat on the sand, shoes off, looking out to sea. 'It's so great to relax like this.' He leaned back and sighed. 'We're running behind schedule, over budget, and everybody's driving me nuts.'

'Why do you work so hard,' I said drowsily,

'make so many movies?'

He paused. 'I guess it's because no matter how much they pay me, I'm always afraid that nobody will ever offer me another job. And there's the money. A lot of people depend on me. My agent, my manager, my family, people on my payroll. So I do what I have to do.'

Colorful sailboats darted across the water, and a flock of pelicans skimmed low above the waves before soaring in perfect V formation into a travel-poster sky.

'You know I'm not stage trained . . . I'm no Shakespearean actor.' He sifted sand between his fingers. 'I got my training doing commercials and on a soap opera. My movies aren't highbrow, but I give every one my best shot, try to be original. But I worry . . . ' His voice trailed off.

'About what?' Who would ever believe he's as insecure as the rest of us? I thought.

'Lots of things. Making the wrong decision . . . I left WFI, the studio I'd been with forever, thinking Titan would be a big improvement. But the way things are going with this picture so far . . . '

'Did you burn bridges? Could you go back?'

'Hell, they want me back, didn't want me to leave, but I won't ever work for that guy again. I've told 'em in no uncertain terms. The studio's not the same since Bernard Gettinger took over. He was big-time in Vegas. To him moviemaking is not an art, it's strictly business.' He sighed, his rugged profile pensive. 'And I worry about getting older, when I can't be the action hero. When the only role I can land is somebody's father or grandfather. I already have to work twice as hard in the gym to maintain the body for action flicks.'

'Why don't you do other kinds of movies, even comedies? Go out on a limb.'

'The few times I did, it broke and I fell off. Fans are fickle. When they like you in a certain kind of role, they're pissed off and stay away in droves when you deviate from that.'

'Try it again. You'd still have action movies to fall back on.'

'Yeah, the ones the critics love to crucify.'

'Hah, they're usually over-educated pseudo-intellectual wannabes with no clue about what the average person really likes. The guy we've got at the paper? If he loves a movie, it is always foreign or incomprehensible. He gave a must-see rave and four stars to an art film last year, never mentioning that it was in French with no subtitles. He assumed that everybody spoke French. Phones rang off the hook. People who bought tickets based on his review were livid. That's a critic. You're a major star. You communicate, you touch people. That's what counts.'

We strolled back to our picnic table, his arm around me. The Australian pines were still moody, the surf still pounded the beach, the wind still played in the treetops, but something was different. The sun, blazing in the western sky, blinded me for a moment and I was not sure what I saw. My T-Bird was still there, but the windows were smashed and all four tires flat.

I did not think we were followed. Apparently, I was wrong. Or perhaps, as I suggested, this was random vandalism. Lance was sure it was not. He was right. *You were warned* said the note amid the broken glass on the windshield.

'Dammit. Stephanie.' I scanned the woods. Nobody in sight.

'She must be gone,' he said, as I brushed glass off the shiny new-car finish. 'It's my fault. I'll have everything fixed. Get you new tires.'

'I have insurance,' I said mildly, surprised myself that I was not more upset. If we let Stephanie ruin our day, she won. He called Niko, asking him to send us a flatbed tow truck and bring us a car.

We waited, lounging at the picnic table, finishing the wine and telling our life stories.

'As much as I gripe about the business,' Lance said, 'I love movies. Always have, since I was a kid. I walk into a theater and my heart beats faster. I'm ready. Ready to be entertained, enlightened, transported. I want to laugh, to cry, to gasp in astonishment, to forget the real world and let the filmmakers push my buttons. I want to sit in that seat and forget who I am and where I am for two hours. I'm so lucky to be part of all that.'

I understood. To a lesser degree my job, the stories I become involved in, can transport me, make me forget my own life.

Niko, behind the wheel of a dark blue Mark VIII, and the tow truck arrived almost simultaneously. He was not happy and became even less pleased when Lance insisted he accompany the tow truck driver and leave the Lincoln with us.

'What are you doing out here? Remember what happened last time you didn't listen? How do you expect me to do my job?' he grumbled, climbing into the truck.

'He'll get over it,' Lance said as they pulled away. We grinned, like schoolkids playing hooky, as I put the things I had removed from the T-Bird into the Lincoln. The truck pulled away, Niko watching us over his shoulder.

'Guess we should go,' I said. We both hated to leave this place.

He bent to brush kiss my cheek, but I turned my head at that moment and something happened. Ten minutes later we were still engulfed in that first kiss. We were making out like teenagers. I vaguely heard the sound of a car pulling up as he bent me back over the hood of the Lincoln. I opened one eye: a harmless elderly couple in an old station wagon.

We ignored them. They stopped to watch.

'Don't they have a home?' the old lady said reprovingly. She and the man sat erect, staring.

We parted lips and glanced up.

'No,' Lance said, 'we don't have a home. That's why we're here.'

We slid into the car, breathless, as the couple continued to stare.

'Isn't that . . . ?' she began.

'He looks like . . . ' he said.

As we drove away, I felt warm and flushed. It was all so romantic, so . . . so much like a movie.

14

The car phone rang as Lance drove me home. 'We're shooting on the beach tonight, instead of at the paper,' he said as he hung up. 'They decided the weather is perfect for a love scene.'

'We could've told them that. What kind of love scene?'

'I'm afraid Van Ness has seen *From Here to Eternity* too many times.'

'You mean that sexy scene in the surf? Burt Lancaster? Deborah Kerr? Watch out for the riptide, it's treacherous. Want me to come?'

He shook his head. 'It's a closed set, as closed as it can be out in the open.'

I nodded. The filmmakers wanted the site kept hush-hush, he said. A stretch of Matheson Hammock, with off-duty cops and security barring beach access. I remembered the scene Lottie had talked about in *Dead by Sundown*. 'Bare-ass naked,' had been her subtle description.

'Will you take your clothes off?'
'Yeah.'
'All of them?'

'Damn close.'

'What about Lexie?' My mouth felt dry.

'Second nature to her, she's an exhibition-ist at heart.'

'I guess all actors are.'

He shot me a quick glance.

'Too bad about the sea lice, the sand fleas, and the Portuguese man-of-war — those are transparent jellyfish with long tentacles. They wash up on the sand but you can't see them. Their sting is pretty nasty.

'Then there's that sand you'll have to lie on. Actually it's crushed coral rock with sharp edges, like ground glass. To say nothing of the wandering homeless, the prurient cops, the paparazzi who will sniff you out, high-risers with binoculars, and all the bad dogs that run loose in packs at night.'

He fought back a smile. 'Sounds like a job for Trent. Wish he could take my place.'

Then I asked what I really wanted to know. 'Do you get aroused during sex scenes?'

He gave me a quizzical look. 'No chance, even for an exhibitionist. It's all very technical. You have to worry about hitting the mark, so to speak. A dozen people are watching over your shoulder. They keep spritzing you all over, so you look slick and sweaty. You have to worry about finding a way

271

to kiss that makes you both look good on camera. No bent noses. You worry about angles, closeups. Charging up and down that flight of stairs was more fun, I swear.'

'Even with Lexie?'

'Especially with Lexie.' His voice took on a hard tone. 'It's a movie, Britt. It's all illusion.'

★ ★ ★

I didn't even bother to check the office for messages. I stayed home alone, plucked *Ground Zero* from a stack of freshly rented Lance Westfell movies, and popped it in the VCR. I sat in my favorite chair, Billy Boots on my lap, and watched, imagining him making love to Lexie on the sand as the surf pounded and the full moon rose.

He exuded heat, even on the small screen. Toward the end of the movie, Lance tenderly touched the cheek of a blonde actress.

I know one thing, Kelly-Marie. The world is a more interesting place with you out there in it.

I spit up a mouthful of the chocolate-cookie-dough ice cream I was devouring right out of the carton and hit the PAUSE button, REWIND, then PLAY. When he said it again, I threw a sofa pillow at the screen, turned off the phone, and went to bed.

The city was quiet at 6 A.M. Sunday, the calm after Saturday night. The neighborhood was deserted and the warehouse was about to blow.

Ziff and the crew were there, including Rad. I pointed him out to Lottie, who had come to watch. 'Looks like a man whose urine specimen would glow in the dark,' she said.

This was my first glimpse of Lance since his big beach scene with Lexie. Word on the set was it was so sizzling the producers had ordered a second sexual encounter written into the script. Lance looked as though the love scene had gotten out of hand. Lexie must have worked him over. Love bites seemed to cover his neck, and there was a bloody gash, closed by stitches, across his forehead.

Ziff claimed responsibility. It wasn't Lexie. The injuries, burns, and bruises on his throat, and the nasty head wound, were phony. Ziff had painted them on for today's scene.

Trent wore identical injuries and was dressed like Lance, except for padding beneath his fireproofed clothes. Makeup concealed his scar, and he wore a black wig styled like Lance's hair.

Though he looked nothing like himself in that getup, Lottie was smitten. 'T-types are hot,' she muttered. 'Did I ever tell you about the stunt pilot I met in Mexico?'

'T-types?'

'That's what psychologists call 'em: T,' she said, lifting an eyebrow, 'as in thrill. Risk takers, people who love excitement, who live on the edge. They're a turn-on. They scale Mount Everest, they sky dive, drive race cars.'

'Yeah, and some freebase, drag race, and rob banks.'

'As American as apple pie,' she said. 'Risk taking is the essence of America.'

'Well, this stunt has been plotted, planned, and diagrammed like a military operation. Not much risk here.'

★ ★ ★

They had already filmed take after take of Lance dashing through the warehouse, gunfire exchanged, bad guys in pursuit. Then they shot a scene with him and Lexie. Her character, Cassie, pulled up at the warehouse in a white Porsche. Tanned and lithe in a white dress, long hair flying, she ran to greet him as he emerged, spritzed and sooty, from what would later appear on film as an inferno. He caught

274

her wrist and they raced back to the car, but before making their getaway he bent her back over the hood in an embrace.

'Don't they have a home?' I muttered.

'What?' Lottie asked.

'Nothing.'

'Remember.' She cut her eyes at me. 'It's jist acting.'

'Hey!' Van Ness applauded. 'Lance doing a little improvising there!'

'Nice work,' Hodges called. 'Not bad.' He looked pleased.

Now it was time for the big blowup.

Lance fought a last-ditch argument, insisting that he should do the run-through as the charges were detonated and fires ignited. He lost.

Nobody was on his side.

Nobody would know the difference, they said, shooting down Lance's contention that the sequence would appear more realistic if he did the whole thing. Somehow his takes and Trent's would magically merge in the final edit, thanks to the technical miracles of modern filmmaking. Plus, Trent was cocked, loaded, and ready to roll.

He seemed almost abnormally calm. This was a one-take scene. Once the warehouse blew up, there would be no chance to try for a better take. Pressure was on, from the fire and police departments as well, to do it before crowds gathered and traffic interfered. A number of bystanders — the homeless, night workers, and others lured by word of mouth — had already gathered to watch.

The series of explosions, controlled sequential detonations, had been orchestrated by Stan Fisher, the film's pyrotechnics expert, who resembled a bespectacled accountant more than a mad bomber. The plans had been scrutinized and approved by the cops and a fire department consultant. This time, as Gardiner Bowles exchanged gunfire with the villains, charges would explode, dropping parts of the structure and igniting fires behind him as he sprinted through the heart of the building. Fisher would activate the sequence, using a panel box with remote switches.

Explosive charges, packed into large steel funnels, were aimed like mortars at specific targets to make the explosions appear far bigger than they really were. The inverted funnels would spit the small explosive charges exactly where they were intended to go. The force would all travel in the direction of the funnel, with no blow-back, leaving few safety concerns.

'All directed and controlled,' Fisher said. Camera angles would make the explosions appear closer to Trent's heels than they actually were. After he safely cleared the door, a final big blast would bring down the front of the building and its heavy steel beams. Simultaneously, four fifty-five-gallon gasoline drums planted behind the walls would ignite. Each drum was a quarter full of gasoline and diesel fuel, then filled with cork that would flare into spectacular fireballs to create a truly magnificent inferno.

The flying debris would be relatively harmless, cork and balsa wood, but fire, police, and security personnel stood by, armed with fire extinguishers. Minor mishaps were known to happen, a fireman told us. Once, during another movie shoot, a chunk of flaming cork hurtled across the street, high above the heads of firefighters and cops, landed on a fire truck, and burned a hole in the air-conditioning unit.

'Lookit them,' Lottie muttered. 'Lookit their eyes. These boys all love playing with fire. Boys and their toys.'

True, from the cops to the firemen to the film crew, each wore the glittery-eyed look of the arsonist in the crowd. All except for Lance, who looked wistful, as though he really would have liked to do it himself.

Fisher wore a hard hat and was perched high on a truck, squinting behind his glasses, the control panel before him. Cameras were positioned to shoot the disaster from every angle.

I always regret seeing any old Miami building come down, another piece of history, lost forever. But this old warehouse was coming down in style.

Three fire trucks, their crews, and a rescue vehicle stood by, as required by the city.

They pushed us all back across the street, everybody but security and fire personnel and the directors and the cameramen mounted on their equipment. Even Lexie, who had disappeared into her trailer, stepped out to watch.

The big moment arrived. 'People, this is one time only!' Hodges shouted through a bullhorn. Both he and Rad wore firemen's coats and helmets.

Lance shook hands with Trent, who gave a jaunty wave to the crowd. He winked at us, strode inside, and found his mark.

Lance and Niko trotted across the street to join the rest of us.

'You were right about the sand fleas,' Lance muttered sotto voce into my ear.

'Ready, Trent? Here we go!' Hodges cried. 'Action! Camera!'

Van Ness and Wendy, to our right, wore earphones, watching a monitor as Trent, alone in the building, began his run, shooting at unseen villains.

Two small explosions behind him. Then nothing. 'Hey!' Van Ness looked up. 'Shoulda been another one. Son of a bitch! Must've been a dud. Dammit!'

I looked over their shoulders. On the small screen, Trent kept running, kept shooting, but glanced sharply back to where that last charge should have detonated.

He was visible now, through the large double doors. A darting silhouette, halfway there.

A deafening explosion rocked the front of the building. The crowd gasped, oohing and ahing, as the street trembled. The front wall blew out and fell, the roof collapsed with a roar. A smattering of applause swept through the crowd.

For a brief moment even I thought the spectacular effect was deliberate.

Then I saw Hodges's face, as he yanked off his helmet, screaming.

'No! *No!*' howled Fisher, frozen atop the truck bed, staring in shock at the panel box in front of him.

'My God!' Niko said.

'This can't be happening!' Lance said. Both men charged across the street. Shouting firefighters in gear were already running toward the warehouse. Two dragged a hose.

Lottie took off down the street at a dead run. I knew exactly where she was going: to her car, for her cameras.

As smoke cleared and the flames shifted, there was a glimpse of Trent on the monitor, pinned to the cement floor by a steel beam. His arms flailed.

'Get him out! Get him out!' Van Ness bellowed.

At that instant, the gasoline mixture exploded, along with all the other charges, spewing a fireball that enveloped Trent.

A cameraman stationed close to the front of the building to film Trent's exit was blown backward, staggered, and fell, engulfed in flames. Clothes on fire, he scrambled to his feet and ran screaming, straight into Lance's arms. He and Niko wrestled him to the ground, beating out the flames with their bare hands.

'No, Lance! No! No!' Van Ness and Wendy both shouted. 'Get back! Get back!'

The monitor behind them was blank, the remote camera dead.

Flames leaped, soaring against the Sunday morning sky. Sirens screamed as more fire rescue units arrived. Lexie stood, mouth open in shock, on the front step of her trailer.

Hands shaking, I began taking notes.

15

Firefighters were unable to remove Trent's body from the warehouse for more than four hours. First the fire had to be doused, then homicide detectives, fire inspectors, and arson investigators began to pick through the rubble.

The 'controlled' sequence of explosions had occurred in nearly reverse order, with the final blast detonating prematurely.

'This can't be, this can't be,' Fisher mumbled, staring at the panel board, until the cops confiscated it as part of their investigation. 'I wired it myself,' he told them. 'It was perfect. I wired it myself.'

Lance wept silently. Niko hugged him. I knew what they were thinking. The victim consumed by flames so fierce that he would have to be officially identified by dental records came this close to being Lance.

Both he and Niko suffered minor burns on their hands from beating out the flames on the cameraman, who had been taken to the burn unit. He would survive. They had reached him before the fire did serious damage.

Ziff blubbered like a baby, whimpering and hugging Lance and everybody else within reach.

McDonald showed up to take charge of the death scene. Tight-lipped and serious, he took no static from Van Ness, who grumbled about the delay and its cost.

'Frankly, I don't give a damn about your budget or your shooting schedule,' McDonald told him. 'Somebody's dead. I'm in charge of this investigation, and it will be done right.'

'It was an accident,' Van Ness said. 'This business has a less than three percent injury rate. It was just our bad luck. Terribly unfortunate, of course, but accidents happen.'

'I don't know what it is at this point,' McDonald replied, 'but I intend to find out.' Detectives took the film and wanted statements from everyone at the scene.

Lexie actually asked whether this meant they would not be reshooting the scene between Lance and her. If not, she wanted to go back to her hotel.

At headquarters, she pouted. She knew nothing about the stunt, but all the cops were eager to interview her. For the first time she didn't totally ignore me. She glared, curling her lip at both Lance and me as we talked.

When I began asking questions for my story, McDonald motioned me into his office.

'Nice crowd you're involved with here,' he said pointedly and settled into his desk chair. 'All the producers care about is what kind of a delay this will cause, and all Lexie Duran wants to do is go play tennis. That poor son of a bitch. This movie and that crowd ain't worth dying for.'

I told him that Trent was sober, eager, and in good spirits when Lottie and I spoke with him shortly before the stunt.

'See any drugs used among the crew?'

'No. You know Rad's history. Do you anticipate some kind of criminal charge? Manslaughter, reckless endangerment, that kind of thing?'

'Don't know what I'm thinking yet. Something went wrong here. This was reckless, unnecessary, irresponsible. The city looks like crap for permitting it. I'll be glad when this crowd gets outa town. We've got enough going on here. Listen to that out there.' He gestured to the rows of desks, mostly unmanned, outside his door. 'Every phone in this office is ringing. We didn't need this. We've got no civilian personnel in on the weekend, we're short-staffed, and the press has gone crazy. We've got 'em calling from

London, Australia, Spain. First news flash reported a fatality during a scene involving Westfell. Apparently rumors spread that it was him.'

'Thank God it wasn't.'

He looked at me sharply.

'Yeah,' he said, unenthusiastically.

'If not for Lance and Niko, his bodyguard, that cameraman would have been more seriously burned, or worse. They acted like heroes.'

McDonald looked skeptical. "Acted' being the operative word. Firefighters were already at the scene. But I'm sure what they did is good publicity for them.'

No point in arguing. 'My understanding,' I said coldly, 'was that Trent checked out all the details of the stunt several times himself. He was a pro. The fire department consultant who worked with Fisher approved the stunt, monitored the setup in the warehouse, and examined all the wiring.'

McDonald nodded. 'We're talking to him now.'

I rose to leave.

'You okay?' he said.

'Sure.'

He gazed up at me with those silvery blues that always knocked my socks off. 'Let's get

284

together soon, for that dinner.'

'I'm kind of busy right now,' I said, and walked out of his office.

I went back to the paper to write the story.

★ ★ ★

Lance called just before eight. 'Finished yet?'

I said I was.

'I'll pick you up.'

'When?'

'Now.'

He was alone, driving the Porsche, or one just like it.

I slid into the car and kissed him. He took his hands off the wheel and kissed me back, hard.

He had ointment on his hands, still wore the clothes he had been wearing on the set, but had washed off his 'injuries'.

The air felt thin, as though only a wispy hard-to-breathe layer of night protected the city from something infinitely bigger and darker above.

We didn't talk; he just drove. The sports car swayed in windy blasts out on the open road. On the radio Selena sweetly sang 'I Could Fall in Love'. For the first time, I listened to the words.

The road grew darker and more deserted

as he drove west. About fifty miles out on the Tamiami Trail in the 'Glades, he let go of my hand to downshift, turned off, and drove a half mile into the wilderness. I knew where we were when I recognized the old jetport. The project had been designed to relieve the overload of commercial traffic at Miami International Airport. Embattled environmentalists fought to block the intrusion into the 'Glades. They eventually won, but not until the main runway had been built.

Novice pilots now practice touch-and-go landings at the deserted site. Our headlights picked up several parked trailers and vehicles used by the movie company.

'Want to see the nuclear reactor?' Lance asked. 'They finally got it stabilized.'

'Sure.'

Far from city lights, the sky was darker than dark, the moon huge, and the stars hung bright and low. The song sung now came from a chorus of frogs, night birds, and critters that live in the saw grass. I was grateful this was not mosquito season, and that tonight's strong winds had blown away the few in residence, probably to Miami Beach.

The headlights of the Porsche lit the way as we walked to a parked jeep. Lance found the keys stashed atop a front tire. As we drove down a rutted trail, the Porsche's automatic lights went out behind us. 'Sure you can find it in the dark?'

'Absolutely.' He lit a cigarette.

'Be careful,' I cautioned with some urgency. 'This is the dry season out here. Drop a match and the whole place could go up.' I remembered the trooper who had stopped a motorist on the Trail. As he wrote the speeding ticket, he smelled smoke. His cruiser's hot muffler had ignited the dry roadside grass, and he lost his car to the flames.

The jeep's headlights picked up an eerie sight. The reactor towered, alone in the wilderness, like an apparition.

'It looks real, like Three Mile Island,' I whispered in awe.

'The whole set is built from disposable material painted to look like concrete, steel, and plastic. Come on. Nobody's here now.' I noticed the blanket he had brought from the Porsche as he helped me out of the jeep.

A wooden platform circled the base of the reactor. He helped me find the three steps in the dark and we stood together, next to the nuclear plant's fake entrance, a movable aluminum door, lying on its side.

'Alone at last,' he said. The night was so dark I could barely see him.

My hands found their way into his hair. Our lips found each other. He spread the blanket out on the deck and we sat on it, our legs over the side, my head on his shoulder.

The setting was like being marooned together on a small island in an inky sea of night. He sighed and smoked. 'This is a good place to think.'

'Or not to think.'

We sat for a long time, listening to the wind sweep across the saw grass, watching Venus, the brilliant evening star, climb the western sky and the seven sisters lead the dazzling parade of winter constellations across the eastern horizon.

'I guess we should go,' he finally said. 'It's a long drive back.'

We got stiffly to our feet. He kissed me, gently this time, his hands around my waist. I pulled away, trying to see his eyes in the dark.

'I won't bite you,' he said, with a hands-off gesture, 'unless, of course, you wanna be bit.'

The moon emerged between two star clusters, breaking free from indigo clouds, and I saw his eyes.

'Bite me.' I opened my arms with a sense of absolute freedom, as though we were lost in space and nothing else mattered.

He sighed. 'My pleasure.'

We eased back down on to the blanket,

entangled in a sweet, slow embrace. That was when I heard it: an engine.

'What was that?' I sat up, a premonition of fear overtaking me in a shudder.

'I heard it too.' He sat up as well. 'Could be a ranger.'

'Maybe he saw the jeep and wants to check it out, to make sure everything's all right.' Forestry officials had been monitoring the site. I tried to reassure myself, without success. 'Do you have a gun?'

'No. Why do you keep asking me that?'

There is something to be said for dating a police officer. A mate who is always armed provides one with a sense of security — unless, of course, he turns the gun on you. There was also something to be said, I thought, for Niko, Dave, Al, Frank, and Pauli. I promised myself to never again resent their presence.

A car door closed quietly but unmistakably, somewhere upwind, near the jeep. 'Think somebody's stealing it?' I whispered fearfully.

Lance touched his pocket. 'Got the keys right here.' He stood up. 'Yo, anybody out there?'

I wished he had not done that. Whoever it was now knew exactly where we were. No answer.

I stood up and took Lance's arm, straining

my eyes into the darkness. The night sounds had stopped.

'Listen,' I whispered.

'It's the wind,' he said.

'No, hear it?' Something or somebody was moving quickly, thrashing through the waist-high saw grass, in an arc, the sounds of water splashing.

'Yeah, I hear it.'

Was somebody dumping something out here? If only it wasn't so damn dark.

Then I smelled it and knew what was happening.

'Gasoline!' I screamed. 'No!'

'What the hell . . . ?' Lance said.

The night lit up with a roar. In a split second a hundred-foot-long arc of fire sprang to life.

'Let's get out of here.' Lance gripped my arm.

'We'll never outrun it,' I said. Tongues of leaping flame had already cut us off from the jeep. Beyond, I heard an engine start up and pull away.

Twenty- to twenty-five-mile-an-hour winds propelled the blowing grass fire into a fast-burning inferno that rolled at us like an avalanche.

Lance turned, his classic body silhouetted in the light from the flames, and hit the deck. Hell, I thought, we are about to die and we never even had decent sex. He grunted, straining, ripping boards from the platform beneath us. What was he doing? I was about to run for it anyway when he caught me, pulled me down, and shoved me into the dark crawl space beneath the platform. There had to be snakes, bugs, rats. I hesitated. He pushed me hard, forcing his body in after me as he yanked the sheet of metal, the false door, down over the opening with a clatter.

'Move,' he demanded, as we crawled forward.

'They'll never find us here.' I fought panic. 'They'll never know what happened to us.' The fire roared like something alive as it rolled over us, crackling, snapping, shooting sparks, an incendiary circus, leaping and dancing. Hot embers fell between cracks, stinging our flesh. I couldn't breathe. The weight of Lance's hand came down on the back of my neck, pushing my face down into what felt like wet mulch. It seemed like forever . . .

Resigned, limp, lungs filled with smoke, I opened my eyes to the dark. The light of the fire had passed, but I still heard the roar in my ears.

Lance was alive. Dizzy and nauseous, I felt

his heartbeat. He was breathing, or was that me?

'Britt?' His voice was a raspy croak.

'Yeah?'

He squeezed my shoulder. 'Was it as bad for you as it was for me?'

'Just about.'

We crept out on to the scorched earth.

'Good God,' I murmured. Flames swept across the 'Glades like waves across the ocean. The entire horizon seemed ablaze. I heard an alarm, from some distant ranger station. The flames moved like wildfire. For the first time I completely understood the term.

The nuclear reactor had melted like a marshmallow, sinking in on itself.

Whoever set the blaze had slashed the tires on the jeep. Stephanie's MO. We drove it anyway, fearing if we stayed on foot the wind would change, putting us in the path of the fire again.

'We almost got killed,' Lance said, his voice painfully hoarse.

'Tell me about it,' I said, throat scratchy, my head aching from the smoke. 'For you, it was the second time today.'

He looked as though the thought had not occurred to him, then said, 'The third time may prove fatal, when I tell Hodges, Van

Ness, and Wendy what happened to the reactor.'

We flagged down firefighters on the Trail. They wanted to know if we had lit a campfire or tossed out a lighted cigarette.

We gave them Stephanie's description and that of the car we last saw her driving, the red Taurus, probably a rental. They did not pass it on the road, but she could be driving anything by now. They seemed skeptical of our story that a shadowy someone we hadn't seen was responsible. The crumpled pack of Marlboros in Lance's shirt pocket did nothing to enhance our credibility.

He dropped me back at the paper and went to break the news to Hodges and the producers. My clothes were filthy and I was a mess. I washed up in the ladies' room, then peeled off my blouse and opened my locker to change into the extra set of clothes I kept there. I took out the hanger with a skirt, blouse, and fresh underwear attached, and gasped. The garments were shredded, slashed by some razor-sharp instrument. Inside, my makeup had been opened, spilled, scattered, the toothpaste squeezed out.

'Oh, no,' I moaned, then whimpered. Miserable, head throbbing, sinuses closed, still shaky from all that had happened, I tried to think. How? I had the only key. When was the last time I had opened the locker? The night the film crew was shooting here, before the flowers came. I had left it open, was in a stall, heard footsteps. She was here! She had invaded this safe, familiar, mirrored room. Rage overwhelmed me. I could kill Stephanie, I thought, if I could just get my hands on her.

I slammed the locker door, tried to tidy my clothes, and went back out to check with fire central. The department was saying only that a 'Glades fire had erupted, origin still undetermined, and that firefighters from Metro-Dade, the Division of Forestry, and Everglades National Park were battling the blaze.

I drove home watching my rearview mirror, checking the shadows as I unlocked the door. I fed the animals, squeezed Murine into my red, itchy eyes, and tried to wash the smoke out of my hair. As I prepared for bed, I monitored Metro's fire frequencies on the scanner. Flames had jumped across the trail, and the road was being closed. Reinforcements were being called in to a command post set up at Forty Mile Bend. More than a hundred firefighters had fanned out to fight the flames.

★ ★ ★

The phone rang at 2 A.M.

'Did they put it out?' Lance asked wearily.

'Wait a minute,' I said, groggy. I turned the scanner back on and listened. 'No. It's worse.' Firefighters and equipment from other jurisdictions were en route to help, under the emergency mutual aid pact. The fire, wreathing the treetops of towering Australian pines, had leaped a drainage canal and the road west of Sweetwater. The duff, a thick mix of crisp foliage and dried pine needles matted on the ground, was burning and blowing in fiery clouds across the south side of the trail toward the Miccosukee Indian Village.

'Jesus Christ, hope nobody gets hurt.'

'You've been with Van Ness and company all this time? How did they take it?'

'Not well.'

I told him about my locker.

'The woman's out of control.' He gave a short, angry sigh. 'Niko's arranging to have one of our lawyers meet with the police chief first thing in the morning. She's gotta be stopped before she kills somebody. This is insane. I can't believe I once worried that she was suicidal. Now I wish she still was. I liked her better that way.'

'I know what you mean.'

'You sound terrible,' he said.

'So do you. Where are you?'

'In bed.'

'Me too.'

'You know, I want to come over there and bite you.' He sounded exhausted.

'Good,' I said, smiling. 'But we both better get some sleep.'

'Yeah, it's been a long day. And I think Niko's got me locked in.'

'Good for him.'

'Good night.'

''Night.'

'Say it.'

'Say what?'

'What you said last time you put me to bed.'

'Pleasant dreams?'

'Yeah.'

I said it.

★ ★ ★

The morning news was bad. This was the driest time of year and the blaze, fanned by stiff winds from a gusty cold front, was racing south, toward populated areas. Reinforcements had been marshaled but were unable to contain the fire. No rain was forecast.

'Oh, no,' I murmured, as I stepped out to scoop up my newspaper. The unmistakable smell of smoke was in the air, carried on the wind from hundreds of scorched and burning acres. The horizon was hazy, and a smoky shroud hung over the city as I drove to the office.

★   ★   ★

Metro fire issued a press release at 10 A.M. Listed among the damage was the movie set, where the blaze had apparently erupted. The next logical question from reporters was whether anyone had been present at the time. The affirmative answer, that the star and a *News* reporter had been on the scene, set off a flurry of inquiries.

During a news conference at noon, the battalion chief ruled out lightning as a cause. The ranger stations, on alert during the dry season, had reported no strikes. Seven hundred families directly in the fire's path, an eight-and-a-half-square-mile area of rural South Central Dade, were being evacuated. Firefighters from the Florida Division of Forestry's Everglades District were waging an all-out battle to save the residential area. Helicopters equipped with 'Ping-Pong-ball machines' were flying low, a hundred feet off the ground, dropping the balls in straight lines. Forty-five seconds later, the chemically treated balls burst into flames, creating an instant wall, a counter fire designed to consume everything in its path so the approaching wildfire would be curbed, starved for lack of fuel. Firefighters from Collier and Monroe counties were gearing up to join the operation. Smoke was causing problems as far south as Homestead and Florida City, and campgrounds were being evacuated fifteen miles west of Interstate 95.

Then the chief opened it to questions. Yes, he said, Westfell did appear to be a smoker. No, smoking had not been ruled out as the cause. No, he did not know what the two of us had been doing out there alone in the dark. And no, he had no idea how the film crew had gained permission to build their set in the federally protected Everglades National Park.

Our publisher and Fred, my editor, and Mark Seybold, the paper's lawyer, asked me the same questions.

'He was upset, stressed out after the accident,' I told them. 'He wanted to be alone. I had never seen the reactor set before, and we drove out there.'

'After dark?' the publisher said.

'Yes.'

'Is it possible that anything you or he did

298

accidentally started the fire?' the lawyer asked.

I explained again exactly what had happened.

Since no eyewitness could place Stephanie at the scene, we could not identify her in print as a suspect. Our story would simply state that we heard noises, smelled gasoline, and then 'flames erupted'.

'Who the hell gave them permission to build that thing out there in the first place?' the publisher asked angrily.

'We're damn sure gonna find out,' Fred said.

'Has to be illegal as shit,' Seybold said, looking grim. 'Do they still have any shooting to finish here in the building?' The publisher chewed his lower lip.

I nodded.

'How the hell did we get mixed up with these people in the first place?' Fred asked indignantly.

I raised my eyebrows. I could have told him, but didn't.

'Can't stop them from finishing what they started in our building.' The publisher paced the office, running his hand impatiently through thinning hair. 'Or can we?' he glanced hopefully at Seybold.

'I wouldn't,' the lawyer said. 'We had an

agreement. If they sued, we could be held liable for the costs of reshooting what they've already done. But we can certainly encourage them to finish up here as quickly as possible, then distance ourselves from the entire situation.'

'When they are in the building,' the publisher instructed, rocking back and forth on his heels, 'I want them monitored and security strictly maintained. The first time they violate the agreement, they're out.'

Janowitz and I worked on the story together. Lottie, who regularly monitors fire channels, had shot spectacular pictures from a chopper before dawn.

People were streaming into doctors' offices and hospital emergency rooms by early afternoon, with allergies, asthma, and chronic upper respiratory ailments aggravated by the smoke.

By late afternoon, the Long Pine Key and the Chekika Recreation Areas were closed, and the boardwalk at the Anhinga Trail, totally rebuilt after the storm, had burned.

The *News*'s lead editorial in the early edition questioned how filmmakers had won permission to build in the 'Glades. Had they circumvented the entire permit process and in doing so despoiled a precious and sensitive Florida resource in the pursuit of profit?

Then McDonald called. 'Thought you'd want to know,' he said. 'We're scheduling a press conference in a couple of hours. That stuntman, Trent Talon. His death was no accident. It looks like a homicide.'

16

The control panel had apparently been tampered with, wires reversed, to prematurely detonate the blast. Search warrants had been served at two locations. Detectives and crime scene technicians were at the trailer, where the panel had been stored from late Friday until the morning of the explosion, and at the production's downtown office. There had apparently been a break-in. The only items missing from an unlocked file cabinet were a blueprint for the warehouse stunt and the schematics for the control panel.

'But who? Why?' After the fire I had wondered whether we had stumbled into the wrong place at the wrong moment, as the set was about to be torched by an arsonist, or whether we were the targets. The answer seemed chillingly clear.

'Somebody wants to kill Lance,' I blurted.

'I wouldn't jump to that conclusion,' McDonald said. 'There are easier ways to do that.' He shrugged. 'Just wait outside Planet Hollywood and shoot him in the head. Nobody has to blow up a building or set fire to the whole goddam county to whack him. From what we understand, the chances of his actually performing that warehouse stunt were remote from the start. Why risk it when you know you're probably gonna take down the wrong man?

'We're looking into Talon's background, his personal life, working relationships, who profits from his death. The usual.'

'But what about the fire? Isn't that too much of a coincidence? We almost get killed out in the 'Glades the same night? Twice in one day?'

'We've talked to Metro fire. Their theory at this point is that careless smoking probably sparked it.'

'Not true. I swear, McDonald. What about Stephanie?'

'We'll talk to her, when we find her. And we are looking into her background. But how realistic is it to think that she could steal the plans and rewire the panel? We have no shortage of crazies, like the lady with the love potion — who is free on bond, by the way. But common sense says: not realistic.'

'Don't underestimate Stephanie,' I warned. 'She has a talent for slipping past security, in and out of houses, hotel rooms, the newspaper. She's capable of anything, and she's dangerous.'

'I said we'll talk to her, but at this point we don't even know if the woman is still in Miami.'

'Oh, she's here,' I said. 'She's here. I can feel it.'

★ ★ ★

The feeding frenzy grew even more manic after the police press conference. Headlines read DISASTER STALKS MOVIE MAKERS. Writers for the tabloids and crews from *Inside Edition*, *Hard Copy*, and *Entertainment Tonight* swarmed into town like locusts. TV newscasts reporting that Lance was present when the 'Glades fire ignited kept playing and replaying a clip from *The Last Gunfighter*, one in which Lance takes a last drag on a cigarette, tosses it aside with reckless abandon, draws his gun, and swaggers down a dusty street. From that, they cut directly to flaming acreage.

The honeymoon was over.

And the fire continued to rage. The Krome Detention Center, a holding facility for illegal aliens located on the fringe of the 'Glades, was evacuated at dusk. Nearly a thousand inmates were loaded on to buses. Visibility was zero, due to the smoke, and a chain-reaction rear-end collision resulted. One hundred and seventy-four illegals — Haitians, Cubans, Dominicans, Salvadorans, three men from Bangladesh, a child molester from Berlin, and a con man from Canada — escaped in the confusion.

Hospital ERs now overflowed with patients suffering from smoke-related conditions. Environmentalists were enraged. Politicians saw which way the smoke was blowing and joined the fray, demanding answers. In the capitol, the governor was ducking the press until the matter could be thoroughly researched, which meant until his advisers decided which of them would be sacrificed and thrown under the bus.

I got back from covering the escape of the aliens, who had vanished into the smoky haze, and found messages from Angel Oliver, Sam Bliss, and a familiar caller who wanted to massage my feet.

Now, I thought, irritated, Angel wants to talk, when I'm as backed up as a cheap toilet. Her timing was lousy. Please call, her message said. Bliss's said *urgent*.

'Britt,' he said, 'we need your help.'

'Swell,' I said, wishing my sinuses would open. 'I can't even help myself right now.'

'You're in tight with the movie crew. You could do us a favor and open the door. Keep it to yourself,' he said, lowering his voice, 'but there's a hit out on Angel Oliver.'

'That's not exactly a bulletin. I was there, remember?' What did that have to do with the movie crew? I wondered. 'Did you find out who wants to kill her?'

'Probably a lotta people, but the one who put out the hit was Darnell.' He sounded sheepish. 'Her ex-husband.'

'She was right! The guy you said was such a nice fellow! How'd you find out? Are you sure? Did he really have somebody shoot at his kids?'

Bliss filled me in. Turned out, police knew about the murder attempt before the shooting, but not the right police, and as we all know, in this age of communication, cops often have trouble communicating with each other.

A PLO member, a kid named Omar, had been shipped out of Miami by his parents and a judge, to save him from the influence of the bad-asses he hung out with. Sent to live with out-of-town family members, he was put to work on a construction crew in Orlando, the same construction crew

305

foremanned by Darnell Oliver. Soon he and Darnell were chatting about how Darnell would like to get rid of his ex-wife down in Miami. Omar said he had buddies who could do the job and made a few calls. Then he bragged to a cousin, who told another cousin, who happened to be a snitch.

The snitch told an Orlando detective that gang members were coming up from Miami for a business meeting at a hotel on the Orange Blossom Trail. The detective and his partner staked out the Orange Blossom Trail Econo Lodge, between a McDonald's and an ABC Liquor store. Sure enough, a carload arrived and there was much exchanging of gang handshakes with Omar in the parking lot. The detectives shot surveillance photos as what appeared to be pictures, information, and a cash down payment changed hands. Darnell was clever enough not to show his face.

The Orlando detectives were gung ho to pursue it, but their supervisor refused to authorize the overtime. He said it was Miami's problem. So they passed the intelligence to a Miami gang unit detective. The car's tag came back as stolen. All they really knew was that 'a dude who works construction in Orlando' had put out a hit with teen gang members on 'a broad who lives near the Orange Bowl in Miami.'

After bullets flew the next day, the Miami detective put two and two together and called his Orlando counterparts. They took their film to a one-hour photo service, then to the airport, where they gave the pictures to the Delta pilot on the next Miami flight. A detective met the plane.

Local gang detectives recognized the PLO members and the car. It was the Bonneville. Bliss and the gang detective flew to Orlando to put the squeeze on Omar at his cousin's house. They needed his cooperation to nail Darnell.

Omar was recalcitrant, but detectives had brought along his probation officer, who threatened to revoke him on the spot. That was when Omar spilled the gruesome details. Darnell was pissed, he said, not only because the clumsy attempt had failed but because the hit men had not followed his carefully formulated plan.

The deal was to abduct Angel and leave her body in a not-too-remote area. He wanted her found. His instructions were explicit. He wanted her heart cut out, so police would attribute the murder to the unidentified serial killer responsible for four similar cases. That way he would never be considered a suspect.

Yuck, I thought. This from the man who wanted only to raise his kids to study hard and be good God-fearing Christians.

During the drive back to Miami, the gang decided that Darnell's plan was too gross for even them to carry out. Dead was dead. However they accomplished the mission, they decided, Darnell would be satisfied. They reverted to their usual method, a drive-by shooting.

Though pissed, Darnell still wanted it done, Omar said. He wanted the killers to take a camera along this time. Before he paid the $1,500 balance, he wanted to see proof that the job had been done his way.

'We need to accommodate him,' Bliss said. 'Much as I'd like to do the world a real favor, we can't actually remove Angel's internal organs. We'll have to fake it. That's where you and your Hollywood pals come in. There's gotta be somebody on that crew who can help us make Angel look dead, so we can take pictures. Then we can put a wire on Omar and have him deliver them to Darnell. We need to be convincing enough that he hands over the money. Then we bust his ass.'

'You want her to look like her heart's been cut out?'

'And her throat slashed, right.'

'I know the perfect guy. But why don't you just call them?'

'It's awkward for us to approach them right now with the stuntman's murder investigation in progress. You have better access, Britt; you're on better terms with them.'

'McDonald know about this?'

'He's the one who told me to call you.'

So much for McDonald's thoughtful advance tip on the press conference and old times' sake. He wanted to use me, as the press and the police so often use each other.

'Maybe you could even write a story,' Bliss said hopefully. 'You know, that Angel was killed by the heart taker. Omar could show him the newspaper along with the picture.'

'Forget it. No way would we print a phony story. But the special effects expert and the pictures, that's doable. On one condition. When you guys bust Darnell, I wanna be there.'

'What for, Britt?'

'Hell, Sam, I almost got killed. Those little SOBs he sent to waste Angel shot at me too.'

★ ★ ★

The movie company was shooting a scene at a small motel down on the river. Security was tight. When Rad Johnson spotted me, he whispered in Wendy's ear. I assumed she would have me launched into the street like the rest of the media. Instead, she and Van Ness trotted over like old friends, eager to know what I had learned about the murder investigation.

They had been 'terribly hurt' by the 'unfair' *News* editorial. Back in LA, even Alan Cappleman, the head of the studio, was upset, they said.

'We lost our reactor,' Van Ness said plaintively. 'And we can't rebuild in that burned-out area. It's a mess. Now we have to find a new location for it.'

'In the state of Florida?' I asked skeptically.

'You think that'd be a problem?'

'Why would it be?' Wendy whined.

In response, I rolled my bloodshot eyes toward the western horizon, obscured by a pall of smoke that made it difficult to breathe at the moment.

'You heard about the escaped aliens?' I said, 'and the incident during the evacuation of the animals at the Metrozoo?' During the confusion, a collection of tropical birds had escaped from the aviary. A number had landed on the small manmade island where tigers run free in their natural habitat.

A zoo handler, trying to save Lulu, the crested Amazon parrot famous for speaking in three languages, fired a tranquilizer gun at one of the big cats. Snowflake, the rare white tiger, was hit, staggered, fell into the moat, and drowned before they could save him.

A TV news crew shooting the evacuation caught the carnage. The piece picked up by the network ended in a poignant freeze frame, feathers afloat on the water.

The producers looked puzzled. 'We didn't tell them to build a zoo way out there,' Van Ness said righteously.

'But you promised that when you finished the movie you would put things back the way they were.'

Lance had emerged from the motel room where they were shooting.

'Knew you couldn't stay away.' He still sounded hoarse but looked buff in a faded blue denim shirt and jeans. This was the first time we had seen each other since the night the fire ignited. Our eyes caught.

'Actually, I'm here to see Ziff.'

★ ★ ★

Ziff was busy fashioning a severed arm for a sequence in which one of the villains would lose a bout with a helicopter blade. He was thrilled that the police wanted his help.

'Painted faces for a PBA picnic? A training

film? I've done dismembered corpses, alien autopsies, vampire hookers, and the walking dead.' He smiled expectantly.

'Remember the news stories about Angel Oliver, the woman accused of starving her baby?'

'Personally,' he confessed, removing his apron, 'I'm sort of a news idiot. I try to stay away from it. It's such a messy world. I don't really want to know all that much. I tend to make my own little world and ignore the rest. You know, it's frustrating, a real downer, because what can you do about it?'

He had a point.

But he couldn't wait to meet Angel, especially after he heard she'd been accused of murder. And he adored the assignment.

'I think I've done that very thing,' he said, an index finger to his lips, black polish gleaming. 'Did you see *Grim Reaper II*?'

'No,' I confessed, 'I tend to stay away from the world of horror flicks. It's so messy, a real downer.'

The caterer had set up a lavish buffet with a river view, under the cypress trees behind the motel, and Lance invited me to stay for lunch. I waited at a shady table while he talked to his agent on long distance. One of the crew, Norman, the Best Boy, loaded his plate with shrimp and sliced steak and sat next to me. Hardly a boy, in his late fifties, he wore work clothes and an assortment of screwdrivers in his belt. He always seemed to be the busiest man on the set.

'So.' I dropped my voice. 'Are you really as good as they say?'

He nearly spit up a shrimp.

'Well, given your title. I always wonder what Best Boy means when I see it in movie credits.'

'I don't go for coffee,' he said indignantly. 'That's what some people think.' He blotted his mouth with his napkin, eager to explain. No reporter had ever asked him the question.

'My responsibilities are varied,' he said, and put down his fork. 'I make sure that all the electrical and lighting equipment works. If it doesn't, I fix it. I make sure that the gaffer, the chief set electrician, and the lighting director have the equipment they need when they need it. The lights take a lot of juice, and we usually use portable generators. I run the power cables from the generator to the set and deliver the right amount of electricity. And I provide the power for the wind and rain machines.'

'Wish you could make it rain now,' I said wistfully.

'Oh, we will. Tomorrow. But only on our set.' He squinted at the horizon. 'Wish we could put it out. It's messing up all the outdoor shots.'

'Tell me about it. So where did the name Best Boy come from?'

'Don't know,' he said, 'but I've got no quarrel with it. I am the best.'

'What do you think happened with Trent's stunt? What went wrong?'

Norman's smile faded, and he sipped his iced tea before answering. 'The cops are right. Whatever it was, it was no accident. Don't say I said it, but it had to be deliberate.'

'Did it take an electronics genius, an engineer, to do it?'

'Not at all, especially with the schematics. It would've been simple. Anybody who can change a light bulb could've switched those wires.'

'You think Trent had any real enemies — ' What sounded like chanting nearly drowned us out. The noise came from the front of the building.

The door to Lance's trailer opened. His big frame dwarfed the entrance. 'What's that?' He looked apprehensive.

'Must be some extras rehearsing,' I said.

It wasn't.

An earsplitting blast from an air horn sounded, and the chants resumed even louder.

'What are they saying?' Norman stopped chewing and listened.

'Ex-tremers?' I tried to make out each syllable.

'Oh, no!' Lance jumped down to the ground. He looked pale. 'It can't be.'

* * *

At least seventy-five men, women, and children surrounded the front of the motel. They wore green ribbons and waved picket signs and horns. THINK BEFORE YOU CROAK said one sign, bearing a picture of frogs on a lily pad. Others said HOLLYWOOD GO HOME!, HANDS OFF THE 'GLADES, SMOKE AT OUR OWN RISK, illustrated by a drawing of flame-threatened wild animals, and DON'T DESTROY TOMORROW TODAY! Two attractive children, young teenagers, a boy and a girl, held a huge green banner, EARTH SCREAMERS.

'Brendan! Shelley!' Lance cried.

'Why'd you do it, Dad?' they chanted. 'Why'd you do it, Dad?'

They continued to chant, shrugging off his attempts to hug them.

'My God, Renee.' Lance turned helplessly

toward a woman carrying a sign that said, NO MARGIN OF ERROR!

In her late thirties, she had a deep tan, crystal-blue eyes, and raven-black hair beginning to gray. She wore sandals, a khaki skirt, and a forest-green shirt.

'Own up to it, Lance!' She brandished her sign at him, the way a believer would brandish a cross at a vampire.

He peered around it, trying to reason with her.

Each time he attempted to speak, shattering blasts from the air horns drowned him out.

He backed off for a moment, rejoining Norman and me. Others from the movie crew had gathered.

'What the hell?' Van Ness cried, hands over his ears.

This must be the first Mrs Westfell, I thought.

'My first wife — and my kids,' Lance confirmed. He looked stricken.

'I thought they were in Brazil.'

'So did I.'

EARTH SCREAMERS, I later learned, had evolved into an ecological SWAT team, swooping into hot spots, wherever there was a threat to the planet.

Several TV trucks and radio news cars

pulled up. Fear replaced arrogance in Van Ness's eyes.

Hodges stepped out of the motel room where they had been setting up shots. He wore a baseball cap over his curly hair and blinked in the sunlight. 'We're going to need quiet, people,' he announced. 'We're making a movie here.'

The shouts and blasts nearly knocked him off his feet.

'People of Dade County,' Renee Westfell said into a bristling bouquet of microphones. 'Before this disastrous fire, Miami's mold and pollen count had hit a ten-year high. Mount Trashmore, your garbage dump, is full and leaking lethal amounts of ammonia into Biscayne Bay. Seeping landfills are threatening your drinking water. The chemical plants and phosphate mines upstate are creating toxic clouds of poisonous gas, clou-uds of ammonia.' The woman was a pro, her delivery superb.

'Ozone damage is killing the amphibians.' Her voice rose. 'The sea grass is dying. Mercury is poisoning the fish, and red tide is killing the manatees. And now the moviemakers who expose and inure your children to violence are despoiling your most precious natural resource for their own greedy motives.

317

'Your politicians sold out to the filmmakers and allowed them to build on environmentally sensitive national parkland, and it now appears clear that careless smoking and reckless behavior by the star is responsible for the fire now ravaging this treasure essential to our future well-being.'

Damn. She's right on target, I thought, about everything but Lance. I saw what was about to happen, too late to warn him. The cameras swung toward Lance and Van Ness, as reporters sought a response.

'That is not true. I swear I did not start that fire,' Lance said. But nobody else heard him. The chants — 'No Margin of Error!' — and the air horns drowned him out.

17

Her lips and fingers were blue, throat slashed, clothes savaged, chest cavity open. Rib cartilage exposed. Blood everywhere. Big eyes half open in a lifeless stare.

The corpse was perfect, except that she had to keep getting up to go pee, apparently a symptom of her pregnancy.

Ziff had done a helluva job. He spilled

blood, spattered gore, and dripped body fluids with an artist's precision and top-of-the-line technique. He and Angel had hit it off from the start as he measured and studied her. Then he had fashioned a mold of her chest, using latex and clay.

McDonald was there, in plain clothes. So was Sam Bliss, and Lottie with her camera. Lance and Niko were there too, free at the moment because the filmmakers had been forced into court for an injunction to stop Earth Screamers from further disrupting their shooting schedule.

'How come, in those movies, you never run out of bullets?' Angel asked Lance as he signed autographs for her children, who were then whisked away. A rookie policewoman had endured six months of calisthenics, torment, and survival training at the police academy to qualify for this assignment, baby-sitting Angel's kids for the afternoon.

'Yeah,' said Lottie, 'and why isn't the movie ever as good as the book?'

'Because they don't read the books,' he said. 'Sam Goldwyn was once shooting a big movie based on a best-seller and was asked if he'd read it. He said, 'A book that good, you don't need to read.' '

I was glad to see Lance smile. We both

felt ragged and looked it. I had seen his eyes as he watched Angel and her children and knew he was thinking of his own. After the encounter with Renee and the Earth Screamers, he had spent lunch muttering, 'It was always me, always my fault. That's how it always was.' I got the impression he had spent the night on the phone with Silverman, his LA therapist.

Ziff had reported morale among the crew as 'lower than a snake's belly,' adding that a Cuban-born cameraman was actually blaming a Castro plot for the company's misfortunes.

The fire, still sweeping south, had closed both US 1 and Card Sound Road, cutting off the only land routes to the Keys, traveled by more than twenty thousand cars a day. With the roads closed, the paper had to hire a cargo plane to deliver the *Miami News* to Key West. Tourists were fleeing Miami and its haze, and the Department of the Interior had launched an inquiry, not of the fire but into how permission was granted the movie company to build the reactor in the 'Glades.

'*Margin of Error* is turning into a budget-blaster,' Lance told Lottie and me over coffee in Angel's spacious new kitchen. 'Every day is money on location, and we're so far behind schedule now . . . ' He shook his head.

Being out, away from the filmmakers, was healthy for him, a good idea, I thought.

McDonald and Bliss were even civil, and their anticipation was contagious. We all shared the same goal, nailing the bad guy.

'Well, what do you think of Angel?' I asked Lance privately.

'She's like Demeter,' he said, 'the ripe and fertile earth mother in Greek mythology. Always pregnant, bountiful breasts always filled with milk. She wandered the planet in search of her lost daughter, Persephone, who was stolen and spirited into the underworld by Hades.'

'Fertile, yes,' I conceded. 'But her daughter wasn't stolen. She starved.'

What we were doing, I realized, could, in effect, orphan Angel's children. If we were successful, the father could go to jail for life, the same sentence Angel faced if convicted in her baby's death. Justice for all but the children.

★ ★ ★

Ziff worked on Angel in the sunny Florida room, as a crime-scene technician video taped the entire process. Supine, on a large

321

worktable, lying on a backboard borrowed from a rescue unit, Angel seemed in surprisingly good spirits for a woman in such a sobering situation.

She and Ziff giggled, whispered, and shared secrets. She must be relieved that the police believe her, I thought, and that if everything worked as planned Darnell would soon be out of circulation. And she had every reason to be happy about her living arrangements. I know I was impressed.

After whisking Angel and her kids out of their bullet-riddled, low-cost housing-project apartment, the cops had moved her into a spacious $375,000 five-bedroom Miami Beach home seized by the federal government from a drug dealer. This was an example of the tools the feds were providing to local cops battling domestic violence.

'Do you believe this?' I whispered to Lottie, as we strolled through the dining room with its crystal chandelier, delivering coffee to the others. 'If we were homeless, Jimmy Carter would build us houses; if we had husbands trying to kill us, the government would put us up in luxury. But no, we're just working stiffs.'

'Where did we go wrong?' Lottie wondered.

'The kids hated that apartment by the Orange Bowl,' Angel was saying, staring at the ceiling as Ziff matted her pale hair with fake blood, a mix of corn syrup and food coloring. 'We were the only ones in the neighborhood who didn't speak Spanish.'

The big backyard, overgrown since the prior owner's arrest, was the perfect place to shoot the pictures. Angel's mutilated body was slid gently off the backboard into weedy centipede grass, amid a wild outcropping of Surinam cherry bushes.

'Geez, think it was a good idea to put her in the poison ivy?' Niko quipped, prompting giggles from the corpse.

'You play dead now,' Ziff demanded, smearing gore on the surrounding leaves with a spatula. 'This is serious.'

Her carotid artery appeared to be cut just left of center so that blood had gushed over her shoulder. Crimson spurts and droplets stained the weeds and leaves.

The effect was horrifying. Unconsciously, we all began to speak in the hushed tones used in the presence of the dead. Most chilling was knowing that this grisly tableau was what Darnell wanted for real.

'Anybody who glances over that fence

will have a heart attack,' I warned. We all had seen real corpses who looked more alive than Angel did now.

'It's high enough that there shouldn't be a problem,' McDonald said.

The cops shot tape, to document the scene, and snapped the Polaroids for Darnell. If they did not convince him, nothing would. Lottie fired off pictures as well, probably too gory for use in the *News* once the story broke, but Ziff wanted prints for his scrapbook.

Bliss lightened the mood as the photo session ended. 'Okay,' he said, 'get the shovel. We can bury her now.'

Back inside the house, Ziff helped Angel remove the phony chest cavity and much of the gore; then we all ate sandwiches while she showered. The kitchen was stocked with boxes and boxes of plastic forks, spoons, tiny packets of powdered milk, sugar, mustard, mayo, and relish. The former owner was apparently big on convenience.

'These are great hurricane supplies,' I noted.

'The only hurricane supply I would need, honey, is enough gas,' Ziff said, 'to get out of town.'

Bliss and Santangelo, the gang unit detective, already had their tickets to Orlando. Santangelo had been recruited into the unit right out of the police academy. He looked seventeen, baby-faced and slightly built. Posing as a PLO member, he and Omar would deliver the pictures to Darnell and pick up the incriminating cash. I called the *News* and had Gloria put me on the same flight, which left in a few hours.

Lance wanted to go along.

The cops were not crazy about it. Our deal had included me only. But McDonald called the chief, who surprised everybody by agreeing as long as nothing compromised the case.

Niko booked two first-class tickets aboard the same flight.

As Lottie and I left Angel's, McDonald called me aside.

'I learned patience years ago,' he said, his expression serious, 'when I was a rookie in robbery, waiting in the bushes for twelve hours for somebody to rob a Seven-Eleven.'

What was this man talking about?

'But I've almost lost it,' he said. 'You're falling for this guy's pitch. I can see the stars in your eyes.'

'What pitch?' What *was* he talking about?

'Fertile earth mother, my ass.'

'You were eavesdropping!' I said, surprised at him. 'Don't you worry about me, I know what I'm doing.'

* * *

Skies were clear, once our flight ascended above the smoke. I switched seats with Niko and joined Lance in first class as soon as we were airborne.

The flight attendants, who usually only acknowledge my existence by flinging tiny packets of peanuts, fawned all over us.

'Not bad.' I sipped the complimentary champagne. 'A pity the flight's too short for a movie.'

'Wish we could keep going.' He sighed and leaned back in the comfortable seat. 'Hawaii, Paris, Mexico . . . '

'I thought you were the man who loved Miami at first sight.'

'I do.' He took my hand. 'It's just everything that's been going down . . . You know.'

The flight was too short.

* * *

Omar, a gangly kid with tattooed arms, was wired for sound.

The high-tech police surveillance van equipped with video and audio tape equipment was crowded: Bliss, in his blue suit, two Orlando detectives, a patrolman in

326

uniform, Lance, and me. Niko nursed coffee and a burger in the McDonald's while we parked outside the Econo Lodge.

Omar had called Darnell to set up the meet. 'Need to see you.' Every word was monitored.

'Can't it wait till morning?' Darnell grumbled.

'No, man, you don't wanna talk about this on the job site. You got cause to celebrate. Somebody just came up from Miami with some pictures you're gonna like. Bring the cash.'

It was growing dark when Omar drove into the lot in a battered blue Camaro accompanied by Santangelo. He had said that Darnell drove a white Ford pickup, so we nearly missed him when he pulled up alongside in what must have been his wife's car, a dark blue Nissan.

'There he is! There he is!' Bliss said urgently.

Adrenaline pumped. As we all stared out the tinted glass, Lance's hand crept beneath my skirt and up my thigh. I flexed my thigh muscles, trapping his fingers.

'Shit!' exploded the Orlando detective monitoring and recording the wire.

Omar had tested the wire while they waited, and we had heard him loud and clear. Now there was interference, a low steady buzz, and static.

Slightly shifting position, I brushed my right breast against Lance's forearm.

The interference vanished as quickly as it had appeared.

'Who's this?' we heard Darnell ask. The three were standing between the Camaro and the Nissan now. Darnell was husky, with light hair. Good-looking, except for a slight overbite.

'Buddy a mine from Miami,' Omar said. 'You don't wanna know his name.'

'Right, right,' Darnell said. His voice bore traces of a southern accent and sounded tinny.

Lance, his fingers still caught between my thighs, was scrutinizing me in the semidarkness instead of the scenario unfolding half a parking lot away. Slowly, I licked my lips.

'We handled everything,' Santangelo said.

'Hope it went better than last time.'

'It went perfecto. We got the job done. Just the way you wanted it.'

'So how do I know?' Darnell sounded suspicious. 'You got something to show me?'

A slim sliver of skin showed between the back of Lance's shirt and the waistband of his jeans as he crouched in the van.

'You bring the cash?'

'Come on, come on,' Bliss muttered.

I put my index finger in my mouth, as though in suspense, then casually removed it and smeared the wet digit across that bare sliver of skin.

I felt him shiver.

'I wanna see proof, first. Did the bitch buy it this time?'

'Here we go,' Bliss chortled. 'Here we go.'

'Do it, do it,' the Orlando detective next to him coaxed softly.

'Lookit this.' Santangelo removed the two Polaroids from his shirt pocket. He handed one to Darnell, then the other.

'Jesus,' Darnell said. He took a step back, holding the pictures up to better see them in the twilight. 'You really did her. She's outa my hair permanently now. How come I ain't heard nothing from Miami?'

'Nobody even knows who she is yet. They just found the body.'

'You really did it,' Darnell repeated softly. 'She suffer?'

'Whadda you think?'

Scribbling notes, I wondered if Darnell was feeling remorse or experiencing second thoughts. He wasn't.

'This picture is worth to me ten times what I'm paying you,' he crowed.

My thighs released their grip on Lance's

329

hand. His fingers advanced.

'She gives me any trouble, maybe we can do my mother-in-law next.' Darnell was talking his way into a prison cell.

The cops in the van were grinning. So was Lance. His probing fingers had reached first base. I wondered if my notes would make any sense when I tried to read them later.

'Get the money,' Bliss whispered. 'Get the money.'

'Here you go,' Darnell said. 'It's all here.'

'Here we go,' Bliss said.

'Nice doing business with you.'

That line was the prearranged signal.

'Let's take 'im!' The van's door burst open as the cops jumped out and ran.

'I wanna jump you. Right here,' Lance muttered in my ear.

'We can't.' I jumped out and ran after the cops.

Marked police cars raced out of nowhere, blocking all the parking lot exits. An Orlando PD SWAT team scrambled out of another van across the street and charged into the lot in full gear. The police presence was overwhelming, overkill if you ask me, especially since they knew Darnell's name and where he lived.

Santangelo was struggling with Darnell,

330

who had stuffed the pictures in his mouth. Omar was walking away, looking skyward, hands apart, pretending he was not involved.

Darnell found it difficult to chew and swallow two three-by-five Polaroids with a policeman gripping his throat.

He coughed them up.

He knew he had been had.

Head down, handcuffed, he sneaked a peek up at Lance, who had followed me out of the van.

'You're him.' He squinted.

'Who?' Lance said.

'Him, you're him!'

'Yeah.'

'Why did you hire people to kill the mother of your children?' I asked.

He mumbled that he had nothing to say.

★   ★   ★

Bliss and Santangelo would return home with their prisoner in the morning. The Orange County state attorney had granted permission for the charges, solicitation to commit first-degree murder, to be transferred to Miami.

'Let's stay up here overnight,' Lance whispered in the cab to the airport. 'We can

331

go to that new hotel at Disney World.'

'Can't. Have to go back and write the story.'

He put his hand on my knee and nibbled at my ear. 'Call it in.'

'Van Ness and Wendy don't even know you're out of town.'

'They'd be pissed if they knew,' he acknowledged, and stopped nibbling.

We discussed Darnell and Angel for the remainder of the ride.

'When you dig a grave for somebody else,' Lance said, 'you always wind up falling into it.'

'Amen.' Niko nodded.

'Great line,' I said. 'I'd love to use it in my story. Is that original, or dialogue from one of your movies?'

Lance thought about it. 'Don't know. Niko?'

Niko screwed up his face. 'Maybe. Sounds familiar.'

'Think it coulda been *Ground Zero*?' Lance said.

'I was thinking maybe *Dead by Sundown*.'

'No, no,' Lance said. Both were lost in thought.

'Never mind,' I said. 'I won't use it.'

★ ★ ★

The sexual tension sparked in the surveillance van was electric. We could not keep our hands off each other. After two glasses of champagne I checked out the rest room. Pretty small on a Boeing 727, and Lance was a big man, but maybe.

I returned to my seat. 'I've always heard about the mile high club,' I whispered. There were only a few other passengers in first class. The entire plane was nearly empty, due to the fire. Nobody was going to Miami unless they had to.

I went first. Lance casually meandered up the aisle and joined me a minute later.

'Where have you been?' I said, when he opened the door.

There was little room to maneuver. I wound up with one foot in the sink, then sitting in it. 'This is never going to work,' I panted.

'We can make it work.' He grunted, breathing hard. 'I've been wanting to bite you all week.'

'Ouch,' I said. The faucet jabbed the small of my back. 'How do people do this?'

Just when it seemed we might be getting somewhere, a cheerful voice advised that all passengers should return to their seats; we were about to land in Miami.

When we ignored it, the flight attendant

tapped on the door.

'We're busted,' I said.

'We can do this,' he said urgently, 'but not on this plane. I can lease a private jet.'

Jammed face to face, we struggled to open the door. What madman designed this bathroom? I wondered bitterly. Who on earth would put a soap dispenser in a place like that?

I stepped out first, avoiding the eyes of the flight attendants, already buckled in their jump seats right outside the rest room. By the time Lance joined me, I could see the wildfire from the air, as we swept in over the Everglades. 'Look at that,' I said. 'It looks worse.'

I was right. The pilot announced that the raging fire had affected the power lines along US 1. The entire Upper Keys were blacked out.

18

I went straight to the paper to write for the final.

Bobby Tubbs, working the night slot, complained about a flood of calls, including

Van Ness, Wendy, the production's publicist, and Wallace Atwater, all looking for Lance. The former were worried about him showing up for work and the last was concerned about the benefit. Channel 7's entertainment reporter had announced on the news at six that 'the final blow may have come to the beleaguered *Margin of Error* production' with unconfirmed reports that the star had packed up and left town. Somebody must have spotted Lance at the airport.

'That's ridiculous. He's right here in Miami,' I said truthfully.

The stack of messages awaiting me included one from the *National Enquirer*. I shoved them aside and called Angel for a quote for my story. 'Now the children and I can go on with our lives,' she said demurely.

'Well, keep your head down and stay out of your old neighborhood until the cops pick up the kids who shot at us. I'm serious,' I warned. 'As far as they know, nothing has changed. You don't want to wind up in their gun sights again.'

The irony of the story was that the same cops who originally arrested Angel had probably saved her life.

'They were wonderful,' she said. 'Did you notice that lieutenant's beautiful blue eyes?'

'Yeah,' I said. 'I noticed.'

Her current boyfriend, she said, was in the Navy. Once everything was straightened out and he was home on leave, they planned to marry.

It would be nice, I thought, if the wedding date arrived before the new baby.

'He loves kids,' she was saying.

Lucky for him, I thought.

'Once my charges are cleared up,' she said, 'we'll have a normal life.'

'I've been wanting to talk to you about your case,' I said. 'What is the current status? Is there a trial date? Are you negotiating a plea?'

'No plea,' she said firmly. 'There's another hearing in two weeks. My lawyer said not to talk to you about it until then.'

I took his number and left a message on his machine.

Before going home, I watched the eleven o'clock news. Renee Westfell appeared on all three local stations, a tape from that afternoon, speaking in front of a crowd of Earth Screamers that had been picketing the *Margin of Error* production office. Their numbers seemed to be growing, despite a judge's ruling that, though they had the right to demonstrate, they could not continue to disrupt filming with their air horns. Some carried signs saying REMEMBER SNOWFLAKE.

There was even a Cuban contingent waving signs that said [ex]COMMUNISTA! I turned up the sound.

'Hollywood must be made to realize,' Renee was saying, 'that making a movie is not the end of the world. Taking care of people and the planet is what counts.' Who could argue with that?

The camera panned the crowd. Seated at my desk watching the monitor, I could have sworn that for a split second I saw Stephanie's face among them. I sprang to my feet, staring. Too late. No way to be sure. It infuriated me that I had to drive home watching the rearview and wondering.

My restless half-sleep was interrupted in the middle of the night by the pounding and the wet kiss of rain. The winter wind blew so hard that a fine spray cascaded through the screens over my bed, and I had to get up to close the windows. Torrential rains still fell at dawn, a blessing for exhausted firefighters and all of us. By late afternoon, the smoke had cleared enough to reopen the road to the Keys, and the island chain was reconnected to the mainland. All told, the fire had consumed more than 3,900 acres.

Uncharacteristically gray skies leaked chilly rain for three days straight.

Now that the fire was out, forestry

personnel had a chance to go back and investigate. They can look at a burn and see how it started. That was not difficult in this case. They found what set it, and it was not a Marlboro. It was a fuel can, commonly called a drip torch. Firefighters use them to set backfires on the ground. When it is tipped, a thin stream of fuel flows over a built-in wick and ignites the ground. The drip torch was marked, owned by the Forestry Service, one of two stolen from the back of a four-wheel drive at the ranger station nearest the nuclear reactor.

Oddly enough, even when reporting that Lance had been vindicated, that smoking was not the cause, the TV news still ran the same clip over and over, of him carelessly flinging away a cigarette just before pulling his gun.

I expected the rain to make everybody happy, but even the downpour seemed part of a grand conspiracy designed to further frustrate and delay the film crew. The day it began they had planned to shoot several rain scenes, including a provocative sequence with Lance and Lexie soaked to the skin, she wearing a skimpy little dress, him in his tight jeans. Perfect, I thought. But no. Real rain, I learned, does not photograph well. The only rain realistic enough for movies is spewed from rain machines operated in clear weather. Go figure.

Not only did they have to wait for the rain to stop so they could shoot the rain scene, the deluge also delayed construction of the new reactor. A developer, clearing land for a west Broward amusement park, leased the film company the property at exorbitant rates. He also insisted that the new reactor be a permanent structure he could later use as a tourist attraction; therefore it had to meet the tough new hurricane code and required architectural renderings, permits, and a licensed general contractor. Both the developer and the country required the filmmakers to provide huge bonds and private twenty-four-hour security.

Van Ness and Wendy were frantic, fielding daily calls from Cappleman's office. Originally budgeted at $60 million, the cost of the film had already skyrocketed to $100 million, and a half dozen lawsuits were pending, including a wrongful death action filed by Trent Talon's ex-wife in Seattle, on behalf of their three minor children.

★　★　★

The lone bright spot on the horizon was the AIDS benefit at Lance's Star Island home.

The cause was good, and whatever positive publicity it generated was sorely needed. Response was excellent. Those who did not buy tables because of Lance's star appeal bought them because everybody runs to see a disaster. At least that was his theory.

Lottie planned to wear her green velvet, so striking with her fiery hair, and I had a wonderful winter white dress with a low-cut back and a shawl of velvet over silk with a lavishly embroidered border, an *au courant* ensemble coordinated by my mother. She was undecided about her own attire: a black velvet evening suit if the night was cold, shimmery gold silk if the weather was hot. She looked beautiful in both.

She had an escort, a nice man named Jules, a widowed cosmetics company executive who had come to Miami to play golf. She was doing much better since the shooting that had solved the mystery of my father's death. For months afterward she had grieved like a new widow. Now, at age fifty-three, a new woman seemed to be emerging. I wished I could say the same for myself.

I had good reason to look forward to the big night. Lance and I had had no time together since the Orlando flight.

'You realize our last big date was Darnell's arrest?' he said by phone the morning of the

340

benefit. 'I'm looking forward to tonight. I'm hoping you leave your beeper home and bring your nightie.'

'What would you say if I left them both at home?'

He said he'd think about it — all afternoon.

★　★　★

Lottie was worked up into a lather herself, that afternoon. The rain had signaled a significant change in the weather. People up north, from Maine to the Carolinas, were digging out after a blizzard, and the first major cold front of the year had rolled into South Florida. Her green velvet would be perfect. She took the afternoon off to have her hair done, but then Gretchen beeped her and insisted she take an assignment. Photo was short-staffed, and somebody had to go out and shoot art to go with the weather story. There were fears that the tomato, snap bean, and strawberry blooms would be damaged and the citrus crop endangered. Farmers were fighting the freeze by sprinkling insulating water on to their plants.

'It's already after five o'clock,' Lottie wailed over the phone. 'Bad enough I have to work tomorrow. She knows I'm going to the benefit tonight. She's doing this deliberately, that bitch. Cocktails are at seven. By the time I go out and find some cold-weather art and shoot it, take it back in and soup it, write the captions and get outa here — then go home, get dressed, and drive over to Star Island — I'm gonna miss most a the evening.'

'Look,' I said. 'Gretchen's jealous because you're going and she's not. Don't let her make you crazy. Just do it. Fast. Then get out. Don't go far. Don't go all the way down to farm country. Pick someplace close. How about over on the Beach, down by Lummus Park? Find some chilly senior citizen bundled up in a winter coat, collar turned up, some old lady in a fur or some — '

'Yeah,' she interrupted. 'I have an idea. I've got it. See you later.'

* * *

I arrived an hour early. Lance was gorgeous in a tuxedo.

He opened the door himself. The house looked stunning. He looked stricken. 'You look beautiful.' He kissed my cheek. 'Bad news.'

'What else?'

'Actually,' he said, shamefaced, 'it's good news, bad news.'

342

'Good news first.'

'Renee let the kids come over to spend a few days.'

'Great. That's also the bad news?'

He nodded. 'They're here now.'

A sleep-over was obviously out of the question. I sighed, then laughed in resignation. 'That's good. You'll get a chance to play dad.'

'But that's not the role I planned for tonight.'

* * *

Candlelit tables with crystal bowls of flowers, ornate silver wine goblets, and exquisite linens were everywhere. I had thought it too cold to party outside, but outdoor heaters had been installed at strategic spots, including under the tables around the pool. An elegant uniformed chef, the glistening bay and a sparkling nighttime view of the skyline behind him, presided over a huge cast-iron skillet as big as my car. The paella had been simmering over hot coals all day. The house and grounds easily accommodated the tables, the guests, and the Peter Duchin Orchestra, leaving ample room for dancing. Not only were there full-service bars indoors and out, there was a third tucked into a poolside courtyard facing the bay, beside a seafood bar with shrimp, oysters, and stone crabs. Nearby, yet another chef grilled tiny potato crepes, serving them up with flourishes of caviar.

Security was tight as a drum. The guest list was checked at the guardhouse entrance, again at the gate, and a third time at the door, with extra security bolstered by off-duty cops.

Lance and I greeted guests at the door. His little girl Shelley, age twelve, joined us. Polite, quiet, and well mannered, she was dressed in green taffeta, a ribbon around her slim waist and a big lace collar. She seemed almost shy until she spotted Monica Atwater sporting a big black bow in her hair and a full-length chinchilla cape. Withdrawing her hand, the child looked up sweetly and said disdainfully, 'Fur is dead.' I could like this kid, I thought. Brendan preferred trailing around after Niko, apparently an old chum.

I thought my mother would swoon when she arrived and found me, not only well dressed but in such a lavish setting. She had to think she was hallucinating.

'I turn into a pumpkin, it all goes away at midnight,' I whispered, then introduced her and her date to Lance.

The matinee idol was on, his claymore smile exploding in 180-degree arcs, knocking out everybody for a hundred and fifty meters.

No one would ever guess at the demons haunting the movie set.

Lottie was smashing in her own tall, tomboy way. 'See, I knew you could do it,' I murmured. 'You're not even late.' Lance greeted her with a hug, turning heads. She was stunning in a sparkly silver sheath. Even Lexie, with Van Ness, Hodges, and Wendy, arched her neck and stared. Lexie's eyes roved the house, as though trying to spot anything she might have missed in the divorce settlement. It surprised me to see her, but the event was positive and the studio wanted the *Margin of Error* principals to make a good showing.

Cameras from *ET* and *Extra* taped arriving guests, conducted brief interviews with Lance, and spoke to celebrities outside the door, but no camera crews were permitted inside to disrupt the evening.

Everybody was there: The Estefans, Madonna and Carlos, Jon Secada, Julio Iglesias, Stallone, even Oprah, who is new to the neighborhood. The Atwaters were positively beside themselves. Lance, the perfect host, moved from table to table between courses, circulating among his guests.

During the second course, I saw Niko step through a side door and scan the crowd. His look was urgent. He found Lance, then whispered in his ear. They high-fived, then Lance turned, did a thumbs-up, excused himself, came to the table, and spoke in my ear.

'More good news. Miami PD just picked up Stephanie on the causeway. All dressed up with someplace to go. Looks like she was about to join us. Had an invitation in her purse and was dressed to kill, they said.'

We touched our champagne glasses. What a relief. The news that Stephanie was out of circulation added to the celebratory mood. Giddy, I wished more than ever that Lance and I could be alone.

Instead I indulged in the dessert, white chocolate pianos with dark chocolate keys, their open lids filled with red and golden raspberries drenched in zambione sauce. Absolutely decadent. I spotted Lottie laughing with Stallone. Turned out he remembered her and the magazine photos she had shot of him. He said they were among the best he'd ever had taken.

All in all, it was a swell night, a huge success that raised tons of money. Guests began to depart shortly after midnight. Most were gone by one. Saying good night to my mother and Jules, I said, 'Call me tomorrow.'

Uncertain, she looked around me. 'Where?'

she whispered. 'At home, Mom. At home,' I said angelically.

★ ★ ★

We wound up in the kitchen as the caterers cleared away the tables. Lance and I sipped more Cristal rose champagne, eyeing each other as the kids devoured countless white chocolate pianos. They had enormous staying power. I would have thought they would have gone to bed hours ago. Niko was hauling huge trays of leftover food out a side door to the garage. 'Taking it over to the food bank at the homeless shelter,' he explained.

The homeless would dine well. 'Nice idea,' I said. 'But why not wait till morning? Surely you don't want to drive around that neighborhood at this hour.'

He shrugged, unknotting his tie. 'Might spoil. I already told 'em I was on the way, and I'm armed and dangerous. No problem.' He grinned. 'Stephanie's in jail.'

'Stephanie's in jail,' I echoed, relishing the words. Sounded good to me.

There was no escaping the kids. They even tagged along when Lance walked me out to my car to say good night. Brendan looked so much like Lance, it was scary. They eyed me suspiciously as he kissed my cheek and helped me into the T-Bird.

'Nice kids,' I said softly.

'At least they're not trying to poke my eye out with a picket sign,' he murmured. 'Not at the moment.'

They stood in the driveway and waved, all three of them, as I drove out. I watched wistfully in the rearview as the family turned to reenter the house together, Lance in the middle, holding his daughter's hand, his other arm around his son.

★ ★ ★

I was mellow and relaxed from the champagne. The evening had been a huge success. This was a good time in my life, and they don't come often. So why did I still have bad dreams and trouble sleeping?

I analyzed my problem, lying beneath my feather comforter in the dark, as Billy Boots purred at my side. Something had gone wrong with my slumber switch, I decided. Turn it on and the lights in the brain go out so it can sleep. Turn it off and the awareness and arousal cells wake up. Hard as I tried, all I could find was the dimmer switch, which kept me drowsy and dopey but awake.

I finally gave up and watched *Island of the*

Dead, starring Lance Westfell. I groaned, smiling and not really surprised, when in a tense moment Lance's character refused to abandon a companion, saying, 'We go down, we go down together.'

* * *

Lottie called from the photo department the next morning, as I drank coffee and read the paper at my kitchen table, headachy and bleary-eyed.

'I'm dead,' she announced grimly. 'I dug myself a shallow grave.'

'Good morning to you too. What's wrong?'

'That cold-weather picture, that's what's wrong. Hell all Friday, Britt. Everything, my whole career, is down the tube.'

The paper was in front of me. The weather story had made the front page. So did her picture. It had been shot on South Beach.

A man, bundled up in a dark coat, stood at the sea wall, his thinning hair lifted by the ocean breeze. Hands jammed in his pockets, collar turned up, he was watching the seagulls. The caption read: 'Winter visitor Solomon Maxwell, 71, braces against the chill, weathering Miami's coldest day of the season Thursday, as the eastern seaboard shivers in a frigid blast. (Lottie Dane/News Staff)'

'Nothing wrong with it,' I said. 'It's fine.'

'He's dead,' Lottie said. 'The man is spitting up dirt. So am I.'

I stared at the photo. Solomon Maxwell smiled at the antics of the gulls. Hale and hearty, he had a twinkle in his eye. It was hard to believe that overnight he was gone.

'What happened? Was it natural causes?'

'How the hell would I know?'

'But I thought you said — '

'Stiff city. Dead since May.'

'How — ?' I began to suspect what had happened and hoped I was wrong. 'You didn't shoot this picture yesterday?'

'No. You know I didn't wanna be late to the benefit. Gretchen foisted the damn assignment on me at the last minute. I was supposed to be off.'

'When was it taken, Lottie?' My voice sounded stern.

'Last winter, February. You know how the desk always plays gimme, gimme, gimme; wants dozens a different pictures, then only uses one. I shot it for the weather story on the coldest day last season. Didn't get used. I remembered that box a unused pictures when we talked yesterday. Perfectly good shot. Why let it go to waste? The man was from New

York, a snowbird. I figured if he was back in town this year, he'd get a hoot out of it; if not, who was to know?'

'Who knew?'

'The widow. She wakes up this morning, opens her paper, and there's her dead husband, like a ghost, all smiles on page one. The caption says he was strolling around South Beach yesterday. She called the desk, hysterical.'

'You're dead.'

'Just drive a railroad spike into the base of my skull, right into the medulla oblongata.'

'Wait a minute. Wait a minute. Don't panic. Take a chill pill.' I got up and paced the kitchen as we talked. 'What's happened so far?'

'When she called, she got Gretchen, who told me. She can't wait to spring it at the eleven o'clock budget meeting. I swear, Britt, this is the murkiest water that's ever been under my bridge.'

'Okay. You need to apologize to the widow and keep her from suing for mental anguish, or whatever. Go see her, for Pete's sake, and make nice, woman to woman. Bring her some good prints of the picture. Maybe it's the last one taken of him. Say you made a horrible mistake. But first, go talk to Gretchen. She owes us big, remember?' We had surprised

351

her and a colleague in a compromising position last year, and when it all hit the fan, we kept our mouths shut and saved her job.

'It's payback time. Tell her we all do things we regret sometimes, but us women in the newsroom have to stick together. She'll know what you mean.'

'That crossed my mind.'

'Remind her about all the big awards you've won, all the hours you work, how you never call in sick, and that your Colombian earthquake pictures made it into the Pulitzer finals. If all else fails, plead temporary insanity.'

'Gotcha.'

Good grief, I thought, after we hung up. It was as though the curse stalking *Margin of Error* had rubbed off on her. Ridiculous, of course.

I called McDonald. 'Hear you picked up Stephanie last night.'

'Right,' he said.

'What have you charged her with?'

'Nothing.'

'Why not?'

'We talked to the woman. We have no evidence, no proof of any crime she's committed. She's an overzealous fan, but the woods are full of them.'

I perched on the arm of my favorite chair.

'So where is she now, the hospital?'

'That woman is perfectly lucid.'

I stood up. 'What are you saying?' My voice shook. 'Where is she now?'

'Don't ask me. She walked outa here hours ago.'

19

'How could you?'

'I'm investigating a homicide. That woman is not a prime suspect at this point. On what grounds would you have me put her in jail? What would your newspaper say if I violated her rights?'

I wanted to scream. 'What about our rights? To be able to live without looking over our shoulders? We almost got killed; my car was vandalized, my locker.'

'Did you see Stephanie Carrollton do any of those things?' He sounded tired.

'No.'

'Do you have any physical evidence or any eyeball witnesses who can place her there?'

'You know we don't.'

'The homicide is my prime concern,' he said.

'But we — '

'We. That's you and Westfell, right?'

'Yes,' I said hesitantly.

'I would think that when somebody chooses a career in show business they have to expect to deal with some loss of privacy. You do have legal recourse; there are steps you can take if you feel personally threatened.'

I huffed and puffed impatiently. 'Did you at least get an address on her?'

'Sure.'

I heard him shuffle papers.

'She's subleasing an apartment on Hibiscus Island. Has a rental car with proper papers, a bank account. This is not a street person.'

No wonder she never missed anything. Hibiscus and Palm are twin islands just west of Star, where Lance was staying. How convenient. I jotted down the address.

'How'd she get a ticket to the benefit?'

'Said she was invited by her fiancé, the host.'

'What was she driving?' I demanded, my fury rising. 'What the hell was she driving?'

'Britt, listen to yourself. What do you — ?'

'Oh, so she gets to know everything about us, but — ' There was that us again. I knew it annoyed him when I said it.

'Okay, okay,' he said. 'She's got an Olds, a

silver Aurora.' He read me the tag number, and I repeated it after him. 'Britt, I'm worried about you.'

'So am I,' I snapped. 'Far be it from you to do anything until it's too late, until there's a tragedy.' I slammed the phone down.

My beeper, in its charger on my bedroom dresser, began to chirp. I was off today; what the hell was this? I ignored it.

I called Star Island. Niko answered.

'Went great last night, didn't it?' He sounded relaxed.

'I know where Stephanie is.'

'In jail?'

I laid it on him.

'Shit,' he said. 'Those bastards. McDonald is a — '

'I'm going over to her place,' I said.

'Wait,' he insisted. 'I'll go with you. You can't go alone.'

He was right.

'What about Lance?'

'Definitely not. It would play right into her hands. That's exactly what she wants, attention from him. She'd love it.'

He was right.

'I'll pick you up at the guardhouse on Star.' It was on my way. 'I'm leaving now.'

'Okay. I'll call her family's lawyer in Boston. So they know where she is.'

I dashed into the bedroom. The beeper began to chirp again. Muttering curses, I rang the office. Gloria said Angel Oliver was trying to reach me. An emergency.

Damn, I thought, punching in the numbers with a vengeance. They probably turned Darnell loose too, so he could stalk Angel and steal their kids.

The truth was not quite that dramatic. She had called a friend from her old neighborhood.

'You're not supposed to do that,' I snarled. 'Did you tell anyone where you were?'

'Not actually.'

Oh, shit, what did that mean?

'They broke into my old apartment there, trashed it.'

'Think it was the people who shot at us?'

'There's gang graffiti all over the walls.'

'Have any of them been arrested yet?' That was something I had neglected to ask McDonald.

'I thought you could find out.'

Swell. I had just slammed the phone down on the man who could tell me.

I called McDonald back. His secretary knew my voice but coolly asked who was calling, a bad sign. She put me on hold, came back, and said I should call the Public Information Office.

The man thought I was calling back to quarrel. Who could blame him? 'Tell him it's about Angel Oliver,' I pleaded.

She came back again. 'You have to call PIO,' she said firmly. I pictured McDonald pouting at his desk. I quickly called Bliss, but he wasn't in.

Sergeant Menendez in PIO said he would have to check with Lieutenant McDonald in homicide to find out if any of the shooting suspects had been arrested and if the detectives were aware of the break-in at Angel Oliver's apartment.

He left me excruciatingly on hold, when all I wanted to do at that moment was jump in my car and race over to Stephanie's apartment to straighten her out once and for all.

He finally came back. There had been no arrests, and the break-in was news to them. Somebody would look into it. I dialed Angel back.

'Do not go over there. Don't even talk to anybody from that neighborhood. Stay away. Looks like all the shooters are still loose. They must know by now that the deal is off and Darnell is in jail, but I wouldn't take any chances.'

She began to grumble, but I cut her off.

'Angel, this is not a game. Too many

people depend on you.'

I pulled on a sweat suit, socks, and sneakers, ran a comb through my hair, and was out the door. The weather was still cold but clear. Niko was waiting when I pulled up to the guardhouse.

He trotted over to my car, wearing sweat pants and a bulky sweater. 'I was beginning to get worried,' he said.

'Angel had a problem.'

'Let's take the Town Car.'

I wanted to snarl about men too insecure to let women drive, but parked and climbed into his car instead. I was in no mood to waste more time arguing.

'What a difference,' he said, smiling. 'You were so glamorous last night.'

'I'm afraid this is the real me, unfortunately.'

'Nothing wrong with it. Just a big contrast, glamour puss to tomboy. Jeez,' he said, turning onto the Palm-Hibiscus bridge. 'She's been right around the corner all along.'

'Basically,' I said, as he slowed down, looking for South Hibiscus Drive, 'I just want to set her straight and get her off our backs.'

'Know how many times cops, lawyers, doctors, her family, and all the rest of us have tried to do that?' he said grimly.

'If we have to,' I said, 'I was thinking that

maybe we could scare her, put the fear into her — '

'Been there, tried that. Nothing anybody threatened could scare her off.'

'Well, what do you suggest we do?'

'If it was up to me I'd dump her in the drink, but that's against the law. We can try to reason, but that's hopeless. Our best bet is to just hang onto her, not let her out of our sight until her family gets somebody out here. They've got a local law firm, and her father was on the phone to them while I was still on the line.'

He slowed down, searching out the address. The residential islands off the MacArthur are all single-family private homes except for a few small apartment houses on Hibiscus.

The building was surrounded by old trees and colorful tropical foliage. The silver Olds was parked out front. 'She's here,' I said, heart pounding. The tag number matched the one McDonald had given me. Niko parked, blocking it in. I was glad now that he was driving. I had seen Stephanie in action. If she rammed a car today, better his than mine.

'What if she wants to leave?' I said, before we got out of the car. 'We can't just tie her up and lock her in a closet.'

'Can't we?' He cut his eyes at me. 'I'm up for it, if you are.' He was dead serious.

'It's probably a crime,' I said. 'But hey, at this point, I'll try anything. The cops won't violate *her* rights. We're the only people who can protect ours.

'Too bad they stopped her last night,' I went on, thinking aloud. 'If she had actually shown up at the house, they could have charged her with trespassing.'

'You kidding? How long do you think they would have held her?'

'You're right.'

We found her name on the mailbox, first initial only. A pleasant, shady walk to a private entrance. A cozy second-floor hideaway with a view, through trees, of the bay. No more shadowy wraith, appearing at will, then disappearing, leaving us frustrated and helpless. We had her cornered where she lived. I liked that feeling of power.

The stairs were stone with Italian tile inserts. We stood on either side of the door so she couldn't see us; then Niko rang the bell. We heard its melodic chimes inside. No answer. He rang again, and a third time, as we stood there in the chilly shadow of a huge ficus tree.

'Think she saw us coming?' I whispered.

'Could be,' he muttered, looking around.

Then he knocked loudly. He leaned over the railing, eyes searching the yard below and the property next door. 'She's gotta be around here someplace.'

No movement inside, only silence.

'Maybe she's out jogging, or taking a walk.'

We went back downstairs. Nobody around. The inside of the Olds looked like a rental. Clean, nothing unusual. Niko squatted, removed the valve stem, and let the air hiss out of the right front tire.

'What are you doing?'

'I don't want her to take off while we're driving around the island to see if she's on foot. She could be watching us from in there right now. If I was her, I wouldn't be answering my door either.'

We cruised both islands, scanning up and down every cross street. No sign of Stephanie. Back at the apartment the Olds was undisturbed.

'Maybe she was so upset about the cops picking her up that she cut her wrists or hung herself.' I began to feel apprehensive.

'I doubt it. If she did something dramatic, it would be on Lance's doorstep.'

We stared at each other. 'She could have gone there on foot,' I said. 'It's quite a walk, but doable.'

He called the Star Island guardhouse, then

the house, on his cellular. Pauli answered. No sign of Stephanie.

'She must be inside.' We went to the door and rang again.

A car pulled up downstairs. Two men. The passenger, a tall skinny young guy, got out, looked around, then spotted us.

'That your Lincoln?' he called. 'You've got us blocked in here.'

'Hey, Pete,' the other man called. 'The damn thing's got a flat. Nobody said anything about that.'

They were from Holiday Rent-a-Car. Stephanie had called to turn in her car and had asked them to pick it up at the apartment. Said the keys would be under the fender, which they were.

Niko moved the Lincoln and helped them change the flat. When they left, we went back up the stairs and began searching for a key. Under the mat, in the flower pot, on the ledge over the door. Nothing. Then I ran back downstairs, fished in her mailbox and came up with two keys on a metal ring. She must have left them for the landlord.

'We're not breaking and entering,' Niko said as he unlocked her door. 'We have a key.' A man after my own heart.

The apartment was pin neat. Wicker,

bamboo, and flower prints. Sunny kitchen, neatly made bed. The closets were pretty much empty, most personal items gone from the bathroom cabinet. Nobody home. In the trash, lots of tabloids, magazines and newspapers with pages cut out. It was obvious whose picture had been on those pages. She must have quite a scrapbook, I thought. A half-full coffeepot still sat on the stove. She left in a hurry, forgot her toothbrush and hairspray. No clue where she had gone.

A elderly woman, emerging from a downstairs apartment with her dog, said her upstairs neighbor had left earlier in a taxi. She did not recall what cab company.

If only I had called McDonald sooner. If only I had not wasted time on the phone with Angel. If only, if only — we might have caught her.

'She knew when she gave the cops her address that we'd be all over her,' Niko said bitterly. 'She's not stupid.'

'With my luck, she's moving into my building at this very moment,' I said.

*   *   *

Lottie and I exchanged half a dozen calls that afternoon as I caught up on my laundry and housekeeping chores. She was suffering the torments of the damned. By late afternoon it appeared that Gretchen had come through. All the photo editor said, in passing, to Lottie was, 'Damnedest thing about that cold-weather picture.'

'Ain't it,' she said vaguely, looking appropriately distressed.

'Hope you talked to the widow.' He shook his head.

'Nice lady, sure have.'

She and Mrs Maxwell, now residing in a Collins Avenue condo, had shared a long and lovely chat. New to town, newly widowed, she had served Lottie tea and home-baked coffee cake. Lottie now had a new best friend, whether she liked it or not.

By day's end it appeared as though blame had somehow fallen squarely upon the shoulders of an inept copy boy who had somehow delivered the wrong file to the photo desk. His sloppy work, or even deliberate carelessness, probably related to the fact that it had been his last day on the job. Now on a trip to Europe, he was returning to Dartmouth to pursue the study of veterinary medicine.

'Don't ever do that again,' I told Lottie, then described McDonald's obnoxious behavior.

'He's jealous!' she hooted.

'Lance doesn't like him either. It's surprising, because in some ways they're very much alike.'

'Maybe Lance is insecure, worried about the size of his pee-pee. A lot a those hunky body-building studs are, you know.'

'Lance isn't.'

'Hell all Friday, Britt! Good for him. Good for you. You have to tell me every little detail!'

★   ★   ★

We were on *Entertainment Tonight* that evening. At least Lance was. My mom called, all excited, saying she saw me in a background shot. I dashed to the TV, missed myself, but caught the tail end of Lance's interview. He rubbed his brow in a familiar modest gesture as he said that the shooting was progressing smoothly on location and that any problems with the production had been overcome. I wondered if he had his fingers crossed.

★   ★   ★

The weather remained clear next day, and the rain scenes could be shot. 'But it's in the forties,' I told Lance. 'You'll catch pneumonia.'

No way to wait until the weather warmed up, he said; every day on location costs big bucks, and the film was so overbudget now it was creating a negative buzz in the industry. Disaster-speak could build into a self-fulfilling prophecy at the box office.

A tropical storm had apparently been written into the story line by another new writer flown in from LA to 'punch up the script'. Kirby Walters, the last script doctor, the one who so hated his hotel accommodations, had been banished back to Hollywood, described to me by Lance as the place bad people go when they die.

Ziff filled me in on the scandal.

Walters's downfall was too many nude scenes on the Beach. None were in the script; they were between his shy college-age son, who had arrived to spend a few days, and Wendy's spoiled, heavy-drinking, pot-smoking, sexually aggressive high-school-age daughter, sixteen going on thirty-five, who had flown in to do the same. In an ugly scene, Wendy had threatened to have the son arrested and the father's legs broken.

Ziff was now convinced that 'both the devil and the anti-Christ are involved in this movie.' Made sense to me.

They shot the rain scene at a remote boat ramp. I wanted to go, but after Gardiner Bowles and Cassie Malone are drenched, the script called for them to, what else, strip off their wet clothes and fall into each other's arms again.

I would have loved to watch, but it was another closed set. Lance advised against it.

'At least,' I told him, 'Gardiner Bowles has an active sex life.'

★ ★ ★

Lance called me between takes, just after dawn. Drenched, wrapped in a blanket, drinking hot soup from a thermos, his teeth chattered.

'Listen,' he said. 'I have to go to LA tomorrow for the *Dark Journey* premiere. It's a bad time to leave, but it's in my contract. I've got to try to support the film, as much as I can. Short trip, two nights and a day, but you wanna come with me? We'll get outa town, go to the premiere, see the movie, spend a little time.'

I heard them revving up the rain machine and calling Lance for another take. The temperature was 42 degrees. The reporter who hated leaving Miami out of fear that she might miss a murder did not hesitate.

'When do we leave?'

I had comp time coming, and took it.

My mother and Lottie were beside themselves about what I should take, what I should wear, what to do with my hair. This was not tossing a toothbrush into an overnight bag to leave town on a story. This was a goddam Hollywood premiere!

Lottie thought I should have my hair frosted. My mother decided my eyebrows and eyelashes should be dyed.

I decided against both.

Then Gretchen called.

'Britt? How much money did they raise at the AIDS benefit?'

'Tons,' I guessed. 'Much more than they had anticipated.'

'You have to be more specific than that.'

'Why?'

'Because it's gone. Along with Wallace Atwater.'

20

Monica Atwater had bypassed the usual channels and called the police chief at home to report Wallace missing. She feared for his safety. He must be the victim of foul play, she said. However, she had not reported his disappearance until the bank began to question Wallace's transfer of the proceeds from the benefit into another account, which he had cleaned out.

Any foul play seemed to be on Wallace's part. He had apparently lost a fortune in bad investments. The money belonged to him, his clients, and lifelong friends whose retirement funds he managed. If anything was left, it disappeared with him. The Atwater bank accounts were empty, money gone, along with Wallace, his passport, and a young secretary named Lynda.

To add insult to injury, Lance's checks to pay for the party had been deposited into the same account. The caterer, the musicians, the florist — none had been paid. Lance paid the bills for the second time, taking the hit with good grace.

But the precious positive publicity and good-will generated by the benefit was about to evolve into embarrassing headlines. And the timing could not be worse. Lance was about to do publicity and interviews for the new movie. The questions could not be dodged. Not only were they disconcerting, they would divert focus from the film he was promoting. I wrote the story, of course, again earning me the undying animosity of the filmmakers and the Chamber of Commerce. I could see their point. I drank the champagne, I ate the chocolate piano, and now I was asking them to show me the money.

'No way you could hold off on it for a while?' Lance had asked, pained.

'No way,' I said.

Monica refused to talk except to insist that the events were totally out of character for her husband, that she trusted him implicitly, and there had to be an explanation. Then she filed for divorce.

★   ★   ★

Our LA plans changed slightly. Instead of flying west together, Lance was booked for New York first, a publicity blitz beginning with the *Today* show. His schedule was tight, it was all hard work, and now he was fighting a cold, from the drenching rain scenes.

He would jet to LA from New York and I would fly out from Miami, alone. Separate flights, I thought, how romantic. But at least we would return together. This is what I need, I told myself, not to be alone, to share time, secrets, and my body with someone who cares. The fact that he was the object of a million fantasies was a definite plus, though I heartily wished he had at least one less fan.

In the days after Niko and I missed finding Stephanie at her apartment she bombarded Lance with greeting cards, novelty gifts, and love letters, all postmarked Miami. Wearing a scarf and sunglasses and driving a blue Buick Riviera, she showed up at Star Island and announced she was Lance's houseguest. When the guard at the gate recognized her and called the house for instructions, she raced away.

She left me messages at the office and on my answering machine, unnerving since my home number had been unlisted since an unpleasant experience several years ago. Sometimes she merely left her name, to let me know she was out there. Other times, she would sing out, in an almost musical lilt: 'You're not listening to me.' Or an ambiguous: 'You see, I told you. Lance and I are in love.' Unsettling, but nothing cops or courts would construe as threatening.

Usually the reluctant traveler, I was ready to get out of town. Lance left for New York, downing large quantities of vitamin C and nursing his sniffles. Dave and Frank went with him. Pauli went on to LA. Niko was not thrilled about staying in Miami, but he had been working closely with fraud and forgery investigators and the missing persons detective in an attempt to track down Wallace Atwater and the embezzled charity money.

★　★　★

I watched Lance on *Today*. He looked bravura but sounded hoarse, and as they came back from a break he was putting away his handkerchief. Touching his brow in that familiar earnest gesture, he gamely fielded questions about the embezzled money, the Trent Talon tragedy, the fire, and other production problems. Skillfully, he kept steering the conversation back to his target topic, his new movie, *Dark Journey*. When he gazed into the camera and confided how much he was looking forward to LA and the premiere, I couldn't help smiling. He was in frigid New York; I was in Miami. Hard to believe that by late tonight we'd be in LA together.

I planned to work a few hours and take off at noon. The magic of that morning's *Today* show faded in the face of real life. A nine-year-old girl had been critically wounded, caught in the crossfire between two carloads of teenagers. The gang unit was working overtime trying to track the shooters. Listening to the scanner as I dressed, I heard the BOLO (Be on the lookout) in the drive-by. They said that the beef might have been between the Brickell Boys and the PLO. The latter still hadn't been picked up, but the dispatcher described them as armed, dangerous, and 'suspects in a thirty-one'. A homicide. Was that a mistake? Or had the PLO killed somebody I didn't know about?

I called Bliss.

'Do you have them in a homicide?' I asked.

'Yep. The Fairborn case.'

'The Metrorail security guard? How do you know?'

'Drugfire.'

Ours was the third police department in the nation to acquire Drugfire, a high-tech computerized program developed by the FBI to work drug-related and gang shootings. A microscope-mounted camera automatically shoots digital pictures of the backs of cartridge cases collected at shooting scenes.

The individual markings, as distinctive as fingerprints, are captured, their images stored. Without even being asked, the computer automatically compares them to stored images from other crime scenes, ranking them in similarity. Casings from the 9mm pistol used to blast away at Angel and me had been compared to eight hundred open 9mm cases already in the computer. A casing from the bullet that killed Randall Fairborn ranked number one.

'It's a match,' Bliss said. 'Same gun; all we gotta find now is the kid using it.' His name: Ignacio Zamora, better known as Iggy Zee, on the street.

'That's great. When did you find all this out? Why didn't you call me?'

'Didn't wanna step in it. The lieutenant was cracking down on us initiating any contact with the press except through PIO. Apparently he's in a mad-dog mood this week.'

'Who isn't?' That was my doing, unfortunately.

'According to gang unit intelligence, Iggy Zee is the only one still looking for Angel. Always gotta be one stubborn little bastard in the bunch. The others couldn't care less about her, they're just watching their own skinny butts.'

'But Iggy Zee must know that Darnell was arrested and the hit is off. Why would he be crazy enough to keep after her? Or crazy enough to keep the same gun, for that matter?'

'They don't think ahead, you know that. They live hour by hour, minute by minute, and worry about the consequences later. This guy, he just likes shooting people, I guess. Word on the street is, he said he was gonna take the bitch out and by dammit, he's gonna take the bitch out.'

'A man of his word. How nice in this day and age. Is somebody protecting her?'

'As if! Think the taxpayers can afford a personal bodyguard for Angel Oliver? She's safe enough over there.'

'Sure. As long as she lies low and stays put. Did you tell her about this?'

'Nah, I called. The kid said she wasn't there, so I left a message.'

'I hope you talk to her,' I said. 'I tried, but I don't think I got through.'

'It's her ass,' he said, his voice deliberately casual. He could not forget the fact that she was also a defendant in one of his cases. I realized that to Bliss there are just good guys and bad guys, us and them, and Angel was not one of us.

My flight was leaving at two o'clock, and

arrival time in LA was 10 P.M. The good news was that I was traveling first class, as Lance's guest. Two brief stopovers were the bad news. I think that even when we die, we will have to go through Atlanta and then Dallas.

I had no time to think about Angel now. But then I wondered. Which kid did Bliss leave the message with? Harry most often answered the door and the telephone, but he couldn't even write yet.

Oh, for Pete's sake, I thought, and called.

'Mommy's not home,' Harry said.

Where was the woman? If she was visiting Darnell in jail, or hiring him a lawyer, I would slap her silly.

'Let me talk to Misty,' I said.

'She went to school.'

That was good news.

'What are you gonna bring me?'

'Who's taking care of you?'

'I'm big now,' he said indignantly. 'I don't need a baby-sitter.'

'Okay, let me rephrase this, Harry.' If those kids are home alone, I swore, I would find Angel and kick her butt. 'Who else is there?'

'Beppo, the twins, the kitty cat . . . ' he recited in singsong fashion.

'Any grown-ups?' I asked sweetly.

'The lady.'

'What lady?'

'María.'

'Good, put María on the phone.'

'She's watching telebision.'

The stringed theme of a daytime soap opera swelled in the background.

'I don't care, Harry, put her on. Now.'

He clunked the phone down on a tabletop and went away. For a long time.

'*¿Hola?*'

'María?'

'*Sí.*'

'Where is Angel?'

'School. She go to school.'

'Misty's school?'

'No, no. Her school. She study to be secretary.'

I could picture that.

'Where?'

'Downtown. Eh, Lindsey Hopkins.'

'What? She's not supposed to go over there.'

'She afraid she miss too much school.'

She said Angel was not expected home until three.

Damn. I looked up the number, then realized calling was probably pointless. The school is huge, on ten acres, a little United Nations with students from forty or fifty countries. It would be quicker to go there and yank Angel out of class myself.

It was eleven o'clock. Niko was picking me up to go to the airport at twelve-thirty. I could do it if I hurried.

I drove over there, cursing traffic all the way, hit the office, and found where secretaries in training were studying, in third-floor classrooms. I didn't wait for the elevator; I ran up the stairs. The halls ended in open breezeways where students lounged over soft drinks or books.

I trotted up and down, peering into classrooms. Angel was seated in a middle row of the fourth room I peered into. Class was in session. They seemed to be working on reading their own shorthand, something I wish I had mastered myself.

I tried to signal but she was absorbed, brows knit, rosebud lips slightly parted and moving, wearing the befuddled expression of a dog trying to read a road map.

I asked a long-haired girl slouching by when classes would break. In less than five minutes, she replied, so I waited, tapping my foot, pacing, checking my watch. From a gym down the hall came the rhythmic counts, cries, and grunts of a karate class in session.

The bell rang and the secretarial students poured out. All but Angel, who lagged behind, talking intently to the paunchy middle-aged male instructor.

This woman was driving me nuts. 'Come on,' I muttered. 'Come on.'

Behind me, at a table in the breezeway, one of the students slowly got to his feet and also seemed to be waiting. Angel emerged just then, her hair loose, face set and serious. Her pregnancy was beginning to show, I thought, or perhaps it was just the cut of her cheap plaid slacks.

'Britt.' She looked surprised. 'What are you doing here?'

'More important, what are you doing here?'

I must have sounded like an irate mother scolding a child, because Angel looked intimidated, then stepped back, clearly alarmed.

'School is good,' I conceded. 'I understand that. But this is irresponsible. To come over — '

'It's one of *them!*' she said. That's when I saw she was staring past me, toward the kid in the breezeway.

Dropping her books, she ran down the hall. I whirled, mouth open, for a better look at the lanky kid who had been sitting, head down at the table. He wore loose, nondescript street clothes, a shapeless checkered shirt flapping over a black T-shirt and khaki cargo pants with half a dozen pockets. He had the look of

379

a gang member: short black hair, traces of a mustache and a goatee, tattoos on his arms, and an automatic pistol in his waistband.

I had seen that face, probably even that gun, before. This had to be Iggy Zee.

He stepped forward with an arrogant I-own-the-world stride, his expression oddly anticipatory.

'Run, Angel!' I screamed, redundant at this point. She had figured it out on her own and was making good time, beating feet down the hall.

He must have remembered me too, but other than a slight squint of recognition, his eyes were empty, nobody home.

Angel turned, glanced back, didn't like what she saw, and began yelping, a series of sounds not unlike attacking Apaches in one of Lance's old movies.

My screams and her yelps drew attention. Faces appeared from doorways, from the gym.

'He's got a gun!' I shouted, at the top of my lungs. I saw he did not appreciate it. He had probably intended to follow Angel quietly, to catch her when she was more vulnerable, at a bus stop or in a stairwell.

He took his eyes off Angel and focused on me, annoyed.

I shrank back, about to follow Angel. I did

not worry about being shot, I worried about missing my plane.

'Get 'im!' A woman darted out from the karate class, petite and hard-bodied with a Dutch-girl haircut.

'Eeee-yaaaahh!' She spun around and landed a circular kick to the center of his chest. Half a dozen women, all shapes and sizes, all clad in white uniforms, stampeded out behind her. Karate cries filled the hallway. Iggy Zee looked startled and staggered back, reaching for his gun, but it slipped and slid down into the leg of his baggy pants. He groped frantically for it as they advanced, kicking and screaming. Flying hands sliced the air. The same woman connected again, with a frontal kick to his groin. He crumpled, mouth and eyes wide open in an agonized expression, right arm still trapped down his pants, trying to free his gun.

A security guard appeared at the far end of the hall. For one brief insane moment I thought it was Randall Fairborn. The uniform and company were the same. I shook the thought and screamed, 'Gun! Gun! Gun!'

The guard was unarmed, shouting into a hand-held radio as he ran.

A middle-aged blonde barefoot woman let loose a blood-curdling cry and landed a

381

karate chop to Iggy Zee's Adam's apple. 'Go, girl!' somebody shouted. Another chop-chopped at his rib cage.

Spitting strangled curses, he yanked at the gun, somehow snagged on a stitched flap inside his baggy pants. I plucked a fire extinguisher off the wall and slammed it down on his wrist.

The breathless security guard, who had been alerted by Angel, pounced as Iggy Zee wrenched the gun free. It went flying and clattered to the floor. Women were still kicking at Iggy Zee when the cops arrived.

Angel was scared. I was frantic about the time. Bliss was elated. Iggy Zee was handcuffed and bruised.

Bliss, wearing his brown suit, yanked at Iggy Zee's handcuffed wrists to more closely examine his amateur tattoos. 'What the hell is this PLO shit?' he boomed. 'Oh!' He brightened. 'I know what that stands for: Puny Little Organ!'

'Powerful Latin Organization,' Iggy Zee said sullenly. 'That's Powerful Latin Organization!'

'Lookit this,' Bliss said gleefully, examining Iggy Zee's 9mm pistol. The grips had been wrapped with tape. 'Know where that's from?'

'No,' I said, edgy. 'I have to leave.'

He ignored me. 'It's from a movie. Now everybody's doing it. Iggy here saw a TV movie where some hit man wraps tape around his grip so prints can't be lifted off it. But it's all bullshit,' he crowed. 'I never saw a case where anybody got prints off the grip; we always get 'em off the metal.' He grinned at Iggy. 'Know what you are? Living proof that a mind is a terrible thing to have. Only thing worse than a punk is a dumb punk.'

'Think it's the same gun?' I asked.

'The lab will tell us soon.'

'I have to leave.' I headed for the stairs.

'Hey, where ya going?' Bliss said. 'Hang on there. We need a statement.'

'I don't have time now, I have to catch a plane.'

'No, no, no. No, ya don't. We gotta get a statement first.'

'I'll be back in forty-eight hours. I'll do it then.'

'No way.' He frowned.

'Look, you've got Angel, you've got witnesses.'

He was adamant.

'Ask the lieutenant,' I pleaded.

He radioed McDonald, wandering toward the breezeway as he did. Did he do that for better reception or so I couldn't hear him? I considered making a run for it.

'Okay.' He strolled back. 'The lieutenant says we can tape your statement here, if we can find a tape recorder.'

A patrolman had one in his car, went to get it, then had to go to Walgreen's for batteries. I was hyperventilating by the time he got back. I insisted on taping while walking to my car in the parking lot, babbling breathlessly.

I didn't even say goodbye to Angel.

I drove home, chest tighter than a drum, grinding my teeth at every red light and dawdling driver.

* * *

Niko paced in front of my door. He checked his watch as I ran from the car. 'Thank God, you didn't give up and leave,' I told him.

'Where've you been?' he said impatiently.

'I don't think we can make it,' I said, nearly in tears.

'You all packed?'

I nodded.

'Grab your stuff!'

'I have to say goodbye to Mrs Goldstein and give her the keys,' I said, as we rushed out the door. 'She's taking care of the animals while I'm gone.'

'Go!' He hustled me toward the Town Car.

'I'll bring them back and give them to her myself.'

We burned rubber. My heart was in my throat. If we were stopped for speeding now, we would never make it.

Leaning on the horn, he wheeled around slower vehicles and drove like an absolute madman. I held on, closed my eyes, and prayed.

He roared on to the access road to MIA at eighty miles an hour. My heart sank as we reached the terminal, clogged with cabs, buses, and airport shuttles. I asked a curbside attendant about my flight. He squinted at his watch and shook his head. 'You'll never make it.'

He told us the concourse and the gate number, then shrugged as I prepared to run for it, lugging my garment bag, overnighter, and purse.

Niko reached for the bags.

'You can't!' I cried. 'They'll tow the car.'

'So what? I'll get it back. No sweat. It's cool.'

I love this man, I thought.

'Coming through!' He snatched the bags and cleared a path through the crowd like a broken-field runner, outdoing O.J.'s Hertz commercial. I charged after him.

At the metal detectors, signs warned

PASSENGERS ONLY BEYOND THIS POINT. He put the bags on the conveyor belt, flashed my ticket, and we both ducked through the arch unchallenged. So much for MIA security. He scooped up the bags and ran on.

He reached the gateway ahead of me. My flight had already boarded. A lone attendant was leaving the desk. The plane was about to depart, the doors closed. Somehow Niko got them opened and me and my bags aboard.

I never would have made it without him.

I turned to hug him at the last moment, but he pushed me toward the jetway. There was no time. 'Go, go, go!' he said. 'Don't worry about anything,' he called after me. 'Happy landings.' He grinned.

The flight attendant helped me hang my garment bag in a closet. I shoved the overnighter into the overhead compartment and sank into my first-class seat, weak with relief. Did the Town Car get towed? Would Niko remember to take the keys to Mrs Goldstein? I put all those questions out of my mind. Nothing I could do about them now. The jet moved away from the gate and inched toward the runway. I was on my way, all of Miami's craziness, worry, and bad news behind me.

When the plane was in the air and the seat belt sign turned off, I went to the rest room.

The small cubicle made me smile and think of Lance, somewhere in the air himself at that moment. His flight would arrive hours before mine. As I made my way back to my window seat, I glanced through the curtains dividing the compartments. A well-dressed woman in coach stood in the aisle, reaching up, adjusting something in the overhead. It was Stephanie.

21

I crouched in my seat the rest of the way to Atlanta, then to Dallas. As passengers disembarked, I hid behind a magazine and sneaked peeks. I would have been thrilled had one of those cities been Stephanie's destination, but I knew where she was going. She was following Lance, as always. The premiere was no secret. The fact that Lance would be there had been reported in newspaper columns and on TV.

Only a few LA-bound flights leave MIA each day. Sheer bad luck had put her on mine. I wanted to confront her, but not at thirty-seven thousand feet. What would happen if she saw me? With my luck she'd go berserk, I thought, hoping she would be served only plastic utensils with her meal. I lapsed into 'if onlys' again, as I gazed out my window at billowy cloud banks as soft and inviting as feather beds. If only I had been on time, Niko and I might have spotted her at the airport. He would have thought of something. It occurred to me that Angel had caused most of my 'if onlys' lately. I vowed to stay away from her once I got back to Miami.

At least I now knew where Stephanie was. I used the in-flight phone built into the seat back in front of me and called Lance's LA number. He had not arrived yet, but I could leave a message. No answer.

I sneaked a peek back into coach after Dallas. Stephanie, her head nestled on a pillow, was dozing as the movie ran.

We roared across a darkening sky, chasing the sun west. Hoping for a nap myself, I turned my face to the window and closed my eyes. But when the flight attendant touched my arm, I jumped like a scared rabbit, heart beating wildly. Would I like a blanket or a pillow? I declined both. Sleep was out of the question with Stephanie aboard. I ate the dinner, which was good, but declined drinks. I would need my wits about me should Stephanie run amok.

An hour out of LA, I tried Lance's number

again. This time an answering service picked up and took a message.

We descended into LAX, the dark of the sea and the lights of the city spread out below. I remained seated as other passengers yanked their bags from the overhead and crowded the aisles. I ducked, pretending to be retrieving something from beneath the seat as Stephanie filed by, rolling a small piece of luggage on wheels.

She looked eager, in a hurry. Sure, I thought irritably, she's refreshed and well rested. The damn woman slept like a baby all the way here, while I fretted and peeked over my shoulder.

Now I was determined not to let her out of my sight.

Once she cleared the plane and was on the jetway, I snatched my bag and moved swiftly after her, retrieving my garment bag on the way. Keeping my eyes on her back, I trotted down the concourse behind her.

She moved briskly, and I had trouble keeping up. My garment bag seemed heavier than ever. I needed one of those little luggage carriers on wheels, I decided. Someone behind me kept shouting, 'Miss! Miss!' If they kept it up, I feared Stephanie might hear it and turn around. I spun to see who it was: the first-class flight attendant. It was me she was calling. Out of breath, she caught me.

'What is it?' I said, annoyed, still watching Stephanie. I was certain I had left nothing behind.

'I think you took the wrong garment bag,' she gasped, a hand over her heart.

'No, this is mine.' Crowd surges were coming between me and Stephanie. What if she spots Lance waiting for me? She would think he'd come to meet her.

'Would you check it, please?' she insisted.

I jerked open the little zippered compartment. The typed card with my name and address wasn't there. A plastic luggage tag was tucked in its place. The name on it was not mine. Focused on Stephanie, I had taken somebody else's tweedy grey garment bag, identical to mine.

'Come with me,' she said cheerfully. 'We'll straighten this out.'

'But — ' Torn between the need to keep Stephanie in sight and my desire for the wonderful little black Chanel knockoff wrapped in tissue paper, tucked inside my bag and now in the hands of strangers, the dress won. My mother had found it. 'It just sings Chanel!' she had said.

Perhaps, I thought, I could still have both. We dashed back to the gate and made the switch, much to the relief of an irritated white-haired wheelchair passenger whose bag I had inadvertently taken. Then I ran like mad, bags banging against my knees, to where I had seen Stephanie last. She was out of sight, of course, and I was handicapped because I had to stop at each ladies' room. I would crack the door to see if she was in line. If not, then I would dash inside to peer under the stalls and check out the feet. No luck.

I emerged into the main terminal and frantically scanned the crowd.

'Britt! Britt! Over here!' Dave, broad-shouldered and blond-haired, was waiting for me.

I put my forefinger to my lips to keep him from shouting out my name again. 'Did you see her? Did you see her?'

'Who?'

'Where's the baggage claim?'

'You've got more luggage?' He looked puzzled and reached for my bags.

'You didn't get my message?'

'What message?'

'Stephanie! She was on the plane!'

She was nowhere in sight. We charged down the escalator to baggage claim. The luggage from our flight was already revolving on the carousel. Nothing. No way of knowing if she had even checked a bag. I suggested we separate. I could go back up to the terminal, while he checked the cabstands down here. But what if one of us did find her? We had no way of communicating. The place was mobbed. It was hopeless.

'Where's Lance?'

'He has to do the *Tom Snyder Show*,' Dave said. 'It's live and he feels lousy. He was taking a nap; then Pauli was gonna drive him.'

Lance had had a miserable flight from New York, Dave said as we drove to the house. The altitude had caused painful pressure in his ears and clogged sinuses. He had used a nasal spray to relieve the discomfort but had apparently overdone it, and now his nose was running like a faucet.

His housekeeper, a plump, smiling woman named Pilar, welcomed me with a cup of hot tea and a bowl of soup. She showed me to a guest room, where we wrestled over my garment bag. She insisted on unpacking and hanging my clothes, then left for the evening.

The huge hilltop house was cavernous: high vaulted ceilings, massive furniture, and marble mantels. Dave had disappeared. A TV blared somewhere, behind closed doors. This was not the welcome I expected.

I showered, pulled on slacks and a fresh blouse, then tried out the canopy bed in my room. The coverlet was crocheted, the sheets silken, and the wallpaper French floral. I wondered how many other women had slept in this bed; then I dozed off.

Something, perhaps sounds in the hall, woke me. Startled and disoriented, I was uncertain for a moment where I was. I slipped out of bed, ran a brush through my hair, put on some lipstick, and ventured out to investigate.

Before becoming totally lost, I encountered Pauli. Turned out that Lance's room was across from mine. He rapped on the door and Lance opened it.

'Welcome to LA!' This was the welcome I had in mind, I thought, as he hugged me. He looked terrible, nose red, eyes watery. He sounded worse and felt feverish. Whichever it was, cold or flu, he had it, full blown. I insisted we go back downstairs so he could eat some soup.

We grinned at each other across a Mexican-style wooden table in a corner of the massive kitchen, under a framed collection of vintage movie posters.

'Worst flight I ever had, except for an emergency landing at Orly once, in Paris.' He blew his nose. 'Thought my head was gonna explode.'

'Let me tell you about mine,' I said.

They didn't get my message because Niko had called to say I was safely on the plane, Dave had confirmed that it was on time, and nobody checked the service.

I told him about Angel and my wild ride to the airport with Niko. It all seemed so remote now. We climbed the stairs, arms around each other.

'I feel like I've been hit by a truck,' he apologized. He definitely had a fever, said he didn't want me to catch the bug, and suggested I stay in the guest room.

'I didn't travel all this way to sleep in the guest room,' I said. 'My resistance is pretty high.' I brushed his damp hair back off his sweaty forehead. 'Let's just take a nap together. If you need anything during the night, I'll be here.'

'Didn't we do this once before?' he said hoarsely. He sat down heavily on the bed. 'I don't think I'm in shape right now to — '

'I know.' I helped him undress and didn't even go back to my room for my nightgown. I undressed, slipped on one of Lance's oversized T-shirts, and climbed into his bed.

This was not the night we had expected. No urge to merge overwhelmed either one of us. He thrashed around, achy and feverish, while I thrashed through bad dreams. This time men with searchlights and long guns hunted me through those dark woods. Stephanie and Angel were screaming, sobbing children scurried through the shadows like frightened animals, and the gun slipped from my hands. I lost it in the weeds . . .

'What'sa matter? What'sa matter?' Lance croaked. I was sitting up, groping, in a panic.

'I can't find the gun,' I said urgently. 'I can't find the gun!' then burst into stupid tears. I had firmly believed that this would not happen here, not with him.

★ ★ ★

'What was that?' he wanted to know in the morning. 'You dream like that often?'

'Yeah,' I reluctantly admitted.

He rolled his eyes and nodded.

His fever had broken during the night but he felt wobbly: throat sore, voice ragged, nose and chest congested.

'I think I'm getting better,' he said hopefully. 'I think it's breaking up.' Squinting, he breathed through his mouth, trying to assess the state of his health.

His schedule included a morning satellite tour of press interviews, a lunch meeting with his agent, and a session with Silverman. 'Dave will take you shopping,' Lance said. 'You're gonna love Rodeo Drive.'

I wrinkled my nose. 'I'm not much of a shopper.' That would be my mother's idea of a dream day, not mine.

'Then he'll arrange a sightseeing tour for you. Okay?' During breakfast, Niko called from Miami with news, a possible Atwater sighting in Hong Kong. He, the cops, and Interpol were hot on the trail of the AIDS money. He had had tea and cookies with Mrs Goldstein and, astonishingly, the Town Car, though ticketed, had not been towed, confirming my belief that cops tow only the cars of those who can afford it least.

I missed Miami and hadn't even been gone twenty-four hours. Lance barely touched the big breakfast prepared by Pilar, checked *Variety* and the *Hollywood Reporter*, kissed me goodbye, and took off with Frank and Pauli.

I explored the house, seeing it for the first time in daylight. The place was a jaw dropper, with a ten-car motor courtyard, an art deco pub for a den, and a lava rock pool with several waterfalls and a sandy beach.

The sightseeing tour Dave arranged for me was not one I would have chosen. LA seemed dry and brown, drab compared to Miami's vivid colors. The terrain was not as flat, traffic was as congested, the pale sky hazy. The limo that picked me up looked like a hearse. It was a hearse. In the next few hours I saw the snug little Spanish-style house where Marilyn Monroe died, O.J.'s Brentwood estate, Nicole Simpson's condo, the hotel where John Belushi overdosed, and the sidewalk outside the Viper Room where River Phoenix breathed his last. The dead stars' tour reminded me of Ziff and the ghoul pool. The driver gave me a free grave map to two cemeteries of the stars. He looked like a mortician, and his spiel made me a bit headachy and depressed. I blamed jet lag or lack of sleep, thought about Bitsy and Billy Boots, and hoped they didn't think I had abandoned them.

I passed on a late lunch at Mezzaluna, the restaurant where Nicole ate her last meal, and asked to go back to the house. Maybe Lance had finished early.

Dave had given me a key, in case I returned before he did and Pilar was not there. He had also informed me that I had a late-afternoon beauty appointment for hair and makeup. How considerate, I thought, hoping it had not been arranged by the same people responsible for my tour.

The hearse dropped me off and I used the pedestrian gate. It was unlocked, which I thought a bit careless on somebody's part. If Lance was still working, I decided, I would find some aspirin and lie down for a while. I was taking the key from my bag at the front door when Stephanie stepped up beside me. She must have been sitting on a stone bench behind the arecas that shaded the entranceway.

'What are you doing here?' She sounded truly annoyed.

She wore an expensive-looking powder blue suit with a ladylike pink blouse. The element of surprise was on her side. For a moment I was speechless. I finally had her and didn't know what to say.

'I'll take that.' She snatched the key out of my hand.

'Hey!' I yelped. 'Give it back! Are you crazy?' Why ask? I thought. I knew the answer. 'Give it up, Stephanie! This is not cool!'

A distinguished-looking older gentleman with a Doberman on a leash heard the racket, peered into the entranceway at us, then rapidly walked off. Stephanie had also glanced his way, and I took that opportunity to try to grab the key but she held it tantalizingly out of reach, behind her back like a child.

'You had better leave now,' she instructed.

Oh, sure, so Lance could come home and find her lurking in his house or destroying it?

'You're nuts!' I screamed and frantically jabbed the doorbell. 'You are going to jail or a padded cell! You'll never get out this time,' I threatened. Even as I said it, a nagging fear gnawed at my gut. Did her oversized Gucci bag conceal a weapon?

No one answered. Did the freaking bell even work? I jabbed it again, then kicked the door out of frustration, again and again.

Stephanie turned away. Maybe I had finally succeeded in scaring her.

'Thank heavens you're here!' I heard her say.

I turned and saw who she was talking to, a middle-aged police officer in uniform, a second, younger patrolman right behind him. They were watching me.

'I caught her trying to break into the house.' Stephanie stepped behind the first cop, who advanced toward me, club in hand. 'Lance Westfell lives here, but he's out right now,' she said. 'I'm his fiancée.'

'Yeah,' I said, exasperated, 'and I'm Princess Grace.'

I knew as I spit it out that it was the wrong thing to say to two strange LA cops. This was not Miami.

'Be careful,' Stephanie warned them. 'I think she's dangerous.'

'I'm gonna get you for this.' I pointed my

399

index finger at Stephanie, who shrank back.

Again, the wrong thing to say, but this entire scenario was simply outrageous.

'Don't let her get away! She has to go back to Boston in a strait-jacket,' I said, as they frisked me.

I explained that she had burned 3900 acres trying to kill us in South Florida, that she might have murdered Trent Talon, that she was Lance's longtime stalker, and that I was his houseguest, his date for the premiere. I added that we were heading back to Miami on an early flight first thing in the morning. Unfortunately, my identification and my plane ticket were locked in the house, in the guest room upstairs.

I realized how this looked to them. Well groomed, well dressed, and well spoken, Stephanie seemed the solid citizen. They had found me kicking on the door of a famous movie star's multimillion-dollar mansion with no ID and nothing but three dollars, my free cemetery map, and a dead stars' brochure in my bag, my blouse and slacks stained by an Orange Julius I had spilled in the hearse.

'I can explain everything, officers.' How many times, I wondered, had these cops heard that line?

Stephanie graciously allowed them to check her purse after I warned that she might be armed. The cop's big hand came up with a dainty lace-edged handkerchief, cosmetics, and her Gucci wallet full of cash, credit cards, plenty of legitimate ID, a picture of Lance, and, of course, the key to his house. They apologized to her and glared at me.

The neighbor with the Doberman was watching from a distance. He knew about Lance's trouble with a female stalker and had flagged them down.

'Ask him,' I demanded furiously.

He was no help. He said he didn't recall seeing me before but that Stephanie looked familiar. The cops decided to keep us both until they could sort it out. They ignored it when I said I had a hair appointment. Stephanie and I wound up wearing little plastic bracelets, sitting on cold metal benches, me on the left, she on the right, in the back of a LAPD paddy wagon.

'Is Lance really taking you to the premiere?' she asked in a small forlorn voice.

I nodded.

'But . . . ' She didn't finish the thought, but I saw as she studied me that she was puzzled, probably wondering what the hell Lance could possibly see in me, especially when he could have her.

The paddy wagon started with a lurch.

'I hope you're happy now,' I said.

'Stephanie, why are you doing this?'

'You don't give up on your dream,' she said earnestly. 'Lance and I are meant to be together.'

'Is that why you want to kill him, so nobody else can have him?'

Her jaw dropped, shocked that I would even suggest such a thing. 'I would never hurt Lance,' she said indignantly. 'Never, never, never! I would do anything to protect him. I'll always love him. He wanted me to join him out here. That's why I don't understand . . . '

'What on earth makes you think that?'

'His messages.' She smiled. 'He sends me messages.'

'How?'

'All sorts of ways.' She cocked her head, still smiling. 'The most special was on the *Today* show.'

'I saw that; he sent you no message.'

'You're wrong. He did it again, last night on the *Tom Snyder Show*.'

'You're imagining it.'

'No. You've seen him take his right hand and gently touch two fingers to his eyebrow when he's talking.' Her curly lashes dipped shyly, and her voice took on a dreamy quality. 'Then he looks into the camera and smiles. That's our secret signal. That's when what he's saying is meant for me. He did it when he talked about coming out here, to the *Dark Journey* premiere. He was saying he wanted me here.'

I swiveled my head, looking for the cops, wishing they could hear this.

'That's how he sends you messages?'

'Only one of the ways,' she said coyly.

'Stephanie, get a grip!'

She regarded me intently. 'Did you ever want something so much that nothing else in the world mattered?' she whispered.

'Sure.' I watched the sky out the small window high over our heads. Miami's sky was so much bluer. 'I get that way about the truth, about stories, on deadline.'

'Do you give up when somebody says no or slams a door in your face? Do you?'

'No, but this is entirely different. Your goals have to be attainable, you have to have some hope of achieving them.'

'I do,' she said simply. 'You don't understand. I'm ready for Lance. I have a lifetime of recipes, funny stories, dreams, plans, and unconditional love, all saved for him. If he's not ready for me yet, I'm willing to wait. Lance is worth waiting for.'

'That all sounds so positive,' I said sarcastically. 'But you left out the parts about trying to kill us, vandalizing my car, slashing tires and clothes, arson and murder.

How do you justify them?'

'Me?' She looked as innocent as a little lamb. 'You're accusing *me* of all those things?' Her expression was one of disbelief.

'Did you rewire that control panel; did you kill Trent Talon?'

'I can't believe you're saying that. I won't even listen to it. I'm channeling my positive energy force to gain fulfillment, peace of mind, and the man I love. I can make it happen. Nothing is impossible. We create our own futures.'

I sighed. 'That's exactly what you're doing, Stephanie, and it won't be pretty.'

She sounded so earnest, so believable, who could blame the cops for listening to her and doubting me? Outside of her obsession, she seemed to function so well in the real world.

They had left a note on Lance's front door. I knew it was only a matter of time before I was sprung.

I expected him to send one of his men, but it was Lance who showed up at the station, with Dave and Al. His nose was running. He wanted Stephanie prosecuted for trespassing and said his lawyers would contact the judge about the restraining order.

He was apologetic. I didn't blame him as much as I did Dave. 'If Niko was here,' I told

Lance, in front of him, 'this never would have happened.'

'Let's go to Tiffany's, I want to buy you something,' Lance said soothingly.

'I don't want anything,' I said peevishly. 'Let's just stop and buy some postcards, so I can let everybody back home know what a good time I'm having.

'Oh, yeah,' I added. 'You know that thing you do?' I mimicked his little hand-to-the-brow gesture.

'What?' He looked puzzled.

I did it again, exaggerating.

'Oh, yeah.' He nodded.

'Stop it! Don't do it again! Especially not in public. Especially not in front of a camera.'

★ ★ ★

I had turned ugly. I guess that's why they took me to a North Rodeo Drive salon to be pampered. I felt like a poodle being dropped off at the groomers. Like a bad-tempered poodle, I wondered if they would ever return for me. The salon staff took me in tow, whisking me off to a small room where they gave me a smock, then steamed my face like a lobster, over water bubbling with aromatic herbs and spices. An elegant woman examined my pores through a huge magnifying glass, shook her head sadly, and asked if I knew the word sunscreen. Then she spread a sticky green clay masque over my skin, slathered my hands and feet with oil, placed heated gloves and booties over them, and left me in a reclining chair with my feet up, swaddled in a fleecy blanket, soft music playing. I fell asleep immediately. Too soon, they woke me, peeled the masque from my face, splashed my skin with rose water, daubed it with moisturizing cream, and unleashed Armando, the makeup artist.

When he finished with his brushes and pencils, crayons and colors, a manicurist shaped and polished my fingernails and toenails while a stylist swept my hair up and off my face in a style I had never worn and could never duplicate, with waves, tiny curls, and dangling ringlets.

Somebody should take my picture, I thought, as I stared in a mirror, awed at the new me. I would never look this good again.

Al rushed me back to the house, where I slipped into my little black Chanel knockoff and joined Lance downstairs. Champagne waited in the limo. 'I got you something,' Lance said, on the way to the theater.

The box was from Tiffany's. A little gold

bracelet linked with Xs and Os, hugs and kisses.

It was all I had imagined. Velvet ropes, photographers, TV cameras, fans waving. Lance held my hand, flashed his megawatt smile, and waved. Pauli and Frank brought up the rear.

Everybody seemed to love *Dark Journey*, and I didn't see how anyone could tell that there had been frantic re-editing and a new ending shot.

I met too many people to remember at the post-premiere party. All Hollywood types, exchanging phony kisses, lips not really touching the other party, as they made sounds like *mmm-whaa*. I felt uncomfortable with all those strangers who kept repeating how 'excited' they were about everything. So 'excited' about the film, about their new projects, about seeing Lance again.

'I'm *excited*,' I whispered to Lance, 'about the hors d'oeuvres. Aren't they great?'

'I'm excited too,' he said, flashing me his smoldery-eyed sexy look. Maybe his cold was breaking up.

We stopped at Spago afterward, to be snapped by the paparazzi, to see and be seen by more of the excited Hollywood crowd, and to eat a tiny pizza.

Everybody else magically disappeared when we got back to the house. Alone at last. More champagne. I fetched my nightgown from the guest room but never got to wear it.

Afterward, I lay next to Lance, thinking. Did I expect too much? Was he a bit disappointing in the stud department? Could it be the steroids he had ingested, buffing up early in his career? Maybe it was because I was overtired. He did still have his cold. And we were both jet-lagged.

He pushed our early morning flight back until afternoon, despite angry words long distance with Van Ness, who wanted him back in Miami to shoot a scene late that afternoon. 'They're lucky I'm coming back at all,' Lance muttered after hanging up. Obviously buoyed, he was feeling more feisty after the *Dark Journey* reviews. It looked like his last film for WFI would be a success; the reviews were terrific. We sunned by the pool and ate a leisurely lunch, interrupted by a call from Miami.

Niko wanted to know if we were sure Stephanie was in LA. The Star Island guard said she had just driven by several times.

'No way she could be in Miami,' I said. 'Unless she has a twin or a double.'

The LAPD was apologetic. A snafu. By the time the paperwork had reached the threat management unit that handles VIP stalking cases, it was too late. Stephanie had already been released on a $50 signature bond in the trespassing case. She could be anywhere, Miami included.

Lance dreaded the return flight and reporting to the *Margin of Error* set, but I was ready to go home to Miami.

'I know what is so odd about this town,' I told him, as our plane climbed and I saw the reddish smog hugging the jagged Pacific coastline spread out below. 'The ocean is on the wrong side. It's so weird.'

We lowered our seat backs and relaxed, holding hands as I described my heart-to-heart with Stephanie.

'The worst lies are the ones you tell yourself,' he said, shaking his head.

He was right. I was impressed. 'Is that yours? Or is it from one of your movies?'

'What?'

'I never know if it's you or a scriptwriter talking.'

'What's wrong with that?'

'Plagiarism.'

'No, it ain't. Hell,' he grumbled, and looked alarmed. 'My ears just popped. Hope I don't have any problems on this flight.' He blew his nose gingerly, then tucked away his handkerchief. 'Now if some talent was paid

Guild wages to write me that line, why shouldn't I use it? Besides, who remembers? Once I learn a line' — he tapped his temple — 'it's in there somewhere. How can I remember if it's something I thought of or something somebody else thought of for me?'

He paused.

'I guess that sounds so Hollywood,' he said bleakly. 'Like all those people at the party last night.'

'Your friends?'

'They are not my friends. Never make that mistake. In the real world, you keep lying to people and pretty soon you're not making a living. In Hollywood, the opposite is true. Shit has integrity in Hollywood. They admire a lie, a good scam, more than they admire real talent. If they don't constantly retail lies, a movie doesn't get made. Under all that hype you heard last night, there is one chance in a thousand that any of those projects will be made. They're shrewd. They use your name . . . Show any weakness at all, and they ply you with alcohol or drugs. If they see that you have a minor weakness for women, money, or booze, they turn it into a major vice. If you're vain, they zero in on that, feed it, and stroke it.

'There is no truth in these people. It's not considered hip to tell the truth. They

410

live in a fantasy world. Hollywood is like prison. If they are twenty years old when they get there, they become even more juvenile. Nobody ever grows up in Hollywood. It's like dealing with an underworld culture, like in prison or a third world country.'

'How do you survive?'

'I'm tough and I'm smart,' he said simply. 'But I learned a helluva lot of things the hard way, and I never stop watching my back.'

★   ★   ★

We approached across the vast dark of the Everglades; then came the lights of the sprawling city below and a semicircle, swinging out over endless black sea broken only by occasional flickering lights on the water.

It felt good to be back in Miami, to hear the sounds of Spanish and experience the raucous chaos of MIA, with Lance's body-guards running interference. Niko was not waiting as planned on the lower level. Pauli went upstairs to see if he might be there.

'Damn,' Lance checked his watch impatiently. 'This is not like him.'

Traffic poured through the fume-filled terminal as we searched the oncoming stream

411

for the Town Car, the surging crowd for the familiar ponytail.

'Call 'im,' Lance told Dave. 'Find out where the hell he is. If he broke down somewhere, we can hop a cab.'

No answer at the house or in the car.

We wound up in a station wagon taxicab that could hold all of us and our bags. The night was hot, the air conditioner didn't work, and the driver had the news in Creole turned up full blast.

Dave sat up front and directed him. A fire truck rumbled slowly off Star Island as we approached. No one spoke, but the look on the guard's face as he opened the gate sent my stomach into a free fall.

Police cars, fire trucks, and a crime-scene van ringed the house, cluttering the court-yard. They appeared to be mopping up, finishing reports, awaiting some final detail before leaving.

Lance was halfway to the house as Dave paid the driver and the others got the bags. As I stepped out of the cab to follow him, I glanced back over my shoulder and saw the medical examiner's wagon approaching over the bridge.

22

Lance swept past the patrolman at the door. 'Niko! Niko!' The cop moved to stop him, but a Miami Beach detective lieutenant inside signaled that it was all right.

'Where is he? Where's Niko?' The lieutenant, Greg Wallace, jerked his head toward the stairs. Lance took them two at a time. The walls at the top of the stairs had been discolored by smoke. The electricity was off and a fire department generator hummed, their lamps providing the light.

I followed Lance. The detective behind me nearly ran me over when I stopped suddenly, frozen in place, halfway up the stairs. The smoky smell of burned wood and insulation had given way to the unforgettable odor of charred flesh.

'Oh, please don't let it be him,' I whispered. The detective wore the expressionless poker face that cops affect when they are not sure what is going on and trust no one.

Voices rose and fell behind us, expressions and expletives of shock and disbelief: Dave, Al, Pauli, and Frank, hearing bad news from somebody down below. Flashes of light from upstairs, camera flashes. Lance should not walk blindly into some terrible sight. Somebody had to explain first.

'Lance!' I rushed after him. 'Wait!'

A fuel can lay discarded in the hall. A drip torch, marked with the Forestry Service emblem. The second of the two stolen from the 'Glades.

'Lance!' Too late, he was in the room.

A loud, almost immediate, crash followed, as though he had fallen or passed out.

Taking a deep breath, I burst inside. Lance had not fallen. The crash came when he had spun away from what was on the bed and slammed both fists into the wall at eye level. His pain was a terrible sight. As terrible a sight as Niko's body.

'You should have told him first!' I turned on the detective. 'They were lifelong friends!'

'I didn't tell him to barge in here.' The detective shrugged.

Lance looked numb, eyes wet, breathing deeply. 'What happened?' he muttered between breaths. 'What the hell happened?'

The body, drawn into a fetal position, was almost unrecognizable, charred like the mattress, the floor around it, and part of one wall. He looked as though he had been wearing Lance's burgundy-colored bathrobe, part of a sleeve still intact. His ponytail and part of his scalp remained.

'Let's talk downstairs.' The detective herded us into the hall.

'We can't leave him alone up here, like . . . like this.' Lance's voice cracked. 'Somebody has to stay with him.'

'He won't be alone,' I murmured. The removal crew from the medical examiner's office passed us on the stairs. 'They'll take care of him,' I whispered.

A neighbor had accommodated the cops by allowing them to use her brightly lit kitchen as a command post. We talked there, around a glass table.

'We thought it was you, at first,' the detective said, almost jovial, 'smoking in bed.' He raised an eyebrow as if that would be the only logical conclusion.

'He didn't smoke,' Lance muttered. 'I'm the smoker.'

'But your house, your room. That *is* your room, right?'

Lance nodded, heavy-lidded eyes shrouded in misery.

'You usually share your bedroom with this guy?'

'No.' Lance shook his head, bewildered.

'What do you think he was doing there?'

'He knew I was coming back. Might have been getting the room ready . . . He had the run of the place. Whatever.'

'What is it you said this guy did for you?'

'Security, personal trainer, assistant.'

'We shot down the smoking-in-bed theory when we found that can of accelerant,' Wallace said. 'Then a dispatcher said she seen you on TV, at something in Hollywood last night. Security at the gate said this guy told 'im he was s'posed to pick you up at the airport. You just get in?'

He wanted to know why we had taken a later flight, why we had been delayed, what time we had landed.

Lance, staring at the floor, raised his eyes. 'Stephanie!' The way he said it chilled my heart.

I stood next to his chair, my hand on his shoulder, fighting my own tears, remembering Niko at the hospital when Lance was hurt, Niko exasperated at Cape Florida, racing me to the airport, ready to lock Stephanie in a closet or dump her in the drink. Did he try? Did it backfire?

'We know who did this.' Lance got to his feet, slowly nodding, fists clenched.

We told the detective everything, then referred him to McDonald and the Miami fire investigators on Trent Talon's case.

'So you're saying that this case, the stuntman's murder, and the 'Glades fire may be related?'

He wore the unhappily incredulous look of a man who likes things simple and tidy, a man just beginning to realize that they were about to turn messy and complicated.

'Hopefully,' he said, 'the post will tell us a lot. What, if anything, he had on board at the time. Whether he was dead or alive when the fire started.'

'Post?' Lance said.

'Postmortem, the autopsy,' I said.

He closed his eyes.

I turned to the detective. 'What about the press?' How had they missed all this? Where were they?

'Been and gone. Had us a riot scene for a while. They were all over us before we knew what we had. Lost interest when they heard Westfell was out of town and it was just some guy who worked for 'im.'

How nice of him, I thought bitterly, to phrase it that way. Thankfully Lance, lost in thought, did not seem to notice.

'When did this happen?' I asked.

'Oh, we had us quite a day,' the detective said. Niko was already dead before we left LA. While we were on the freeway to LAX, Miami Beach fire had two calls, almost

417

simultaneous, one from the alarm company monitoring station, reporting that a smoke detector had activated at the Star Island house, the other from a neighbor who saw smoke.

The fire department had worked fast to contain the blaze. Smoke had damaged the entire second floor, but the actual fire had been confined to Lance's room.

★　★　★

We spent what remained of the night at my apartment. Pauli slept on my living room couch. The other guys went to a nearby motel.

Silent, angry, grieving, Lance did not want to be held. He kept getting out of bed to use the phone in the kitchen. He talked for a long time to Niko's married sister in Saddle Brook, New Jersey. A longer time with Silverman. I heard him weeping.

He took a suite at the Fontainebleau in the morning. We both had to go back to work. The movie was so far behind schedule there was no way to take more time. And Lance was presented with pages and pages of new dialogue to learn, written by the latest imported scriptwriter. The story line had changed so much that it was totally unrecognizable and incomprehensible. Hodges and Van Ness were fighting bitterly about it. Wendy was on medication, and Lexie had turned into a raging prima donna, showing up late on the set and throwing tantrums.

The only good news was that the cops were now seriously searching for Stephanie.

She had been released about an hour after I was, according to LAPD. Airline records showed her aboard the next flight to Miami, probably because she heard me tell the cops that we planned to fly out first thing in the morning.

The Star Island gate guard picked Stephanie from a photo lineup as the woman he had seen and reported to Niko. Niko had been right when he told Lance that she had been sighted. She was in the neighborhood. Soon after, he was dead.

Miami detectives had dug into her past and learned that as a troubled preadolescent she had set fire to her family's summer home in Cape Cod. Her only arrest unrelated to stalking Lance was for teenage shoplifting, nothing violent. But she had dropped out of college for a semester to strike out on her own after a dispute with her parents. During that time she had worked briefly for Western Electric, reading diagrams and wiring telephone company components.

Not enough for an arrest warrant but enough to elevate her to number-one suspect in Trent Talon's murder, as well as the 'Glades fire. Police issued BOLOs with her picture. Watch orders were placed on my apartment, the Star Island house, and the movie locations. LA forwarded the proper paperwork to hold her on the stalking violations once she was picked up. But where the hell was she? Suddenly scarce, she looked all the more suspicious.

Lieutenant Wallace shared with us the results of the medical examiner's initial report. The doctor had seen a trace of congealed blood at the scene, and his suspicions had been confirmed. X-rays showed a bullet still lodged in the occipital region, at the base of the skull. Though Niko had been shot first, the incineration had not been postmortem. Soot in his larynx and trachea meant he had been alive, if just barely, when sprayed with gasoline and set afire.

He had been fully dressed, down to shoes, socks, and wristwatch. Lance's robe still hung in the closet. Niko had one the same color. The big house was often chilly. He must have thrown it on over his T-shirt and trousers.

420

Wallace said the fatal shot was fired from the balcony, along with two others. Two slugs were lodged in the wall. The killer, hiding in Lance's room, must have slipped out the French doors, then fired through the glass when Niko approached to investigate a noise or for some other purpose.

'She thought it was me,' Lance said. 'It was me she wanted to kill. She thought we had come back earlier; it was my room; we looked alike.'

After seeing me in LA, she caught the first plane out, then beelined for his Miami home, lying in wait to ambush Lance when he arrived.

It made sense, in the obsessive world of a single-minded stalker, but something nagged at me. I had nearly believed Stephanie's sad sincerity in LA. Was my judgment that bad? She was talented at convincing people. Everybody believed her. That was how she had been able to get away with so much for so long. Like the slick swindlers who bilk thousands with ease from the same bank tellers who invariably question my fifty-dollar check.

It had to be her. If not Stephanie, who?

★ ★ ★

In the days that followed, I did my job but never relaxed. The gun in Iggy Zee's possession when he was arrested was the murder weapon in the Fairborn case and one of the guns fired at Angel and me. Cops had picked up the other shooter and three more gang members. One flipped, agreeing to testify against the others in the homicide and attempted murder cases. All were being held without bond.

My eyes constantly searched crowds and traffic for Stephanie. I startled easily. Grew more edgy and cautious. Put my gun back in the car and carried it with me into my apartment, even though I felt queasy handling it. I double-checked my smoke alarm and bought extra batteries. Something new had been added to my bad dreams. I kept waking up smelling smoke.

Lance had asked the first night if I wanted to join them at the Fontainebleau. I didn't but almost wished I had when two pushy tabloid reporters appeared on my doorstep. Our picture had appeared in the *Enquirer*. WESTFELL STEPS OUT WITH NEW LOVE WHILE BODYGUARD IS SLAIN IN MIAMI. Lance was furious. I was heartsick. My mother was thrilled and said the dress looked great.

I said nothing to the reporters. Just got into my car, as one of them snapped pictures, and drove to the office. Even a word would only encourage them. It felt so bizarre to be on the wrong side of a press frenzy. The entire world seemed topsy-turvy.

★　★　★

I went to meet Lance for breakfast at the Fontainebleau and was surprised to encounter Lexie, just leaving. She brushed by me angrily, without a word. She looked as though she'd been crying.

'She's upset about Niko,' he explained. He had been everpresent when they were married. 'She's also jealous and mad as hell at you.'

'Jealous?'

'She saw your picture in the tabloids. That's intruding on her turf. She has to be Queen Bee.'

★　★　★

He hated hotel living. The day after the police released the crime scene, he dispatched a platoon of workmen and painters. Two days later, he moved back in, though not to his old room, which was kept closed. The faint smell of smoke lingered, but he went there only to sleep.

Niko's sister kept calling, wanting to claim his body. The delay was that the ME office was having trouble obtaining his dental records from LA, the final formality in such cases.

* * *

'The kids saw you on TV,' Angel said cheerfully, as I worked on a story about the latest *chupacabra* sighting. But what she had really called to say was 'We're in the movie! Do you believe it?'

Angel and her kids had been hired as extras on *Margin of Error*, thanks to Ziff. Their big scene was in a shopping center, as Lance, pursued by the bad guys, raced through the mall, bullets flying. They played a mother and her children ducking for cover. A plucky teenage girl, played by Misty, strolling by with friends, screams and runs.

Not much of a stretch there, I thought.

I hated to be negative but had to ask. 'Aren't the kids just getting over the trauma of the real shooting?'

'Nah, they're fine. They're having a ball. And we get paid!'

She was thinking about registering, as a group, with a talent agency. The model family. The hearing in her manslaughter case was coming up and she was optimistic.

'Have they caught that awful woman yet?' she said, asking about Stephanie.

Life is strange. I could not believe I was having a friendly chat with Angel Oliver about some other awful woman.

An intern was filling in for Gloria, taking messages. She approached my desk as I said goodbye to Angel. 'Somebody was trying to reach you,' she said brightly.

'Who was it?'

'Some woman.' She glanced down at the message she had scrawled. 'Said her name is Stephanie. Said it's important.'

'Why didn't you signal me to get off the phone? Do you realize who that was?'

The intern cocked her head to one side and blinked, her mouth open.

'Do you read the paper?'

The answer to both was an obvious no.

Stephanie had left no number. If only I had not been on the phone with Angel. If only Gloria had not been on her break. If only.

The message was on my machine at home that night. She sounded hysterical.

'Britt, make them stop saying those terrible things about me! You know they're not true. I've got to talk to Lance. To make him listen. He'll believe me . . . Don't force me to do things I don't want to do.'

She called Lance numerous times as well. She got Dave, Pauli, Frank, and their voice mail, but Lance was never in when she called. Police and the telephone company installed a trap on the line, but she always hung up before they could trace her call.

★ ★ ★

I covered Angel's hearing on the fourth floor of the Richard E. Gerstein Justice Building. Braced and invigorated by the cool, breezy weather, cops, lawyers, victims, and witnesses in suit coats and shades trotted briskly up the sun-dappled front steps. The pace of the place picked up as the temperature went down.

Bliss, in his blue suit, conferred with the prosecutor outside the courtroom. He shook his head at me as the attorney went inside. 'She's gonna skate,' he said.

'What . . . ?'

'See for yourself.' He held the door open for me.

Angel was already inside with her attorney, smiling like the belle of the ball. For the first time since I had known her she wore a dress, a navy blue number with a little white collar.

426

Her public defenders had worked vigorously. Their presentation was impressive. This was the first time I ever heard of intestinal atresia. The criminal charges were based on the police investigation and the findings of the chief medical examiner who had determined that Cynthia did indeed appear starved, body wasted, stomach empty, at the time of her death.

Detective Bliss had found that her bed was a blanket in a cardboard box and that a sister, a child herself, was often the caregiver, with the mother away.

The defense had countered by hiring a noted pediatric pathologist to study Cynthia's entire record, with revealing results. A premature baby who weighed only three pounds at birth, Cynthia suffered from a number of medical problems, including serious neurological deficits. Nurses had made several unsuccessful attempts to bottle-feed little Cynthia. She had trouble sucking and gaining weight, they noted, describing her condition as 'floppy', as 'limp as a rag doll'. Hospitalized for two and a half months, the baby was tube-fed until the day doctors sent her home with Angel, who was referred to a high-risk clinic for follow-up.

Twice, Angel carried the baby to the clinic,

taking two buses to get there. Each time, her records could not be located in the computer. Each time, she was referred back to the hospital, two more bus rides away, where clerks shook their heads, told her she was in the wrong place, and sent her back to the clinic.

Both sides told Judge Let-'em-go Joe Turrell that after examining her medical history, they now concurred. Baby Cynthia would have died anyway, even with professional care; in fact, she did well to survive fifteen months. All agreed that the manslaughter charge should be reduced to a single count of child neglect.

Angel pleaded no contest in exchange for six months probation. A social worker would visit and report to the court on the well-being of the other children. I found myself hoping that someone would tip her off to bring something for Harry. For the first time, I was not incensed by one of Let-'em-go Joe's rulings. Obviously relieved, Angel practically skipped out of the courtroom. So did I, relieved that after this story, Angel was out of my life for good.

As I drove back to the office it occurred to me that lately nobody was really what he or she first seemed to be. Not Angel, not Darnell, not even Lance. The man I expected to be arrogant and shallow when we met was somebody I could actually love, if only I didn't feel so damn numb all the time.

Back at the office I made the mistake of answering the phone before finishing my story about Angel's day in court.

'How high were those strappy high-heeled sandals you wore in Hollywood?' the caller breathed. 'Three and a half inches?'

I was about to hang up when he said, 'Do you change your shoes when you drive? You ever drive that flashy T-Bird barefoot?'

How did he know what I drove?

'Saw your pictures in the tabloids,' he said. 'The one in your car didn't show your feet.'

Urgent sounds resonated in the background.

'You're watching X-rated cable, aren't you?' I said accusingly.

He hesitated. 'Not exactly.'

'Well, what is that?'

'I don't subscribe,' he said defensively. 'It's scrambled. It's better that way, just glimpses, little flashes, a thigh here, a foot there. It's more exciting,' he confided. 'More like real life. I don't pay for it.'

Nice, I thought, and slammed down the phone. Now this sicko knew what I looked like and the model car I drove.

The final scene at the paper was shot in the pressroom that night. I stayed to watch the villains pursue Gardiner Bowles and Cassie Malone in a deadly game of hide-and-seek, down into the pressroom where huge rolls of newsprint weigh 2,000 pounds and giant ink drums measure four feet around. Shot and wounded during a knock-'em-down drag-'em-out fight, Gardiner is hurled back onto the web, his bleeding body moving inevitably toward the press. Cassie struggles bravely with the last bad guy still standing. The villain breaks away and flees, as she scrambles to hit the emergency STOP button. The machinery slows down, then cuts off, just in time. Cassie cradles Gardiner in her arms, weeping, 'Don't die! Don't die!'

The scene gave me the creeps, as they shot it again and again.

Lexie had to clean up and change clothes for each take because of the fake blood gushing from Gardiner's gaping bullet wounds, courtesy of Ziff, who once more outdid himself in the gore department. Wardrobe worked fast on Cassie's four identical dresses. By the time Lance bled all over the fourth, the first was again fresh, quick cleaned and pressed.

The final take was the best, Lance's face so etched in agony, his moans so real, that I nearly wept. He really is good, I thought, and wondered if he was thinking of Niko.

'You were amazing in that last take,' I said, as Pauli drove us back to Star Island. 'Anyone would swear you were really in pain.'

'I was,' he said. 'Lexie was digging her fingernails into the back of my neck.' He touched the area just below his hairline and winced. 'Think she drew blood. She always liked to do that.'

The man really did have claw marks deep in the back of his neck.

Pauli turned down the street to Lance's house. A party was winding down at a neighbor's home. A number of cars and a catering truck still remained.

Still wide awake and restless, we strolled out to the pool deck overlooking the bay. It was windy and cool in the dark, about a half hour till dawn.

'Who else is there?' I asked, as we gazed out over the water. 'Who else wants you dead?'

He looked at me oddly. 'How romantic.'

'Just in case it isn't Stephanie,' I said. 'What if it wasn't her?'

'Since when are you Stephanie's new best friend?'

431

'Just humor me. I'm trying to figure this out.'

He leaned against the wrought-iron railing, his back to the lights dancing on the water. 'Well, let's see. You could start with everybody who paid to see my last picture.'

'Be serious.' I made a face and stuck out my tongue.

'Don't point that thing at me unless you intend to use it.' He reached for me, but I eluded his grasp and slipped into a comfortable lounge chair.

'This could be important.'

He sighed and sat in the chair next to mine. 'There's both my ex-wives . . . your ex-boyfriend, the cop.'

'Who else? Somebody obviously doesn't want to see this movie finished. What would happen?'

'The studio would collect the insurance.'

'How much?'

'At this point, with all the cost overruns, they might barely break even.'

'How much do they stand to make if it's released?'

'The way it stands now?' He paused and gazed out at the misty skyline. 'It's got to be a blockbuster to do more than break even.'

'And if it flops?'

432

'If it's a disaster, the studio could be in trouble.'

'How bad?'

He shrugged. 'If Carolco could go belly up, anything can happen. They've been on shaky financial ground since the summer disasters last year. Overhead is huge. Cappleman has padded the payroll with all kinds of friends and relatives. There are more big budget productions these days, and marketing costs are on the rise. It's tough for any studio to make the money back, and this one's had a string of box office bombs.'

'Is there anybody else out there that you're worth more to dead than alive?'

He turned to face me, the chair creaking under his weight. 'You're suggesting that the studio might decide it's cheaper to kill me for the insurance money than risk a major financial disaster if *Margin of Error* flops?'

'I'm not saying they held a stockholders' meeting and took a vote, but maybe somebody . . . people get killed for a lot less every day. Look at Darnell Oliver, hiring those kids to waste Angel. I'm just thinking out loud, considering the possibilities.'

'With any luck,' he said, leaning forward, elbows on his knees, expression thoughtful, 'we should wrap soon. Only a few days of shooting left.'

'Are the scenes critical? Could the movie be released without them?'

He thought about it. 'Hard to say, at this point, what could be done in editing.'

Dogs started to raise hell somewhere close by, their barks carrying over the water. The all-night partyers must finally be going home. I shivered, and Lance leaned over to put his arms around me.

'Want to go inside?'

'No, I want to see the dawn.'

'But you're so cold.' He eased off his lounge chair on to mine, cuddled me close to his chest, and began unfastening my skirt. Slipping it off as I raised my hips, he drew it down over my feet, then straddled me and began unbuttoning my blouse as he nuzzled my neck and began rocking against me.

'I'm beginning to feel warmer.' I forgot the topic of our discussion, until I heard sudden thrashing in the shrubbery.

The dogs we just heard must be running loose, I told myself. But my heart beat wildly. 'Lance, what is that?'

'Let's go in the house.' He pulled me to my feet, peering into the dark.

I snatched up my skirt and hoisted my blouse, which had been pulled down off one shoulder.

'Nooooooh!' A woman's high-pitched howl

of panic. A gunshot rang out a split second later and the leg of my lounge chair splintered. We were no longer using it; we were halfway to the house.

Lance was shouting for Pauli to bring a gun, and call the cops.

Pauli stumbled out the French doors. He must have been dozing. He looked dazed and held a handgun. Dave appeared a moment later, hair in his eyes, shirtless, wearing only undershorts. He was in excellent shape.

'Who was screaming?' he demanded. 'Was that you, Britt?'

'No, son of a bitch! It's her, it's her!' Lance said. 'Goddammit! Give me the gun. The bitch tried to shoot me! Give me the gun!'

Pauli ignored him and charged past us, followed by Dave and Frank. Al was on the stairs. He had a shotgun.

I dialed 911, while trying to hang onto Lance. 'Don't go out there! She's got a gun!'

'I can't live this way,' he muttered, slamming his fist against the wall. 'No more. I can't live like this. I hope they kill her.'

23

Cries, sobs, and shouts sounded in the night. Some were mine, as I struggled to keep Lance from rushing out into the dark.

'They've got her! They've got her!' I peered through the mullioned windows. Stephanie was being dragged unceremoniously through the shrubbery, toward the house, as a faint blush of dawn streaked the eastern horizon. Pauli had forced her right wrist down until it was just a few feet off the ground. Her left wrist was grasped in Al's big fist, over his head, nearly lifting her off her feet, as though announcing the winner in a prizefight. He held his shotgun high in the other hand. Stumbling, struggling, stretched between them, Stephanie was screaming at the top of her lungs. Dave and Frank marched behind them, the latter with a handgun.

Police cars howled across the bridge.

'Lance! Lance!' Stephanie shrieked hysterically. 'Are you all right? Lance! Are you hurt?'

Lordy, I thought, the neighbors must be so sick of this. I knew I was. The police should build a substation here. They would save the gas spent speeding to the scene of the crimes.

* * *

They had not found Stephanie's gun by midmorning, despite police divers, a metal detector, and a dog. The theory was that she had either stashed it among the trees and the lush foliage on the west side of the house, tossed it into the bay, or pitched it up on to the roof of the cabana, the boathouse, or the main house itself.

Lance ignored her frantic pleas to see him. His only revenge was to deny her what she wanted most.

He sent her a message instead, instructing the cops to tell her that if he ever had the chance he would put a bullet in her head himself. I was sure he meant it.

He remained agitated and reluctant to even talk to Lieutenant Wallace, who showed up about an hour after Stephanie was taken to headquarters, paraded before a gauntlet of photographers and TV news cameras.

'I don't like that son of a bitch,' Lance muttered. 'He's the one who said Niko was 'just some guy who worked for me."

'I had hoped you missed that,' I said. 'Sure, he's insensitive, but he doesn't mean it. He's just been on the job too long.'

The morning glare was hard on our eyes after being awake all night. We talked to Wallace in the great room, over a pot of coffee with the blinds closed.

'Either of you see or hear anybody else out there when this all went down?'

The answer was no. Neither had Lance's bodyguards.

'Here's what we get from Stephanie.' Wallace spoke directly to Lance, ignoring me. 'She's itching to tell you her story, that she didn't do any of these things she's accused of. So she comes over here last night. Sees you come home. She waits, hoping to catch you alone, when she sees somebody in the shadows at the side of the house. She thinks it might be you and follows him back behind the pool bar. She hears voices, which hadda be you and Britt, here. The guy she followed is watching you.'

My face must have reddened at this point.

Wallace's eyes lingered on me speculatively before he went on.

'Then she sees this guy try to pop a cap at you. She panics, yells at 'im, and grabs for the gun. It goes off, he smacks her up the side of the head, knocks her down, and hits the wind. By the time she's back on her feet your guys are all over her.'

'Did she recognize the man with the gun?' I asked.

Lance frowned, with an expression of disbelief.

'Says it was too dark. She was more interested in watching what he was watching, until he pulls the gun and tries to smoke you.'

Lance did a double take. 'You're not buying that? In other words, she's saying she deserves a medal, that she saved us from some imaginary intruder? Bullshit. That's like the crazies who torch buildings so they can rescue the victims, play hero, and get their pictures in the newspaper.'

'That's her story.' Wallace shrugged. 'She tells it well.'

'She always does.' I remembered our first meeting just outside this very room. 'She can be very convincing.'

'Finding the damn gun would help us a lot,' Wallace said. 'We're having no luck so far, but that's not unusual because of all the silt on the bottom of the bay. She is all bruised up,' he added.

'From my guys when they tackled her! Here's what really happened,' Lance said. 'She cried out in protest when she saw us — ' He hesitated.

'Displaying affection,' I said.

'Right,' Lance said. 'That's when she shot at us.'

Made sense. But what if . . . 'Did security at the gate see anybody else leave?'

Wallace shrugged and shook his head. Any other night at that hour, the guard might have noticed. But cars were leaving the neighbor's party. Nobody scrutinizes departing motorists. For them, the gate opens automatically.

'This fucking woman has made my life miserable for years.' Lance paced the room, eyes exhausted. 'New York, LA, now here.' He turned to the detective. 'Isn't there a test to see if she fired a gun? That would settle it.'

'Right,' Wallace said. He closed his notebook and got to his feet.

'I never want her to see daylight again,' Lance told the departing cop, who turned at the door.

'Oh, she won't be going anywhere for a long time,' he said. 'I can guarantee you that.'

★ ★ ★

Go to jail and you are entitled to a phone call. That's singular. So how did Stephanie manage to call me four times that day? Most were messages.

'I warned you,' I said, when we finally connected. 'Everybody warned you,

440

Stephanie. You wouldn't listen to me then, so I won't listen to you now.'

'But somebody is trying to kill Lance,' she protested. 'You have to stop him.'

Was she a split personality, a multiple personality, or what? Nobody was buying her story. I wouldn't either, except . . . if only they would find her damn gun.

'What did you do with it, Stephanie? Is it the same gun you used to kill Niko?'

'I hated Niko. He was trying to keep me and Lance apart. But I never would have killed him. I wouldn't physically harm another human being.'

'Maybe from outside on the balcony you thought he was Lance.'

'It wasn't me, but somebody did. That's what I'm trying to tell you. You have to listen to me. Somebody is trying to kill Lance!'

'Would you be willing to take a polygraph test?'

'Of course. Absolutely.' She showed no hesitation. I had only asked to see her response. The tests are notoriously unreliable on the medicated or mentally deranged.

* * *

The GSR test, gunshot residue, came back inconclusive that afternoon. Sterile swabs,

441

used on different parts of her hand, had been analyzed for gunpowder. Traces were present, according to the lab, but not enough to be conclusive. What was found could have been sustained while struggling with a gunman as his weapon fired.

What if she was telling the truth? The existence of a more deadly stalker was a long shot. But if there was one, Lance remained in danger and a killer was still free.

Stephanie called again, and I told her to put me on her visitor list.

The noise and chaos of the women's lockup unleashed a rush of bad memories. They took my bag, patted me down, and checked my tape recorder. Stephanie looked pale and disheveled, and a large bruise had purpled the side of her face. She wore no pearls this time. We talked into microphones, heavy plate glass between us.

'Is Lance all right? Is he very upset?' Despite all the trouble she was in, she was still obsessed over Lance.

'Of course he's upset. He's been shot at and missed, two friends are dead, his neighbors want to lynch him, and all this has totally disrupted his life, the movie, and maybe his entire career. Other than that, he's swell.'

She bombarded me with questions about him. Where he was, what he was doing, wearing. What did he say about her?

The less we discussed Lance, the better, I thought.

'I just haven't had any messages,' she said fretfully.

'You mean from the TV?'

'No. Phone messages.'

'Well, this may come as news to you, Stephanie, but you can't take calls in here.'

'I pick up the messages about Lance. I've called and called, but there are none.'

'What are you talking about? Where do you call?'

'My service. I had it transferred down here.'

'What kind of messages? Who leaves them?'

She shrugged, with more than a trace of self-importance. 'Lance, or whomever he has call me with the things I need to know. Where he'll be. Where he's staying.' She paused and smiled fondly. 'Who he's with, where he wants me to be. Sometimes he sends kisses.'

'You talk to him?'

'No,' she said impatiently. 'It's a monthly service. I call in and they read me my messages.'

'That's ridiculous. How could — '

'No, it isn't,' she snapped. 'How do you think I got your home number? Lance left it for me on the service.'

I swallowed, stomach suddenly queasy. 'I wondered how you got it.'

She nodded. 'He told me where you live, too. And he left word that he would be in LA for the premiere. Even told me what flight to take. But' — she pouted — 'he didn't say you would be there.'

My mouth felt dry. 'When did you start receiving these messages?'

'I always used the service, back in Boston. But Lance didn't call until after the time in New York, in his hotel room. I was so depressed after he married Lexie. I was afraid we would never be together. I didn't want to live and I did something stupid. I just wanted to die. But then, after I got out of the hospital, something wonderful happened. The messages began and I saw hope, that he did care, that I just had to be patient — '

'Why would he leave messages telling you where he was and then have you arrested?' I felt bewildered, as though this was another crazy dream.

'That,' she said, misty-eyed and shaking her head, 'is something I have to talk to him about. There is so much I don't understand.' She looked up at me, grey eyes inquisitive. 'Why? Why did he get involved with you?'

'I'm going to find out,' I said. 'This is insane.'

She gave me the number.

★ ★ ★

The service was office style. For seventy-five dollars a month, live operators answer calls twenty-four hours a day with a generic greeting. No voice mail.

'Miami office. Can I help you?' a cheery voice asked.

'Stephanie Carrollton, please.'

'She's not in, would you like to leave word?'

'When do you expect her?'

'She calls in regularly to pick up her messages.'

I called back in twenty minutes. 'This is Stephanie Carrollton,' I said. 'Any messages?'

'Nothing at the moment, Ms Carrollton.'

'Nothing from Lance?'

'No messages at all since you last checked. Sorry.'

'How long do you keep my messages?'

'They're usually destroyed after you pick

them up, Ms Carrollton.'

'No old ones there?'

'Let me see. There's something in the box here, from Sunday night. Umm, you got this one.'

'Could you read it?'

'Sure. *Lance works late tonight at the News, then goes back to the house.*'

'That's it?'

'That's all.'

'Would you save that one for me, please? I'd like the hard copy. Along with any other old messages of mine that you can find. I'll have someone pick them up.'

* * *

I slept with Lance that night, searched his eyes, and saw only honesty and affection. Of course, I realized, he was an actor and I was not in my right mind.

24

While Lance slept I searched his desk, his wallet, and his address book and scrolled through the files in the computer room down off the kitchen. His schedule, the production's daily call sheets, and e-mail memos from the *Margin of Error* office were all in there, but I did not find Stephanie's number or anything else that appeared incriminating. That did not mean it was not him.

I crept back into his bed, as guilty as a thief in the night. 'What'sa matter?' Lance mumbled. 'Where you been?'

'Couldn't sleep,' I said truthfully.

'Nothing new. Join the club.' He pulled me close.

As his breathing became slow and rhythmic, my mind raced. The chain of evidence would be broken if I picked up the messages, and they would lose any value in court.

Whom could I trust?

I slipped out of bed again.

* * *

447

'Britt, are you all right?'

McDonald sounded sleepy but not angry that I had called him at home at 2 A.M. I wondered if he was alone.

'Where are you?'

'It doesn't matter.' I gave him the number and the address of the service and explained. He instantly understood the implication.

'You think the son of a bitch deliberately led her on for some reason?'

'I don't know. I don't think so.' I was near tears. 'I don't know what to believe. It could be somebody else.'

When I went back to bed, Lance was sitting up. My heart sank when I saw his face.

'What's going on?' he asked me.

'You tell me,' I said.

I told him about my visit to Stephanie and about the messages.

'But who?' He leaned forward, peering into my eyes as though something disturbing lurked there. 'You think it was me? You believe her?'

'Somebody's been fucking with that sick woman's life.' I stood and paced the room.

He was slumped in an armchair now, smoking a cigarette, eyes smoldering, wearing only loose pajama bottoms. 'And somebody's been fucking with mine.' His voice had a razor edge.

I began to get dressed.

'Where do you think you're going?'

'Home.'

'You can't leave till we settle this.' He stabbed out his cigarette. 'Look at me,' he said, moving between me and the door. 'You goddam know better, and if you don't, you should be ashamed to be here.'

I sat abruptly, face in my hands. 'Well,' I said, after a moment. 'Let's brainstorm. Stephanie said the messages began after her suicide attempt in New York. What was happening in your life then?'

He took a deep breath. 'Me and Lexie were going down the toilet.' He reached for the cigarettes on his desk, lit another, then exhaled. 'I was leaving WFI and about to sign to do this picture with Titan.'

'What else?'

'I dunno.' He raised his eyes and his hands in a helpless gesture.

'Try.'

'I was working on *Dark Journey*, skirmishing with WFI because they didn't want me to leave. They wanted to keep me there.'

I thought for a moment. 'At the *News*, we have on-line access to everything published about both studios, about you, about Lexie, at around that time. Let's go search through them, see if anything rings a bell. Maybe we can come up with some lead . . . '

He grabbed a shirt. 'I'll get Dave and Al.'

'Wait! How do you know you can trust them? They could be on somebody's payroll.'

'That's crazy.' He snorted. 'I'd trust those guys — '

'You say you didn't leave those messages. Then who did?'

We slipped out of the house in the dark and took my car. My gun was in the glove compartment. I thought about it as I drove to the News, conscious every moment that the man beside me might not be who I thought he was at all.

Streets were deserted. The only lights in the sky came from incoming jets as they broke through the cloud cover that hung over the city.

The security man was missing from behind the glass at the employees' entrance. The News was probably shorthanded again, which would put him on rounds through the building, or perhaps he had taken a break.

We settled in at my desk, at the computer terminal. I tapped into the library system, summoning the world and its data bases to my fingertips. Lexis-Nexis; Dialog; Data-Times; Cypress, which accesses Dow Jones and other financial services; SEC reports from the Internet; and Baseline, rich with biographies of entertainment figures, their past work, the budgets of their films in progress, and industry financial reports. We began scrolling through stories in search of something, I wasn't sure what, printing out whatever appeared interesting.

'All these old films of yours,' I said. 'All WFI.'

'Right, I've been with them since the start.'

'Hmmmm. Does Titan have life insurance on you? A keyman policy for this film?'

'Sure. That's not unusual.'

The newsroom was eerie at 3 A.M., the silence broken only by the click of my computer keys and the steady hum of the printer.

'There were more stories about you last year,' I muttered, 'than about Fidel Castro, Mother Teresa, and Newt Gingrich put together.'

I glanced up, to refocus and rest my eyes for a moment. We were not alone. A man stood, silent, just feet away, in the shadows from the lobby's dim light. I experienced the same moment of madness, the same gut-wrenching sensation, as when I saw the Lindsey Hopkins security guard and mistook him for poor dead Randall Fairborn.

I blinked. But the specter remained the same. Oh my God, I thought. Tears stung my eyes. 'Oh my God,' I murmured aloud. He wore black and a ponytail.

Lance looked up from the printout he was reading. I heard his sharp intake of breath.

'Christ!' He sprang to his feet. 'Thank God you're alive!'

'Too bad I can't say the same for you, amigo.' Niko stepped forward, a dark snub-nosed .380 automatic in his hand.

'We thought you were dead,' I said stupidly.

He smiled. 'Exactly what you were supposed to think.'

'Who was he?' I asked.

'Somebody who won't be missed.' He sounded impatient.

There was a sound, a movement behind him, and I realized that he had a companion. A woman lingered in the darkened lobby.

'Hey, babe.' Niko spoke over his shoulder. 'Take the keys, bring up the car, and put it right next to hers.' He tossed a set of car keys in her direction. She stepped forward and caught them, onehanded, in midair, the light bouncing off her blonde hair.

'Okay, honey,' she sang out. I had seen her only once before but would never forget her face: Karen Sawyer, the woman on the elevator, the fan who had sprayed the love potion in Lance's eyes.

'Niko,' Lance said. 'What are you doing?

What have you done?'

'It pains me to say this, amigo, but some people are worth more dead than alive.' He did not look pained.

'You sent those messages to Stephanie, didn't you?' I said.

He sighed in exaggerated fashion. 'I was afraid somebody might listen to her. Lucky it was only you, and I heard in time.'

'How?' Was he tapping Lance's phone?

'Let's just say I have friends in the right places.' The gun still pointed at us, he plucked a sheet from our stack of printouts and scanned it. Tongue at the corner of his mouth, he raised an eyebrow.

'Not stupid,' he said admiringly. 'Good thing I'm nipping this in the bud.'

'I trusted you,' Lance said emotionally. 'You were the only one I trusted. How could you do this to me?'

'It's always you, you, you, isn't it, Lance? Didn't you think I'd ever get tired of it? We started out equals. You never admitted it, but I was the better ballplayer in high school; now you'll have to agree that I'm the better actor. Yet somehow we wind up with you the star and me the gofer. Is that fair?'

'You coulda quit.'

He smirked. 'Consider this my resignation.

453

Sign off that terminal. Bring those printouts,' he ordered, waving the gun at me impatiently, 'and your purse. We don't want to leave any mess behind. Let's go.'

'Somebody at Titan didn't want him to finish *Margin of Error*,' I said.

He smiled suavely. 'Right pew, wrong church.'

We were marched down the shadowy hallway toward the employee entrance. My eyes searched for the security guard, or for some late-night sports reporter or movie reviewer who might wander into the office. But even the cleaning crews had long since left for the night. The back of my neck tingled in fear. I thought he would shoot us there. He was going to kill us. He had to kill us now. Lance knew that too. He reached for my arm.

'No touching. No sudden moves. Just do what I tell you.' Niko obviously enjoyed giving the orders for a change.

If we were going to die, I had to know why.

'What is this all about? Why does somebody want Lance killed?'

'Think about it. Death does wonders for a career. You'll be a legend, Lance. Look what it did for Selena, for James Dean. Instant legends. The kid only made three movies. If he'd lived, he wouldn't be an icon. He'd be an old man nobody remembers.

'But the big bucks keep on rolling in. Look at Marilyn Monroe and Elvis. Still making more money than they ever did when they were alive.'

'WFI,' Lance said bitterly. 'They own the negatives, the library, all my films.'

'Now you're getting smart,' Niko said. 'Do you have any idea of the revenue stream that your death or disappearance will generate from video cassettes alone? If you never finish a movie for another studio, they own it all. Your entire body of work, your image on coffee mugs, T-shirts, all that shit, in perpetuity. Merchandising rights. A fucking gold mine. You'll be immortal.'

'This has nothing to do with her,' Lance said.

'Nobody ever said life was fair. Too bad, Britt. No offence.'

I tried to take a deep breath but had trouble inhaling.

'I told the cops — McDonald — about Stephanie's messages,' I said. 'He'll put it together.'

Lance looked startled. Niko looked surprised but unperturbed. 'You wouldn't do that; it might make macho man here look bad, and you've been having far too good a time to do that. You don't want to lose your piece of the action.'

455

'You misjudge me, like I misjudged you.'

'How much is Gettinger paying you?' Lance said. 'He hired you, didn't he?'

'Tch-tch, Lance. You know all you need to know.'

He pressed the elevator button. Somewhere, downstairs, I heard it clunk and grind into slow motion. Once we were in his car, if that was where he was taking us, we were totally at his mercy and I saw none in his eyes. Did we have a better chance out there or here in the building? At least I knew the building.

The doors slowly yawned open and he waved us inside with the gun. Who had died in his place? I wondered. How did he manage to find a victim with hair long enough for a ponytail?

'Hit lobby,' he said.

I punched three. Watching Lance, Niko didn't notice I had hit the wrong floor. I hoped Lance did. I caught his eye and glanced toward the control panel, hoping to give him a high sign.

The elevator lurched to a stop. The doors began to open and Niko stepped to the rear to follow us out. As he realized we were on the wrong floor we both broke into a run.

'Hey! Halt!' Confused for a moment, he hesitated for a split second to check the floor.

The cafeteria doors might be locked. No time to check. I burst through the other one, into the stairwell, Lance right behind me. I dropped my purse and let the printouts scatter.

'Let's go! Let's go!' As he passed me, he grasped my hand and dragged me, as we dashed down the stairs. Karen Sawyer was waiting, I thought. Did she have a gun? Was she capable of using it?

Too late. No way would we make it far enough to find out. Niko crouched, cursing aloud, at the top of the flight behind us and squeezed off a shot. It hit the poured concrete stairs and ricocheted off the metal railing with a clang. I winced, as we dove out of his line of fire, through the doors to the pressroom.

The sign on the wall said, FOUR DAYS WITHOUT A LOST TIME ACCIDENT. 'No!' This was no place to be trapped, to try to hide and wait for help. No one would be here until 6 A.M., when the dayside crew arrived to run advance advertising sections. Niko would have the rest of the night to hunt us down like animals.

'Where then?' Lance demanded.

Niko's footsteps pounded down the stairs behind us. No time. No place else to go.

The presses were silent, the shadowy machines like huge dinosaurs in repose. The

457

acrid odor of their inky breath hung on the air. We ran toward a ladder to the catwalk. If we climbed up and lay flat we would be hidden from Niko's sight.

'What are you doing?' I cried as Lance broke away. He sprinted to the control room, mashed the buttons that start the presses, and killed most of the lights. With a rumble, the machinery slowly began to turn and pick up speed.

We scrambled up the ladder as Niko burst in the door.

I didn't know whether an alarm would sound, but hopefully security would hear the presses running and investigate. The noise would prevent Niko from hearing us, but it also masked from us any sounds he made.

He seemed to be groping the walls for a light switch. We reached the first tier of the double bank of catwalks and crouched away from the edge. I wondered if there might be an emergency telephone up here somewhere.

The web that threads paper through the rollers was moving like an endless conveyor belt. Pressmen work on the catwalks to monitor the ink feed, conduct inspections, and make repairs. The catwalks are kept clear, a strict safety rule. I groped in vain for anything a worker might have left behind, anything that could be used as a weapon. The presses stirred up the ink particles in the air and my eyes burned. The dinosaurs were awake. Their voice was deafening.

Lance suddenly touched my shoulder. Niko was climbing the ladder at the other end of the catwalk, already halfway up to our level. He nudged me and we moved, scrambling the ten feet or so to the ladder that stretched to the top level. I went first, Lance behind me. I felt, rather than heard, a bullet slam into the wooden platform and moved faster. He had seen us. He knew exactly where we were.

On the upper level, I slipped and kicked something over as I turned to take Lance's hand. A spill of the oil-based ink had left a slick spot on the catwalk. What I had kicked was a bucket of wiping rags left behind. A tool, some sort of narrow wrench, lay a few feet away.

I guided Lance's hand over the slippery spot to warn him it was there. He nodded and took the wrench. I clung to the pail.

Niko clambered onto the top level a hundred feet away. He stood searching, then spotted us. 'Go!' Lance shouted in my ear. We hunched as we ran, trying to make ourselves into smaller targets. I wondered how many bullets he had left, if he was carrying more ammo.

The roar of the presses was so deafening that I wasn't even sure whether he had fired more than once. With one in the stairwell, that left him at least four more in the weapon.

Lance stopped. Niko had reached the spot where the ink spill was and ran full tilt, gun in hand. Waiting for a sure shot before he fired.

Lance drew back and heaved the wrench like Dan Marino releasing a pass. The powerful throw spun it through the air, end over end. Niko saw it coming, as I flung the pail with both hands, sending it rattling along the platform, the rags spilling out.

Shielding his face, evading the wrench as he ran, Niko saw the pail at the last moment and leaped over it, startled. Pail and wrench both missed him, but suddenly he teetered like a tightrope walker in trouble, arms windmilling to regain his balance on the slippery surface.

His left foot skidded out from under him and he plummeted off the catwalk, but, like an acrobat, in midair his right hand caught onto the moving conveyor belt. I did not see his gun; he must have lost it. The belt moves papers up through an opening in the ceiling to the fifth floor. It carried him along, lurching in our direction for several moments as he dangled, clinging to it one-handed. As he drew closer, swaying in

460

sheer space, I saw that he no longer had an acrobat's grip on the belt. It had him. His hand was caught in the metal jaws that normally feed paper through the mechanism. I did not hear him scream, but saw his face.

He plunged suddenly, as blood exploded through the air. His fingers, half his hand, still rose, moving along without the rest of his body. Whether he still had the gun no longer mattered. He glanced off a steel support girder jutting out from the first tier. The sound of the impact as he slammed into the folding machine below was lost in the pulsating roar that filled the space around us.

Carried along, his head at an impossible angle, his body finally jammed against the unforgiving steel framework where teeth pull the paper into folds. We scrambled down the ladders. There is zero tolerance, no clearance where the machine was trying to fold him like a newspaper, but his hair was caught. Before we reached the emergency shutoff button, the ponytail was gone. So was his scalp.

The dinosaurs shuddered into blessed silence as a paunchy middle-aged security guard burst through the double doors. Seeing us, he crossed his arms, brow furrowed, mouth open in an indignant expression.

'What do you think you're doing in here?' he demanded, glaring at me. Then his eyes narrowed at Lance.

'I'm sorry, sir,' he said, 'but the movie crew has finished in here, and my orders are that you no longer have access to these premises.

'You know better,' the guard muttered, turning to me. 'I'm gonna have to report this.'

Then he saw Niko and his eyes widened.

25

Niko was definitely dead this time, his neck broken.

Karen Sawyer drove away when she saw the patrol cars. They pulled her over at 36th Street and the Boulevard.

She denied everything. Said she'd had trouble sleeping, had gone for a drive. But we were not the only ones who had seen her at the *News* building. A totally independent eyewitness could put her in the parking garage. His name was Harvey Shimmel. They stopped him as he, too, tried to drive off. He had seen her and had apparently been waiting for her to leave. The cops asked us to step outside to see if we recognized him.

We did not. Small and pasty-faced, the man smiled in recognition as though he knew me. On the front seat of his car was an orange and black pair of knee-high fire department boots.

'Hey, wait a minute!' I said. 'Those are mine.'

Somebody had broken into my T-Bird. Nothing else was taken. Not my gun or my roll of quarters for tolls and meters; only my boots.

The officer leaning into Shimmel's car found a high-heeled shoe, then a sheer stocking. They were not mine. 'This guy could be a robber.' The cop held the stocking up, mistaking it for a makeshift mask.

'No,' I said. 'I know who he is.'

* * *

Much of the mystery was solved when police learned Karen Sawyer's place of employment. She worked at Stephanie's answering service, got the job shortly after the movie crew arrived in Miami. Sullen, she refused to talk at first, though police were certain she and Niko knew each other in LA.

When she did talk, all she would admit was that they were lovers, that she did as he asked

463

because he promised a huge payoff and a future for her in movies. He had divulged few details about the scheme and had never named the source from whom the big payoff would come.

The total truth may have died with Niko. The FBI and police in both South Florida and California are still investigating the murders and the plot to scuttle the film. They found that WFI is in financial trouble, floundering in red ink, stripped of many of its assets by those operating it, but more proof is needed for a prosecutable case, proof that may never be found.

The threat to Lance has hopefully been eliminated because the details were exposed and because both the FBI and Lance's attorneys have talked to Gettinger — who, of course, claimed to know nothing. He has his own problems, with creditors closing in and a possible collapse of the studio. WFI's attorneys suggested that Niko was freelance, working on his own.

Our best guess is that the man whose body was left in his place was selected during one of Niko's charitable forays to the homeless shelter's food bank. He would have had no difficulty luring a street person to Lance's house with the promise of money, food, or clothes. Missing persons reports have yielded nothing. The homeless are rarely reported missing. Lance, of course, will continue watching his back. He's used to that. Unlike the image the public has of film stars, it is lonely at the top. Whom can you trust? If anything, Niko's 'second death' hit Lance harder than the first. It is tragic to mourn a friend, but somehow sadder to realize you never had one.

Stephanie was flown back home by private plane and is being treated in a Boston psychiatric hospital.

They finished *Margin of Error*. In light of the events surrounding it, there was no wrap party; the crew just left town quietly.

Margin of Error took so long to finish that Lance would have no break between movies. He stayed on for a few more days before flying to England to start shooting his next project, another Titan film.

The night before he left, we had a late dinner and then stopped by the paper to pick up some prints Lottie had left for him, pictures she had shot of him and his children. The building was quiet and we sat at my desk, where we first met.

'Come with me,' he said, eyes intense.

'Is that a proposal?'

He paused for a long moment. 'No.'

I understood.

'What do you think?' he asked.

I shook my head and shrugged. 'What would I do?'

'Be with me.' He looked hurt.

'And when you're working? Which is most of the time.'

He didn't answer. Finally, he said, 'You're sure?'

'My judgment's been way off on a lot of things lately. But I'm sure.'

He studied me. 'How could you want this,' he asked, glancing around the newsroom with the contempt I saw that he still felt for most reporters, 'more than you want me?'

'I don't. It's not this. But every once in a while, there comes a story. A story that blows your mind. One where you know you've made a difference. That's what makes it all worthwhile. That and the anticipation. It's addictive, because you never know when it will happen. It could be tomorrow, next year, or five minutes from now, but when it does, nothing in the world is as important. Maybe I'm as obsessed as Stephanie, in my own way. But this is my home, and Miami is a helluva news town. If I took off with you I might miss something.'

He leaned back in his chair, long legs stretched out, stared at the floor, then raised his eyes to mine. 'Would your answer be different if this was a proposal?'

My turn to pause. I smiled at him. 'No. I can't compete with Hollywood.'

'Hell, Britt. Hollywood can't compete with you.' He leaned forward to touch my hair.

'That's a nice thing to say. Where did you — '

'It's original.'

I got teary-eyed.

'Another time, another place,' he said, 'this would have worked.'

'Another time, another place, we never would have met.'

★ ★ ★

I rode with him in the car to the airport. 'I can't say I'm sorry to say goodbye to Miami,' he said. 'It's been a trip. You're the only thing I'll miss.'

We walked to the concourse, his arm around me. I tried not to think of the last time I had come here, rushing to catch a flight. 'This new movie will be fun,' he was saying. 'I get to fly a helicopter.'

'Nice.'

'Of course, then I have to hang from it as it careens between the mountains . . . '

'I was afraid of that.'

' . . . and ride the top of a speeding train. We're negotiating now on the film that I really want to do after this one.' He paused. 'It's a comedy.

'This isn't goodbye forever,' he said.

'I know,' I said. I would see him again, as long as I had the price of a ticket.

The driver took me back to the paper. I arrived at my desk suddenly cheerful, and full of hope for the future. I knew what I had to do.

Before I could make the call, my phone rang.

The caller was one I didn't expect to hear from again.

'What's happened, Angel? Is everything all right?'

She shushed the children playing noisily in the background and then bubbled over. 'I think I've got this job, Britt! I can start part time, with no benefits now, then switch to full time after the baby arrives. We can even get medical coverage!'

'Good for you, Angel,' I said, relieved that there was no problem. 'I guess school paid off.'

'Sure did. I'm going back for my second interview this afternoon. What I need to know is, can I put you down for a reference?'

'Sure,' I said doubtfully. 'I guess so. Where is it?'

'The *News!*' she trilled. 'They need a secretary in the advertising department. I'll be working in the same building as you! Is that neat, or what?'

*   *   *

I punched in the number I wanted as soon as Angel got off the line.

'Lieutenant McDonald, please.'

'Who's calling?'

I told her. Surprisingly, he picked up.

'Some time ago,' I said, 'you gave me a list of professionals to call. You know, to decide who to see for some help. Remember?'

'Of course I do.'

'I lost it.' Then I thought, No more denial. This is the time to be honest with myself and everybody else. 'Actually,' I said, 'I never wrote it down. I didn't bother. Do you still have it?'

'I think I can put my hands on it.'

'Good. I need it now.'

We do hope that you have enjoyed reading this large print book.

Did you know that all of our titles are available for purchase?

We publish a wide range of high quality large print books including:
Romances, Mysteries, Classics, General Fiction, Non Fiction and Westerns.

Special interest titles available in large print are:
The Little Oxford Dictionary
Music Book
Song Book
Hymn Book
Service Book

Also available from us courtesy of Oxford University Press:
Young Readers' Dictionary
(large print edition)
Young Readers' Thesaurus
(large print edition)

For further information or a free brochure, please contact us at:
Ulverscroft Large Print Books Ltd.,
The Green, Bradgate Road, Anstey,
Leicester, LE7 7FU, England.
Tel: (00 44) 0116 236 4325
Fax: (00 44) 0116 234 0205

STRANGER IN THE PLACE

Anne Doughty

Elizabeth Stewart, a Belfast student and only daughter of hardline Protestant parents, sets out on a study visit to the remote west coast of Ireland. Delighted as she is by the beauty of her new surroundings and the small community which welcomes her, she soon discovers she has more to learn than the details of the old country way of life. She comes to reappraise so much that is slighted and dismissed by her family — not least in regard to herself. But it is her relationship with a much older, Catholic man, Patrick Delargy, which compels her to decide what kind of life she really wants.

THE SANCTUARY SEEKER

Bernard Knight

1194 AD: Appointed by Richard the Lionheart as the first coroner for the county of Devon, Sir John de Wolfe, an ex-crusader, rides out to the moorland village of Widecombe to hold an inquest on an unidentified body. But on his return to Exeter, the Coroner is incensed to find that his own brother-in-law, Sheriff Richard de Revelle, is intent on thwarting the murder investigation. But Crowner John is ready to fight for the truth. Even faced with the combined mights of the all-powerful Church and nobility . . .

SLAUGHTER HORSE

Michael Maguire

The Turf Security Division is surprised and suspicious when playboy Wesley Falloway's second-rate horses develop overnight into winners. Simon Drake investigates, but suddenly there is a new twist — someone is out to steal General O'Hara, the star of British bloodstock, owned by Wesley Falloway's mother. With a few million pounds at stake, lives are cheap; Drake finds himself both hunter and quarry in a murderous chase where even his closest associates may be playing a double game.

MERMAID'S GROUND

Alice Marlow

It's been five years since Kate Williams' beloved husband died, leaving her with two young children to raise. Now she's built a good life in one of Wiltshire's prettiest villages, and she has her dream job, as gardener at Moxham Court. For the last year, Kate has had a lover, roguishly attractive Justin Spencer, but he won't commit to more than a night here and there. When she takes in a male lodger, Jem, Kate's secretly hoping his presence will provoke a jealous reaction in Justin. What she hasn't reckoned on is exactly how attractive Jem will turn out to be.

HOT POPPIES

Reggie Nadelson

A murder in New York's diamond district. A dead Chinese girl with a photograph in her pocket. A plastic bag of irradiated heroin in an empty apartment. A fire in a Chinatown sweatshop. The worst blizzard in New York's history. These events conspire to bring ex-cop Artie Cohen out of retirement and back into the obsessive world of murder and politics that nearly killed him. The terrifying plot uncoils first in New York — in Artie's own back yard — then in Hong Kong, where everything — and everyone — is for sale.

NOVEMBER TREE

Ann Stevens

Rowena and Phyllida are both sixty-something, and both on their own — so what better than sharing their declining years? They have known each other for fifty years — and there's something to be said for the devil you know. But who said that retirement would be peaceful? Amidst demanding relatives and with a new suitor on the horizon, it looks as though the future is far from predictable, bringing past resentments and a festering secret to the surface. As the tension rises and tolerance falters, the long-suppressed truth threatens to erupt in a most unpredictable way.